NEW YORK WOMAN . . .

Her name is Jessie Bourne. She was born in New York, lives there, and never dreams of leaving . . .

She knows the town like the back of her pretty hand, from crowded tenements to glittering mansions, from pushcarts on the sidewalk to the exclusive world of the theatre and swank eatery . . .

She is ever-so-wise in the ways of the city—and terribly foolish in the ways of the heart . . .

"Recommended"

—LIBRARY JOURNAL

"Highly readable . . . admirably done"

—NEW YORKER

MARCIA DAVENPORT was born in New York City and started her writing career at an early age. In addition to novels, she has done much musical comment and criticism, and has traveled and lived throughout Europe. Her novels include the widely read THE VALLEY OF DECISION, MY BROTHER'S KEEPER and THE CONSTANT IMAGE.

Available in Popular Library reprint editions

EAST SIDE, WEST SIDE

Marcia Davenport

POPULAR LIBRARY • NEW YORK

POPULAR LIBRARY EDITION

The chorus of the song, "On a Sunday Afternoon," quoted on page (23): Copyright 1902 by Harry Von Tilzer Music Publishing Co., 1697 Broadway, New York; Copyright renewed 1929, and assigned to Harry Von Tilzer Music Publishing Co. Used by permission.

The chorus of the song, "My Mother Was a Lady," quoted on page (26): Copyright Edward B. Marks Music Corporation, R.C.A. Building, Radio City, New York. Used by permission.

In Memory of
MAXWELL EVARTS PERKINS
with gratitude for
this and all his work;
with love and sorrow.

PRINTED IN THE UNITED STATES OF AMERICA

I

MONDAY

I

Jessie Bourne liked to wake very slowly in the morning, gradually feeling the coming to life of each of her senses. She was a light and nervous sleeper and she had learned long ago to keep daylight and noise from her bedroom. The heavy silk draperies at the windows were made with interlinings of black felt, and she slept with these curtains closed except for a narrow space through which the delicious live air of New York refreshed her. When she began to wake at a moderately late hour of the morning, between nine and ten, the room was almost perfectly dark and she liked to lie still for a time, letting her eyelids roll open, and her ears begin to accept the distant noises of the day. At other hours she might scarcely notice the pleasant hootings and chuffings on the river far below, but now she took deliberately the time to hear them; it was her way of insuring that she would feel calm and good humored when the moment came really to begin the day. She might lie slowly waking in this way for ten minutes or a quarter of an hour, sometimes face down, her arms folded on the cool pillow-linen; sometimes flat on her back, hands and feet quietly crossed in a formed symmetry which she found soothing, like any pattern of neatness, precision, or regularity. Presently she would feel quite ready to be awake; there would pass through her a pleasant current of energy, a sense that light would be welcome now, and that a change of mood to the crisp accents of the day would be natural and unforced. Then she stretched up her right hand to the small enamel bell which hung at the headboard of her bed, and pressed the button twice.

The door opened quietly; Josephine knew Mrs. Bourne's antipathy to household noises such as roughly handled doors, echoes of kitchen sounds, or carelessly loud voices and footsteps. Perhaps if Jessie Bourne had had children she would have compromised some of her exacting habits, but there had been no discipline of that sort. On the other hand, Josephine realized, there was Mr. Bourne. He was a door-slammer from choice as much as chance. She understood what had made Mrs. Bourne's prejudices what they were.

Josephine drew open the heavy pale pink curtains and closed the casement windows. Brilliant sun poured into the room. There were two tall banks of these casements, forming a corner east and north, and beneath them an old-fashioned window-seat which Jessie Bourne had had built in, like all the interior architecture of this apartment. The building dated from the booming late nineteen-twenties when the fashionable cooperative apartment house epitomized whopping stock market profits and canny paper-pyramid financing. Almost all such apartment buildings had long ago passed through the wringer of deflation, bankruptcy, and abandonment of their rights by original stockholders unable to maintain them; but Jessie and Brandon Bourne still lived here, after seventeen inharmonious years, and Jessie's attachment to her home was passionate. Every morning she was newly glad to see it; she had never lost her appreciation of its charming personality, its dramatic beauty of outlook up the magnificently bridged East River, its solidity and permanence in contrast with the meaningless cubbyholes which most apartment-houses offered, the slight and carefully tended shabbiness which the years had spread upon it.

Jessie was a snob in her own way, and that consisted of belonging to the special fraternity of people born upon Manhattan Island, who had lived upon it all their lives and would not consider themselves alive if they should have to live anywhere else. This had nothing to do with social position or family or privilege. On the contrary, it was for instance upon going to the nearest drab public grammar school, to register for Election Day, that Jessie gloried most in her native fraternity. There the cops on poll duty and the tenement housewives keeping the election rolls and the taxi driver who had left his hack parked outside and Mr. Goldfish who kept the candy and news store on York Avenue all shared with Jessie their clannish treasured pride: they belonged here, nobody else really could. And when one had lived for so many years at the same address one never even gave one's name as one's turn came in the line. The four women would look up from their big books and the chief clerk would smile, "Hello there, Mrs. Bourne," and all four would turn the heavy books to the B page without being told. That was a good way to be a snob, Jessie thought. A cosy, folksy way—if snobbery meant keeping to a tight little club of right-by-birth which no outsider could ever enter. And these other members of the club were not in the least impressed by her residence in the luxurious apartment-house poised on the edge of the river and towering over their five-story coldwater walk-ups half a block away. They knew her for one of themselves.

While Josephine went to fetch her breakfast tray Jessie slid out of bed and into her mules with one smooth motion and went into the bathroom. Splashing water on her face she drew relaxed deep breaths, with a sense of pleasure that this was the beginning of a good day. Sometimes it was not like this, sometimes she felt strained and jangled of nerves and that gave her foreboding. The clean flavors of soap and toothpaste were refreshing, and the light dry fragrance of the eau de cologne which she sprayed on her neck and wrists. She did not examine her reflection in the mirror. Her only reaction to an involuntary glimpse of her face as she shut the mirrored door of the medicine cupboard was momentary amusement at a habit which she had formed years ago, of scrubbing her face with soap and hot water at bedtime and then carefully making it up as if she were going out. In those days it had seemed so important to look her best for Brandon. And now she had the benefit of never looking like death when she rose in the morning.

She had a sharp sense of Monday as she went back to bed, where Josephine had shaken out and piled the pillows high so that she could sit up against them; Monday with its springboard feeling from which she would dive into a new week.

The October sun was glorious streaming through the rosy silk voile glass curtains, which were never drawn across the centre bank of east windows because the view up the river was too beautiful to obscure. There was nothing more perfect in its pattern of small delights than this first hour of the day; the smooth, heavy linen sheets embroidered with garlands and boldly monogrammed, the silk crêpe blanket cover which Jessie had made herself, banded with blonde binche lace which had belonged to her mother; the breakfast tray across her knees with its plates and covered dishes and graceful eggcup of Chelsea porcelain abloom with pink roses; the four morning newspapers which she would read with the professional thoroughness that she had never lost since the hardworking days on the old *World*. The pile of mail was enormous, but Jessie knew that most of it was advertisements, begging letters, and requests to lend her name for the benefit affairs of charitable organizations and to committees for pressure groups, public luncheons and dinners, and fund-raising projects. She would pitch most of that mail into the wastebasket, still thinking as she had all through the war of this wanton waste of paper at a time when the public was urged to save it.

The orange juice brimming in the tall glass was exquisitely cold and delicious, tingling on her tongue. The coffee was steaming hot, hot as possible, blacker, stronger, fresher, than the coffee in any other house she knew. Anna was an artist and a perfectionist in everything that she made, but her coffee was the measure, Jessie thought, of her genius. Jessie herself could cook like an angel if she felt like it; her own coffee was superb, but never in her life had she tasted coffee like this of Anna's, unfailingly wonderful day in and day out. Into it Jessie poured a quantity of boiling hot milk. The resulting drink, without the desecration of sugar, was one of the good things that made all the rest of life seem better. Good coffee with lots of hot milk had been important in this way all her life. It went back to school in France, to childhood summers in Austria, to the dark winter mornings in the basement dining-room in the old brownstone house on West Eighty-fourth Street, where she vividly remembered her mother in a trailing, frilled petticoat and a quilted black china-silk jacket, sitting with her elbows on the round oak table and holding a big cup of such coffee in both hands, huddling over it for extra warmth because houses were much colder in those days than now; and it seemed to Jessie anyway that winters, when

8

she was a little girl on the West Side, had been far more severe. She could remember to this day the agony of suffering from icy, numb feet in spite of long stockings and woollen drawers, flannel petticoats, warm clothes such as little girls did not wear nowadays. Jessie saw them trotting about all winter with bare legs, short socks, and low shoes, and certainly she never heard of a child crying as she used to cry from the pain of cold feet and chilblains.

She drank her three cups of coffee, the first with her boiled egg and hot buttered whole-wheat toast, the other two with the morning news, which she read with close attention and with sharp, almost violent reactions. She read carefully the lead editorial of one of the great morning papers which, she knew, had been written by her friend Clyde Pritchard. She had known Clyde Pritchard for twenty years, he had given her her job on *The World* as little more than office errand-girl. In those days he had written editorials so brilliantly compounded of factual precision and fighting idealism that he was inarguably the most respected young name in American journalism. Jessie had worshipped him. But in those days there had been no public issues vast enough to challenge Pritchard at his best; and now that the world was punch-drunk and staggering amid its ruins, plunging and foundering for lack of leadership and articulate conviction, Pritchard had almost nothing to say. Jessie read his editorial twice, the second time with a sense of lost, dead hope. In all those words he challenged no heart, lighted no torch; evidently he was more than content to follow the obscure and timid policy of his publisher. Does that happen inevitably, Jessie wondered, at fifty-odd years of age and thirty thousand dollars a year?

On a different sort of day this troubled mood, partly personal in its restlessness, a sense of uselessness and inadequacy, partly impersonal, a thing of profound spiritual sorrow and anxiety—such a troubled mood might have settled upon her for any length of time. But today as she laid the newspapers aside, Jessie felt the rebound of her good spirits, the same sense of pleased contentment and calm in which she had awakened. She lay back upon her pillows and stared for a moment at the ceiling, on which the sunlight danced and rippled, as if reflecting itself from the surface of the river sixteen stories below. Jessie stretched her body slowly, pressing her fingers against the lean frame of her hips, arching her neck against the pillows and indulging in a flash of childlike guilt for her small vanity, her satisfaction that she did not have to struggle like most women whom she knew, with the battle of flesh and pounds. However, she had many threads of grey in the curly mass of her rich brown hair, but that had no special meaning at her age of thirty-eight because premature greyness ran in both sides of her family. Jessie's hair had been greying for more than ten years. She remembered her mother, quite grey before she was thirty, saddled with the interminable nuisance of keeping her hair tinted with henna, one of those old-men-of-the-sea from which one could never be free if one had once taken it up. Jessie had sworn never to be so bothered, but she was clever enough also to realize how much fresher and smarter she looked with her hair just as it was, naturally curly, cut quite short, brushed cleanly away from her forehead and temples and crisply upturned at the back of her neck. I am a Pharisee, she thought, every time I go to Paul's to have my hair washed and my nails done, because I feel so smug at not wasting time and money on permanent waves and facial massages and all that sort of rot. You know perfectly well, her cynical mind assured itself, that if you needed or wanted permanent waves and facial massages and green lacquer on your toenails, you would have them all and supply yourself with pressing reasons why they were essential.

She smiled at the sunlight on the ceiling, at the bowl of pink roses and carnations on the small pearl-colored baroque table in the window corner, at the wonderfully successful monotone in which she had conceived this room where she spent so many of her hours, its cool bowl-like sweep of the same odd shade of muted pink, a color tinged with white and in some fabrics, like the dull ribbed silk of the curtains, the thick crushed nap of the carpet, showing silver. Walls, doors, mouldings, floor, the damask upholstery of the baroque chairs and stools that she had found years ago in Vienna, all of it was a continuous monotone of the same identical shade, much of it dyed together in the same vat, varied only by the textures in which it appeared, the soft contrasts between wool and plaster and wood and silk. It was and had been for years her deepest comfort, her refuge, in many ways the only peace she had; a shell into which she fitted herself, curling and hiding away from everything that lay without, like the defenseless soft things which live in shells and can only find peace shut tight inside them.

She had such peace this morning, she had it deliciously; and as she lay smiling at the ceiling and stretching her toes

10

against the cool tightness of the linen at the bottom of the bed, she knew still better why she felt so serene, why this was so surely a good Monday, the beginning of a good week, or as good a week as there could be for her. Brandon was away. He was away somewhere in Virginia, she did not know exactly where, and the fact that she did not precisely know, and certainly did not care, was a large part of the serenity in which she lay secure. For a long stretch of wretched years she had cared desperately where he was, and with whom, and for what, but now it was only blessed and the essence of peace not to know or care or have to see him, not to throb with suspense when she heard his step or his voice. She did not know just when she had begun to realize and recognize this, it was too profound a thing to have happened precisely in time, it was a long evolution. One day during the war the product of its ponderous workings had come into her possession; but even then she had not grasped it whole and suddenly. She had, rather, examined it very slowly, turning it over between her hands, learning to know its shape and weight and meaning, gradually growing accustomed to it and now at last accepting it with relief and satisfaction.

The crystal clock on the table beside her bed said quarter past ten, at which Jessie sat up suddenly and reached for her blue leather engagement book. The bedside table was wide and low, just the height of the broad French bed. On it were an alabaster lamp with a rosy shade, a silver thermos jug of icewater, a gold pill-box containing the means by which Jessie sometimes had to resort to quiet and sleep, a telephone, a small Chinese white jade cat, and an old photograph of Jessie's dead mother, Rosa Landau, in a yellowed ivory frame.

Jessie Bourne looked at the page of her blue book headed Monday, October 15th, and then again at the clock.

"My God," she said aloud, "I must hurry."

She rang for Josephine, stepping out of bed, and said, high over the roaring of the hot bath-water, "Tell Anna and Sarah I am dining out tonight and Wednesday. I'm not sure yet about tomorrow. And I asked them both to change their day out this week from Thursday to Friday, I have people dining here. You are in, aren't you?"

"Yes, Mrs. Bourne," said Josephine. "I am off on Wednesday." She scowled at the windows. They had been washed only last Friday, but nothing could keep them clean outside, with all that smoke from the boats. And it had rained last week. Jessie laughed at the maid's expression. "My mother

11

used to say," she said, "that she could always make it rain. Just have the windows washed . . ."

"Muller's called on the telephone just now," said Josephine. "They said it will cost fourteen dollars to weave the burn in Mr. Bourne's new grey suit, and should they go ahead with it."

Jessie paused in the bathroom doorway, exchanging a glance of silent mutual exasperation with Josephine. It was not the fourteen dollars that they minded so much as the interminable struggle with Brandon Bourne's habits. Jessie shrugged. "Tell them yes," she said. She wished she dared tell them simply to patch the suit and send it back; she would add it to the bundle that was going to Europe. There flashed across her mind the vision of Brandon's wide double clothes-closets bare and empty, if only she had the courage to make them so, and to sweep away with their contents much that he himself had come to mean. She thought about it as she stepped into her bath, with a recurrence of the doubtful, uneasy mood of half an hour ago. It was as if a lowering cloud hung dark over the vista of her existence, but she knew too that there must be some alternative to sitting idle in its shadow, acquiescent merely because it was there. It was too easy to ascribe all this sense of uselessness and waste to Brandon; it would be dishonest and unfair.

Scrubbing her knees and ankles vigorously with a hard brush, she wondered suddenly what life might have been like if she had never stopped working. A great deal better, I should imagine, she thought; and now she speculated why she had ever been content to allow a combination of circumstances to make of her something which her heredity and all her instincts deeply scorned: an idle woman. Never mind the so-called "work" that you do for charity and all that, she thought; you would do it better if you had made something of yourself. She put down the hand-brush and began to cover herself with lather from the floating pink soap which smelled deliciously. Just because *The World* had disappeared, and she had married, utterly wrapped up in Brandon Bourne to the exclusion of every other consideration; and just because she had rationalized that at a time of depression she had no right to hold a paying job when some other person badly needed it, these excuses she found now to have worn themselves out. None of them any longer had any meaning, and a measure of accomplishment resulting from her own work would have

12

yielded more than meaning by now; it might have held the answer to brooding questions otherwise unanswerable.

Ah, well, she sighed; and then she shook her head briskly, partly to clear it of these heavy thoughts and partly to whisk water from her ears. Here was this week which held a number of pleasant possibilities; she began even to think ahead to Thursday night when some of her own friends were coming, people who liked smoked sturgeon, and stuffed breast of veal, and cheesecake, all things that Brandon hated.

"Squabs!" she said violently, kicking her heels in the foaming water. "Filet of beef! Turkey and cranberry sauce! Breast of guinea hen! Ice cream and petits fours! Fooey!" She burst into a cadenza of not very expert song and finished her bath in a mêlée of cheerful noise.

II

Horace Howland had directed that Mrs. Bourne should not be kept waiting in the reception room and she was ushered straight through that austere cavern of dark polished panelling and leather upholstery to his office bright in the morning sun. The old gentleman moved across the room to greet her, and Jessie thought, with the pleasure that was always part of seeing him again, how much he himself was the handsomest ornament of this splendid room. She put both her hands into his and pressed them affectionately as he kissed her cheek.

"I am so glad to see you!" she said.

He smiled, holding a chair for her, and answered, "Then why not oftener, my dear?"

"Oh, Horace. We all run around in such a witless way."

"Not I," he said. "Not any more. And," he added, "I am vain enough to claim that I did not run about witlessly even when I had the energy to do so."

"No," agreed Jessie. "I'm sure you didn't. What a heavenly view this is. If I were you I'd live down here."

She looked out the broad windows down over the panorama of the harbor, the curve of the Battery, the broadening sweep of brilliant blue water churned with ships and ferries and tugs and barges as far as she could see. From this height their detail was almost indistinguishable, but a great hulk was moving up The Narrows, so dwarfing everything

13

about it that the transports and freighters looked like small swimming insects. Her heart, she believed, really pumped harder at the sight.

"Look," she said, pointing. "That must be the Queen Mary. With troops."

He nodded. "Extraordinary. She brings in nearly fifteen thousand men every fortnight."

Jessie sighed as he turned from the window to seat himself. She said, "I will be so glad when I can go again, Horace—you cannot believe how badly I want to get away."

"I know a man who says that the trouble with America is the restlessness of its women."

"Oh—I suppose. I think it's more a matter of wanting to eat our cake and have it too."

"Which are you doing now?" asked Horace Howland. He was sitting back, very straight in his chair, with his hands propped together from the elbows. He looked at her over his knuckles and added, "Or have you achieved the impossible?"

Jessie shook her head as he pushed a leather box full of cigarettes towards her across the desk. She did not take a cigarette. She sat quite still, her eyes moving slowly from the majestic view to the man opposite her, no less handsome now when he must be at least seventy than he had been as she remembered him from her childhood, the most constant of all the elements which had filled her mother's sparkling world. With him and about him there had always been that atmosphere of dignity, of permanence, the calm grace of manner which never varied no matter in what surroundings or with what people the man might find himself. And Horace Howland during his lifetime had surely found himself with everybody. To Jessie he personified the essence of aristocracy. She wondered too why it was that Brandon, whose background was so much the same, lacked this quality which made Howland both important and charming. And in all the members of Brandon's family the quality of assurance too often appeared to be mere arrogance.

Howland was speaking. "How much you look like your mother, Jessie!" There was wistful warmth in his voice. "Much more than ever before, somehow."

"I love to hear that," she said. "People have been saying so rather often lately. It must be age."

"Age! The old gentleman held up his strong, veined hands and shook his head. "You seem like a child to me. But then, of course, you always will."

14

Rather abruptly he leaned forward and opened a heavy canvas folder full of papers and legal documents. He selected the second paper from the top, the pile having been arranged in a certain order, and said, "We really should get on with all this, Jessie. I ought to think of it as an ordinary matter of business, I spend all my time at this sort of thing, but somehow—" he looked up, placing his spectacles across his nose, and sighed.

"You never really believe that she will not walk into this room and tell you that she's changed her mind about everything."

He laughed softly. "Precisely. It is quite dull to find all these matters proceeding according to the terms of her will, only because she is not here to change them."

"You miss her as much as I do," said Jessie.

He looked across at her with warm appreciation. He thought Jessie Bourne extremely pretty but to his taste not beautiful, for she had not the classic, mature beauty of her mother with whom he had been in love for thirty years, for whom he had remained unmarried, though without hope that she would ever marry him. He had been the cornerstone of much of Rosa Landau's life; her constant companion, her adviser, her beau, her man of business, her perfect, dependable friend always ready for every imaginable demand upon his time, his presence, his boundless grace and charm. He must have been her lover, too, before she had married; those who knew them well had always assumed that; but long, long ago. It seemed impossible that she had not married Howland but instead, the great driving noisy bull of a man who was Matthew Kernan. It was typical of all three that their lives resolved as they had; that Kernan should live briefly, spectacularly, and abundantly, and that Rosa should guide her relationship with Horace Howland to the fine, deep friendship that had lasted all her life and past her death, until now.

For here sat her daughter Jessie, in a strange way a modernization of the personality and the beauty of the Rosa whom Horace Howland had loved. Here Rosa's breadth of bone and face and coloring were sharpened, lightened, and made contemporary in the process. Rosa had had broad shoulders, full arms, a classic column of a throat, abundant hair; a late-nineteenth century form of beauty ideal to Horace Howland's eyes. In Jessie Bourne he saw and sensed the speed and vibrance of the present day; the short, crisp hair which he knew could be dressed with a few strokes of a comb; the small, trim wrists and ankles shaped for the abrupt brevity of today's clothes, joints in which Howland imagined that he could perceive the nerves as clearly as the neat bones and taut muscles. He was conscious of the animation of her face with its features smaller than Rosa's; the nose short and slenderly bridged, the eyes wide apart, dark grey, heavily lashed, and more often than not half closed in a smile which was not necessarily expressive of merriment. He had seen Jessie Bourne's face when it was remote, cold, thoughtful, disdainful, or reflective of antipathy for a person or an idea; and yet those strange eyes would appear to be smiling because they were lowered and partly closed. It was when she really laughed that Jessie looked up and straight at one, opening her eyes very wide for a moment before they went almond-like again, their pupils seemingly pin-pointed because they were so much in shadow. When she was amused the outer corners of her eyes turned gay; they moved up, lifting the fine skin into small upward lines which failed to frighten Jessie despite all the warnings of the hocus-pocus world of beauty experts.

Horace Howland was thinking as he had often thought before that it was no wonder that Jessie differed so much from her mother. After all, Matthew Kernan had been the extremest possible opposite to the dark subtle warmth of Rosa Landau. Yet he had been just as earthly as Rosa, just as gusty, quite as much the solid common clay which loved to feel itself the substance of the sidewalks of New York. Howland himself, for all his Knickerbocker ancestry, had been the outsider, sometimes quite wistful, amidst those initiates. He had always understood, when all their shrewd and worldly friends had not, why Rosa had married Matthew Kernan. In the same way he understood much about Jessie which she herself had never really comprehended. He had watched her for years, moving about in a pattern of attractive futility which he knew could not satisfy her and from which the certainty of her eventual breaking-away was as clear to him as the resemblance to her mother, only latent before, but emerging with dramatic accent now. It seemed natural too to him that this should begin to assert itself when Jessie was approaching forty. And by a coincidence she caught up his thought now.

"I am so nearly forty," she was saying, "that I am beginning to feel I ought to plan every minute of the rest of my life."

"You have no idea how silly that sounds to me," he said, dismissing her with an affectionate expression of reproach. "At my age. Now really, my dear, do let me get on with these papers. I have all sorts of details to turn over to you and then I hoped that perhaps you would lunch with me at India House."

"Oh, Horace! If I'd only known sooner. I should have loved it but I told that ghastly sister of Brandon's I'd meet her at her club. Let me call her off." She reached for the telephone.

Howland put up his hand, looking at Jessie over the tops of his spectacles. "Certainly not!" he said, as he might speak to a child. "I understand you young people think nothing of such rudeness, but you are not going to indulge in it on my account." He took a beautiful coin-thin platinum watch from his waistcoat pocket and looked at it. "What time are you to meet Millicent?"

"One-thirty," said Jessie meekly.

"Then you shall leave here at ten past one. We have an hour." He put the watch back in its pocket and Jessie remembered vividly, with a pang which seemed never to strike less sharply, the Christmas when her mother had given the watch to Howland, the last Christmas of Rosa Landau's life. She had been ill for a long time past, with Jessie and her closest friends watching her in mute anxiety and suspense, for Rosa Landau would not confess to them what they could too tragically see for themselves. Jessie remembered that entire year as the most terrible, most disastrous of her whole life. Pain and waste and tragedy had penetrated every part of it, even the parts remotest from her mother, who was dying at the same time. That last Christmas, therefore, was a quiet one, no big party, no buffet supper with suckling pig and coddled goose-liver and hot rum punch and boundless champagne.

All that had grown up around the fact that Mat Kernan, though he had clouded his own ecclesiastical status by his marriage to Rosa, had never missed a Christmas Eve Mass in his life, and had precipitated the first of those famous parties before Jessie's birth, by coming home to his pregnant wife with a dozen of his closest old friends, all former altar-boys of St. James's like himself. The next year the party had mushroomed to include everybody from the boss superintendents, Riordans and Nolans and Lynches, of the Kernan Construction Company, to the theatre people, the singers, dancers, song-writers, newspaper writers, and Broadway favorites who were Rosa's friends; the Tammany crowd who came were Mat's oldest cronies.

After his sudden death in the crash of an I-beam from a cable hoist during the Queensborough Bridge job, Mat's friends began to drop away from the parties, and from the changing frame of Rosa's life, especially after she moved from the ponderous homely brownstone of West Eighty-fourth Street to the compact, chic, limestone of East Sixty-sixth. It was only natural that the Christmas parties evolve from the lusty conviviality of Mat's time to the quieter, more elegant, but wittier gaiety of Rosa's own. The parties changed from Christmas Eve to open house all Christmas afternoon, buffet dinner, music, games, a great festive exclamation-point in the middle of the winter for more interesting and famous people than Jessie could possibly remember now. Yet all that had thinned and faded, toward the end, to the gentle veiled mood in which Jessie was remembering her mother, thinking of Rosa Landau as she was that day, very thin, very frail, but vivid like the glint of gold thread in old brocade, putting a flat silver-ribboned box into Horace Howland's hand as he leaned down over her sofa and kissed her tenderly. Jessie's eyes smarted for a moment; she swallowed hard and drew a long breath and Horace Howland covered his notice of that by bending his head over his sheaf of papers.

"It will be on the twenty-second, Jessie"—he glanced at his desk calendar in its onyx frame—"that is, one week from today, that the trust terminates and I am to turn over the securities to you outright. I think all the documents are in order, but the chief thing that you must do today is read through this accounting and—" he looked up, smiling, "sign your acceptance of it if you approve."

"Suppose I disapprove?" Her eyes were twinkling.

"You would be a very tiresome young woman and I would deeply regret ever having wasted a moment on your affairs."

She put out her hand and picked up the long technical accounting in its blue legal binding and began to read it. Howland took a cigar from the humidor built into a drawer of his desk, clipped it, and lighted it carefully with an old-fashioned match. He saw that after the first paragraph or two Jessie was not really reading the accounting, but that her eyes were skimming down the pages without any concentration at all. She sensed that he was watching her and she looked up and laughed.

18

"Really, darling," she said. "You didn't think I would read every word?"

"Quite all right if you do not," he said, "but at this rate I could have embezzled half your fortune or given it to some crackpot scheme to save the world or——"

"It was perfectly safe with you," she murmured, reading. "Mother was the proof of that. And I always knew at least that you would never give any of it to Brandon."

"Why should I? He appears to have his own earnings."

"Oh yes," she sighed, laying down the document. "But if he had not had, you would not have given him any of my capital —even though you had the power to do so. I wonder if I will have as much sense."

Horace Howland hesitated. His natural reserve, a deep instinct to hold himself aloof from the private troubles of any other man, would ordinarily have kept him from a word of question about Brandon Bourne now. Howland was a man of the law who specialized in matters that suited his discriminating mind and referred unpleasantness like divorce and its concomitant disorders to another firm whose partners did not object to this type of practice. He knew Jessie Bourne to be consistently reticent, a woman who never discussed any aspect of her marriage with anybody. Stubborn pride would have kept her silent if exacting taste had not. Howland concluded that something very upsetting had happened to bring her to this uncharacteristic point of readiness to talk, and he asked her, finally, feeling that that was what she wanted of him. But she only shook her head.

"No," she said. "Nothing unusual at all, nothing definite. Nothing has happened."

"But that remark about Brandon was very unlike you, Jessie."

She looked up, her face rather puzzled, and answered, "Yes it was. But you know, Horace—something queer must be going on in my mind. I've always had thoughts that I would not tell anyone, but nowadays every once in a while one of them just pops out. Without my thinking about it. And quite often I don't care a bit. Nobody could be more surprised than I!"

"Something," said Howland very slowly, "has become more important to you than the privacy which you believed of the utmost importance before."

Jessie leaned back in her chair and again raised her eyes to look frankly into his. "You must be right," she said.

He was prepared to drop the matter now. Since she knew him so well and had made up her mind anyway, she said abruptly, "I would give my immortal soul never to have to see Brandon Bourne again."

"But," said Howland quietly, with no indication of surprise or other comment, "you have not come to this state of mind suddenly."

"No. The only difference now is that somehow I've got ready to admit it to myself. And I don't suppose I shall ever do anything about it, Horace. I so loathe all that sort of thing. I have such scorn for all the people I know who think nothing of marrying and unmarrying and remarrying as casually as they go somewhere for a holiday. And also—" she paused and drew a long breath. "Also of course I am too proud to confess I have made a failure."

"It takes two to fail at that," said Howland, "and in this particular case Brandon's ways have been public knowledge for so long—the only comment your friends would make, I should think, would be wonder that you had not given up years ago."

"That is exactly why I never would give up," said Jessie. "Brandon is a rotten husband but so is nearly everybody else. And I was going to be the woman who stuck it out even if all my friends gave up and divorced their husbands who were actually much less miserable to live with than Brandon. I was determined to be different." She took a cigarette and lighted it with an expression of revulsion; she hated to smoke and only did so under strain. "In fact," she added, "I mean to keep on being different still. I mean to stick it out."

"Why?"

"Oh because now—" she gestured at the legal document lying between them. "Now I shall have this money outright and if I left Brandon it would seem——"

"You mean 'they will say'——"

"Well—what does it matter? The truth is that I could not endure the implication that I had dumped him as soon as I came into this property, because I was unwilling to share it with him. That's not like me and it's not true."

"No," agreed Howland. "You are a decent woman. Like your mother."

"And there's another thing, you see. Mother. She would be scathing if she were alive and had to watch me leave Brandon. She would think it undignified and irresponsible, and she would be right."

20

"It was your father who was the Catholic."

"Yes, but I scarcely knew him seriously, Horace, I was so young when he died. He had no influence over me at all. But Mother's contempt for divorce was far more realistic and worldly than Father's religious scruples, I am sure of that. She was so wise. She always knew what went on, she accepted it because she was too knowing to be shocked at anything that people did. Except when they threw over their responsibilities. That was the one thing she blasted them for. Otherwise—" Jessie gave an expressive shrug.

"Is Brandon really so serious a responsibility? After all, it is not as if you had children."

"Only to my—what would you call it—my conscience? That must be why I am talking to you, Horace dear. I suppose I think of you as my conscience because Mother set the pattern so long ago. For herself."

"Not really," he smiled. "Not at all. Actually she did many things against my advice. When I really believed I should convince her of something I almost had to pretend to believe the opposite."

"Like dealing with a man," murmured Jessie.

"Your mother was like a man in many ways. But she was the most charming and feminine woman I ever knew."

"Ah," said Jessie. The sound was a sigh rather than a word. Rosa Landau's charm, her personality, the radiance with which she had illumined the lives of those who knew her, would not die so long as a friend of hers survived.

"Horace," said Jessie softly, "do you know that you have never told me how you met Mother—or where, or when?"

"Strange." The old gentleman took off his spectacles and turned to gaze away for a moment at the view from the window beside him. "Strange. I believe she was so much a part of my life that I have scarcely thought of the precise moment when she entered it. She was always already there."

Jessie looked at his clear, serene profile which in late years had taken on the beauty that comes to fine heads in old age, handsomer by far than the careless good looks of youth. And this man's face was profound, seasoned; it reflected a layered richness of experience going far back into a wise, a warm, complete life. She found herself realizing that no contemporary of hers would ever have such a face on reaching Horace Howland's age. And she said, suddenly, "You are the living proof that all this about missing life if one stays unmarried is nonsense."

21

"But," said Howland, "I did not miss Rosa, at the very right moment. Marriage would have been irrelevant, that is true, but Rosa in those years———"

"Tell me, Horace, please! How you met her, at least."

"It was in 1904," he said softly. His eyes roved towards the curve of the Battery, and out across the sparkling sapphire Narrows to the islands and the farther shores. "On a Staten Island ferryboat, one Sunday afternoon."

They were silent for a moment, while Howland continued to gaze out the great windows, and Jessie sat watching the tender expression of his face, imagining how these same fine features must have looked so long ago. It was not difficult to see him as he must have been then, already a successful young lawyer, just thirty years old.

It would have been difficult, indeed impossible to find in all the city a man more favored with every grace of looks, birth, money, privilege, brains, and extraordinary charm. Nobody was more in demand, nobody more doted upon by the great hostesses, by the mothers of debutantes, by the dowager queens to whose boxes at the Opera he was commanded. And no man was better liked by his own men friends, none so popular for their club dinners, and for other dinners at Delmonico's and the Broadway lobster palaces with the famous public beauties of the day.

But he was a man of more poise and balance than most; of the greatest delicacy of taste; of qualities of heart and character without which he might have been as well liked by the world, but a barren companion to himself. He had handsome, stately rooms in a splendid old house on Fifth Avenue near Washington Square; and his book-lined walls, his piano, his old mahogany and silver plate and Irish crystal, his family portraits, his few, carefully judged paintings, the beginnings of a lifetime collection, were better keys to his real nature than the qualities for which Society admired him. Also he was very loyal. It was his habit, no matter what invitations he must refuse in order to do so, to go every Sunday afternoon to visit his mother and dine with her at the old Howland mansion at St. George, where she lived as five generations of Howlands and Archibalds had done.

He enjoyed the sail across the Bay, and even in the coldest weather could be seen in his tall hat and fur-lined greatcoat, standing on the upper deck of the ferryboat, his handsome face high-colored in the sharp salt wind. In warm weather his winter costume was replaced by a wide boater with his Har-

22

vard club ribbon, and by dove-grey suiting superbly London-tailored, with fawn-colored gloves and a beautiful malacca stick. It was on such a Sunday, at the end of May, that he stood facing the gracious low hills of Staten Island, their fresh green rising from the glorious blue Bay as it swept round from the Hudson on its way to the sea. He was thinking of many things more rewarding than the mass of diversions with which his calendar for the coming weeks was filled. He heard laughter and singing from the benches along the deck behind him, and that was commonplace because the ferry-ride was so popular a Sunday outing with boisterous crowds from the tenements and sidewalks whom he had no occasion otherwise ever to see.

"On a Sunday afternoon," they sang, with swinging accents and full spontaneous harmony. Men's voices and women's; there must be eight or ten of them, and one particularly warm and ringing soprano which, to Howland's knowing ear, was not that of an amateur like the rest. A mezzo; not a spectacular voice, not a great one; but distinctly the voice of a personality, and one that did not sound altogether unfamiliar to Howland. The chorus rang out, framing the fine warm voice:

> *"On a Sunday afternoon,*
> *In the merry month of June,*
> *Take a trip up the Hudson or down the Bay,*
> *Take a trolley to Coney or Rockaway,*
> *On a Sunday afternoon,*
> *You can see the lovers spoon,*
> *They work hard on Monday*
> *But one day that's fun day*
> *Is Sunday afternoon!"*

For a moment, as the song ended in a bubble of laughing and chatter, Howland had a queer and wistful sense of loneliness, a striking thought that these gusty and vigorously natural people knew so much better than he and all his world how to enjoy life. They seemed to know how to enjoy the city which he loved in his own reserved and justly proprietary way, but which they were making so spectacularly their own. Howland stood there imagining just what faces and what personalities, what curly black heads, strong bold features, and loud, show-off clothes were grouped on those bench seats behind him. It was quite unthinkable to turn around and look at these people, it would be in the worst possible taste, and quite out of character; but that was what Horace Howland did.

The group was precisely as he had known it would be. They sat ranged along the ferry rail, all young and florid and bursting with open-mouthed laughter, the men with their arms round the girls, and the girls, high-colored, overdressed, pretty and lively, holding their big hats against the wind.

"Dat's a boid!" Howland heard a coarse bass voice say, and somebody else made a remark in a thick ugly language, accompanied by an unmistakable gesture of spread hands and shrugged shoulders, at which the girls tittered. But Howland ignored them; he was now staring frankly at one young woman who stood apart from the rest as dramatically as the voice which he knew now to have been hers had rung out over the chorus.

Her face was Rachel, it was Esther, it was Ruth, it was the face of great, ancient, noble beauty; it spoke of strength and fortitude and tenderness, it was eloquent of humanity and the richness of a simple heart. But it was young too, it was a girl's face. The hair above it shone bright brown with the clean vigor of youth, and the charming scoop hat, the tight, high collar with its white snowdrop ruching, were the perfect frame in all their freshness and style for this treasure of a face. And Howland was not really surprised that he recognized the girl, for such a personality if one had seen it ever before would have made its lasting impression. The girl was Rosa Landau, who had created a minor sensation in her first part as the soubrette in *The Lilac Girl*, which was still the year's great hit on Broadway.

But to see her now, at this distance of a few yards; to see the lovely high natural color, the sparkling dark brown eyes, huge and wide under straight, classic brows; to see her animation and gaiety among these friends who were obviously the companions of her tenement childhood, was a new and compelling experience for Howland. He knew as many actresses and dancers and operetta singers as any other young man of his world, but his astonishment lay now in the discovery that Rosa Landau was infinitely lovelier here than he had already thought her in the theatre. It crossed his mind that he must not stand and stare at her in this rude way, but he had never in his life wanted so irresistibly to look at a woman. And in a moment his steady gaze had the inevitable result. Her great brown velvet eyes looked up and saw him and, presently, spoke.

24

She was surrounded by her own friends, any of whom among the men would have made a horrible scene if Howland had dared to approach her, but that of course did not occur to him. He stood quiet and silent in his place at the front of the ferry and for a moment which was not nearly so long as it seemed, exchanged with the eyes of Rosa Landau a look which told him all that she might in days or even weeks have said. She was as innocent, as "good" in the phrase of the day, as her orthodox upbringing could make her. The usual life of the theatre had not touched her. Howland remembered now, watching her, that no man of his acquaintance had ever mentioned meeting Rosa Landau or taking her out. He could see now what her life really was; this was the way she spent her leisure, among the young people with whom she had grown up in the strange life of the East Side, which drew the sharpest imaginable line between its own daughters and the swarms of wretched whores who lived and plied their trade in the very same stinking tenements and rotting holes where the strictest rituals of family life were observed.

Howland knew nothing of the lives of such people; they were as foreign as the slums and ghettos of Poland and the Russian Pale and Rumania and Lithuania from which they or their parents, in the past twenty years, had emigrated. He did not know, for instance, how it could be that these young women in Rosa Landau's party could be so well-dressed, in smart summer muslins, with brightly trimmed hats. He did not know that they spent their lives at the sewing-tables of downtown sweatshops, or possibly, the most skilled among them, at the great Fifth Avenue dressmaking establishments. He did not know of push-cart bargains or "fire sales" where a shrewd girl could pick up damaged material for a dress which, cut and sewn by the same talent that made the clothes of Howland's mother and her friends, with stained or burnt lengths eliminated, and touches of exquisite hand-work added, produced the charming picture that he was enjoying now. He was fortunate in what he did not know, he was an enchanted and an enraptured young man; and to all his other pleasures he could add now the knowledge that this beautiful girl, who would grow, he saw, to far rarer beauty, understood what his eyes had so ineluctably told her. He turned away, just before the instant when it would have been embarrassing to have held her gaze a moment longer. Behind him he heard the laughter and the voices, the repartee that he did not fully understand, the cries of "Anh, Rosie, c'mon! Sing!"

They all took it up, and Howland heard their queer inflection, the thickening like a nearly soundless "k" on the end of the word as they clamored, "Singk, Rosie! Rosele! Singk!"

And again, as the dark, smooth voice rang out in the fresh wind, he felt the lurch at his heart, the helpless response to the mood of a song really as silly as a song could be.

> *"My mother was a lady*
> *Like yours you will allow,*
> *And you may have a sister,*
> *Who needs protection now,*
> *I've come to this great city*
> *To find a brother dear,*
> *And you wouldn't dare insult me, Sir,*
> *If Jack were only here."*

Again the laughter and the eager talk and the demands for more songs. Some they sang together and some she sang alone. Howland did not look at them again, but as the ferry approached its slip at Staten Island, and he saw his mother's barouche waiting on the dock, with old red-faced McCarthy standing beside the chestnuts, he felt a sharp regret that the trip was over, and some sense of indecision as to how he was to see Rosa Landau again. He stood aside, indulging his reluctance to hurry off the ferryboat as the party of Sunday trippers moved along ahead of him. He was behind Rosa Landau, watching her graceful back, her charming figure in its long ruffled skirts; and he saw in a sudden stroke of luck for which he had scarcely hoped, that a jagged shred of wire protruding from the open ferry gate was about to snag the ruffles bundling along behind her. He stepped forward quickly and said, "Miss Landau! I beg your pardon."

She stopped of course; astonishment would have stopped her if Howland's voice had not. She turned her head and saw him there and asked, her brown eyes wide, "But—how do you know my name?"

He smiled, pointing at the threatening wire, and said, "You were about to catch your gown. Forgive me."

"Thank you," she said, sweeping the skirt aside, "but—how did you——"

She was not in the least used to her new fame, such as it was; she was almost blushing. Yet he knew that she was glad he had spoken to her. He saw the rest of her party a pace or two ahead, the men watching him and glowering at him, the

26

women's faces inquisitive. He could not detain her a moment. They must move along.

"I have had the pleasure of seeing *The Lilac Girl*," he said quietly. "One does not forget Rosa Landau."

She looked at him again, and though the moment was as brief as possible, he was satisfied with what he saw in her extraordinary eyes.

"Would you let me call for you at the theatre tomorrow evening?" he murmured, so low that the nearest of her friends could not possibly have heard him.

She moved forward, not looking at him now, and speaking also in a whisper with her lips nearly still. "My sister doesn't let me," she breathed. "But—yes."

Jessie Bourne touched her eyes with her handkerchief and sat forward in her armchair, her face pale, her grey eyes strained. She did not speak for a time. She looked past Horace Howland's shoulder at the great blue view beyond him, at the sweep of water where with all the intensity of her heart and her imagination she had followed his meeting with Rosa Landau. There was nothing to say. Presently she turned her head to Howland and stood up, as he did, and placed her hands in his as he came around his desk.

"Thank you, Horace dear," she said. He bent and kissed her cheek, and walked with her across the room and out through the long panelled corridor and the reception room to the elevator. As they stood waiting for it he took the platinum watch from his pocket and said, "See what we can do with time when we make it serve our memories! We have been so many years away, you and I, and still you will be on time for your engagement with Millicent."

"I wish I could stay and lunch with you," said Jessie. "I am in no mood for Millicent."

She pressed his hand and smiled, feeling quite shaky still, and stepped into the elevator.

III

At the corner of Broad Street and Exchange Place she hailed a taxi and told the driver to go to The Assembly Club at Park Avenue and Sixty-fifth Street. The man started along towards Wall Street saying, "I'll go up de East River Drive."

For a moment Jessie did not notice what he had said. Her mind was still full of Horace Howland's story. With his eloquence and his warmth, his sincerity and the vivid beauty of his love for her mother, he had stirred Jessie's own memory to echoes of long ago, of times and impressions buried so deep underneath the mounting contrasts of years that only some extraordinary impulse could set them moving. Howland's last words stayed clear in her ears now; she sat back in the cab and let them echo as he had quoted them, for she too could imagine the partly shy, partly mischievous way in which Rosa had spoken of her sister. Auntie Esther. Auntie Esther who had brought up the whole family, working, laying down the law, ruling the home with love and austerity, and carving out of penury a life for five dependent women with a pair of cutter's shears. Auntie Esther. Only a handful of forgotten neighbors from the old days had ever realized that Rosa Landau was the masterpiece of her eldest sister Esther; that Esther, nearly twenty years older than the baby Rosie, had shaped and trained and guarded and schooled the child, stubbornly bringing into bloom a flower in the dungheap of an Orchard Street tenement. "My sister doesn't let me . . ." Jessie sat back and let her memory wander, and doing so, stared out the cab window at the thundering traffic of South Street, the rusty bows of the freighters nosed in rows at the piers, the dirty bulkhead of the river.

"Driver!" she exclaimed, sitting up suddenly. "Wait. Don't go straight up the Highway. I——"

He slowed down a little and tipped his head backwards, with his eyes on the madhouse of the street and his right ear cocked towards her. "Hanh, lady?"

"I want to go through Orchard Street," said Jessie. "Turn left along here someplace."

"*Orchard* Street?" The traffic light changed then and the driver stopped the cab with a bump. He stared at Jessie in his rear-view mirror. "Watsa idea," he said. "Ya tryin'a lose time?"

She smiled. "No. I know what I am doing." She looked at his hack license fastened on the front wall of the cab. His name was Louis Goldwasser. "I just—I want to look at it. I want to see what it looks like now."

His shoulders hunched in a slow, comprehending shrug. The light went green and he put his groaning motor into gear. "I get it," he said, working his way toward the left-turn corner at Grand Street. "On'y I wouldn' a t'ought *you'd* be

28

in'arested in'a old Tent' Ward." He looked into the mirror again, and again shrugged. "*Nu*—ya neveh know."

The traffic westbound on Grand Street was very heavy, a crawling, jerking mass of towering evil-smelling trucks, interspersed with the battered ancient sedans and dirty taxicabs in which people got about who had business down here. It was only a short distance, but Jessie's driver had to inch and hump his way, weaving right and left of the hulking trucks, calling down on himself the bawled curses of their drivers. As they reached Orchard Street the hackie said over his shoulder, "Ya still wanna go t'rough here, lady?"

"Why of course. I said so."

"Okay," he said. "You ast for it." But he shook his head as if pitying his passenger's dimwittedness. Jessie almost expected him to tap his forehead.

"I'm sorry to hold you up like this," she said. "I'll make it worth your time."

"Oh, it's all'a same to me. Ya get everyt'ing in dis racket."

"And drive slowly through Orchard Street," Jessie added.

He cackled quietly. "Try 'n do anyt'ing else!"

She sat forward on the edge of the seat as he turned into the first block of Orchard Street from Grand, and moved along towards Delancey. She looked quickly from side to side, right and left at the tenements, all looking so queerly neat and empty and brushed up, so strange and unnatural. This was not at all her memory of that summer afternoon years and years ago . . . twenty-eight, twenty-nine years, she speculated, I couldn't have been more than nine . . . Auntie Esther had taken her out that day, she could not remember now what she had been doing in the city at all on a hot day like that. Perhaps it was the dentist . . . no, it was because we were sailing for Europe. And Mother had a lot of things to do and Fräulein had the day off and Auntie Esther took me out . . . Her face puckered with concentration. "It's further up," she said suddenly to the driver. "Near the corner of Rivington Street." She looked and looked for the house; this one, no; that, no. Oh how silly of me, she thought, how could I possibly remember having seen that house? She did remember how much more crowded the street had been, she remembered the swarms of yelling children and fat dirty women and pushcarts with cackling peddlers in derby hats and black beards . . . garbage in the gutters . . . the sidewalk barrels outside the stores, the smells, the stinks, herring and kosher pickles and thicker, stranger smells that she did not

29

know . . . and now it looks so empty and quiet and almost neat. How queer, I never realized . . .

She could not remember the house at all, there was no way of telling it and of course she had never been inside it anyway. And they all looked alike. But Auntie Esther came sharply to her mind, standing there on the corner of Rivington Street holding Jessie tight by the hand and pointing to the watermelon stand with a dirty old man beside it. "Did your mama love watermelon!" Auntie Esther had said, wagging her handsome grey head. She was so wonderful to look at, Auntie Esther, so richly and quiety dressed, and she stood there perfectly natural in the midst of all that hullabaloo. "Did she love it! She was always teasing me for a penny for watermelon." Jessie had asked, round-eyed, if Mother always got the penny, and Auntie Esther had answered gently, "Nearly always. I tried my best. But sometimes I couldn't afford a penny. Sometimes Gran'ma took every cent for bread or soup-meat. But if Rosie was a good girl" (she did not quite say 'goil' but there was a suggestion of it)—"if she was a good girl I tried to give her a penny. She bought cocoanut too. She used to say it lasted longer than anything else she could buy with a penny. Sometimes she took all day to make up her mind what to buy . . . if it wasn't summertime with watermelon. But in the end she bought a penny hunk of cocoanut. She said she didn't like the taste, but she could keep on chewing it all day long and it was hard to swallow so it lasted. . . ."

The spasm in Jessie's throat was a sharp buffet back to here and now, her eyes were too wet to see anything more. She leaned back against the torn cushion of the cab and swallowed and drew a long breath.

"All right, driver," she called through the window. Her voice was quite changed from a few moments before, quite cool, light, impersonal, the voice of a busy, preoccupied woman. "You can go back to the Highway now." The driver made a right turn into Houston Street, heavily shaking his head. "Women—*mishugeneh*—" he said, but Jessie did not hear him. She sat staring at the fascinating sights along the River as the cab churned uptown, craning her neck to see what she could of the Brooklyn Navy Yard, and wondering what on earth was going to happen to all that stuff, to all those men, to everybody she knew, to millions of people she did not know, now that the war was over. She was going to

be nearly twenty minutes late for her appointment and that
was one thing which did not worry her at all. She stepped out
of the cab as the giant snob of a doorman at The Assembly
Club opened the door, and handed the driver four new dollar
bills. "That's all right," she said, dismissing the change, and
walked quickly to the entrance. The hackie sat looking after
her for a moment, wagging his head a little with a puzzled
squint in his eyes.

A page stepped forward as Jessie entered the black and
white marble lobby of the Holy of Holies, the club so exclusive that Jessie herself would not have been acceptable for
membership if she had married a man ten times the social
superior of Brandon Bourne, who was already considered
impeccable. But Brandon Bourne's name did not mitigate a
matter like Jessie Kernan in the eyes of the board of Gover-
nors of The Assembly Club. Jessie's mother had been on the
stage. That was the less unforgivable of the two indelible
counts against Rosa Landau Kernan. Jessie was precisely such
a person as the self-perpetuating admissions committee of the
club was dedicated to exclude. She felt a derisive satisfaction
in the knowledge that she would not join the thing anyway, if
the entire membership should vote to invite her.

"Mrs. Fielding is in the Blue Room, Madam," the page
murmured, leading the way. Jessie followed him with a cynical twitch of her lips. She knew her way to the Blue Room
which was the only one where members were permitted to
entertain outsiders. The fiction was gravely observed that any
person invited into the Club from outside darkness could
never have been there before, and must be accompanied by a
club servant in such a way as to stigmatize her as publicly as
possible.

Millicent Fielding rose stiffly from the hard armchair in
which she had been sitting, and gave Jessie her weak, evasive
handshake. Jessie said a word or two of regret at being late,
but Millicent Fielding, as capable of irritability as any woman
she knew, only curved her narrow lips into a perfunctory
smile and said that it did not matter. So she wants something,
thought Jessie; I wonder what. Oh well, it will come soon
enough.

"Would you like a cocktail?" asked her sister-in-law. Her
cold, weary manner suggested that she thought before-lunch-
eon cocktails a vulgar depravity.

"Please," said Jessie promptly. "A martini. Dry."

Mrs. Fielding pressed a bell. A tall, disdainful, middle-aged maid in the elaborate club uniform of dark green with ecru organdy appeared at once.

"One martini," said Millicent Fielding, at which Jessie could barely suppress a laugh. She wanted to say, "Point your finger at me, Millie, the biddy would understand." Instead she realized that this gauche stiffness of Millicent's was proof that she must be really upset about something. Millicent was a bore and a small-minded anachronism of a woman, but she had as much savoir-faire as anyone else of her sort. Jessie felt sorry for her and moved impulsively to put her at ease. She laughed lightly and said, "Do order something for yourself, Millicent; you look as tired as I feel." Jessie had not felt so well or so little tired in months.

"Well—and a dry sherry," added Mrs. Fielding. "I am tired, Jessie. I—" she stopped speaking and closed her mouth as if admonishing herself about something. Her flat, light grey eyes were uneasy. What a wilfully unattractive woman she is, Jessie thought. Her features are not bad. Her figure doesn't matter, at least it's neat. You can do anything with hair. Those hands and feet, of course—Jessie looked quickly across the room, careful not to make Millicent uncomfortable. The hands and feet were the long, narrow, bony sort which have been described from time immemorial as "aristocratic." To Jessie they were merely sterile. Long, thin fingers, narrow nails conservatively manicured and lacquered with colorless polish, a dry look of rigidity about the joints which stated that these hands were not, by Jessie's instincts, hands; they did nothing. Hands should be strong and supple, flexible, warm. Good hands always look warm, even outdoors on a freezing day; bad hands look cold and bluish. That was one of Jessie's irrational quirks. Her own hands were large in proportion to her small wrists. Her fingers were generous, rather heavy for their moderate length, the tips blunt and capable of hard use, well-cushioned, the nails of medium length, growing straight to their rounded points. Long nails which curved inward were another of Jessie's phobias; they reminded her revoltingly of talons. She had been hand-conscious in this way ever since she could remember, and now she thought once again of her mother in an echo of the mood of this morning.

Rosa Landau had had good hands, large, warm, soft and brown, with the heavy spatulate fingers of talent and her heredity. They were hands incapable of idleness, they had been trained to a needle, like those of the whole family that Auntie Esther had raised. And Rosa in turn had taught Jessie as a very small child to sew, to knit, to crochet, to tat, to embroider, to set the finest possible hemstitching and the daintiest beaded seams. Jessie could not remember her mother alone or at leisure amidst her intimates without some sort of fine needlework in her hands. And Jessie herself, in addition, had another talent. She could go to the kitchen, on Anna's day out, to peel onions and grate cheese for a risotto that would put her best friends into ecstasies two hours later, or to cook anything else for which she was in the mood.

Millicent Fielding, here, had no notion that such good, solid stuff entered one's life through the use of one's hands. Poor thing, thought Jessie, at the same moment rebuking herself for the meanness of feeling superior to Millicent. She finished her cocktail and followed her sister-in-law to a table in the corner of the dining-room which adjoined the Blue Room, the dining-room to which members took their guests. The brief, chastely printed menu on the thick white card with the gold club crest was precisely as uninteresting as the women who came here to eat it. Jessie selected consommé and a mushroom omelette knowing that both would bore her as much as Millicent's conversation. The food was daintily served, too daintily; there was something about the fine crisp toast, the prim small portions, the swift, expert, feminine service which irritated Jessie intensely. I am an idiot, she thought, why should I let this stupid place annoy me and spoil my mood when I have had such a lovely day up to now? She smiled gaily at Millicent, determined to overcome her inward ungraciousness, and using secretly a mental device that she had contrived long ago. In a situation like this, finding herself enclosed in an unpleasing atmosphere, she would deliberately throw her mind to the extremest possible opposite; and doing so, break the sense of being cornered in irritation or boredom. So as she looked about this really handsome room, with the brilliant October sun making radiance of the glassware and silver, and this warm loveliness failing to animate the stiff women about her, she thought mischievously of the kind of lunch that she would really have enjoyed, in a place grotesquely different from this. A place like a certain diner-wagon downtown on the way to the Holland Tunnel, where truck-drivers and taxi-drivers liked to eat; a place where the double-thick hamburgers were grilled, along with the toasting buns, while you watched, and the coffee was

33

fresh and good and always boiling hot, and the voices were growling and good-natured and terse. The kind of place where Jessie in the old days used to make Brandon stop to eat, when they went off on motor trips, because it was easy and rough and in its ridiculous contrast to everyday life, the beginning of getting away and letting down. Millicent Fielding had never in her life been inside such a place; she would have starved before unbending to the mere idea.

Her conversation up to now had been snips and bits of personal and family news. Mama was feeling much brighter these days (old Mrs. Bourne was well past eighty and an unremitting trial to every soul unfortunate enough to be bound to her by blood, duty, or obligation). Then Millicent said that it was really such a relief that the war had ended when it did because the poor young girls, these past years, had been cheated of their debuts and now Iris could look forward to the parties that were her right. Of course there were a good many young men still away in the Army and Navy, but they would probably be about town during the holidays and after all, the uniforms really are decorative at parties, aren't they? Of course things won't be really normal this season, Millicent sighed; there are so many of these benefits and things to raise money for all these foreign countries; did Jessie suppose we would have to go on feeding them and hearing about them *forever?*

"I for one," said Millicent, in the manner of all the Bournes when they spoke in the first person, a calm assumption that their opinions and wishes could not possibly be contravened, "am bored to death with them all. Haven't we done enough for them by winning the war?"

Jessie restrained the impulse to answer that we had not won the war, that it was not yet won and that it would not be won until the horrid messy starving foreign countries about which Millicent was complaining were all put in order again. It was not worth the trouble to pursue such a thought with Millicent. She would never understand because she did not want to. She had been good during the past four years, she had worked hard as a Nurse's Aide, for British War Relief, for the Free French, the Dutch, the Navy League; she had not knowingly broken a rationing rule, she had kept her motor car in storage, she had had a hard war by her lights; and now she wanted to reap her reward, in gasoline and cream and roast beef and no more high taxes and polite service once again from those horrid people in the shops, who had become too incredibly insolent; and she expected as a matter of course that all the appointed components of her scheme of things should fall at once into their proper places and remain there. Jessie wondered now whether Millicent ever really read the newspapers, or whether she opened them from the middle break to the Society page, after an uncomprehending glance across the headlines, whose subject such as strikes, Congressional inquiries, war-criminal trials, international conferences, the atom bomb and that awful Soviet Russia could only seem to her like the most annoying refusals on the part of all these tiresome people and countries to settle down and let life get back to normal.

But Millicent is uniquely chicken-witted, Jessie reminded herself; a great many women like her are perfectly aware of what is going on and perfectly aware that the ruin of their world is beyond any king's horses or all the king's men. Yet even those women are just as absorbed in all of Millicent's nonsense as she is. Jessie looked about the room and noted them. They all had a certain uniform appearance which might have been defined by their clothes and their shoes and their coiffures, but which was really a state of mind to which a woman was born, not one that she could ever possibly assume, not even after a lifetime of assimilation into this particular stratum of society. Jessie herself had moved in and out of it, because of her marriage to Brandon Bourne, for a great many years, yet she was as conspicuous a contrast to the other women in this room as if she had been lunching here in her nightdress. Her clothes were smarter and more daring and worn with crisp, flaring chic, but they came from the same establishment, or others much like it, where these discreetly-suited women had had their clothes made for generations. Jessie saw three women at a nearby table scrutinizing her and commenting to one another in the indirect way which could never have descended to the level of outright gossip but which implied by their bearing and their eyebrows and the set of their heads that Jessie was still a curiosity among them. She marvelled at the way in which these women managed to make of their special little world-within-a-world a Boston, a Philadelphia, a Richmond; an island of privilege and the tranquil past in the midst of disruption and the agitated present. And then she almost laughed aloud at the sudden thought that other women, in other equally circumscribed groups, made their own strange small islands of unchanging identity in the midst of this vast coagulum of

35

extremes which was her New York. She thought of the Hungarian store on Second Avenue where she went occasionally to buy paprika and poppyseed and vanilla beans and kümmel seeds, where hardly a word of English was spoken, and the fat customers with kerchiefs or boudoir caps on their heads greeted one another with the casual acceptance of long acquaintanceship that also served the members of The Assembly Club.

Jessie realized suddenly how bored she was by Millicent's petty, vacuous talk, else her mind would never have strayed to such a ridiculous extreme. She caught herself up, hoping that nothing had been said to which she should have given an answer. But Millicent was still murmuring that she did so hope things were settled enough so that Iris could have a proper debut, but how it was still difficult to make many arrangements, and the prices of everything were perfectly outrageous, and there was not really enough time to do things properly, but nobody had known last spring what to expect with the war still on, and finally, with a stitch of perplexity in her forehead, that Iris somehow did not seem as interested in her own plans as Millicent thought a young girl should be; in fact sometimes she thought that Iris hardly took her debut seriously at all. Millicent thought the young girls so strange nowadays, Iris and her friends; sometimes she scarcely understood what they were talking about.

If you dropped in at El Morocco about half past one some night you'd find out what Iris really talks about and with whom, thought Jessie; but one of the few real bonds that she had with any member of Brandon's family was her promise to Iris never to tell Millicent or any of them when or where she ever saw Iris. A woman like Millicent was so easy to deceive, and her own family had been doing it for so long that Jessie almost jumped when, after they had left the table and had gone back to a secluded corner of the Blue Room to drink their coffee, Millicent bit her lips, stared uneasily at the floor for a moment, and then, flushed with distress, softly blurted, "Jessie, do you know a woman named Isabel Allen?"

Jessie put down her cup and weighed her answer for the briefest possible instant. She said, "Certainly. She's been around for years."

"I know." Millicent wove her dry, stiff fingers together. "I wondered if you knew her."

"Yes. So does everybody else." That was a way of telling Millicent one thing, at least, for which she was evidently

36

fishing. But Millicent said, "That was what I wanted to talk to you about, Jessie. You see——"

Jessie had seen, from the first mention of Isabel Allen's name. She felt sorry for Millicent, not because of the position in which she found herself; most married women had to get used to finding themselves in that position; but because for some reason Millicent had found it necessary to lay aside her stubborn pride and admit the situation and confess her distress about it. Jessie did not suppose that Millicent could be physically jealous. If she had ever been capable of enough sexual expression to make anything real of living with Evander Fielding, the faculty had atrophied long ago. Jessie doubted if it had ever existed. This distress of Millicent's was clearly caused by public mortification or by fear of it, and Millicent must be at the end of her rope now, to have gone to such a length as to talk to Jessie. The pale, cold, forbidding woman sat stiffly, almost inarticulate with embarrassment, and Jessie realized that only by grasping the nettle herself could she be of any help to her sister-in-law. She said, "Van doesn't—he couldn't—want to *marry* Isabel?"

Millicent swallowed and shook her head.

"Then—" Jessie spoke as gently as she could. "After all, we've all got this kind of thing to deal with, Millie. I don't think Van is being any more conspicuous than any other man." She shrugged. "They all do it."

"But you see," said Millicent, "it's Iris that I am worried about. Why, Jessie, we *can't* have this going on while Iris is coming out. Things are so hateful now, nobody knows who is safe and who isn't. All these dreadful night clubs and places no young girl would ever have been allowed to go when—" she stopped and breathed heavily and tried to speak calmly. "Of course Iris does not go to these horrid places yet—" Jessie looked carefully across the room and kept her face expressionless—"but it will be impossible to forbid her to go where her friends go this winter. And I—I'm told—" she stopped helplessly.

Jessie nodded. There was no use denying Millicent's admission that Van Fielding took Isabel Allen to all the most publicized places, where the last barriers of demarcation between the different elements of metropolitan society had long since gone down. It made no difference whatsoever who was old family, who the big money, who the theatre and Hollywood, who business, who the newspaper crowd, who the brains and talent, who the *soi-disant* demimonde, and who the outright nobody on the up-and-up. All that was required for inclusion in the galaxy was money (or access to somebody's money) and to be news. Yet the scribes and chroniclers of that strange, cruel, yet intimate world, the newspaper gossip columnists, had their own code about it. They did not mention by name married men in their connections with other women, so long as the men were not separated from their wives. Let a man move to a hotel or to his club, and the lid was off, but that had no bearing, Jessie felt, on a situation like that of Van Fielding. She said so now to Millicent, as tactfully as she could. She even said, "I know those chaps well enough to know that they wouldn't print anything about Van. I wouldn't worry so if I were you, Millie."

"That's not exactly what is worrying me," said Millicent wretchedly. "It's that I don't want Iris to go about and see—and meet—" she turned scarlet again. "Why," she almost gasped, "things have got to such a pass in this horribly cheap way everybody behaves—Iris might even see her father in one of those places. With that—that woman."

"Might!" thought Jessie. Again she dared not look at Millicent. She wondered what Millicent would say or do if she knew that Iris and her father had already evolved a modus vivendi which was a simple exchange of protection between thieves. The situation was so impossible of evasion that Jessie, not many days ago, had marvelled at the sangfroid with which she had seen Iris, in the company of a disreputable man named Jack Spanier, stroll past her father's table at El Morocco and nod coolly at him and Isabel Allen. And Jessie almost never went to such places, she loathed them; but if on her rare visits she invariably encountered Van Fielding, it must mean that he was out on the town every night of the week. Jessie found herself wondering by what combination of lies Iris must keep her mother hoodwinked about her own doings. And the whole truth, so cynically and expertly manipulated by Millicent's husband and daughter, made of her concern such a preposterous triviality that Jessie did her best to induce Millicent to forget it. But Millicent would not be induced; on the contrary she shook her head and said, "No, I have closed my eyes to everything that Evander has done for years, but this year he has got to consider Iris first. I will not have her mortified the year she is making her debut."

Jessie could have told Millicent that Iris was incapable of mortification, at least on any such count as this, but that would have been cruelty. She wondered then why Millicent had not appealed to her husband directly; after all, he was not a scoundrel and Jessie would have expected him to understand Millicent's plea and to be fairly decent about it. Evidently that had not happened, because Millicent must have been really cornered and in despair to have brought this up with Jessie. A great deal of time had gone into this futile meeting by now and Jessie was longing to break away. But she sensed that for all her talk, Millicent had not yet come to the real point of her problem. Jessie said, "Look here, Millie, why don't you tell me what you really wanted to ask me about? Wasn't it something more than just asking if I knew Isabel?"

Millicent Fielding looked up quite honestly at Jessie. She said, "Yes. It was. I thought—" She pinched her lips together. Jessie was too clever for her. She said, "Really, Mill. You didn't want *me* to talk to Isabel!"

Millicent sat more stiffly upright. "I don't see why not," she said. "You say you know the woman."

From Millicent that was almost an insult but Jessie ignored it. She only shrugged and said, "Everybody knows everybody. I don't really understand how it's happened you have never met Isabel yourself. You'd be surprised the houses she's invited to. Like a lot of gals."

"It's a perfectly disgusting world," said Millicent angrily.

"Well, neither you nor I can do anything about it so you might as well relax. Millie, you didn't seriously think you could get me to go to Isabel Allen and ask her to give up your husband?"

"I—somebody will have to do something," said Millicent. There was an edge to her voice that made Jessie narrow her eyes and think a little.

"If you are seriously asking my advice," said Jessie, "the only thing I can suggest is to talk to Van perfectly frankly yourself. Tell him it will be a big favor if he will just agree not to take Isabel out to public places this winter. After all, you don't care if he sleeps with her or not."

"Jessie!"

"Oh, I'm sorry. Either you're realistic about these things or you're not. But to ask me to go and turn on the throbs with Isabel—why, it just doesn't make sense, Millie." She paused. "I wouldn't have done it when she was living with my husband—why should I make myself ridiculous about yours?"

"Oh." Millicent looked stunned. *"Brandon?"* Her voice was choked with shock and disbelief.

39

"Yes," said Jessie coldly. "Brandon. You didn't think he would overlook a special job like Isabel in making the rounds, did you?"

"Oh, how can you be so vulgar," breathed Millicent.

"It all depends on what you consider vulgar," said Jessie. "Isabel has slept with most of the attractive men in town and been kept by a lot of them. I used to be told that was vulgar. But what beats me is how she always looks like a candy angel. With that spun-glass hair and those languid, drifting ways of hers. Actually she's as hard as marble—and probably tougher."

"Then," said Millicent, her voice dull with misery, "you won't help me?"

"Well, I can't, Millie. You don't realize what you're asking. Isabel would only laugh at me and ask me if I had lost my mind and did I want to see her new sables. She'd know you had put me up to it and she——"

Millicent had sunk back against her chair and was holding her handkerchief to her lips, staring over it at Jessie. Jessie was planning in another moment to put on her gloves and get out of here; this was too futile and too painful. But now she saw that Millicent's trouble, whatever it was, was still unstated, and it also dawned on her, in a stroke of perception which revised her former estimation of Millicent's wilful naïveté about her daughter, that Millicent was not altogether the fool that she seemed. There was a hard look in Millicent's cold eyes. Jessie leaned forward and said, "Why don't you tell me the rest of it, Millie?"

Her sister-in-law hesitated and Jessie could see her struggling with her pride. Then Millicent said, "Evander is spending so much money on that—that—creature—that—oh, Jessie!" This ordeal was really intolerable for her.

"There will not be enough for Iris's debut," Jessie finished. "Is that it?"

Millicent nodded miserably. There was silence for some time. Then Jessie said, "He never really recouped that big loss at all, did he?"

Again Millicent answered silently, with an embarrassed shake of her head. It was and had been for years an intolerable ignominy that for all the importance and the position of her own family and her husband's, neither of them were wealthy at all; neither had any appreciable capital. The Bournes had been poor, by their own standards, for two generations. The old lady, early widowed, had brought up her

40

son and her daughter to the life that she considered their natural right, and in doing so had used up the last of the means left her by her husband. It was agreed (with charity on the part of some observers) that Millicent, whose only dowry had been good family and a pale, fleeting prettiness, had done extremely well in marrying Evander Fielding. At the time he was well-to-do. But now as Jessie sat confronted by her sister-in-law's problem, she thought once more how complete an anachronism was the life of the Fieldings. Evander Fielding had lost most of his money in the stock market crash of 1929; and instead of digesting that loss over the intervening years, and making whatever adjustments might be involved, he and his wife had each continued stubbornly to live by standards and measures that had actually ceased to exist. In his case the measure was money; in hers the aims and the rules of a world which she considered fundamental and eternal, and which in fact was only a frail, antique veneer where it appeared to survive at all.

Jessie was not surprised to learn this most recent truth about Evander Fielding's circumstances. He seemed to spend money lavishly, but that was often done, in the words of Jessie's friends, with mirrors. And it was also very often the case that a man like Fielding, resentful of his domestic financial burdens, lashed back at the dullness and the circumscription of his life by blowing in everything that he managed to keep out of his family's hands.

Still, Evander Fielding was a man who would normally see to it that his daughter had her debut, and Jessie also suspected, knowing him, that if he could find the money for Millicent he would only too willingly give it to her, as the best way of insuring her leaving him to his own concerns. He must be in far worse straits than his wife could suppose, if he had already refused her. Jessie had no choice but to ask Millicent that; otherwise she was wasting her time.

Millicent answered with stiff lips. "Evander says that this is a great deal of money for him at the present time; he cannot promise to give me all I will need for Iris and it is hardly any use—I mean——"

Jessie nodded. Millicent was right about that; if one were going in for the undertaking of a debut one had to do it or not do it. One could not draw a line across the middle of the intricate procedure and stop to economize at this subscription or that new dress.

"How much do you need for Iris's debut?" asked Jessie

abruptly. Millicent's lips tightened; such a question would seem in execrable taste to her. "I mean," said Jessie more gently, "how much did you ask Van for?"

"I—we agreed," said Millicent, groping for any phrase that might lay even a shred of dignity over this humiliating exposure, "that we would have to count on about ten thousand dollars."

"And you think that if Van stopped—ah—seeing Isabel Allen he would be able to let you have the money?"

Millicent said "Yes" almost inaudibly.

Jessie sat back for a moment and looked away from her and said, "Millie, I don't believe you are right about that. I honestly do not think that Van can raise ten thousand dollars for Iris, or for Isabel Allen. He doesn't—" she paused. "See here, Millicent, I can't talk about this unless I tell the truth. I know it is very unpleasant for you, but you simply cannot grope your way through a jungle blindfolded. Do you understand me?"

"I suppose so."

"Well—I am merely trying to tell you that Van does not keep Isabel Allen. I mean he doesn't pay her rent or—or—you know."

"How do *you* know?" said Millicent in a queer blurting way.

"Because I know who does pay her rent—or gives her the money to pay it. Isabel is not just a straight cut-and-dried job, you know. She keeps up a semblance of an identity of her own. She has a small part in some show about once every two or three years, and so she manages to be called an actress and not just a—a—" Jessie paused and laughed. "You are so hard to talk to, Mill; if only you wouldn't act so shocked!"

"I am shocked."

"No, you're not. Not really. You only think it's expected of you to seem shocked. Anyway, those girls like Isabel all live about the same way. They look like ladies, you know; probably you don't want to be told so, but they do. And no matter where they came from, Arkansas or Alabama or Iowa, they all learn to talk in a certain chah-ming, tinkling way—until they take on a few too many or get a little excited about something and then you hear the old R's start to grind, or the twang come through, like the brass underneath the plating on a piece of junk jewelry. And everything else about their lives is pretty much the same. They always live at the best possible addresses, and they give the most amusing cocktail parties in town, and they are very careful to know a few really wellbred prominent women and the women know them because—" Jessie paused and Millicent, frowning, asked, "Why?"

"Because, Mill, you cannot get many important and interesting men to come to your parties unless they have a good time there."

There was a moment of silence and Jessie, anxious to get away, said, "So you see, Isabel keeps several irons in the fire at a time, and for all that, she appears to be quite artlessly on her own. Of course she seldom pays her bills but that's a technique all of itself. And even when she gets one real ace in her hand, with a chance to get herself paid up and a lot of new clothes and furs collected, she never keeps him long. So if I were you, I wouldn't make any more fuss about Van and Isabel. You won't get the money for Iris by doing it, and you will humiliate yourself—unnecessarily. Van will get tired of Isabel anyway, but then there will be somebody else instead. There always is. The only thing you really want is to be able to keep your head up and see that Iris has her debut the way you want her to. I'd be glad to give you the ten thousand for that, Millie. You ought to have it."

Jessie was careful not to look at Millicent Fielding then, for she knew as if she were watching it that the unhappy pallid face had turned scarlet and the cold hands had gone into a hard, twisted knot. Jessie knew before she spoke that her offer would not be received with relief or welcome, but that it would seem to Millicent Fielding like a searing insult. Yet there was nothing else to do. Jessie was only aware of the really horrible pass to which Evander Fielding's finances must have come, if he could not raise such a sum as this; and she expected, too, what Millicent would say when she spoke.

"That is very kind of you, Jessie," said Millicent, breathing between the words. "I could not—I mean we—of course—a loan——"

Jessie shook her head, gathering up her gloves and handbag and purposely forcing a tone of brisk gaiety.

"Nonsense," she said. "It's nothing, Millie, really. I would like to do it and nobody else will know a thing about it. Certainly not Van," she added, with a laugh. She stood up, forcing Millicent also to her feet and thanking God silently that the ordeal was over. "I'll put the check in the mail when I get home. I loved lunch. I simply must run now, I'm frightfully late."

"I—" Millicent would have tried to thank her but Jessie

43

forestalled that by glancing at the crystal watch attached to the clasp of her handbag and gasping, "Oh my God, I forgot I had a three o'clock fitting at Bergdorf's. It's nearly half past. Good bye, Millie, give my love to Mama Bourne."

She pronounced the word "Ma-*mah*," which was how their mother had taught Brandon and Millicent to address her. Jessie had thought when she first knew them how affected it was; a meaningless Anglicization of the French, sufficiently mispronounced to appear the exclusive creation of the Bournes. And I sent her my love, thought Jessie, hurrying out of the club and starting down Park Avenue. If I ever said a more hypocritical thing in my life, I do not know what it was.

IV

The appointment for her fitting was not for today at all, but for tomorrow. Jessie had seized upon it as the quickest excuse for breaking away from Millicent, which would be an equal relief to both of them. She trotted southwards along Park Avenue in the direction of Fifty-eighth Street, for she had left Millicent at the door of the club, and it seemed decenter to be going in that direction. Having started, she was happy to be there on foot anyway. It was as beautiful an October day as there could possibly be, and to Jessie that meant a day for the spectacular display of her beloved city, imposing as the setting for bold and lavish jewels. Stepping out of the house this morning, to breathe the brilliant air which seemed like an elixir poured from the great blue bottle of the sky, she had wanted to skip like a small child for sheer excitement. Surely no sky anywhere could be as exhilarating as this amazing sky embracing the towers of New York. Perhaps this was because it was almost surprising to find any sky here at all; or trees, or grass, or flowers.

The city was indeed a creature, brawlingly alive but made of stone and glass and brick and concrete; and yet it breathed and spoke and smelled and sounded, waked and slept, froze, thawed, and sweated as all the country world of plants and animals had never seemed to Jessie to do. She knew that she was wrong; she knew that her prejudice seemed preposterous and wilfully outrageous to all her friends who loved their country places in Connecticut and Bucks County and New Jersey and Long Island. They can have them, she thought, whenever the idiotic argument began anew. She loathed the country, her life in these past six summers when she had been cut off from Europe had been one continuous refusal to be trapped by any circumstance into renting or buying a country place. There was no greater incompatibility between Brandon and her. Perhaps, she thought, I detest the country so violently because it holds no resources for me to turn to when Brandon lets me down. Since life had taught her with cruelty amounting at times to violence that Brandon in one way or another would always let her down, she saw no reason for expecting ever to relax her guard.

She thought now as she walked down this great beautiful arrogant avenue of her city, that perhaps her passionate attachment to it was a secret weakness, a confession that she needed its size, its power, its drive, its might, to bolster her in her uncertainties and to give her reassurance through her sense of oneness with every strong brick, girder, and square of paving. Never, never for one instant in her whole life, had she ever felt the loneliness and desolation that many people knew in this city; never had she thought it cold or hard or heartless; never had she found its worst uglinesses forbidding.

She remembered an afternoon in the past summer when Brandon had gone off to spend a week end at Glen Cove with people who bored her to sullen stupidity. She had seen him leave, with a happy acceleration of the sense of bliss that his absence gave, and after he was gone she had wandered about the apartment, dripping with the horrible sweat that accompanied the worst kind of summer weather in New York; sweat that was made even more dreadful because of the grit that rolled in through the windows which one had to keep open at times of the day, or suffocate altogether. So it was not sufficient to clean and dust a house once or twice a day in such weather, but once in every few hours. Even that she did not mind; her scheme of life included the means of coping with it, and her house, prepared for summer, was designed in its washable rugs, its fresh chintzes, its dark awnings and its cool Venetian blinds, to withstand the effects of the city summer as gracefully as Jessie herself.

That afternoon she had taken another of the innumerable cool baths, with handfuls of fragrant salt and splashes of eau de cologne, that punctuated such days; and then she had lain reading in a chiffon nightdress on the long French couch in her bedroom, covered for the summer with glazed white chintz. When she could in this half-secret, relaxed summer way deliberately go off into a world where she felt her heart and her brain to be alive, leaving her body content in the place where it loved best to be, she knew a pleasure which Brandon with his tennis, his swimming, his friends, his gregarious restlessness could not comprehend in any degree at all. She remembered then the impulse that she had had, that same foully hot evening, to wander out after the sun went down, an ugly red threat for tomorrow, behind the roofs on the other side of town, and watch the people, her neighbors who lived through this perforce and not from choice, as they made the best of their lot.

They appeared to enjoy themselves and she had no doubt that this was the truth. In these years since she had lived at the edge of the East River she had learned for the first time the life of the real people of the city, the people who never left it or went anywhere else at all, except possibly to Coney Island or Bear Mountain or out to spin along the growing networks of parkways in their small clattering sedans crammed with children, the family mutt, and Pa's coat swaying on a hanger by the window. Until she had first gone over to the East River to inspect the half-finished new building in which she and Brandon had selected their apartment from plans, Jessie had lived almost her whole life along the central spine of Manhattan Island, that long strip of wealth and smartness bounded by Central Park on the west and Lexington Avenue on the east. The banks of the East River in those days had been an unknown wilderness of slaughterhouses, coal docks, and miles of five-story coldwater railroad tenements. These were a different sort of tenement from the frightful raddled warrens of the downtown slums; these were not slums at all. They were simply the places where the solid common masses of the city's basic millions lived. Above all, Jessie knew now, these people were self-respecting. However else their life might differ from the screaming, stinking, teeming life of the real slums, Yiddish and Italian and Negro, the great demarcation lay in the intangibles of custom, habit, and standards, as well as in a matter of dollars.

The word "poor" was so dramatically relative in a city like this. These neighbors of Jessie's were of course poor by any contrast with her or even the least wealthy of her friends, but they were immeasurably better off than people whose monthly rent averaged only twenty dollars less than theirs. Twenty dollars to Jessie was perhaps a pair of shoes, possibly the flowers for a dinner-party, Mr. Goldfish's bill for newspapers and cigarettes, not by any means a handbag, a blouse, or a piece of lingerie. But twenty dollars marked the whole difference in millions of lives between the furtive shame of the slums and the tough, cheerful existence of this vigorous majority.

It seemed now in retrospect unbelievable that one could have lived much of one's life a three-minute walk from the abrupt dividing line at which this world began, and never have had an actual knowledge that it was there, but for the accident that a few fashionable people had had the imagination to "discover" the East River in the nineteen-twenties. Now Jessie was saturated in the sights, the personalities, and the argot of the broad shabby avenues and dingy cross-streets which lay between the elegances of the East River apartment houses and the old boundary of the rich and privileged at Lexington Avenue. And she loved what she had learned, she knew a feeling of friendliness and cosiness and a queer sort of security, such as she imagined a worm might find in a cocoon, from her contacts with these people. Small discoveries, one by one, had led her to a real knowledge of how they lived.

She remembered how, years ago, she had wondered why on earth she used to see these housewives coming out of basement shops invariably kept by somebody named Tony, carrying spouted cans of kerosene. What did they do with kerosene? Jessie would have said that it had no possible use except in old-fashioned oil lamps which she knew these people did not use, because through their lace-curtained windows at night she had seen the bright glare of electric lights. Kerosene in New York City?—kerosene was rural, it belonged to the remotest imaginable back country. And then she learned the meaning of that casual New York phrase, "coldwater flat." It had literally never occurred to her that here in the metropolis of the nation of universal automobiles, radios, and plumbing, central heating was a luxury, and hot water did not gush from everybody's taps as it did from hers. She found that her neighbors bought kerosene because they burned it in the portable round sheet-iron stoves with which they heated their five-room flats, and she found that out by seeing the stoves for sale in the endless cluttered hardware stores of

Second Avenue where, by nosing around, she could learn many other things of these people about whom she had never thought much before.

She learned above all one great comprehensive fact: the life of the neighborhood, the life of the block. She learned that certain neighborhood stores were far more than mere places at which women bought their food and their supplies. They were like clubs, presided over by somebody named Louis or Max or Joe, who in many ways was the arbiter of local custom and habit. This man, the grocer or the butcher or the corner druggist, knew the most intimate details of family life in the neighborhood; and he knew it from the women themselves, to whom a new pregnancy, or a letter from a son in the Army, was an event to be shared with the whole block. The proprietors of deluxe establishments on Madison Avenue might know just as much about the private lives of their customers, but they would know it as gossip siphoned from servants and especially from the arrogant coldblooded cooks to whom most rich women left their marketing.

This neighborhood life was altogether different; meagre, sometimes uncomfortable and always incredibly circumscribed, but warm and natural and very distinctly organized according to its own special standards. It had its own code for its wives, its daughters, its small children. Its men were artisans, bus drivers, policemen, firemen, tradesmen, hackies. Its children attended the grim and gloomy public school where Jessie went to vote; they played on the sidewalks and in the streets, on the stoops and in the doorways the same games that Jessie knew her own mother had played, hopscotch and skipping-rope and jacks for the girls, ball and shinny for the boys. They wrote with colored chalk on the pavements and copings "Mae loves Walt" inside a heart and arrow, and sometimes other things which Jessie, glimpsing them as she walked past, would have liked to stop and scuff out with the sole of her shoe. They built bonfires in the gutters at the slightest provocation; on Hallowe'en and Thanksgiving and often just for the hell of it; they roasted snitched sweet-potatoes and apples in the ashes, and after Christmas, when people threw out their dried-up Christmas trees and left them lying in the areaways beside the chained ashcans, the kids went wild with joy and whooped around the leaping fires half the night, with their mothers leaning out of upstairs windows yelling, "You! Harry! You hoid me! You come in'a house this minnit or I'll tell ya Pa to lick ya!" And

Harry, before obeying, would bellow in the rough roar of all his kind, "Hey, Skinn-ay! I gotta scram. My old woman's sore."

She had reached the corner of Fifty-ninth Street, with the traffic light gone red against her, and she stood there wondering why this particular street should remain so persistently a relic of an earlier, ugly day. It must be the crosstown trolleys, she thought, but why should that leave three of the four corners occupied by crazily obsolete buildings? This must be some of the most valuable land in the city. And there sits that hideous garage, which has been there ever since I can remember, and which would have been torn down twenty years ago if things happened consistently in this town instead of in their own peculiar way. I suppose that site belongs to some miserly heir of a rich family who is content with the rental from the garage and has never seen a reason for replacing it with a modern building.

The light changed and she stepped off the curb, to continue walking downtown without precisely knowing why, except that the walk had formed the obbligato to a certain train of thought to which she felt her mind involuntarily returning, because it was that kind of mind, accustomed to finishing what it began. She often thought about the full, flavorsome life of the real people of the city, the big, common, vital hordes toward whom she felt herself so strongly drawn; perhaps that was why she had been thinking about them and their life in summertime when, in a sense, they came into their own after Jessie's kind had fled to the country. Then if she found herself in town she had a sense of remaining from choice in the suffering city, to share even the illusion of the life of these neighborhood people.

That was why, on that cruel evening last summer, she had gone out in a dark linen dress and flat thin shoes to walk slowly westward along the teeming street, and lose herself among the heavy, patient women at the open windows with growing plants along the sills; among the young, rapidly fattening mothers grouped in knots of two or three, each with an oscillating foot on the crossbar of a baby carriage and an eye on one or two small fry toddling in a safe circle nearby. There was evidently some demarcation of age or size in their conventions about their children, below which it was perfectly proper to save themselves the trouble of taking a child into the house, or waiting until it had wet itself, by helping it to piddle neatly in the gutter. And Jessie was always slightly abashed by her own faint shame at this sight which proved her to be less honest than these casually natural women.

It was on evenings like that that the intolerable heat drove the people from the minor privacy of their small homes into the communal life of the street, where it was not really cooler but where it seemed at least easier to breathe. Camp stools and kitchen chairs made their appearance on the sidewalk; Pa, his collar or his whole shirt left off and his work done, benevolently handed out nickels for Dixies and Popsicles; Ma who had counted that he would be along, bought PEACHES, SWEET and JUCY from the huckster leading his miserable hired horse and plaintively wailing his second-grade wares up towards the open windows. The kids played around the blocks of ice which Tony kept standing by the curbstone, snitching a chunk whenever they dared. In many a block somebody had taken a wrench and had illegally turned on a fire-hydrant, which was shooting a geyser into the street. The leaping, howling, wildly excited kids were jumping half-naked into and out of the cool stream, wrestling and rough-housing and splashing. No passerby would have dreamed of objecting; if he got splashed that was his own laziness, he could have crossed the street.

And Jessie had walked on past all this, queerly uncomprehending why she was there, and what had drawn her from the exquisite refuge of her own house to mingle with this heaviness of dirt, heat, smells, noises, ugliness and sweating, bawling people. To say that she enjoyed being here, that she would choose it voluntarily in preference to the summer life of Europe which she loved, would have been very false. But this was an honest and an interesting way of making the best of things as they were; or it seemed so until Jessie looked carefully at the open windows along both sides of the street, and saw small blue-starred service flags in so many of them that it seemed as if every home in this whole mass must have a man away in the armed forces. Making it possible for me to go back to Europe again one day, she thought with a sense of shame; what is there in my life to show that I am worth their doing it?

By that time she had reached Third Avenue, the boundary of this world and its ugliest, most odious feature because of the Elevated which blighted it and made it a gehenna the whole length of the Island, from the sinister enclave of the Bowery to the innocuous but gloomy miles up here. Jessie thought with pity of the dire necessity that must force people

50

to live in these tenements with the hideous trackage almost touching their windows, the ear-rending trains crashing by, and the passengers in the trains often abating the tedium of their ride by staring in at the windows past which they were whizzing, upon the completest domestic intimacies of the people inside. Then she realized that the human creature can get used to anything, and is quite capable of strong attachment to any habit, even that of living in a flat abutting on hell in the form of noise, dirt, darkness, and lack of privacy. Possibly many of them liked it; even certainly some people on Second Avenue and across town on Sixth and Ninth Avenues missed the El in the shadow of which many of them had lived their whole lives; they must feel unnatural, denuded and bat-eyed at the sudden change.

It was the knowledge that there really were uncountable, anonymous thousands of such people, whose instincts she could far better understand than those of men and women whose dearest dream was to escape to the country, that had kept Jessie standing for a moment on the street corner, her face sticky with sweat, her body damp and feeling unnaturally heavy in the heat, her skin specked with grit spewed in the wake of the hateful trains. She stood there thinking not of iron and brick and unwashed windows and fire-escapes with milk bottles illegally kept upon them, and nasty rumpled bedding spread on window sills where there was no air to cure it, and grimy crumbling backyards with mazes of squeaking clotheslines overhead and savage derelict tomcats miaowling on the fences; but all these and many more of sights and sounds and smells and memories bulked deep and heavy in her mind while she did think, with sharp volition which she knew, herself needing beauty and serenity, to be perverse, "I love it, I love it. It is me, it is mine, I love these people even though I do not know them. I do not need their names, nor talk, nor time to spend with them, I do not need to find them one by one and bring them into the walled island of my life, nor do they want me in theirs. It is only enough to know that they are here, that they like me are rooted in this noise and strength and power and mass, and utterly content to be so. I am happy, my life is no more complete than any other, whole beautiful worlds in which I love to be are blighted or obliterated, all my pleasures and my escapes are crushed. Yet for this moment I am happy here. More than this moment would be a falsity, the most absurd of poses, but this moment is a true one and it gives me happiness."

Then she had turned and walked slowly back eastwards towards the river and her cool, delicately remote home whose quiet and privacy and beauty mocked the very emotions that had brought her out on such a hot summer evening to wander through the hard world of her neighbors.

And now on a radiant October afternoon, walking through a part of town as polished and carefully mounted for display as one of Cartier's windows, she remembered how very small a bit of her beloved city this arrogant beauty was, yet how integral to its complicated personality, like the Mainbocher dress and the diamonds which Jessie might put on to receive guests for a dinner that she had cooked herself, wearing an old jumper and one of Anna's aprons.

The clock on the New York Central tower said ten minutes to four, and Jessie paused with a smile to realize that her brisk walk and the interwoven embroidery of her thoughts had carried her as far as Fifty-seventh Street, where she had not intended to go at all. Oh well, she thought, now that I am here I might as well run over to Fifth Avenue and do those errands I've been putting off. She had wedding presents to send to the daughters of two of her friends. She always sent china or linen, and the shops from which she bought these were the same where her own best-loved things had been bought, where her mother had shopped ever since she could remember, and where Jessie never quite lost the faint sense of herself as a young girl in a bygone world. An establishment like Plummer's china shop was one of the legacies from that good gone world which seemed to Jessie to have the fullest right to survival, because it sold fine and beautiful things whose value really began with their use, things which developed taste and the knowledge of a fascinating art, whereas Jessie's memory of other luxuries of the vanished world, such as imported motor cars with custom-built bodies, marked them deteriorative anachronisms which probably never would, and certainly never need come back into use.

But notwithstanding Fifty-ninth Street, nothing could remain unchanged if it were to survive in this city, and so the shops which Jessie visited now had had to swim with the current. She had loved the old original Plummer's in Thirty-fifth Street ever since shopping-trips with her mother as a very small girl had been the greatest possible treat. She missed the old small, dark shop, but she had to confess the convenience of this newer one, which was exactly why it had been put here. She bought a dozen Spode plates for Margaret

Kellway's daughter and succumbed as usual to the temptation of wandering through the department where antique china was on display. And, while the sight of the long tables with whole dinner services of glowing, noble old Crown Derby and Worcester and Lowestoft made her feel almost limp with pleasure, she felt at the same time a mingling of shame and consternation and something very like horror at the reasons why these irreplaceable treasures were here, shipped out of the great houses of England by the descendants of the families for whom they had been made. That the life of these houses was disappearing from the world was no personal concern of Jessie's; but that much of this treasure, so subtle that only real love and real knowledge could appreciate it, was passing into the hands of the most hateful people thrown up by the convulsion of civilization—that was painful.

It was the rich scum of Europe, with their refugeed millions, their vast suites in expensive hotels, their nauseating greed, their arrogance, their vile manners, their tax-dodging, their phony citizenships in silly little tropical republics, their disgusting dinners in the finest restaurants where they gorged on black-market butter and prime meat while their own countries froze and starved and the captains and waiters sometimes audibly wished them frying in hell; it was such people into whose hands these treasures were passing. They were being clever, they were putting their money into things; and while they made public scenes, screaming at manicurists and tipping them five cents, they would in the next hour count off twenty-five hundred dollars from a wad of cash in their pockets for such a service of antique china as Jessie was admiring now. They filled the art galleries and auction rooms, they blew up the prices of lovely things which sane people bought judiciously once in a great while, hoping to live with them for the rest of their lives, to extremes where nobody but a fool would complete. Jessie could well have afforded to indulge her love of old English china at this time when there was so much of it to be had; but not on these conditions. The thought made her shudder.

Out on Fifth Avenue again she walked on, thinking, "Oh, it isn't only the refugees, actually; there are just as many people like me behaving every bit as badly. Look at Mollie Hildreth." Who, last year at the height of the war, had told Jessie with delighted pride of getting a dozen pairs of nylon stockings at "only twelve-fifty a pair, my dear, isn't that dreamy?"

It was a surprise to Jessie that she herself should go on in the same old way of habit, shopping, asking people to dine, thinking—not too much, but enough to achieve results—about her clothes, putting time and effort into nonsense like the precise shade of pin-red roses which she liked to place, massed, in the corners of the drawing-room. Of themselves these habits were all perfectly graceful, perfectly legitimate; people who existed oblivious of them were unpleasant and unattractive to know; their ways and their conversation were usually as barren as their houses. It was of all rationalizations the easiest, in a mad distorted time like this, to tell oneself that the clothes and the flowers, the good things to eat, the theatres, the gay restaurants, the motors emerging from storage, were all here in the unscathed United States, intended to be used; and what possible help could it be to Europe now to make the false gesture of abjuring comfort and abundance in America? One could not achieve the only connective that would make sense, the sending to those who needed it anything that one might be willing or eager to go without oneself. But Jessie, nonetheless, was deeply uneasy. Her sense of trouble, of growing inner distress, and of some impending action, decisive yet involuntary, which would bring her outer life into step with this inner one at which she seldom actually looked, was very strong just now.

She was coming out of the shop where she had bought a second wedding-present, and was about to enter the discouraging contest of looking for an empty cab to hail, when she saw a large, blowzy woman coming towards her, a vague smile on her face, and a particularly tiny toy caniche high-stepping along beside her on a fancy scarlet leash. The dog was a ridiculous contrast to its mistress. Jessie's involuntary amusement appeared to be a pleased greeting as the pair paraded up to her, the woman saying, "Jessie . . . haven't seen you in ages . . ." and Jessie replying, "Hello, Lorraine. How are you? What an enchanting dog."

"Is beautiful, precious, adorable dog," said Lorraine, making a squeezed-up face of vapid rapture at her pet. The dog woofed from its absurd fuzzy muzzle and pranced up to the corner lamppost to lift its leg.

"How've you been?" asked Lorraine. She spoke in the smooth, casual drawl, with the sliding vowels and swallowed R's which had been the hallmark of a certain clique, a caste, a generation of debutantes who had attended two or three fashionable schools to which they sent their daughters now.

Jessie too had been among them at school, though never really one of them for many reasons; the visible and audible ways in which she had always differed from them were clearer now than then. Her speech was more clipped and delicate if she were in a mood to feel precise, but it could also sprawl into slang, profanity, or the natural argot of sidewalk New York which was utterly foreign to her former schoolmates.

"I've just been lunching with Millie," she said.

"Gahd," murmured Lorraine, shaking her head lazily. "Poor Mill. Do you remember, she used to be pretty?"

"Mm . . . she's a bit older than we are," said Jessie, as if to ascribe all of the changes in Millicent to her age. But Lorraine said, "She really has a foul life."

Jessie's thoughts hopped quickly over the highlights of Lorraine's own life, which had hardly been a fragrant one, and had left their marks all too permanently. And Lorraine had been the arbiter of her own existence, whereas poor Millicent had been only the innocent bystander at hers.

"Who hasn't?" Jessie laughed. Lorraine laughed too. There was in their mirth a note of peculiar understanding; it was not a thing of affection or congeniality or even friendliness, simply of explicit fact.

"I wonder if Mill will ever get a come-uppance," said Lorraine slowly.

Jessie was rather surprised, not because Lorraine should slide into talk about her sister-in-law but because there was in the remark something more serious and more immediate than in the usual idle gossip.

"Oh," she said, "this doesn't mean anything . . . any different . . . you know . . ." Jessie shrugged her own words to pieces purposely.

"I don't mean just Van," said Lorraine. Jessie was rather startled but she only opened her eyes a little wider and let Lorraine drawl on. "Mill would be a fool if she weren't used to Van. Of course it's a kind of a thing now . . . he isn't really likely to blow up in Millie's face. But if he doesn't, Iris will."

Jessie would have sworn two hours ago that nothing imaginable could ever make her take a swift and angry stand in defense of Millicent or, in fact, of any member of the Bourne or Fielding families. But some twist in the words of this woman made her react sharply. To her amazement she found that she was stopping just short of blurting, "Not if I can help it." She was silent. She began conspicuously to watch for an empty cab, as a sign to Lorraine that she meant to break away.

Lorraine added in the same vague drawl, "Cynthia doesn't like Iris . . ."

Considering Lorraine's own marital and extra-marital history, and its incidental impingement upon her daughter Cynthia, there remained only the atavism of her undeniably patrician birth to explain what she had said. Jessie understood perfectly. She smiled meaninglessly and said, "Well, those girls, you know . . ." and then, beginning to walk on, "It was nice to see you, Lorraine."

"Call me up some time. Let's lunch," said Lorraine.

"Yes. Let's do . . ."

Jessie waved lightly, murmuring "So long," and started up Fifth Avenue. She would walk until she found a cab; at least she would be on her way. She resisted the temptation to turn and look once at the backs of Lorraine and her dog. She knew that she would be vastly amused at the spectacle in rear elevation, but just now she did not want to be amused. She felt annoyed. It was a great many years, a forgotten passage of years, since Lorraine had had enough importance to Jessie to evoke any feeling at all. On the rare accidental occasions when they met they had always moved on this same plane of tacit, slightly sardonic understanding. But today, and it seemed preposterous to suppose that a non-existent loyalty to her horrid little niece Iris should be the reason, Jessie walked away from Lorraine feeling resentful and protesting and disturbed. She was cross too because so many moments of this day had been lovely ones, except for the false notes struck by the personalities of some of the women about her at luncheon, and now by Lorraine who had been banished from her hereditary niche by many of them. But she was one of them still, and so was Millicent, and for some reason Jessie found herself saying almost aloud, "Cold. Cold. Frozen, empty, heartless plaster casts. All of them. God on high in heaven, how I hate them."

And this was surprising to her because she would have said by now that that world had done her all the damage that it could ever possibly do, and she was far, far beyond hating it. She was also far beyond singling out in memory any of its members upon whom to lay the burden of her bitternesses. So she was surprised, even while one lobe of her brain was derisively reminding her that she did not care a tinker's damn any more, to find that Brandon of whom she almost never thought in absence unless he forced some unpleasantness upon her, had somehow moved up into her mind, and was occupying it now. I do not want to think about him, she told herself, and certainly not because of anything suggested by Lorraine. Yet she was thinking about him, about happenings of long ago over which she could no more feel emotion now than one can recall literally the sensation of excruciating physical pain once it is past. And because such thoughts are very difficult to exorcise once they seize the forefront of one's attention, Jessie was for the moment powerless to turn her back upon them.

V

Ridiculously, she always thereafter associated green peas with her first shattering discovery about Brandon, because she was shelling peas when the blow fell. She was shelling the peas because like everybody the world over, she and Brandon had need to economize in the crushing depression of that time. When she was given the alternative of moving to a smaller, less expensive apartment, or of doing the work of at least one servant and remaining here, she chose the latter.

"I am such a wonderful cook," she had said, with the braggadocio shared by all born cooks. "Why not just be the cook myself? Then we can keep Katie——"

"Maybe we can," Brandon had said.

Thus it happened that Jessie was alone in the kitchen, shelling the peas, when the dry cleaner's delivery boy rang at the service entrance to pick up the clothes to go out. Jessie took the things that Katie had left on a kitchen chair and was about to hand them to the boy when he said, "Sure the pockets are empty?"

And so in the most banal way possible, in an insultingly common way, she made that first discovery. She ran her hands automatically into the pockets of Brandon's blue suit, while the delivery boy stood waiting and whistling a tuneless noise through his teeth. She found the pockets of the coat and the waistcoat empty and all of the trousers pockets also, except—again that vicious dig of the banal—she encountered a folded, crumpled piece of paper. She tossed it onto the kitchen table, among the empty pea-pods which she would sweep into the garbage can, gave the clothes to the boy, and sat down to finish shelling her peas.

Her hands were busy and her eyes unconsciously remarking the blankly familiar, as eyes do when fingers are repeating an automatic process which it is not necessary to watch. So as the shelled peas plopped into the bowl in her lap, she saw without realizing that she was seeing it, something scrawled in pencil in Brandon's handwriting upon the margin of the piece of paper, which had been folded up so that it was very small, and carried in that trousers pocket long enough to become grey and frayed. There seemed to be, she remembered later, a deep hollow within her head or her breast, and something which seemed like a roaring noise that also caused her hands to tremble, as they forgot the peas and very, very slowly reached for the paper . . . unfolded it . . . smoothed it out . . . and read that which only her naïve, ecstatic, innocent love for Brandon could have prevented her guessing before now.

It was the crash of the shattered crockery bowl and the pattering of green peas as they fell and rolled all over the kitchen floor that brought her to her feet, shaking, stupefied, clinging to the edge of the table and staring at the piece of paper which had the appalling cruelty to inform her not only of her husband's infidelity but of the precise details concerning it. In future years as this inexorable, repetitive thing would happen to her, she would find that the fact of his unfaithfulness increasingly lost the power to hurt her, but she grew steadily more bitter, she hated him more blackly, for his clumsiness in effecting that she always find it out.

On that day she was too overwhelmed to think in degrees, in comparisons, of taste or discretion or, least of all, of the plain truths about the nature of man. She had read enough of the world's literature, she had lived enough in the orbit of cynical and mundane people, to take it for granted that this was an elemental fact; yet her youth and her ardent, possessive, pitifully romantic concept of marriage for herself and Brandon had lulled her into the unreality of believing (had she ever faced the thought up to now, and she had not) that this could not happen to her. That, indeed, was what she felt her numb lips whispering as she stood clutching the edge of the kitchen table with cold, damp hands.

"It can't be so . . . oh, God, don't let it be so . . . don't make me believe it . . ."

But she must believe it because she had such proof before her eyes that she would have been truly a child, instead of merely furnished with the emotions of one, if she had been unable to interpret what she had read. And though she was in no condition now to distinguish, among the whole tormenting set of facts which if any was the most hideous, she would realize later that next to massive physical disgust, bitter humiliation was the cruelest. For the woman in the matter who had written the letter was a friend, a girl with whom she had gone to school, somebody she knew well.

"Oh," she moaned, bending over the table as if a cramp had gripped her vitals, "oh, I thought . . . I thought . . ."

She was driven already to such silliness as grasping at the straw of what she might better endure of all this if she must accept any part of it. She was telling herself already that she would have found it more bearable if the girl had been a tramp, a prostitute, a nobody . . .

Moving heavily, dully, slowly, without much awareness of what she was doing, she picked up the piece of paper between the tips of her right thumb and forefinger, dropped it into the kitchen sink, and put a lighted match to it. She stood holding the edge of the sink, wondering whether she would vomit into it, while the paper flared, blackened, curled up, and disappeared. She ran a stream of water across the black spot where it had been, turned off the tap, and left the kitchen, walking with thick, plodding steps. Moving through the front hall of the apartment on her way to the stairs, she saw Katie in the drawing-room and she called to her in a strangled voice, "I— I'm not well, Katie. I've left a mess in the kitchen."

The maid came towards her, eyeing her narrowly; and if Jessie had had her normal perceptiveness, she would have realized that the sharp expression of the woman's face betrayed the suspicion that Jessie must be pregnant, in which case Katie Mullen would promptly leave. No waitin' on thim sick cows for her, thank ye, and no jobs where there was babies and nurses. Katie had had enough of this job anyway; she was all put about by the Madam's messin' in the kitchen where no lady had any business to be. Her conclusion was therefore that this could be no real lady, and her eyes were stony as she stood looking at Jessie, standing a little above her on the stairs clutching the handrail, horribly pale. That's it, thought Katie, but Jessie was too wretched to notice or care. That'll be enough for me.

"Just—if you'll just clean up the bowl I broke—we shan't be in for dinner——"

"Me neither," said Katie, with the astonishing insolence which sometimes cracks the veneer of a superficially well-trained servant. "Clean up yer own mess, Ma'm. I'm leavin'."

"Why—why—Katie—" Jessie stared, puzzled but indifferent, at the hard, sullen face, and without further words began slowly to move, step by step, to the upper story of the duplex apartment. She dragged herself through the charming hall, of whose silvery walls with Chinese tracery she was so proud, into her beautiful bedroom, and as far as the side of her soft, wide bed. Perhaps she had meant to fling herself, in an immemorial gesture which she had not yet been driven to make, down upon the bed to sob; but standing there beside it she could think only of Brandon lying in it with her, making love to her, Brandon who had now defiled and befouled this bed in which she would never, never let him touch her again . . . And then her tormented brain conceived the picture of Brandon, vivid and horrible in another bed, in another house, in a place whose address she knew, with another—with—oh, no, she gasped aloud, shuddering. *Lorraine*. She felt blind with hatred, shame, and disgust, but not blind enough to blot out the picture of that girl, that woman, who would not even have the mercy to be anonymous. With a groan Jessie sank down upon the floor beside the bed, and with her face buried against the edge of it, submerged herself in black unconscious misery.

This had happened in mid-afternoon. A woman in this state of hysteria cannot really know whether she has remained conscious or whether as she may suppose later, she has fainted because consciousness was intolerable. It was a fact however that Jessie would never know how long she had remained suspended in that dark pool of abandoned time and paralyzed will. The first sound of which she was aware was the one that she had anticipated with terror ever since the first impact of this shock: the slam of the front door down in the entrance foyer which would announce that Brandon had come home. She had known for hours, though it was her stubborn will not to count how many hours, that this noise would rouse her and introduce a new and dreadful phase in her relationship with Brandon. Though he had habitually slammed the heavy front door in this way ever since they had lived here, and though she had always detested the crude, unnecessary noise, she had never thought it symbolic of something savage and terrible in Brandon. She had been in love with him in such a way that his every entrance into her presence, whether from a neighboring room, or into the house after any absence, had caused her to tremble, to catch her breath, to feel momentarily disembodied as the whole entity of herself, mind, muscles, nerves, fled the bounds of her control to hang upon the fact that he was there. She had nearly always been able to conceal that this was happening to her, for even in her most ingenuous youth she had had the counteracting example of her clever mother and she had, after all, grown up in a thoroughly worldly milieu. Even when she could not put the knowledge into practice, she understood what was expected of her as a woman and why this had as much to do with her own self-preservation as with the graces and conveniences of society. But in 1931 she was young, only three years married, and desperately in love.

In later years she was to look back upon that day and think of the appalling pity that such experiences, when a woman has them in her vulnerable youth, are the materials for the creation of a shell; a cortex as lustrous, as fascinating, as intricate, as marvellously fine in detail as her wit and skill can make it. And by the time that she has shaped this partial or perhaps complete work of art she looks back upon the raw materials which were its components with reluctance, humiliation, or even shame, as the owner of a beautiful house surrounded by flowers and shrubbery remembers his dismay at the sight of raw ground, piles of discarded scaffolding, masons' mixing troughs, the litter and rubble left after building is done.

Thus, though Jessie knew that the wise and balanced thing to do in this matter was to pretend that she was unaware of it, her youth and her passion and the nature of her love for Brandon swept that course out of the question. So far as she could see, and she could naturally not see one hour beyond the devastating present, this was the end of her life. She wanted to die. She wanted to commit suicide. She wanted to punish Brandon by proving to the world that he had killed her. In such a frame of mind, the great slam of the front door announcing his entrance was the overture to high tragedy. But she was responding to the realest and most crushing emotion that she had ever known, consummately sincere and artless, when Brandon strolled into the room and found her still huddled on the floor. She had heard him coming through the house, switching on the lights which the delinquent Katie should have turned on by now as she drew the curtains in each room, for it was already dark. Jessie heard the click of the electric switch in her doorway, and Brandon's startled, fluid voice exclaiming, "Jess! Why, Jess—what the——"

She did not answer. She heard him cross the room in a few strides, she felt his hands under her armpits as he raised her up and laid her on the bed. She shivered, recoiling from his touch.

"Jess—" his hands gripped her shoulders anxiously— "what's the matter? Are you sick?"

She opened her eyes and in their suffering heaviness he saw what she knew. And she saw his eyes, in their odd vivid blue, change swiftly from anxiety and real concern to angry, stone-hard defiance. She saw the flicker of temper as his blond brows twitched together and she knew at once that he was incapable of remorse or guilt or regret, that he was only furious at whatever mischance had flung this mess open between them. She wanted to turn her head and again shut away the sight of his face, but before she could answer that impulse she saw the flare of his nostrils, the movement of his lips downward into contemptuous scorn which showed his supicion that she had been spying upon him. At that she said with cold disgust, "You ought to know it was your own carelessness. Oh, how I loathe you."

He crossed the room to stand with his back turned, staring through the windows at the dark river below, his hands in his pockets. His attitude was flat and defiant, cold like the glaring glass panes which should be covered now that night had fallen. He said nothing and Jessie lay stiffly on the edge of the bed where he had placed her, her left forearm folded across her eyes. After a time she heard him move and then he said, "Well, I suppose you'll have to make a melodrama of it. But before you start I'd like to ask you: what else did you expect?"

"What?" Against her will Jessie found herself sitting upright, braced by her trembling hands. She was scowling with shock.

His shoulders moved in a reflection of rough irritation. But he turned and seated himself in a low armchair, lounging on the end of his spine as was his habit.

"After all," he said, "this is the way things are. You've

always been an unrealistic child but you'll have to learn some time."

"*I'll* have to learn!" She leaned forward, breathing with difficulty and almost strangling with the sensation of hatred for the face which had the power to evoke the most intense passions in her. "Why should I learn? Why should this happen to me?"

"It has nothing to do with you," he said, whereupon she cried, "Stop!" and clapped her hands over her ears. "I might have known you would say that," she said.

"Then if you knew it, what are you raising all this hell about? Why don't you believe it?"

"Because it isn't so!" she cried. "Does my—my toothbrush have nothing to do with me? My bath sponge? My—anything that touches me—oh, Brandon!" she gasped, "you are so vile. You've done something so foul, so *dirty*—" her voice broke off in a sob and her face fell into her cupped hands.

"Jesus Christ," he said. There was a long silence. At last she heard him move in the chair and he said, "Look here, Jess. I really meant that. If I knew how to explain I'd try. I wish you'd make some effort to understand."

"Why should I? To excuse you? I shall never, never——"

"Hold it," he said. He had a way of using such phrases, left over from the football field or the crew or the hockey rink where he had distinguished himself in his Harvard career, about the academic part of which little was ever said. "I know just what you feel like now, Jess. I can tell you——"

"No, you cannot," she said. "You could not possibly know what I feel, you are incapable of it. You will never understand because if you could, you would never have done this in the first place."

"Well then," he said, "that seems to be that." He rose and started toward his own room adjoining hers. The flippancy and coldness of his manner had the very effect which he had most wished to avoid; Jessie sprang from her bed, stood for an instant clenching her rigid fists, and burst into a screaming temper.

"Oh no," she cried. "No it's not! You've got to understand what you have done to me. You've killed me—*killed* me, do you understand?"

She stood with her raised fists trembling in the air and her face contorted in a spasm of rage and disgust. He looked at her quite coldly, with little expression at all.

"You've killed everything in me that had any meaning," she said. "You've done everything to destroy me."

"Oh come on, Jess——"

"You see? You're so vile that you don't understand what I am talking about. You've not only been unfaithful to me and a liar and a cheat and a sneak—you have torn me all to pieces, robbed me of my dignity and my privacy and—oh, my God—you—you——" her voice trailed into incoherence.

He sighed. From his annoyed, patronizing attitude Jessie could not tell whether he had ever anticipated this scene as the inevitable consequence of his actions, but his next remark was as obvious as those that he had made already. Its effect was only to enrage Jessie more. He said, "Nobody can rob you of your dignity. Nobody can injure your dignity but you yourself. You're doing quite a job of that right now."

"And Lorraine Wilkes? You don't consider you have degraded me by this—this—thing with her? If you had had the first instincts of a normal human being it would have been impossible for you to have anything to do with a friend of mine, *a woman I knew!*" She ended her words with a rasp of pain, again hiding her face in her hands. "Brandon," she said, "for God's sake if you had to do it, why wasn't it some—some—I don't know—some kind of woman that could never have known me! Have you no pity at all?"

"It never occurred to me," he said, "to regard my wife as an object of pity."

The gasp which was Jessie's response sounded as if icewater had been flung over her. She moved backwards with two or three dizzy steps and stood staring at him, the back of her hand across her open mouth.

"You have no idea," she breathed at last. "None at all . . . oh, don't you *know* why this hurts so, Brandon? Don't you understand what I am going through?"

He looked colder, harder, more bored than she had ever seen him.

"I understand at least," he said, "that you are indulging the passions of a jealous, possessive woman. Making yourself as unattractive as you——"

"And you?" she cried, interrupting wildly. "What have you been indulging? And why? For God's sake, Brandon, will you tell me why? Why you did this at all, why you had to humiliate me—a woman whom I—" she broke off and tried to catch her breath and bring her voice under control. She knew how far she had gone in every way towards making herself quite as unattractive as Brandon had said; worse, in descending to uncontrolled ugliness which she herself would detest even more than he; for she was fastidious and he was not.

Brandon had been standing in the doorway to his own room, but now he sighed in a manner of resigned patience and moved across to seat himself again in the chair by the windows. He said, "If you would take my advice, Jess, you wouldn't insist so on talking about this now. You're all worked up and you keep demanding explanations which will only upset you more if I make them. Besides," he added, running his fingers nervously through his heavy blond hair, a habit which was accompanied by a queer cold staring expression of his blue eyes, "besides, there are no explanations. There are only certain facts about life which you are evidently determined not to learn."

He tapped a cigarette on his thumb nail, and lighted it. The first billow of smoke struck Jessie's raw nerves revoltingly; she pressed her lips together, sinking back slowly to sit upon the edge of her bed, something which she would ordinarily never do. But she was reaching now that depressed plane in an emotional upheaval where the instincts of fight and fury and resistance crumple, where, though she might have wished to go on in her course of hysterical temper, she had no more strength to do so.

She sat with her eyes on Brandon, waiting for him to speak. He was smoking and looking in a characteristic way in her direction, but not at her, so that she felt suddenly as if by his action he was disembodying her, removing her from entity. She knew that by now she must be a dreadful sight, with her hair rumpled shapeless, her eyes strained and hollow, her skin sallow, her lips colorless; she would not blame any man for preferring not to dwell upon that. But as she watched his cool, handsome face with its curious plastic quality of reflecting his mood even when he would have chosen to conceal it, she drew a long and fluttering breath which felt as if it had the faculty to turn ice-cold the air that it carried into her lungs. Her eyes hung in a stare almost stupidly helpless upon her husband's face. And she knew that she was seeing him not only as of now, of this moment; she was seeing something that she would have seen countless times in the past, had she had the realism or the disenchantment to see it. His face was as it often looked when he made love to her. It was sculptured, carved, flat, remote; the eyes shone with a queer hard light. Because the sensation and the experiences of her own love for him had been up to now a simple unicellular world, within which it had never occurred to her to question the completeness of his part, she had accepted all his ways in love, the extreme joys that he gave her as well as some mysteries like this remote expression of his face.

But now its meaning struck her with a crash. She knew that with another woman his face must be as she had always known it in love. The image was revolting, but the knowledge was clear. The strange cold intensity of that expression must mean and had always meant that Brandon Bourne in climactic moments was absorbed solely in himself. To him no woman's identity could be more important than his own, but Jessie had heard of the cruel commonplace by which a man while making love to one woman would invest her with the identity of another; and women did the same to men. The thought horrified her, and she shivered in retrospective disgust as she weighed the possibility that Brandon might in her arms have indulged in the perversity of imagining her to be— Oh, God, she thought, swerving from the hateful image—no. I cannot bear it.

Yet because she felt a compelling necessity to know something by which to prove what she now suspected of Brandon, or else to possess any tangible truth however painful, she said, "Brandon. Are you in love with Lorraine Wilkes?"

Her voice was ragged and muffled.

He raised his eyebrows, moved his shoulders, and looked at her without speaking, as if to deplore her naïveté in thinking that the matter could have any connection with being in love. So she understood clearly that excitement and pleasure had been his only purpose, which indeed had had nothing to do with her. But to understand the facts made them no easier to endure. For now she felt certain of her suspicion that to him all love-making was equally a matter of his own primary satisfaction, and for that reason he would diminish the identity of any woman, if not momentarily obliterate it. Probably that was how he had felt when making love to her.

She was much too close now to her own wretchedness to wonder how she could be so deeply in love with such a man, but the explanation would be clouded in any case by his power to arouse her and give her profound pleasure. She only said now, "All the same it was really a cruel thing to do. If you were only seeking—whatever it was—why did it have to be——"

66

He shook his head, sighing over what appeared to him her stubborn obsession. But there was more reasonableness, in his glittering blue eyes than he had shown before, and he said, "You see, that's part of why a man does these things. And it's exactly what you can't take. You think you would feel less upset if she had been a job I'd picked up somewhere, or that sort of thing. But what I see in Lorraine is something that was born in the midst of—unimportant, maybe—but do you understand?"

She nodded, her mouth fixed hard to control its trembling.

"And with you, sometimes I—" he paused. "I feel the difference between us. Not that I don't like it. I do like it. I wanted to marry you. But I knew I was stepping out of my own world. And I know I said the hell with all that." He was quick to remember that, knowing what was passing through her mind. "And I meant it, too. I still mean it. You had something right from the first that fascinated me. I'd never known anything like it before and most of the time I'm damn glad to have it now. But you know—you see what I mean——"

He paused to give her the opportunity to agree and to make the explanation simpler for him. But she only sat perfectly still, looking at him and waiting for him to continue.

"Sometimes," he said, "I get to feeling restless—fed up. Like a fish out of water. You're pretty strong meat, Jess. You're intense and—and——"

"I see," she murmured. Not an Anglo-Saxon, she thought with sarcasm. Not the Ivy League. Or the Junior League, what the hell. She was startled by a sudden swift, hot, piercing sense of violently arrogant pride; it was like a kick in the small of the back, which she might have recognized as the spurt of a charge of adrenalin into her system. Her nostrils flared, but her mouth was cold and she said quietly, "Go on."

"Well, there's the reason, Jess. Sometimes I just—I feel I want to get back where I belong. Not always, not even often. But sometimes. And a girl I've known all my life, a girl like my sister, somebody I've known since dancing-school and summers at Southampton and——"

Jessie wondered if he could know the wave of fury and disgust that was sweeping through her. She sat stiffly, as he paused, and presently she said, "Of course it does not matter that I happen to have known Lorraine and the rest of those—those girls most of my life too. That she was in my class at school. That I would expect you to treat me in their eyes as you would one of them whom you might have married."

"Well," said Brandon uneasily, "it's—you see——"

"Oh, I see," she assured him. "I see perfectly. I am just exotic enough, with my queer background and my fascinating, popular mother and all the petting we've had from bored people who made exceptions of us because—oh, how do *I* know because?", she cried suddenly in anger. But at once her voice dropped again to its cold controlled level. "Just different enough to be interesting and a little piquant, but not different enough to deserve a special loyalty. Oh, I wish you could understand me, Brandon!"

"I do," he said. For the first time there was kindness in his voice and for the first time an expression on his face of something so mild as gentleness or regret. "You may not think I do, Jessie, but—" he paused, having no words ready.

"Protection," said Jessie, so low that he had to strain to hear her. "I am trying to tell you that I need to be protected from women like Lorraine Wilkes and all the rest of them who think that you are their rightful property by some kind of primeval law. They think little enough of stealing men from one another—but from a woman like me!"

For a moment he appeared to be touched, but very quickly his face turned cold again and Jessie knew that she had blundered. To his natural arrogance as a man, beyond his cold personal conceit, it would be intolerable to hear her refer to men as pawns or chattels. He looked at her, frowning, and said, "Only an impossibly possessive woman would say a thing like that."

Once more her face fell into her hands, this time in real despair. There went through her mind the thought of rising and flinging herself down on her knees beside Brandon's chair and pleading with him to any degree of abandonment, to consider her love for him and the ways in which it made her helpless. But in her brain the dark small halls of judgment echoed to the knowledge that this would be a falseness. And after these hours of tearing misery she was both too exhausted and too coldly clear in prevision to be able to delude herself further. She knew now that for a time she would have Brandon in an interval of peace, because he would wish to lull her back into a mood that would spare him the nuisance of scenes and strife. No such affair as the one upon which she had stumbled would be worth continuing if he preferred to remain married to her. But Jessie knew that the burden of love lay upon her; and because of this she knew also that henceforward so long as she remained the prisoner of this love, every woman was her potential enemy. She knew too that being a prisoner she would partake of the sensations of a jailer. Not tonight nor even for years to come would she realize that she, not he, would be the one turned free when she should lose all of her possessive passion for him.

She heard Brandon rise again from his chair and come across the room to her, and she felt his arm go round her shoulder and draw her towards him until her face was hidden against his chest.

"I'm sorry, Jess," he said. "The one thing you can believe is that I didn't mean to hurt you."

Her tears started to flow, though she tried to control them. Since he had taken this step, her bruised nerves began to strain pitifully toward the hope that something in tenderness or gentleness beyond the sparse measures that were his habit would come forth now to give her comfort. It seemed to her that if he should speak to her in some term of endearment, since it was never his way to do so, that would be a token by which she could guide herself to solid ground. He did bend down and kiss her, and his arm was strong about her shoulder, but he was silent. Jessie could not restrain exhausted sobs. After a time he spoke again, his voice matter-of-fact and cool.

"Why don't you get put together now, Jess," he said. "It's nearly ten o'clock. You get dressed and we'll go down to Twenty-One and have something to eat."

VI

Riding down Park Avenue in a filthy, raddled taxicab on her way to dinner, Jessie looked at the great imposing sweep of the avenue in the dusk. For many reasons she disliked the street, but as a sight it was undeniably beautiful. She sat watching the two dense streams of traffic slide past the grass-plots under which the New York Central trains make themselves heard just enough to bring to mind the vast vague westward space from which they come, where the people like to tell one another that New York is not America. And Jessie laughed at the thought, rather inclined to satisfaction that it was true.

Just now, with the clear autumn evening at its perfect moment of deep cobalt blue before it should sink into darkness, with the lights twinkling and the tall apartment houses arrogantly handsome in spite of many things which they concealed, Jessie could not help smiling with pleasure at the familiar sight. As the cab racketed up the slight rise at Seventieth Street and then down the long, smooth slope below Sixty-eight, Jessie imagined as she had many times before what the real shape of the green, hilly island must have been before it had been flattened and paved and groomed to accommodate the city. She could still faintly remember the uppermost reaches of this street at a time when the tracks had run naked up its middle, and the vacant lots had really been a wilderness of trash and goats and bonfires.

She was sitting gingerly upon the edge of the seat, with her skirt tucked carefully close to her legs to keep it off the dirty floor, and as she passed a party of four, laughing and sleek in a smart black landaulet, she thought that there was no reason why she should not take her automobile out of storage and use it now; not to do so was almost an affectation. And yet so strong had been her instinct not to plunge recklessly backwards into an attitude whose very name "normalcy" was a reproach to thoughtful people, that she had postponed putting the motor car into commission.

She began to think about the house to which she was going and the people whom she would probably see there. It was not, she thought, Park Avenue as a street that she disliked, but the apartments which were part of it and many people who lived in them. Park Avenue as an address was symbolic of something, especially to outlanders, which she resented in her native love for her city as the loyal members of a family resent the public messes made by its black sheep, whom they nevertheless will not repudiate. Park Avenue was the symbol of the floaters, climbers, and wind-bag successes whom Jessie detested not so much for themselves as for the false note of discord which they struck in her feeling for her home. They were the people whose most irritating phrase was, "When I first came to New York."

This was in a way descriptive of George and Maureen Stillman, to whose apartment she was going now. She was fond of them, they were good friends and really stimulating people, but George Stillman was nevertheless one of the Dick Whittingtons of Park Avenue. He had succeeded far more creditably with his brilliant editing of a good newspaper than the ordinary smart-money business fraternity who had come from the Middle West or the new South or some place else. I wish they had stayed there, thought Jessie. What a snob I am. Yet I know precisely why I hate these people. It is because they are the rootless, heartless, hard-boiled element which gives us our reputation for being what we are not. You have to be born here to live in it by your heart, not by your wits.

It was a few minutes past eight o'clock when she stepped from the elevator and pressed the doorbell in the outer foyer of the George Stillmans' apartment. She stood looking at the apple-green walls hung with commonplace flower prints in mirrored frames, thinking while she waited that the door would be opened as usual by some new servant whom she had never seen before though she came often to this house. Jessie would have pitied Maureen Stillman for her utter ineptitude at running a house, except that Maureen and George Stillman were the least pitiable people one could imagine. They had a fascinating life, they were charming, Maureen was gay and warmhearted, George was brilliant and really important, they had many devoted friends; and if it was their nature to live in an uproar of cheerful confusion, crazy hours, and domestic turmoil, one accepted that along with their genuineness and generosity and warmth.

The door was flung open, not by a strange, sullen biddy, but by George Stillman himself, grinning and shouting "Hello, Jess!" He was a short, heavy bull of a man with a clever red face, rumpled hair, and the appearance of having thrown his expensive clothes at himself; the front of his soft evening shirt was already bulging away from his waistcoat. He was carrying a telephone instrument in his left hand, with a length of cord ending in a jack-plug looped around his arm. With his right hand he lifted the short mink cape from Jessie's shoulders and dropped it on a bench in the hall as they walked on into the living-room.

"Is it bad tonight?" Jessie asked him. He laughed. She was referring to what his friends called Stillman's telephonitis, which did resemble a disease in its effect upon him if he could not have constant access to a telephone. He became jumpy, inattentive, and sometimes rude, because nothing could ever take precedence in his mind over the pressure of the news. He had been managing editor of *The Press* for many years, and had recently also taken charge of the news department of a broadcasting company which the publishers of his newspaper had bought. George had telephone jacks scattered through every room of his apartment, like electric light outlets, and he carried his telephone wherever he wished to be, plugging it in as he sat down.

A knot of people was gathered about a squat mirror-topped table before the fireplace, sitting upon a pair of chartreuse-colored velvet banquettes. Maureen Stillman jumped up and greeted Jessie affectionately. She said, "Hello, darling . . . you know everybody . . ." She waved her hand at the group. Her manner was as inelegant as her husband's, but she herself offered the single surprising contrast to the careless, taste-less hodge-podge in which her menage was pitched together. She was very pretty, looking far younger than her forty years, and she was beautifully dressed.

Jessie was smiling and nodding at friends, shaking hands with the ones nearest her, and murmuring, "Hello . . . Good evening . . . Thanks . . . Hello, Bucky. How are you, Marge? . . . Fine . . ."

George Stillman at her elbow roared in his usual way, "You remember Mark Dwyer, Jess? I've been trying to seduce him for a week. Can't get a tumble. You try."

The tall officer, who had been talking to his hostess, turned and shook hands and Jessie said with surprise, "Why—yes. I do remember you. But——"

"No reason why you should," said General Dwyer. "It's been a long time."

He moved aside so that she could take his place on the banquette, and drew up a chair beside her. The Stillmans went off to greet more guests at the door. General Dwyer handed Jessie an old-fashioned cocktail.

"Is this what you want?" he asked. She nodded and said, "It was stupid of me to seem so surprised. But of course you've changed."

"Who hasn't?" he asked, fishing all the fruit slowly from his drink and laying it in an ashtray. "Why do they put this stuff in perfectly good bourbon whiskey?"

"Some do, some don't," said Jessie.

"That means you don't at your house."

She laughed. "They taught me to make old-fashioneds at Twenty-One. Years and years ago."

"You're quite preoccupied with years."

"Not necessarily. I was really wondering where I did meet you. But now I know—you were on *The World*."

"That's right."

"But the silly thing is that apparently I never connected

72

you with—with—" she was tactful in her instinct not to talk about his reputation which was now very impressive to any person like herself who had been deeply absorbed in the war, and who would know the names of men who had led commands or accomplished important missions or accompanied the President to his meetings with Mr. Churchill and Josef Stalin.

Yet already, with the war only a few months ended, it seemed strange to see a man in uniform. Dwyer was a Brigadier, which was nothing particularly notable in the Air Force. Most of the high-ranking Air officers whom Jessie had known had been far younger than Dwyer. His left sleeve bore three years of overseas stripes and he had evidently been awarded all possible decorations, with oak leaf clusters, combat stars, purple heart, everything.

He turned his head over his shoulder to answer a question which Oliver Whitelaw had asked him.

"That must have been in Bari about the end of '43, Buck," he said. "I've never seen him since. I'm not sure he ever came through that Ploesti deal."

He turned back to Jessie and said, "Who is that blonde woman coming in?"

She looked across the room.

"Elizabeth Betts. Mrs. Philip Betts, I mean she was."

Dwyer's heavy black eyebrows moved slightly. Jessie observed that he was appraising the beautiful, masklike face not for itself but against the measure of some knowledge of his own.

"You probably know her . . ." Jessie spoke vaguely.

"I know her husband," said Dwyer.

"Her former husband. They were divorced some months ago."

Dwyer moved his shoulders in a slow gesture. The motion had not the flippancy of a shrug, but rather the heavy acceptance of something inevitable.

"Cheap business," he said. "Betts is a jackass." He frowned and drew down the corners of his mouth. "A Wac captain . . ."

"It seems to me I hear about one of these things every day," said Jessie.

"Only one? You must lead a very isolated existence."

He shook his head at the ominous-looking canapés which were being passed by a maid; smears of some unidentifiable substance spread on crackers, with yellow and green

73

curlicues. Jessie refused them also and her eye met Dwyer's and they both laughed.

She felt warm and at ease and at the same time surprised that she should recognize this so consciously. Mark Dwyer was to all effects a stranger, and she was not accustomed to the sensation of immediate pleasure in the company of any stranger. Yet she found that she was more aware of him than of the Stillmans and their other guests with whom the room was filling up. She liked Dwyer's looks and his personality and the almost abrupt directness of his manner and his speech. He was a large man, not only tall but heavy as well. There was bulk in his presence. If he were not in good shape, she thought, he would incline to overweight. He was talking again with Oliver Whitelaw who was called Bucky though nobody had ever appeared to know why. Whitelaw's manner with Mark Dwyer was surprising. It was tinged with an attitude which Jessie would have thought faintly deferential in anybody else. Forty-five years in the midst of, and in the past decade as the owner of, one of the very great fortunes of the United States had not tended to make of Oliver Whitelaw a man who would bring this suggestion of deference and almost of humility to his contacts with anybody.

Jessie turned and began to chat with the man sitting at her other side on the divan, an old friend named Henry Greenberg who was a celebrated lawyer. He had a gentleness and benevolence of manner which Jessie knew to be highly deceptive; it invited ingenuous and indiscreet people to confide in him. He seemed such an appealing human cushion upon which to fling themselves, burdened with their troubles, and his manner assured them tacitly that all their secrets were safe with him. Jessie had suspected for a long time that he was the source of many sensational items which appeared in the most notorious of the tabloid newspaper gossip columns.

"How's Brandon?" he asked her, in a tone which informed her that there was nothing about her life with her husband that he did not know. At the same time she was surprised at her own lack of resentment, for, ordinarily loathing people who pried and gossiped, she could not help being fond of Henry Greenberg. Somehow he evoked affection.

"Fine!" she replied with enthusiasm. "He hasn't had a vacation since he got out of the Navy, so he's down in Virginia with the Claymores."

She saw the faintest imaginable flicker of silent comment in Henry Greenberg's spectacled eyes, and she added a smooth lie without pausing. "I'm going down for the week end. It's heavenly this time of year."

"Why don't you come out to Sands Point instead?" asked Greenberg, his soft voice kind and easy. "You know you like us better than those horsy friends of Brandon's."

"Of course I do, darling," she laughed. "But I really want to be with Brandon . . ."

Her mind was even then asking why on earth she should bother to tell these things to Henry Greenberg who was probably no more taken in by them than she was by him. At that point Mark Dwyer took the empty glass from her hand and asked her if she would like another cocktail; a dour-faced maid stood waiting with the tray. Jessie's eyebrows went up in reluctant peaks.

"I don't want another," she murmured to Dwyer. "Wouldn't you think . . ."

Dwyer took another cocktail but said, under his breath, "Why the hell don't they eat? This is my third. I'm getting boiled."

"When I come here," she murmured, scarcely moving her lips, "I have a cup of soup at home first."

"Bright idea, but why not stay home altogether?"

"Why did you come?" she retorted, laughing.

"Because I had a hunch I would meet you."

"Nonsense. I think I had better follow up that introductory remark of George's . . . such good taste . . ."

Dwyer indulged in a facetious grin. "You'd better be careful to remember exactly what he did say. Or you may find yourself taken up on it."

"I was not referring to his concluding remark," said Jessie primly, "but to his opening one. From the look of things," she said, circling the room with her eye, "George has been offering you a very snug berth on *The Press*. And you have been playing hard to get."

"Not playing at all," said Dwyer. "I just don't want the job."

"Evidently he thinks you can still be impressed into it," said Jessie. "Good evening, Alec." She held up her hand to that of Alexander Lowden, who had crossed the room and was standing before her and Mark Dwyer.

"Evening, Jess. Hello, General."

Lowden had the faculty of looking every inch what he was; very rich, very well exercised and turned out, very powerful physically and in personality; also very, very cautious. He was imposingly handsome, in his late fifties, with fine color, white hair, and a confident expression which to Jessie, who knew him well, was belied by the peculiar indirectness of his glance. He had the sort of eyelids which almost suggest the double-lidded contour of the turtle, whose eyes may be at one moment uncannily bright and shrewd and at the next open, but glazed and inscrutable. He was the publisher of *The Press*, and like many others in his position, had acquired his footing there through his marriage twenty-five years ago to the daughter of the founder.

"How is Serena?" Jessie asked him, knowing exactly what he would answer.

"Fine, thank you, splendid," he said. "But you know—she never wants to dine in town when she can be in the country."

Mark Dwyer saw so faint a twitch of Jessie's lip that he turned his head to avoid Lowden's eye.

"Must be lovely now," said Jessie.

"Lovely," said Lowden. "The chrysanthemums are magnificent. Serena is having a big exhibit at the——"

"Tell him to go to hell," snapped George Stillman into his telephone across the room. "Tell him to shove it up. I settled that yesterday."

Maureen Stillman moved at last towards the dining-room door, chirping, "Food, everybody. Dinner." Jessie rose from her place, chatting with Lowden. She saw the look in Mark Dwyer's eye as he heard a hum-humming banality from the publisher. She turned her head towards Mark and winked her left eye slowly.

The food was execrable. In most houses where one ate as badly as here, the conversation and the personalities were equally dull and one soon learned not to go there. But this particular group tonight was typical of any dinner at the Stillman's. One knew that each guest was an individuality of color and importance (except for a wife here and there, like Marge Greenberg, who had to be asked); almost always there was some pivotal reason why most of the people had been brought together, and the reason was usually a dramatic one well ahead of public knowledge. Jessie was seated between Mark Dwyer who was on Maureen Stillman's left, and Norman Feiner the playwright, whose work since before the war had all been done within the secrecy of the White House, and assuredly not for the theatre. As they were spooning at, but not eating, the canned consommé made sickly with "cooking sherry" and bits of avocado, Mark Dwyer murmured to

Jessie, "Some of the wheels around here have about a dozen interlocking gears."

"Oh, yes," she said, glancing at Bucky Whitelaw. "You know him better than I do."

"I don't want a broadcasting company or stock in the newspaper or a share of Norman's play."

"No," she laughed, "but Bucky's associates want to buy you."

"How subtle you are. If I knew you better I——"

Norman Feiner turned towards them and said, "Have you had any fun since you got in, Mark?"

"Not specially. I haven't given up hope, though." Dwyer moved his left eyelid in such a way that Feiner could not see him, but Jessie could. "How's the play, Norman?"

Feiner said, "Bad, I'm afraid."

"Oh, you always talk like that," said Dwyer. "I've heard that all before."

But Jessie knew that Norman Feiner had reason to be worried about his play, which was opening on Wednesday evening. It would be his first production in five years and his friends knew that he needed badly the money that a hit would make for him. But the advance reports from out of town had been discouraging. She liked Norman Feiner, and she liked Mark Dwyer's evident affection for him; she understood that the two men had become intimate friends during the gravest crises of the war. She asked Feiner now how he came to be here tonight instead of at the theatre in the last preparatory agonies over his play.

He shook his head. "I couldn't take any more," he said. "I've made so many changes in the past four weeks on the road that no matter what I did now I'd only meet myself going backward. It's got to take the rap now the way it is."

"But I hear it's wonderful," said Jessie.

"No it's not. Nothing that anybody writes now is wonderful and don't let them kid you about it. Or themselves."

Mark Dwyer said, "I'd rather be a bootblack than have to write a play or a novel today. You poor wretch, I'm sorry for you."

"Why?" asked Jessie.

"Because," said Feiner, "the actual daily realities that happen are so overpowering and they come along so fast that they squash your piddling little creative ideas the way you'd step on a cockroach. Euripides and Dante and Shakespeare and Tolstoy would have trouble digesting what we're living through. Or competing with it. Or else you would have to be one of them as a writer to keep going through the atom bomb. Or—or the death of a President Roosevelt." His dark, sensitive face was sombre.

"He's right," said Dwyer. "Who has written any real plays or novels during all this?"

"You sit down at your typewriter," said Feiner bitterly, "and catch sight of the morning paper and say, 'Oh, who the hell cares!' One day's news makes tommyrot out of everything you wrote yesterday and for months before."

Jessie had to bend away as the fat red hand of a clumsy maid moved past her nose to change her plate. Phyllis Whitelaw on Feiner's left began to talk to him, and Dwyer said into Jessie's ear, as she leaned his way, "You smell wonderful."

Her eyes opened wide but by the time she had turned her head to stare at him she had forgotten to be shocked. She burst out laughing and said, "For a minute you made me think I was a stuffed shirt. I never heard of such a thing."

"No? You mean you don't know you smell good? Like crazy you don't know it."

She shook her head. "I mean I would expect you to choose your time and place."

"Well, the way it's been," he said, "there's never any time and there's never any place. There's just whatever minute you happen to grab. Oh, my God."

She followed his humorously despairing glance at the approaching servant, staggering with a platter of roast turkey garnished with sliced oranges and blobs of cranberry sauce. The overcooked turkey was hacked, rather than carved, and experience had taught Jessie not to do much about taking a portion.

She was really uneasy about the persistent mischief of Mark Dwyer's remarks, but as the whole table was a buzz and clatter of talk and laughter, punctuated by cheerful profane bellows from George Stillman, with everybody having a very good time, she could not trouble to muzzle Mark.

"Besides," she said aloud, "you are grown up. You can mind your own manners."

Maureen Stillman was talking in undertones with Alexander Lowden on her right, and Jessie saw that for the moment she would not hear anything that Mark Dwyer might say. But Jessie knew too the reflex instinct by which a hostess can hear and see almost everything in addition to the matter upon which she appears to have her attention. Jessie actually envied Maureen Stillman her sublime indifference to the haphazard way in which things were done in her house. The service was grudging and tentative because no servant had ever remained here more than a few weeks; the pace of life and the wild irregularity of the hours in the Stillman household drove away the cooks and maids like stampeding sheep.

"Jesus," muttered Mark, jabbing at something on his plate, "when I really needed a blotter for those goddamn cocktails . . ."

"*Voici la spécialité de la maison qui arrive,*" said Jessie with her lips almost closed. By some ridiculous accident she knew that Mark Dwyer and she had the same tastes in food; she could anticipate his reactions now.

"Don't tell me," he said. "Don't spoil the surprise. Let me guess." His head was turned away from the pantry corner where the servants went in and out. Jessie's grey eyes were wicked, bent upon her plate though she would have enjoyed exchanging a glance of outrageous raillery with Mark. "Sweet potatoes with marshmallows, I betcha," he said.

"And green peas," she whispered.

"Boiled. In lots of water. And ice cream for dessert, Mother!"

"Shut up," she hissed. "Talk to Maureen."

But she was saved from the moment that she dreaded, a suspended blank over the shift of the conversation, by the other end of the table where George Stillman was talking into his telephone.

"I don't give a damn if it's Joe himself!" he said, in the low, sharp snarl which was his telephone voice. He had a peculiar delusion that because this voice was so much quieter than his ordinary roar, people about him did not hear it. "Leave the story where McGrady put it, with a two-column head." He slammed the telephone into place and snapped, "Bastards!"

"Who?" asked Jessie of Mark, as the conversation began to rise again.

"Probably," said Mark, "the worried staff of a certain Embassy who have been told to keep a certain report out of tomorrow's papers. Or to get it toned down, at least."

"Well, really, don't they know about American newspapers?"

"Don't they just! But don't *you* know, Baby! Times have changed since *The World.*"

"Sometimes I think that performance of George's ridiculous," said Jessie. "Nobody else runs a paper that way. They all go home and act like anybody else. George is like a Hollywood idea of a newspaper editor."

"The queer thing is," said Dwyer thoughtfully, "that what you say is true, but George Stillman is the ablest newspaper man I know, and certainly the most honest. So if he wants to act like a prima donna, what the hell. Some drink. Some—" He shrugged his shoulders.

"But you won't work for him."

Dwyer's expression became hard.

"Not now." He smiled suddenly and kindly and said, "It would be the most natural thing in the world to tell you about it, but I don't know why, and this isn't the place anyway. It'll keep until I take you home."

He turned abruptly and began to talk to Maureen Stillman. Only the bone-deep habit of curtaining emotion behind a charming, open, yet inscrutable smile stood by Jessie now; for something in Mark Dwyer's voice, rather than in his words, had caught at her with startling force. She swallowed, as if to clear her ears of the impact, though it was not in her ears that she felt the sharp throb of response to what he had said.

"—tell her too, Norman," Jessie heard Phyllis Whitelaw's cold, bored drawl on Norman Feiner's farther side. The worst thing about Phyllis, dark and moody, was her manner; she could be more human than one would guess from her rude, often sullen personality. She was as near to laughter now as she could ever be.

So Norman Feiner repeated the one about the man who was cutting his lawn with the manicure scissors, and while they were all enjoying another laugh, Maureen Stillman rose and the women followed her from the room.

They returned to the ugly living-room for their coffee, which Jessie could scarcely find the courage to drink, knowing from experience that it would be lukewarm, bitter, brownish water. She poured most of her cognac into it and swallowed the dose quickly like medicine. Phyllis Whitelaw flicked an understanding eyelid, and presently Jessie found herself in Maureen Stillman's bedroom with Phyllis, who was one of those women who detach themselves in this way from groups, to talk with some of them about the others.

"God, I feel like hell about Liz Betts," she said, inspecting her blackened eyelashes in Maureen's hand-mirror. "That bastard."

"She looks like death if she forgets herself," agreed Jessie. "But I really think it is more hurt pride than caring about Philip. After all, it isn't as if——"

"Oh, I know. Philip's been like everybody else. But these damn fools. If they've gone on fifteen or twenty years keeping up a kind of arrangement why do they have to go and make their slobbery official now?" She spoke in supreme oblivion of the fact that she herself was her husband's third wife and that her adamantine determination to break up his second marriage and get him for herself had been the most lurid of public slobberies only five years ago.

"It's the war," said Jessie. "Nearly everybody is in some kind of mess. Look at the Shaws. And the Beckmans. And Dorothy Wyler. And Joe and Minnie Kahn. You would have sworn nothing would ever happen to them." (And there, she thought, taking care to keep her face expressionless, but for the grace of God go you, my girl. Phyllis Whitelaw had the shrewd and tearing eyes of a buzzard.) "Every one of those people is forty or older. They have all been married for years and been through the grinders—but they're all breaking up now like icicles in a thaw. It's in the air, that's all."

"But the damn fools want to marry these jobs they've been shacked up with!"

Jessie longed to remind Phyllis that she had wanted to marry Bucky Whitelaw, and had managed to make him think that that was all his own idea, too. But she only said, "Not all of them. With some it's just restlessness. Or the men finding out that war is not hell, and marriage is—at least when they're that age."

"You're not so wrong at that," Phyllis said, narrowing her eyes. "Those fellers had a holy hell of a wonderful war in London." She knew perfectly well what her own husband had done there, but neither that nor any other provocation would ever pry loose her grip upon Bucky and the Whitelaw millions. Yet she was generous with them. Jessie remembered other hostess's-bedroom talks when Phyllis Whitelaw had been the subject of the discussion, and when some female cynic had explained Phyllis's generosity on the grounds that it gave her a sense of power over her friends. When a point was made of Phyllis's enormous contributions to charity, to war relief, and to all sorts of liberal, antifascist, and international causes, the same commentator had sniffed, "Conscience-money."

Jessie did not have that kind of mind. She might be naïve, she thought, but she preferred to give people credit for the decent things that they did.

Phyllis came out of the bathroom, pulling down the sides of her girdle and swearing at the woman who had made it.

"That bitch used to charge a hundred and twenty-five dollars before the war for French elastic," she snorted, "and now it's a hundred and ninety-five for *that!*" She snapped the edge of the girdle against her thigh. "Crap!"

"Collart asked me fifty-five dollars for rayon nightgowns the other day," said the mild voice of Marge Greenberg who had come into the room and joined the talk.

"Did you pay it?"

"My God, no."

"Well, what do you do?"

"Wait." Mrs. Greenberg shrugged her thick round shoulders indifferently. She was a heavy, dull, but kindly Jewish woman who was so thoroughly merged with her husband's identity that she was accepted despite her ponderousness wherever he went. Everybody liked Marge because they did not have to bother to make conversation with her. "This won't keep up long," she said. "I've got enough nightgowns."

Maureen Stillman came in, opened a drawer at the sight of which Jessie winced, and pawed through the clutter until she pulled out a purse. "I forgot to leave the money for those extra hens in the pantry," she said. "Wouldn't it be awful if I *cared* about servant trouble!" She giggled and said, "Come on back inside, girls, you can't have much left to do here."

"Not much," said Phyllis Whitelaw, yawning.

Jessie walked through the main hall of the apartment as far as the open door of a small library which adjoined the living-room. A radio was turned on there, with the eleven o'clock news from Station WPRS, but nobody was listening to it except George Stillman who was sitting on the edge of a desk, telephoning. The front doorbell was ringing; Jessie heard new voices in the entrance hall, and she knew that the usual late Stillman evening was beginning. People would wander in and out for the next three or four hours. She stood still for a moment, trying to decide whether there was anybody here other than Mark Dwyer with whom she really wanted to talk. She intended not to be conspicuous by any more notice of him, or from him, for the rest of the evening. It happened then that he came out of the dining-room with Bucky Whitelaw and Norman Feiner, and across the intervening space she saw him looking for her. When his eye met hers it was with a glance of peculiar calm, a quiet, intimately informing glance which told her that he had spent the past half hour reasserting his decision to men who had all tried to make him change his mind.

Once again Jessie sensed the surge, almost like a blow, of direct understanding which had struck her at the dinner table. The physical force of this was frightening, for it was unmistakable. But, she thought, this man is a stranger. *A stranger*. She turned quietly, shutting out the sight of Mark Dwyer and the whole large room full of people moving here and there, settling in pairs and groups to talk and drink; she walked over to a chair near George Stillman's desk and sat down in it as he finished with the telephone. He grinned at her and said, "Say, Jess, do you know Mark Dwyer well at all? I wasn't sure."

"Not the least well," she said. "He was a reporter on *The World* when I was filling inkwells around the office—you know how long ago that was. I might have seen him three or four times then and never again until tonight. Why did you ask?"

George made a half-comic face.

"I was looking for a *femme* to *chercher*," he said. "I've tried everything else. It's no good, and I thought maybe a woman could persuade him."

"What is all this, anyway?" asked Jessie. "What is the job you want him to take?"

"Foreign editor. Of the paper and this." He jerked his thumb at the radio. "He'd be so good it makes me drool. His war experience alone would put him in a class by himself so far as handling the whole goddam mess is concerned, but he was a hell of a good foreign man on the *Trib* for ten years before he joined the Army. Damn fool. He should have stuck to his muttons."

"Why?"

'Because guys like that don't grow on bushes. Well, I guess it's no dice now."

Jessie shook her head. "I can see why you think he is crazy, George, but he must have some awfully good reason. Did he tell you what it is?"

"Not so it makes sense to me. The damn fool isn't getting out of the Army now and he is going back to Europe next week to do whatever it is he thinks is better than my job. Son of a bitch. I like him, too."

"He likes you. He says you're the ablest man in the newspaper business."

"Thanks. Nuts. What do you want to drink?"

Jessie managed in a short time to move into a group that had gathered about Therese Street and Mart Ferguson, the acting couple who were to open on Wednesday in Norman Feiner's play. They had come up from the theatre where another three hours of rehearsal had gone into weak spots in the second act, and they sat limply slouched on a couch, depressed and exhausted. Therese Street looked every day of her forty-six years and Ferguson's face was hollow, pasty, and dissipated. On the stage he always looked like a sculptured god, and would again on Wednesday; but now he only said, "Oh, George, gimme another drink for Christ's sake," and leaned back with a groan, closing his eyes. Norman Feiner sat on the arm of the couch with his arm around Therese's shoulder and said, "Never mind, honey. I love you. God loves you. It'll be all right."

"You will, anyway," said Renée Feiner, Norman's wife, to Therese. "Even if it's not another *Roman Holiday*, you and Mart will make it seem like one."

Therese looked up at Renée and said, "You're the only nice woman in the world. No wonder he loves you so."

"I love you that way, hambone," said Mart Ferguson, "but *Oy!* my head."

It was past midnight and Jessie was watching for a chance to break inconspicuously away. People were moving about, some leaving, others arriving. She drifted with Elizabeth Betts and the Whitelaws to the foyer, having said good night to Maureen. Mark Dwyer and Alexander Lowden were also at the front door, and George Stillman, noisily cordial as he sped them away. They all went down in the elevator together, and Dwyer asked the man to call a taxi.

"I can drop you," said Bucky Whitelaw as they walked out to the street. His car was at the curb.

"Never mind, thanks, Buck, the man's got a cab now . . ."

"We'll take Liz," said Phyllis. "Good night, you're coming Wednesday, aren't you?"

The Whitelaws were giving the party for Norman Feiner and the Fergusons after the opening on Wednesday night. Their car moved off and Dwyer asked Lowden if they could drop him.

"Just at the corner of Sixty-eighth Street, thanks," he said. "I'm stopping for a minute."

When he had gone, Jessie laughed and said, "It will be quite a minute."

"One of those," said Dwyer. He leaned back, having given Jessie's address to the driver, and propped his feet against the jump seat. "You'd take that for granted about him."

"I'm almost sorry I didn't tell my sister-in-law about him today," said Jessie. "Just because he's so ridiculous."

"What's it got to do with your sister-in-law?"

"A lot," she said, with a laugh. Ten thousand dollars was quite a point in the case, she thought. "Wouldn't it be funny if Alec Lowden got upstairs there and found his babe out as usual with Van? But I suppose she handles things better than that."

"What's the deal?" asked Mark, with lazy curiosity. "Sounds gummy to me."

"It is. That's why Alec Lowden is such a fool. He is so terrified of scandal and so pompous about himself . . . and the result is that he's the laughing-stock of the gossip circuit. He keeps this job there in the good old-fashioned way but he never dares to be seen anywhere in public with her. So she does her circulating with my brother-in-law Van Fielding, who doesn't give a damn about gossip or scandal and I suppose in times like these he's right. His wife is burned up about it, though."

"It certainly makes Lowden the pink-eyed rabbit of all time," said Mark. "You mean the great man is willing to share his dolly's favors with your brother-in-law?"

"What can he do?" Jessie shrugged. "Isabel Allen is nobody to sit by the fire in a back street and wait meekly for her true love."

"Oh," said Mark. "Isabel Allen. I see."

"You can imagine how much she cares about Alec Lowden or Van either," said Jessie. "As a matter of fact it is very convenient for Alec to have all the talk concentrated on somebody else. In fact it's very convenient all around. Everybody gets what they're after and week ends Alec goes home to Serena in that marble barn at Westbury and entertains the Great of the Earth."

"*Pfui,*" said Mark Dwyer. He was sitting very quiet, relaxed but not slouched or sprawled as many men would be. Again Jessie sensed the profound calm which permeated his personality and which seemed to her the most attractive and welcome quality that a man could have. The cab was going across town from Park Avenue to the River, and it stopped, therefore, at each crossing to wait for the traffic light to go green. Each time that the corner arclight threw its beam upon Mark Dwyer's face, Jessie was conscious of making an effort not to turn her head and look at him. When they reached her house, Mark Dwyer said nothing at all; there was no question either of good night or of whether he was invited to come in. He paid the cab and followed Jessie through the entrance hall and into the elevator.

VII

"Are you hungry?" asked Jessie, as Mark dropped his overseas cap on the table in the hall.

He looked at her, opening his brown eyes very wide in derisive surprise and answered, "For God's sake, what do you think? You had the dinner too."

They laughed and she led the way to the kitchen, switching on the lights as she passed through the dining-room and the pantry. She could not read Mark Dwyer's thoughts and she did not know that to him any place so beautiful, so serene, so orderly, so exquisitely kept was in its way grotesque against the greater images which pressed upon his mind with all the force of primary urgency. But he felt too the capacity to appreciate a moment or a place of peace and beauty just for its contrast to permanent reality.

Mark followed Jessie into the kitchen, looking about with a judicial eye. He took in the shining white tiled walls, the red rubber-block floor, the great marble-topped table in the centre of the room, the ranks of heavy copper pots and saucepans hanging from hooks, the huge, cumbersome black hotel gas range with its banks of baking, broiling, and warming ovens.

"If you had one of those white enamelled stoves that looks like anything else but," he said, "I'd be ashamed of you."

"What do you feel like eating?" asked Jessie. She waved at the vast refrigerator and said, "Look and see."

Mark had already opened the first door and was looking inside with practised interest. He took out a jar of herring in sour cream and said, "This I would expect of you. And black bread." Which Jessie had taken from a bread box and set out on the table.

"There's some sweet butter in that crock," she said. "Not much—but what you can get nowadays. How about this?" She handed him a cold roast of beef, half carved, the bright, marbled meat red and white on the browned rib bones. She put a Canadian cheese on the table, a small covered earthen terrine, some hard-boiled eggs, and a white enamel container full of crisp wedges of celery and Italian finocchi.

"Do you," asked Mark, with his head in the refrigerator, "make a practice of staging these little scenes?"

"You must remember that I grew up in a house full of ice-box robbers."

"You grew up, anyway." He backed out of the icebox with a bowl of cold boiled potatoes in one hand and a jar of sour cream in the other.

"You'll find beer in the pantry icebox," said Jessie, arranging things on the table. "Or do you want milk?"

"*Milk?* For the love of God, why?"

"Oh, you know, everybody always tells you it's the thing men crave most when they get back from overseas. So I thought—"

"I will tell you what I do crave most when I feel good and ready to talk about it," he said. "In the meantime, I was weaned so far as I know at the age of about twelve months and I hope I've stayed that way."

Jessie laughed, getting white crockery plates from a cupboard and paper napkins from a drawer.

"As a matter of fact," said Mark, carving roast beef, "that American craving for milk and ice cream and all the rest of their infantile tastes and habits is part of the same unholy mess they make all over the place. They're wonderful in a real squeeze. But the minute it's over they turn into squalling brats again. Immature. Snot-nosed. *'Mama, I wanna go home!'* His deep voice rose in a savage mock whine. "Christ, if we had an army of male adults to depend on now! Or if it isn't their fault it's their damned Mamas and their yellow-bellied Congressmen with *'Bring the boys home.'* Boys! Boys my—" He stopped speaking abruptly and after a moment's silence came around the table and drew out a chair for Jessie, bowing and flourishing a kitchen towel.

"This herring is balm to my soul," he said presently.

"I love it too. In fact it's my secret vice," said Jessie. "Sometimes—you'd never believe it!"

"What?"

"Sometimes I eat a little piece of it for breakfast. If I've been up terribly late and wake up feeling cranky and jangled. You know?"

He nodded. "Of course."

"It feels so good then," she said. "Soothing."

"Sure. I bet I know where you get it, too."

"Smarty. The label's right there on the jar."

"Never mind, I haven't looked at it. The herring comes from a gentleman named Mr. Poll at Lexington Avenue and Seventy-eighth Street."

"Why—you're right," said Jessie. "How in the world can you know a thing like that when you are scarcely ever in the United States, from what I've gathered."

"My dear girl, I can be away from where I belong for years on end and not forget elemental necessities to my pleasure like my old friend Poll. How is he, anyway?"

"Fine. He always calls me sweetheart."

"Sure. I bet lots of fellas do."

"Only people like him. You know, the butcher and the green-grocer where I've gone all my life—that kind of people."

"People," said Mark with his mouth full. "That's all."

Jessie smiled. Once again, in a word or by a note in his deep, comfortable voice, he had struck that chord of natural understanding in which there was not now, never would be, the necessity to ask or to explain small questions. She looked at Mark Dwyer with the knowledge that he would not feel that she was staring or scrutinizing. His hair was iron grey, almost white at the temples, and very thick. It was curly, and he wore it cropped short so that his skull was covered with crisp, springy waves. Jessie knew that he must be at least forty-nine years old, possibly fifty. She knew too, though she could not have said whether from instinct or because somebody had told her, that he was a self-educated man who had had a hard struggle to get his footing, and had surely done more kinds of rough and heavy work than he himself would remember now.

Also his eyes were not young. They were brown like the darkest brown velours; and they were tired and wise and quiet. Jessie saw that they had the habit of minute observation; they were set in deep sockets under heavy lids, with sharp wrinkles at the corners. She saw two qualities vividly in his eyes and for both of them she felt the most profound, spontaneous sympathy. One was sorrowfulness, the undramatic sadness which comes of mature adjustment to the truths of life; the other was the gentlest kind of humor.

This was a man who would mean something profound and universal in using a word like 'people'; and also something easy and plain and gay. Jessie said so.

"Sure," he answered. "I don't pretend that men and women like that are the only ones I want to know, but they make a good foundation for the fancier kind that you add on later. I ought to know. I am one. And so are you," he added in a queer sudden way, looking round the great rich kitchen as if to remind Jessie that this was a different milieu indeed from one that would more exactly reflect her origin.

"You have the most peculiar faculty," she said, "for conveying that you know a great deal about me which as a matter of fact very few people know at all."

"But I am right," he said. He did not see any reason for telling Jessie also that during his hours at the Stillmans' house he had found out as much about the state of her marriage as he wished to know.

"You are just a lot smarter than I," she laughed. "I've been trying to ticket you, but something slips every time I think I have all the pieces in place."

"Does it, now," he said. But the Irish twist on his words sounded artificial and Jessie said, "That's just what I mean. I start from the premise that you must be a nice Tammany mick from way back, but then those pieces begin to slip."

He laughed with delighted gusto.

"You're a quick chick, in the language of my Army juveniles," he said. "Your instinct is exactly right. The Irish in me is nothing but a fine, phony veneer."

"Then," said Jessie, with a puzzled frown, "what———"

"Oh, my story is not so queer. It's just one like thousands of others that happen in a place like this. For instance, I've been amused all this time sitting here in this apartment with you, when I remember this whole neighborhood from the soles of my bare feet since years before any swell ever dreamed of living here. We used to go swimming in the river out there where your front windows are—the whole gang of us. My gang and then of course the gangs from other blocks, Jesus, the fights we used to have."

"You mean," asked Jessie, almost breathless with fascination, "you lived around here?"

"All my life, until I lit out to get to work."

89

Jessie sat back, her hands limp in her lap.

"It's the most wonderful thing I ever heard," she said. "You can't imagine how wonderful I think it is."

"Be thankin' ye," he said, with a wink.

"But now I'm really curious. Who—who *are* you anyway?" she asked.

"The poor orphan of some good plain folks with a name you couldn't pronounce, who——"

"Then your name is not really Dwyer?"

He shook his head. "Not originally. Not Mark either. In fact, it's neither Mark nor Dwyer nor good red herring."

"But—then—what is it? Really?"

"Miroslav Mráček," he said, with a grin. "Mirko to you." Jessie's mouth was wide open with astonishment.

"Then how," she asked, "in God's name did you get the Mark and the Dwyer? From thin air?"

He was enjoying her amazement and he chuckled before he answered her.

"Not at all," he said finally. "My stepfather's name was Dwyer, God rest his soul. Timothy Dwyer, the sweetest Irishman who ever lived. He was a cop at the Nineteenth Precinct. He adopted me after he married my mother, so the name is mine legally, but I wasn't born with it."

"And the Mark? Your first name?"

"Oh, that just happened when I first went to school. Mama used to call me Mirko, but they couldn't understand what I was saying when they asked me my name. So they called me Mark and it stuck."

"I never," said Jessie, leaning back in her chair and folding her hands in her lap, "heard such a story. Such a fantastic story."

"Oh yes you did. Remember that. Your own is probably just as fantastic—or funny—only you don't think so, being too close to it. Or else perhaps you'd as soon forget some of it, most people would. But in this town everybody's got a queer story—if they really belong here."

"Of course you're right," said Jessie. "Tell me yours, anyway. Who were your parents? From where?"

"Czechs, that's all. Simple as that. With a drop or two of Slovak mixed in among the ancestors somewhere, that must be where I got these." He gave her a mock stare with his brown velvet eyes. Jessie sat silent, almost gaping with astonishment.

"I can see all the questions you'd be asking if you weren't

so dumbfounded," he said. "So I'll save you the trouble. I was born in a coldwater railroad tenement on Seventy-third Street right off First Avenue. All the Bohunks lived around there, still do, as a matter of fact. My old man and Mama came here from the old country in about 1893 or '94, I guess."

"Why?" asked Jessie. "I mean how?"

"In a boat, stupid. Like millions of everybody else's immigrant parents or grandparents including your own."

"What did he do, your father?"

"He was a cigar-maker. Practically every Czech in New York was, they used to be in the old country too. Only of course in those days nobody called 'em Czechs. They were 'Austrians,' or maybe Bohemians, politely, or else just Bohunks. Like the Slovaks were 'Hungarians' because nobody knew the difference. Anyway, they all stuck together the way greenhorns do, and they all lived the same way and did the same kind of work."

He opened a fresh bottle of beer and poured it out into Jessie's glass and his own. He drank a long draught and went on talking.

"The cigar factories were right there around First Avenue and Seventy-second Street——"

"They still are!" exclaimed Jessie, as if she had made a great discovery.

"Of course they are! Only nobody seems to think anything has a beginning or any roots around here. They think it all springs up like weeds. And it doesn't. That's not true. There used to be a big cigar factory named Kerbs & Spiess, and they employed all these Bohunk cigar-makers, men and women both. They used to send an agent over to the old country once in a while, to cigar-making towns, to get new blood, and that's how it happened that practically everybody on our block where I was born was related to everybody else and to somebody back in Sedlec, in the old country."

"Where's that?"

"Sedlec? Oh, it's a village near Tábor, one of those places so small it just gets on the map. Bigger than Lidice—but that got on the map."

Jessie saw his face go grim. Already she understood why. When he began to talk again after pausing, she was sitting with her chin cupped in her hands, her elbows on the marble table, fascinated with his story.

"So when I was a little kid I got it laid on pretty thick. Pa never spoke much English and Ma's was always peculiar, though she learned as time went on. She always talked Czech to me, though. My God, she was pretty. I don't suppose a modern American would think she was, but the way I remember her, she was something you could eat with a spoon. We used to go to church at St. John the Martyr in Seventy-second Street, and I was an altar-boy and all that. I remember Mama used to belong to the Women's something-or-other, they used to embroider vestments and things for the priests. You know how all those women are about embroidery. Terrific."

Jessie knew only vaguely, but she nodded her head.

"And they used to do up the white nightshirts we wore when we served Mass, my God, I've forgotten what in thunder you call them."

"Surplices," she murmured.

"Sure, that's it. Surplices. And the long gowns we wore under 'em were cassocks. And we used to look like such angels in those linens and laces . . . and when I think what we were really like underneath!"

He drank more beer. Now that he had started on these reminiscences it was clear that he was enjoying them hugely and that he had not thought about all this for years.

"Well, the rest of it is pretty simple," he continued. "I was six or seven years old, I guess, when Pa died. He had been sick for a long time, I remember. And Ma got more religious than ever, she used to spend half her time in church. And Tim Dwyer used to watch her there. No man with an eye in his head could have helped watching my Ma. It was a funny parish, about half Czech and half Irish, but in those days they used to preach the sermon and all that in Bohemian. It's changed a lot now, of course. But the Irish and the Czechs got as much stirred together there as people like that ever do. Not an awful lot, they usually stick to themselves. But they did marry sometimes, the way Ma married Tim Dwyer. As a matter of fact," he added, "I remember the parish used to have people in it with names like Božena McCarthy and Patrick Hovorka. You probably don't realize how funny that really is."

"Did you like your stepfather?" asked Jessie.

"I loved him. The story would be more romantic if he'd been a drunken bum who beat me, but he wasn't, he was wonderful. I knew him better and loved him better than my own father. He and Ma had three kids right away. We lived in different tenements all around the neighborhood, you know, people move for some reason or other. And then when I was about fourteen everything happened all at once. Tim Dwyer got killed by a runaway horse he was trying to stop and Ma died in childbirth with her fourth kid, and there I was in the middle of all these relatives who moved in on the situation. Tim's people took his kids and distributed them around among the aunts and cousins, and I was supposed to go to Ma's brother. But——"

Jessie interrupted. "Have you got relatives around there now?"

"Have I!" Mark grinned enthusiastically. "My uncle runs a pork store on First Avenue—"

"No!" exclaimed Jessie. Her eyes were liquid with excitement. "You mean one of those marvellous shops where they have Prague hams and all those things?"

"One of 'em?" Mark roared with pleasure. "The best, Madame. The very best. Vaníček's, if you please. Gee," he added thoughtfully, "they probably haven't had any hams for a long time. But believe me, they've got *something* wonderful to eat, or they wouldn't be themselves."

"You mean," she asked, still fascinated like a child, "one of those lovely stores with a picture of a fat brown ham tied with a blue ribbon?"

Mark leaned across the table and put his hand on her cheek. "Sweet," he said. His voice was suddenly very deep. Jessie's first impulse was to turn her face from his eyes and try to hide the rush of emotion which had made her breath catch, her eyes fill with stinging tears. Instead she found herself looking straight at him, at his face changed from calm firmness to a clear and soft reflection of profound feeling. There was not, there could not be, the slightest effort on the part of either to conceal anything. They sat silent until the moment of itself had slipped away. Jessie drew a long unsteady breath then and asked in the lightest tone she could manage, "Tell me what happened next."

"Oh—the rest is one of those things. I didn't want to stay with all those relatives of Ma's, and I had been pretty badly socked by all that had happened. So I cleared out and got to work."

"You ran away?"

"Sure. I couldn't stay around where anybody knew me on account of the truant officer and being too young to get working papers and all that. So I—oh, well, it doesn't matter really. I just kept on going and somehow or other I finished school and got through college in between jobs. Or during them."

"Where were you then?"

"Oh—everywhere. Akron. Cleveland. Chicago. Buffalo. All sorts of places."

"What sort of jobs did you have?"

"What do those places sound like?"

"Mills and factories and——"

"Exactly. I told you it wasn't very important. A tire plant or a wire mill or a packing-house, what the hell. I ate."

"Where did you go to college?"

"Illinois. And just when I finally graduated along came 1917 and I went to France. When the war was over I stayed there for quite a long time working for a new press syndicate that some people were trying to make a go of. But it went broke and I came home to New York and went to work on *The World*. The rest——"

He turned to change his position and said, "I've talked about myself enough now. I've finished with all the part that matters anyhow."

"Oh," said Jessie.

They sat silent. Each was thinking alone and apart. Mark Dwyer lit a cigarette and sat smoking, staring up at the ceiling with the abstracted expression which reminiscence may bring to any face. And Jessie, unconsciously making on the white marble table a neat pattern with her forefinger of a few brown crumbs, gazed down at it, slowly pushing a crumb here and there, as if this were some symbol from which she could read many things which otherwise would remain mysteries.

But after a time she raised her head and said slowly, "I have a better idea now of what it was you did in the war. It was liaison with all those—the people you have been talking about. I mean their country."

"Partly," he said. "There were a few of us who did a little of everything. I got so used to its all being secret that it never occurs to me to talk about it now. Besides, once those things are over, there's something corny about harking back to them. Most of what we did would sound like a mixture of *Superman*, Eric Ambler, and Jules Verne."

"You mean the O S S," said Jessie. "I suppose the Air Force was just a—a——"

"No, it was the Air Force I joined, in 1942. And then one

thing led to another, not entirely without plan. I'd worked all over Central Europe and the Balkans, and lived there all those years when I was writing for the *Trib*. So I had a little knowledge about a lot of places and things, which proved to be just as dangerous as the old saw says." He smiled. "But also I had had the reasons for this war all ground down into me, right to the bone, long before the U S ever got into it. Years before. So by the time my outfit got to North Africa and was making plans around somebody who could speak any of those lingos, it was simple who the somebody was going to be. That was fine, I'd tried to set it up that way."

"Do you really speak a lot of those languages?"

"In a way. If you speak Czech, Slovak is almost the same thing, and you can communicate with Serbs and Croats and Poles and almost anybody . . . even Russians."

"I should think the *Trib* would have tried to keep you as a war correspondent."

"Oh, they did. But my God, I couldn't have stood that! Even less than this thing now," he added.

"Something tells me that you really have no business to be sitting there," said Jessie. "Alive. I suppose parachuting into enemy territory is just an afternoon's exercise for you."

Dwyer raised one forefinger and shook it at her slowly.

"I told you," he said, "I had talked enough about myself, and I meant it. Look." He pointed at the clock set into the kitchen wall. It said a few minutes past two-thirty. "I'm going home now, as soon as we've cleared up."

"We don't have to clear up," she said. "Except to put the food away."

He helped her, and also went about stacking the plates and other things in the sink. He was methodical and automatically neat.

"Where is home?" Jessie asked him suddenly, because he had used the word and made her curious.

"Nowhere," he said. "I've been loaned the apartment of a friend for the rest of the time I'm here—the rest of this week. In the Ritz, for God's sake."

"Lucky to have a roof over your head," said Jessie, because that was the most banal remark she could have made and she felt untypically clumsy and disturbed.

When they went back through the dark quiet rooms to the foyer, they paused, passing the open doors of the drawing-room. All in darkness, it was not possible to see the room and Jessie had no thought of turning on the lights. For the great centre bank of windows overlooking the river, a dramatic expanse of glass, was always left uncurtained at night if the weather was fine. The damask curtains were drawn over the smaller windows at the farther ends of the room, throwing the magnificent illuminated view of the river into full relief. Tonight the moon was shining brilliant white, the sparkling, radiant full October moon which seems never in any other month to be so spectacularly beautiful. The great round dazzling ball hung high in the sky, like illuminated ice, filling all the darkness, indoors and out, with breathtaking radiance.

Jessie walked slowly into the room with Mark Dwyer. She stood quietly before the windows, gazing down at the shimmering water, a rippling, live brocade of black and silver far below. In the distance, up and down the river as far as one could see, the silhouettes of the great bridges were all blacked out, but their spans turned jewel-like by threads of twinkling lights. More lights sparkled on the islands and the farther shores; high overhead the moon made them appear yellow fireflies in the supreme whiteness of its glow.

Jessie did not speak, nor Mark. They stood looking at the fantastic beauty spread before them. Jessie felt her pulse knocking in her throat, a strange and urgent sensation. She felt Mark Dwyer standing close to her, a little behind her. There went through her the impulse to put out her hand and place it in his, but she did not move. And though she would not have felt the least surprise if he had touched her now, it was also no surprise that he did not.

When the silence had been filled, as water fills a hollow in the sand, he said, "My dear, may I see you again? Tomorrow? And as much as possible before I leave?"

"Yes." Jessie had no other word to add to that.

She felt his hand rest lightly for a moment on her hair. And though she knew that if she moved or turned towards him, he would take her in his arms, she stood quite still. Perhaps she did not want him to touch her and find that she was trembling. In a moment they moved away from the window, across the dark room and out to the foyer where the electric light felt hot and coarse in Jessie's eyes. Mark Dwyer picked up his cap from the table and smiled at her, with curious gentleness as if to reassure her, should she need reassurance for any reason.

"You did not tell me lots of things you promised," she said, keeping her voice very light.

96

"I still have time," he said. "I'll call you in the morning. Ten? Eleven?"

"When you like."

"Good night." He strode out into the elevator hall, turned, and blew her a kiss with his forefinger.

Quietly Jessie closed the door.

II
TUESDAY

VIII

There was a note from Brandon in the mail, scrawled in his strange giant handwriting on the delicate blue notepaper of Claymore Hall where he was staying. Jessie was surprised. Brandon never wrote to her, nor she to him, when they were apart; if it were necessary to communicate they telephoned or wired.

"Dear Jess," he had written. "Sorry bother you Left town forgetting Mama's birthday youll do wont you thanks B."

These few words, run almost continously together without punctuation, covered more than two sides of the folded paper. On the fourth side were more scrawls, which Jessie read: "Nice here too bad youd hate."

She could not help smiling. Whatever their differences in tastes, and especially this irreconcilable one about the country, they had at least reached a plane of agreement to disagree in which each had resigned any attempt to influence the other. All that was left was an occasional bit of lazy banter like that postscript. Yet in Jessie there was so deeply ingrained the dislike of failure that even now she sensed a twinge of regret not entirely free of guilt. She could have made Brandon much happier than he was now, if she had not so stubbornly refused to have any part of a life in the country. But it was he, the other side of her brain reminded her, who had failed to build any of the human foundations upon which such a life would have rested . . . oh, *rats,* she said almost aloud, stop chasing round and round that hen-and-egg circle . . . what does it matter now?

She made a note on tomorrow's page of her memo pad to send flowers and a gift to Mrs. Bourne. There had been times when, at the lowest ebb of her troubles with Brandon, she had detested the way in which he turned to his mother; she knew the old lady to be incapable of seeing anything but perfection in her son. And it had seemed hatefully unfair that in circumstances in which any and all women should hold together in the necessity to make men build solid ground under their feet, a man could escape to the approval of some woman who would not hold her place in the line.

But now those thoughts and emotions seemed immeasurably far away, and unimportant besides, and Jessie was only aware for the moment of a feeling of unusual kindliness for old Mrs. Bourne and for Brandon too. She felt in fact even more serene, more content this morning than yesterday; calmer, and yet at the same time vibrant with a new pleasure in being alive. She was not at all conscious of having gone to bed extremely late, something which she ordinarily disliked and which found her taut, strained and depressed in the morning, with the hollow-stomached sensation of having had too little sleep.

Josephine came into the room carrying a small horn-shaped crystal vase from which floated and trembled two delicate sprays of tiny butterfly orchids, white with rosy throats.

"How *lovely!*" said Jessie, holding up her hand for the card. "Put it here."

She smiled at the exquisite blossoms as she was slitting open the florist's envelope.

"I like you," she read in a square printlike script, slightly backhand, precise, and written with a broad pen so that the lines were thick and black. There was no signature.

"And," thought Jessie as Josephine answered the telephone which was buzzing, "I like you."

Josephine covered the mouthpiece with her hand and said, "Mrs. Lee."

"Hello darling," said Jessie, taking the instrument. "How are you?" This was her closest friend, whose voice she was always happy to hear.

"What about all these bits and pieces this week?" asked Helen Lee. "We left it in the air . . ."

"Mmm . . . let's see. How was the farm?" Jessie wanted a moment's time in which to make plans in her head.

"Wonderful. We just came in this morning. You were silly not to go up with us."

"No I wasn't," said Jessie, trying to make her voice non-committal.

"Oh, so?" she heard Helen Lee laughing and then, "You sound covered with cream and canary feathers."

"Why, you—" They both laughed and Jessie could see as if through the telephone wire the lovely sensitive mouth, the vividly expressive eyes, which made Helen Lee's smile one of the most beautiful that she had ever known. It was more than beautiful; it was full of heart and warmth as well as wit.

"Well, what are we about to do?" asked Helen. "There was something about dinner with us tonight and something about Norman's opening tomorrow. Don't tell me Moddom's changed her mind."

"No," said Jessie. "If you'll behave yourself and not drive me into a mess of double-talk, I'll call you back in a few minutes and we'll get everything set."

"Yes darling," said Helen.

"And none of that vanilla frosting on your rapier," added Jessie tartly.

"No darling."

They were by now conversing more in laughter and in tones of voice than in words. Helen would of course see through any screen that Jessie could possibly raise across a thought, a whim, an identity, a piece of news. And no matter what she saw, no matter what her mischievous badinage with Jessie herself, it did not matter in the least against the greater truth of Helen's loyalty. Jessie knew the stature of this woman in friendship, a quality that had proved her almost noble in comparison with the poor slack thing that the average person turned out to be.

And Jessie treasured the lightness of Helen Lee's touch; it had warmed and illuminated her life for a great many years, leaving buried in good earth where they should be the strong roots of their mutual devotion.

"Let me know when you can," Helen was saying. "It

doesn't matter what you do tonight, it was only family . . ."

"You're an angel. I won't come tonight, and I will call you in a few minutes about tomorrow. We're all going—but we could shift things around a bit, couldn't we?"

"Why not? 'Bye, darling."

Mark Dwyer telephoned almost immediately, as Jessie had expected.

"Thank you for the butterflies," she said. She wondered as she did so how it was that flowers, waiting like charming blank pages in the shop where they were chosen, should have the faculty of assuming the personality or the thoughts of their sender, to the point of taking on real individuality, of smiling at one as these flowers were doing now.

"Are you dining with me tonight?" asked Mark.

"You hadn't made it so specific. I had to guess."

"Well, you've guessed. And what about tomorrow? Norman's given me seats for his play."

"I would love to go with you," said Jessie, "but I've already got tickets——"

"Well, give 'em away."

"The only trouble is I was supposed to go with Sam and Helen Lee and Preston Shaw. I could easily get disentangled from the Lees, Helen wouldn't mind at all. But that would leave Preston on my hands."

"Oh, hell. Unhand him."

"Mark, I can't. He's been invited already and besides, the poor chap is in a terrible state and you would not think of asking me to be rude to him if you knew all about it. He is no special friend of mine, but . . ."

"What's the matter with the fella?"

"Oh—perhaps you're used to these things, you said so last night. But he is not. He got back from years in the Pacific to find that his wife had thrown their whole life into the ash can . . . it's a horrible mess. I'm really sorry for him."

"Poor devil," said Mark. "Look here, what are you doing, all dining together?"

"Oh—half dining. We were going to have a drink and something to eat and then go to the Whitelaws' party afterwards."

"Well—can't I horn in somehow? Unless you're ashamed to be seen with me in all that famous company."

"Don't be silly. Why can't I tell Preston we're going to be six instead of four and get another girl for him? Or will you pick her?"

"I don't know any girls or women. Never touch the stuff."

"Very well, I'll leave it all to Helen. Preston is her friend anyway."

"I like you," said Mark. "You're tractable."

"That's your error, my dear."

"What time shall I pick you up tonight? Where do you want to dine? Twenty-One? Colony? Voisin?"

"Are you particularly set," asked Jessie slowly, "on going any place? I mean is that what you came back to New York for?"

"No. Why?"

"We could just dine here. It is—" Jessie stopped speaking. She did not know exactly what she had meant to say.

"We could," Mark Dwyer was saying. "And with your permission, we will." Jessie knew that he was pleased. "What time?"

"Eight? Eightish?"

"Ish," said Mark. "Earlier. Good bye, sweet."

The connection clicked and Jessie found herself sitting with the dead telephone in her left hand. She was staring out at the dusty green tops of the trees over on Welfare Island, and at the sunbeams streaking high over the brilliant blue water. It was a lovely day, lovelier than yesterday which had been such a delight. It was a different day from any that she could ever remember, she thought, slowly putting the telephone in its place, and then picking it up again to dial Helen Lee's number.

She was dressed and ready to go out a little after twelve, and she stopped in the kitchen to say good morning to Anna and tell her about dinner. The old cook beamed at her with the devotion which Jessie was wont to say nobody could possibly deserve. Her good fortune in having in her house such people as Anna and the waitress, Sarah, in addition to Josephine, was no doing of her own; it was simply part of her legacy from her mother, which had included a great deal more than mere tangible property. Anna was vaguely "Austrian" by definition, which after forty-odd years in the United States, covered a general Central European origin which she had almost entirely forgotten. Sarah was Irish, of course; a strapping grey-haired woman with a needle eye about her work, a fierce devotion to Jessie, a sniffing snobbishness about the ratty state to which Society had descended, and a fanatical Catholic orthodoxy so extreme that when meat or poultry

102

had been ordered on Fridays she served it with a frozen scowl.

She had never since the day of Jessie's marriage called her "Miss Jessie," considering that to be a slovenly mannerism akin to sweeping dust under the rug. Sarah was a woman whose opinions were close to bigotry, but her virtues were simple and few and splendid. Compared to her, Anna was a featherbed of docility and sweetness and patience. Jessie had often teased them by telling them that between them they ruined her life, Anna by making other people's food uneatable and Sarah by applying a martinet's standards to general existence as well as to her own work.

Anna was making noodles, rolling out the deep yellow dough on the white marble table. It would no more have occurred to her to buy noodles than to use canned soup. Either thought was only exceeded in disgracefulness, as a lazy American trick (though she was belligerently proud of her American citizenship), by the fact that such things "would not taste."

She stopped wielding her rolling-pin, waddled around the kitchen table, and pulled out a chair for Jessie, dusting it off with her apron in case any flour might have drifted onto it.

"Don't stop the noodles, Anna," said Jessie, in the comfortable tone that they used when speaking together, for both understood these matters so thoroughly that much of their conversation took the form of shrugs and nods. The rolled paper-thin dough must be folded up for cutting before it began to stiffen.

"Just two for dinner," said Jessie, as Anna's heavy, work-hardened hands manipulated with marvellous lightness the wide sheet of paste into a long multiple fold. Then Anna covered it with a clean towel to "let it rest," dusted the flour from her hands, and sat down ponderously opposite Jessie to the all-important discussion of what to have for dinner.

"Soup I make it now," she said, and if Jessie had privately meant to order some other kind of soup, she decided at once that Mark Dwyer would enjoy Anna's noodle soup better than anything else in the whole repertoire anyway.

"I know," said Jessie, sniffing towards the stove where a thread of perfumed steam floated lazily from a large simmering pot. "You know what you can do about it before I go out, too."

Anna chuckled.

"Meat?" she said, in the resigned tone with which good (and, therefore, somewhat spoiled) cooks had been meeting this sore subject for a long time past.

Jessie decided as usual that it would be best to telephone the butcher and ask what there was before she fixed upon something that she would not be able to get. She and Anna put the rest of the menu together, upon the tacit understanding that the guest who was expected would appreciate real food, planned without concession to anybody who could not understand it. Sometimes there were such people to be considered, and then there had to be a compromise here and there. "Leave out the garlic," or "go easy on the kümmel," or "send in the sour cream separately."

Anna rose, the consultation finished, and went to the bread box. She cut the heel from a loaf of rye bread. Then she took a long, slotted steel spoon, went over to the stove, and poked about in the soup pot until she came up with a piece of sawed marrow-bone on the spoon. She shook the marrow from the bone onto the crust of bread, dashed it with course salt, ground some pepper over it, and handed it to her mistress. Jessie stood near the stove, exquisite in a slender black cloth suit with a gilet of citron yellow lamé, a hat made of six sharp black, green, and yellow quills, and a string of sables looped over her arm. She ate the marrow with an expression of beatific sensuality. Anna grinned as she started to cut the noodles. Jessie, having finished, was peacefully licking her fingers when Anna's cat Putzl made an entrance from a room beyond the kitchen.

He was a giant; pitch black, with a heavy, square, tigerlike head and a prim white waistcoat. He walked imposingly, moving his powerful muscles under the dense shining fur with arrogant vanity. He leaped to a high stool and informed the company that he was interested in the proceedings.

"Do you want to *nasch*, Putzl?" asked Jessie. "Do you want a chicken heart?"

Putzl's bright green eyes had been fixed on the sunny windows until the pupils were fine black lines. This made him look his most commanding; he turned to Jessie and said yes please. From such a large, formidable cat his polite high "mrrrrrrrrrrrhoo" was ridiculous.

Jessie now fished in the soup pot, ignoring Anna's fussing about her clothes, until she brought up a chicken's heart on the slotted spoon. Putzl sat quietly waiting. He understood that the waving spoon meant that his tidbit was cooling.

Presently Jessie offered it to him and he ate it daintily, champing it all up and swallowing it like a connoisseur, slowly so that he savored it well. Then he thanked Jessie by standing up on his stool with his back arched high, and rubbing his jaw against her sleeve while he purred extremely loud, in slow rhythm. Then he sat down again, pouring his black bulk into a handsome pattern on the white stool, with his heavy tail curled round his haunches, and began, very gentlemanly, to wash his front paws and his face.

"*Na,* Putzl," said Anna. "Shame, beggar. You."

"He's a snob," said Jessie. "The other day I offered him a piece of smoked salmon. He only sniffed and strolled away."

"He likes best from the soup pot," said Anna, shrugging.

Passing through the pantry Jessie said good morning to Sarah, told her what cocktails and wine she wished for dinner, and went upstairs to her room to wash her hands after her delicious lapse into greediness. She was just in time to reach Marguerite Barnard's house for luncheon at one. Mrs. Addison Barnard was standing in the doorway of her drawing-room greeting the dozen-odd women whom she had invited to lunch. This was not a social occasion, and the guests understood that well. They were hand-picked from among the best-known, ablest, and most influential women in New York. Most of them were hard-working professionals in various fields. All of them knew one another well—not for personal reasons though some were, naturally, old friends— but because they had worked together many times in the past for public philanthropic undertakings like the one upon which they were engaged now.

They formed the Executive Committee of the Women's Division, with Mrs. Barnard in her classic place as chairman, of the annual drive to raise funds for the amalgamation of war-relief and social service agencies that had been formed at the beginning of the war. This was to be their final campaign, and they were committed to raise an enormous part of the seventeen millions of dollars which was the quota of New York City alone. Such an effort was never planned without women like Marguerite Barnard and the group who were coming to her house today. She greeted Jessie Bourne warmly and Jessie moved on into the beautiful room panelled with magnificent *boiserie* brought long ago from France, when the double-width limestone house had been built in a quiet tree-lined block east of Madison Avenue.

The women were entering in groups of two and three; they

were all prompt because most of them had come from their offices and had allotted a precise amount of time to this meeting. Jessie saw Serena Lowden sitting on a divan across the room, and went over to speak to her. Mrs. Lowden smiled and patted the empty place beside her. She was a very old friend, a friend of Jessie's mother, like Marguerite Barnard; both women had carried over to Jessie their gentle and gracious affection for Rosa Landau. Serena Forbes Lowden was some twelve years older than Jessie; Mrs. Barnard was old enough to be her mother.

Mrs. Lowden asked, "How are you, dear?" as they took small glasses of sherry; and then, "Have you seen Horace lately?"

"Just yesterday," said Jessie. "I was down at his office because Mother's trust is about to terminate. He was so sweet. He actually thought I would ask him what he had done with things these past ten years."

"Can it be ten years!" exclaimed Serena Lowden. "I cannot believe it. I have never got used to it."

"Nor I," sighed Jessie. "And—" it seemed to Serena Lowden particularly generous that Jessie said softly, "I believe that Horace misses her the very most of all."

"It is quite wonderful," said Mrs. Lowden, "to have had a person like Horace Howland a part of one's life ever since one can remember."

Jessie nodded, for she had had exactly the same experience. Horace Howland, who had been a close friend of old Nathaniel P. Forbes, was the trustee and adviser for Forbes' only child, Serena Lowden. Old Forbes had tied up his estate, including control of *The Press*, in such a way that Alexander Lowden could have no share of it. Beyond his title and his salary, he was kept by the dead hand of his father-in-law perpetually a hireling. Those who knew him best believed that it was just as well.

An enormous woman loomed before Jessie and Serena on the divan, greeting them in a bass voice. She was grotesque in every way, her plain black dress a tent well-made of the best possible material, her lank grey hair cropped off with no thought of shape or plan, her face a ruddy bas-relief of undulating flesh, with a small nose lost somewhere in the middle, her eyes devastatingly sharp, intelligent, and shrewd. She was nearly six feet tall and she weighed all of two hundred and fifty pounds.

"Jessie," she said, as if she were checking up on a culpable

106

schoolgirl, "you didn't come to my cocktail party last week!"

"I was so disappointed, Althea, really I was. But I did telephone and tell your secretary."

"No fool you," boomed Miss Althea Crowe. "It was a horror."

"Then why," asked Serena Lowden mildly, "give such a party?"

"My dear Mrs. Lowden, there are dozens of reasons for participating in polite rackets but you are evidently fortunate enough to be able to pick and choose. Or stay aloof. I am a wage slave."

"Poor thing," said Jessie, laughing, as they joined the group that was following Mrs. Barnard downstairs to the dining-room. Althea Crowe was the editor of the women's magazine which had the largest circulation of any periodical in the United States. The possessor of a mind like carbon steel, a woman who read for relaxation Plato, Dante, Chaucer, Marx, and Hegel all in the original, a terrific gormandizer and drinker, a wicked poker-player, she was responsible for purveying to millions of American women the marshmallow-flavored fiction that they loved, the cooing advice about their babies, their marriages, their menus, their dressmaking, their pineapple and peanut-butter salads. And when she thought it timely she also slammed into the front of her magazine a cold, cruel article about juvenile delinquency, world economics, adultery, illegitimacy, venereal disease, or the world trend toward state socialism. She was one of Jessie's oldest friends.

The luncheon went off quickly; there were only three courses, light, delicious, and swiftly served, and all the women kept the talk upon the job that had brought them here. Jessie was seated between Oliver Whitelaw's sister, Mrs. Everett Duncan, faded and timid and generally thought of as pathetic; and Mrs. Thomas Renshaw, a vivid, smiling, pink-cheeked woman of about thirty-five, who was considered the ablest organizer of civic and community activities in New York. She exuded good will, energy, and intelligence; she was a woman of little imagination, but she bubbled with frank, healthy charm.

"Mrs. Renshaw," said Marguerite Barnard, who was now standing at one end of the cleared luncheon table, upon which nothing remained but the flowers, the water goblets, the ashtrays, and the coffee cups, "will head the general coordinating committee to which the chairmen of all the subcommittees will report. The other members of Mrs. Renshaw's committee are Mrs. Prentiss Wall, Mrs. Everett Duncan, Mrs. Walter Bernheim, Mrs. Clarkson Satterlee, Mrs. Francis McCosker, Miss Genevieve Debevoise, Miss Rita Wyeth, and Mrs. Sidney Weinberg, with Mrs. Brandon Bourne as secretary."

There was some general discussion of procedure; particularly close attention to the work of the Labor Division about which Minna Zalkin of the CIO spoke briefly; a reminder that there remained less than three weeks in which to complete final arrangements before the opening date of the fund drive; and the luncheon broke up precisely on the stroke of two fifteen, with most of the women making their way at once to the entrance hall, where maids stood waiting with their furs and coats. Marguerite Barnard had indicated to a few women that she wanted a moment more with them, and presently Jessie found herself in the small ground-floor sitting-room with Mrs. Barnard, Serena Lowden, Althea Crowe, and Dorothy Renshaw.

"I thought," said Mrs. Barnard, "that we had better just take this up while we have the chance . . . it is not really important but we ought to be quite clear about it." Her kindly well-bred face appeared peculiarly cold as it became plain that she was about to mention something distasteful; she bit her lips which were as usual without artificial color. "I presume," she said, her voice pitched low, "that some of you know—know of—a Mrs. Emily Sanders?"

The four women looking at Marguerite Barnard now glanced variously at one another, then carefully at nobody in particular. It was evident at once that each of them knew the person whose name Mrs. Barnard had mentioned, but it remained for Althea Crowe, who had no reticence about anything, and no diffidence in the presence of anyone, to volley out, "Know her? Enough to know she's a crook and a phony!"

Jessie could scarcely restrain a smile, though this was certainly no time to show amusement. She knew Mrs. Emily Sanders, for the same dreary reason that she had occasion to know by sight or by name many other women, some more, some less questionable in reputation. On Serena Lowden's sensitive face there was an unconscious expression of something like disgust or disdain; and Dorothy Renshaw's visible reaction was one of vigorous dislike.

Mrs. Barnard hesitated. Having asked for information, she

had it now from the expressions on four silent faces, but she appeared reluctant to give her own reasons for having brought the question up.

Dorothy Renshaw helped her by saying, "After the snarl in the books at the Allied Aid, I think we all——"

"Well," said Marguerite Barnard rather hurriedly, "it is that sort of thing that I—where I have had reason in the past for feeling as I do. Of course I am sure that Mrs. Sanders is a very hard-working person," she added.

"For one reason particularly," said Althea Crowe in a tough, matter-of-fact tone. "I know her game, Marguerite—you've said enough."

"You see, she is on a newspaper now," said Mrs. Barnard, not looking at Serena Lowden whose expression made it clear to Jessie, even had she not known it before, that Mrs. Emily Sanders could quite as probably have been on *The Press*; and that she had not got her present job without trying first, by familiar tactics through Alexander Lowden, to land herself on his newspaper, a manœuvre that had been quietly blocked by Serena Lowden.

"She has been giving it out," Mrs. Barnard continued, "that she is to be my executive assistant in this Fund campaign. She has been——" Mrs. Barnard coughed and bit her lips—"going about to the offices of many people whom we all know, or calling them up on the telephone and—you understand. I am simply trying to say that we cannot have this—it is unfair to the women who are really going to do the work."

"That's the most charitable light you can put on it," said Althea Crowe, sniffing. "The woman is a fraud. She has a mania for horning in on anything that has a lot of big names and publicity attached to it. You can't put three prominent names together anywhere without finding hers stuck on behind with horse-glue."

Jessie Bourne and Dorothy Renshaw both burst into a helpless laugh. Serena Lowden's lips twitched and even Mrs. Barnard smiled faintly.

"Althea's summed it up," said Dorothy Renshaw. "We all know a lot of other women who do some part of the same thing. Sweet charity—give me a leg up."

"No, it would really be quite unimportant," said Mrs. Barnard, "except that this woman is so noisy and so ubiquitous and so insistent upon getting at people. And it seems that her position on the newspaper makes it more annoying because—I cannot imagine why—she is said to have some influence there. If we repudiate her as we should, she may try to induce her editors not to support the Fund vigorously—and of course we need all the newspaper cooperation that we can get."

"I will ask Alexander to speak to John Carhart about it," said Serena Lowden quietly, though she had her misgivings as to whether the publisher of a rival newspaper would see much reason for tolerating such a suggestion from her husband. Still, she guessed quite accurately at Mr. Carhart's personal situation in the matter, and in those circumstances he would surely find it wise to cooperate with the other newspaper publishers in their plans to support the Fund.

"I think that will be a great help," said Mrs. Barnard. "And for the rest—we all understand that Mrs. Sanders has no connection with our committee. That will become clear to the public as time goes on."

They all moved out to the front hall, offering lifts to one another. The butler hailed a cab into which Althea Crowe heaved herself, with barks and grunts loud enough to drown out the shrieking of the ancient springs. She bellowed at Dorothy Renshaw and Jessie that there was plenty of room; they were all going down Madison Avenue anyway, so come along.

The cab drove off and Serena Lowden raised her eyebrows in surprise that her motor was not there. Then she remembered that she had told her man to stop and pick up an order at the Vendôme; she was going straight out to the country.

"Probably they did not have it ready," she said. "He's been delayed."

She walked back into the small reception room with Marguerite Barnard to wait for her car.

"That's a nice child, that girl of Rosa's," said Marguerite Barnard thoughtfully.

"I am very fond of her," agreed Serena. "Of course I see her through Horace's eyes, just as we used to see Rosa when we first knew her."

"It goes to prove that there can be exceptions to everything," said Mrs. Barnard. "I remember the first time Horace Howland asked me if he might bring Rosa Landau here to tea—I told him I thought he had lost his mind. I was young and brittle then, and I drew the lines so tightly!" She laughed softly. "I told him certainly not, I remember—but he would not take that for an answer."

"It was that quiet determination of his that overrode all sorts of things for her."

"I asked him if she had been divorced. Really, Serena, I am ashamed now to think what a prig I was. But it seemed so important at the time. And when he said no, she was a widow——"

"Ah, she was a darling," said Serena. "I suppose none of us would ever have grown so fond of her if she had not been gentle and full of charm. But she was very different from us, of course."

"Of course. The difference was like a lovely warm glow— not just a blazing fire. What a pity that there are not more people like her."

Both women glanced through the window, but Serena Lowden's car had not yet appeared. She took a cigarette from her case and lighted it, saying, "You were a wonderful friend to Rosa, Daisy."

"Oh, I loved her dearly. And I think her friendship gave me far more than anything I ever did for her. Once I knew her well I was even more ready than Horace to fight battles for her. Of course there were battles."

"But she would never have lifted a finger."

"Never. She had such character—a combination of honesty and the most sensitive taste. She used to say to me, 'Daisy, I am a nobody and I will never pretend to be anything else.' Of course that was just why I did not want her treated like a nobody."

The two women sat silent for a moment, Serena Lowden thinking of the extraordinary lengths to which Marguerite Barnard had gone to lead Rosa Landau and her daughter past the small, powerful group of men and women who had always stood at the innermost social bars. She said, thinking aloud, "She really never did pretend. I am sure that was why we all had such wonderful times at her house. To tell you the truth, Daisy, none of us has ever created such an atmosphere of gaiety and warmth."

"I know. But she was unique, Serena. You might find other places where it could have happened—London, possibly, or Paris. But not here. You could not have had troops of people from Broadway and the lower East Side all following in Rosa's footsteps. But she had a right to people's respect. She earned it."

They were both thinking of the serious qualities of Rosa Landau which were not evident when they thought of her as

111

the spirited and fascinating hostess of the most interesting house that they had ever known. Rosa giving a party, where the guests were, for those times, a daring blend of elements who might otherwise never have found themselves under the same roof, was a very different woman from the one whose quiet and often anonymous good deeds had gradually brought her the regard of the most substantial and responsible people. Such loyalty, once established, was not lightly put aside. "In fact," said Marguerite Barnard, pursuing the thought, "she did more for us than we ever did for her. Horace's judgment about her was sound."

"You do not forget, of course—you might almost say—he brought her up."

"Rosa Landau was born with quality," said Daisy Barnard. "She may have been a lily in a mud puddle. but Horace had the good fortune to find it."

"And she never married him," mused Serena Lowden.

"Of course not. She had too much taste." They rose, for they saw the motor drawing up before the house. "I wish the child had not married Brandon Bourne," murmured Marguerite Barnard, as they walked out to the hall.

Serena Lowden gave her friend, in parting, a poignant look which suggested that marriage in general held a great deal to be regretted.

IX

Standing still in the middle of the fitting-room, Jessie reflected that she had often found this the place and the time for fantastic thoughts. She had never asked herself exactly why. She had a sense of stimulation in being shut up here with the skilful, painstaking, patient men and women who made fine clothes; a sense not only of appreciation for their craftsmanship, but of intimate understanding of how they worked. This thing of tailoring and dressmaking, of the inborn art of cutting, of the instinct to pin and shape and rip and mark and pin again; this common understanding of the use of hands, this standard that no detail might be less than perfection; all this Jessie felt to be ingrained in herself no less than in the Italian fitter, the Lithuanian-Jewish tailor, the now middle-aged sewing-girls upstairs at the machines and finishing-tables. And though the beautiful things that they made by hand were seeming anachronisms in a world of department-store racks crammed full of slick, smart, mass-production, the whole gigantic industry would be quite helpless but for this tiny fertile seed.

"Don't you think a little more there below the shoulder, Mr. Max?" Jessie was watching the fitting in the broad triple mirrors, but at the same time she was thinking of many other things too. "You see?" She bent her arm forward and the grey-haired tailor nodded quickly. Snip—click—and the basted sleeve was out of the jacket entirely. There, she thought. That's just what I mean. The way he's setting that sleeve over again. He turns it an eighth of an inch in the armhole and the whole jacket hangs differently.

The door opened and a model from the negligée salon swept in. She took three long steps one way, two the other, whirled and disappeared. Jessie had not even noticed the color of the gown that the girl was showing; she had no interest in negligées at the moment and she did not want her attention distracted. Mr. Max was working now upon the soft, standing collar of the jacket, which was one of the most difficult things to drape perfectly. He ripped the seam at the edge, snipped at the muslin interlining, and pinned to it once more the fine dark grey cloth which now flowed into place in a smooth sweep.

"You are wonderful," said Jessie. "Really you are."

He smiled and shrugged, but whether his silence was of habit or because he had pins in his mouth, he found it unnecessary to say anything.

He finished quickly, and after asking for one more fitting two weeks hence, he left the room carrying the pinned costume over his arm. Jessie stood in her chemise, waiting for Miss Flora, who always fitted her dresses. Miss Elsie, her vendeuse, bustled in, carrying some blouses, and apologizing for Flora's lateness.

"You have no idea what it's like around here now, Mrs. Bourne," she said. She had the drawn look, tense about the eyes and the corners of the mouth, which was the pathetic mark of her trade; it came of never being free of the agony of aching feet, and never feeling really rested.

"I *have* an idea," said Jessie, shaking her head. "I saw them all out there in the big room when I came in. The place looks like a railroad station."

"It's worse," said Miss Elsie. "Honestly, I'm glad if a lot of people have been striking it rich, Mrs. Bourne, but if you had to handle them all day long——"

Jessie was examining the blouses. She moved them one by one along the rack where Miss Elsie had put them, shaking her head as she inspected the materials, the sewing, and finally the price tags.

"Sixty-nine fifty for *that*," she murmured. "Look." She held up the shoddy synthetic stuff to the light, fingering with distaste the coarse machine stitching and the careless seams inside.

The two women exchanged a look of comic disgust. Miss Elsie was as hard-boiled, as sleekly black-dressed, as carefully dyed and waved of hair, as heavily corseted as all the rest of her hard-working kind. But she had known and served Jessie Bourne for a great many years and she had known from the first better than to try to sell her anything. Jessie was a woman who chose what she wanted. Her taste was crisp and sure; she had no concern whatever for "what they are wearing," only for what she liked. She bought fewer clothes than many women of her means, and wore them longer. And now that real silks and other fine materials were almost unobtainable, she bought very little at all.

"This one really takes the cake," she said, pushing the last blouse aside.

"Well, you know," murmured Miss Elsie. "Ready-to-wear—"

"Ready for somebody else," said Jessie.

"I'll see how long Flora will be," said Miss Elsie, scooping the blouses together. "I'm so sorry to keep you waiting, Mrs. Bourne." She left the room.

Jessie went and stood at the window, looking down over the lovely familiar view of the Plaza, the Girl with the Bath-towel facing the Sherman Statue, and the long, smiling panorama of the Park, with sparkling towers rimmed along its sides like candles round a birthday cake.

"How sweet it is," she thought. "My God, I do love it so."

If she stood there letting her memory play, it would find nooks and corners, green spaces, lovely frosted black-and-white nights, music, the breathless anticipation of childhood for a party, the agonies of girlhood when the mysterious alchemy of "popularity" might suddenly curdle and throw a helpless young thing into the torments of the damned . . . "getting stuck . . . being a flop . . . a flat tire," that was

114

what they had called it in her day, the cruel shining sure ones to whom that never happened. Dancing-school, there in the Plaza across the way, and later the big, crucifying parties to which many a girl would hysterically plead not to have to go . . . tea-dancing downstairs in the Grill, which years ago had vanished in the strange way that hotel places do . . . Mademoiselle or Miss Somebody or Fräulein . . . nobody *else* always has a chaperone, Mother! . . .

And presently because nothing could have surprised her more, there cut across her mind, wandering in this tiny and least important fragment of long ago, the echo of the words: "I ought to know. I am one. And so are you." People. The city's real people, the plain ones, the ones without Names. The ones who work here, in these rooms behind me . . . not the ones I played with down there.

She stood very still, trying now to hold impossibly within the single fragile shell of her mind the bewildering parts of her own self which, one against the next, were fantastically unrelated. It isn't possible, she thought, puckering her brows and shading her eyes with her hand as if the afternoon sun, moving over the westward edge of the Park, could be blinding her. How can it be, how can I know where I belong, or to whom?

But she did know. The instinct now to recognize, to admit at last what she knew, was overpowering. And now it has a name, she breathed, not quite aloud. A name. A face. A voice. I know where there is earth beneath my feet, flesh if I reach out my hand. Suddenly her eyes filled with tears. She drew a long breath and, closing her lips tightly, heard the wisest, calmest counsel which her own good sense, forged in the fires of misery, could give her. To wait, to be still, to learn, to be wise, even old, as she could pitifully not have been in those years of the heartbreaking parties and the life to which they had led.

Miss Flora was fitting the last of the three dresses which Jessie was having made. It was a dinner dress of dark bottle-green Lyon velvet, with a crushed drapery of brilliant scarlet silk jersey crossed over the breasts. A twist of the scarlet jersey was drawn down through slashes in the skirt, and the décolletage could be covered when one chose with a long-sleeved jacket of the green velvet. It was a striking, dramatic dress, and both the vendeuse and the fitter were sincere in their enthusiasm about it. Jessie knew very well that compliments were their stock in trade; but they had too much intelligence, and they knew her too well, to ply her with empty flattery.

It was a long time since Jessie herself had felt the sharp thrill of feminine excitement which a really wonderful dress can give. It had been, in fact, years, now that she thought of it. She stood very still, critically examining the dress and her own reflection in the mirrors. She had a good figure, good shoulders, a high, girlish breast, neat lean ribs narrowing to a small waist, hips perhaps a little too flat.

Above all she carried herself with the light, stretched, flat-backed posture, her head high and her arms quiet, which her mother had drilled into her with remorseless severity, in the years when other girls of her age were obsessed with acquiring the debutante slouch.

"Is that tight enough, Mrs. Bourne?" Miss Flora had been fitting the sleeve of the jacket. She knew that Jessie wore her sleeves long and very tight through the forearm. Perhaps the habit was a bit of vanity, for it flattered Jessie's dainty wrists. Jessie flexed her arm and nodded, adding, "It's really beautiful, Miss Flora. Especially here." She laughed and patted the velvet which had been fitted like skin itself across her flat diaphragm.

"My word," said Miss Elsie admiringly. "Imagine being able to wear that and *eat dinner* in it!"

They all laughed; but it struck Jessie then, with an inner thud which diminished her pleasure, that her first faint thrill at seeing herself in the dress had been a vibration of the primeval instinct that she wanted to please a man by wearing it. Now she realized that the gown would not be finished for a fortnight at least—a week, possibly two weeks, from next Monday. For a moment she felt disappointed in the most infantile way; she could have cried. And then she caught herself, suddenly serious and almost appalled. She was no flirt, she did not mean ever to flirt, this had been the most trifling of notions . . . No, said some other part of her reason, no; not at all. She put the back of her hand to her eyes, as if to clear her brain for saner and more prudent thoughts; and just then she heard someone come into the room and she opened her eyes. It was her old friend Bertha Meyer, who had run the dressmaking part, and many other parts, of this establishment ever since Jessie could remember, and before. The connections went back, indeed, farther than Jessie herself could know, for Bertha Meyer had known Rosa Landau and her family long before Jessie was born.

"Hello, Bertha dear!" said Jessie.

Miss Meyer, who was one of the most impassive women in New York, made a comfortable sound which could mean a greeting, and stood looking at the green dress with a calm surgical eye.

"It's lovely, isn't it?" asked Jessie. One would almost think that she had designed the dress and wished Miss Meyer to approve of it.

The neat grey head wagged slowly and Miss Meyer said, "It's nice."

"You were pretty coony about your pre-war velvet," said Jessie.

"Well, I gave you some, didn't I?"

"I'm trying to thank you. But I may have been a little fresh about it."

"I'm used to it." Bertha Meyer sat down in the corner while Flora was extricating Jessie from the pinned dress, and sighed wearily. "My God," she said, "if I'd ever known the business would come to this."

"What? The zoo outside there?"

Bertha Meyer nodded again. "You never saw anything like it. They'll buy everything in sight. Anything. The carpets, maybe. They want to walk out with it. Pay cash off a wad to choke a horse and take it home off the model's back."

The fittings were finished. Elsie and Flora gathered up their things and left the room. Jessie put her hair in order, fixed her face, and began to put on her clothes.

"Miss Meyer!" The head of a vendeuse popped into the room, her expression a combination of exasperation and panic.

"I'm not on the floor," said Bertha Meyer.

"But——"

Miss Meyer only shook her head. The woman went away. Bertha Meyer looked past Jessie's shoulder into the mirrors and said, "You look a lot like your mother, Jessie."

"Really?" Jessie smiled warmly.

"Different. But you remind me of her. When we were girls."

"It's so queer," said Jessie. "When I think of the things you know that I wish I knew . . ."

"Nothing so special." She shrugged. "We all lived in the same block. Did the same things. Had the same kind of jobs. Only Rosie was different."

"That was Auntie Esther," said Jessie slowly.

117

"Sure."

"Bertha," asked Jessie, slowly fastening the snaps which held her yellow gilet in place. "Bertha, how long have you been in this business?"

"My God. Thirty—let's see—two—three—oh, about thirty-five years. We were down at Thirty-seventh Street then. Your Auntie Esther's place was just around the corner. Do you remember it?"

Jessie nodded slowly, staring into the mirror, seeing not only the soft grey elegance around her here, and the quiet ageing woman in the French armchair, but many other things of this same special world, things of long ago.

"The Place" was what Auntie Esther and her sisters called it. It was one of the very best small dressmaking establishments in the city, occupying the second floor of a business building in the block west of Fifth Avenue. "Madame Esther, Modes" was painted in flowing gilded script across the plate glass front windows. The Place was a citadel, a world, a matriarchy, a vivid intensity of sounds, smells, colors, heat; a core of such magic that a little girl of six thought it the most wonderful of all places in which to spend the day.

Auntie Esther was the queen. Just as she had always ruled her family with calm and justice and an inflexible but kindly will, so she ran The Place and the forty-odd women who worked in it. Auntie Esther had carried the responsibilities of a man and a breadwinner since her early girlhood, but she was the most feminine of women in appearance and in her ways.

There she stood, handsome, tall, firmly corseted, elegantly dressed, wielding with her heavy brown hand the ponderous cutter's shears that were the foundation of her reputation. Her cutting-table was an artist's easel, though the little girl watching round-eyed as the shears closed on some piece of rich velvet or brocade could not understand why a spectator might gasp at Madame's daring. A child, waiting eagerly for permission to pick up a snippet of shining lamé or pussycat velvet for her dolls, would not know that Auntie Esther was risking a great deal of money invested in magnificent French materials, should she ever make a mistake or cut in such a way as to waste part of a length. But Madame Esther did not make mistakes.

"Oh," the child would cry, dancing up and down upon arriving at The Place, while somebody took off her coat and bonnet, "I love it here!"

She was allowed to trot about wherever she liked. In the "front room" there were small tables loaded with books of fashion-plates from which the customers selected their models, though Madame Esther never failed to improvise her original ideas upon them. Jessie could spend hours poring over the pictures. If the little girl popped into a fitting-room while a fitting was going on, everybody stopped work to make a fuss over her, for many of the customers were well-to-do Jewish wives and mothers who adored children, and especially the child of Rosie whom some of them had known since Orchard Street. They all held an intense personal pride in her.

"Na! Goldele!" The kindly, well-fed faces would beam, the puffed and ratted heads would wag, the big, bulging bosoms in the beribboned corset-covers would almost spill over as the women bent down to hug the child.

Little Jessie would sometimes be lifted up and set upon a stool or a chair in the corner, and often she was asked to "sing a song," while the fitting went on.

Cheerful and shrill, the child's voice piped:

> *"H-A-double R-I-G-A-N*
> *Spells 'Harrigan'!"*

Then there was Auntie Esther's cutting-room, with the glaring drop-light hanging above the cutting-table. And then beyond that the most exciting place of all, the big, steamy, smelly, crowded workroom where the "girls" sat at long tables, their dark heads bent over their work in a continual shrill babble of Yiddish, Italian, and broken English. Jessie could not imagine another place where there could be so much to see, to hear, to watch, to smell, to ask questions about.

Over by the big dirty wired windows were the sewing-machines, where dark-skinned, round-shouldered, intent women kept the treadles flying so fast that you could scarcely see the needles work, while the machines burred and whirred and the flat, fine seams flowed out under the women's hands.

Up and down the length of the room sat the hand-workers at the finishing-tables, making before the eyes of the fascinated child the most wonderful things. One girl would be working in bugles, embroidering them upon the frailest chiffon, peering through her thick eyeglasses into the box where the glittering little tubes of glass were kept, picking

119

them up one by one on the point of her needle. Another would be pinking lining, which Jessie thought the prettiest of sights. Another would be covering tiny muslin buttons with smooth grey satin, making ready to sew dozens of them down the front of a handsome afternoon dress. Others would be boning collars, setting hems, making tiny fine silk button-loops, binding, whipping, beading, working with lace and ruching and velvet piping and soutache braid and other things whose names the little girl did not know.

The smell of The Place was one to remain in the nostrils for a lifetime. It was first of all warm, sometimes much too hot; the heavy smell of steam rose from the pressing-boards over in one corner besides the gas rings, where the flatirons stood ready all day long. The smell was human too; the smell of too many not very clean women crowded into too little space. There was too the dry strange smell of fabrics, not so literally an odor as a texture for the nostrils, just as velvet or satin or broadcloth had each its own texture for the fingers. The gas smelled, often so strongly as to make some girl ill. There was always the smell of coffee in a tall grey agate pot standing on one of the gas rings. And finally there was the pungent smell of food, for the girls brought their lunch to The Place, and laid aside their work to eat there at the long littered tables.

The child was goggle-eyed over the things that they ate, and though Auntie Esther always took her round the corner to Fifth Avenue to lunch at Maillard's, Jessie hoped not to be away while the girls were eating. For they ate the strangest, greasiest, spiciest food that it was possible to imagine, reeking with garlic, and the fascinated child loved to watch them doing it. Each girl brought her sandwiches in a greasy brown-paper bag. The Italian girls ate great hunks of crusty bread with salami or cheese or pickled olives and peppers. The Jewish girls ate rye bread or enormous crusty semmels, split and filled with dark red meat which, Jessie learned, was called pastrami. Or they ate bologna or corned beef or sometimes slices of pungent bright pink fish which they called lox, a far cry from the delicate Nova Scotia salmon which would one day be the *pièce de résistance* of Jessie's buffet table.

And having eaten with their fingers these reeking, greasy foods, of which, Jessie would think in later years, they could never have washed away the traces, they would go back to work upon the most fragile silks and chiffons, the palest

120

colors, the most expensive trimmings. And nothing ever seemed to be damaged; the gowns were finished and pressed and sent out, and the business flourished, and Madame Esther's reputation, built partly upon her superb work, partly upon her rich personality, endured years past the day when Rosa Landau finally induced her to close The Place and retire. To this day, when she moved in certain concentric circles which embraced business, Broadway, the arts, the old-time life of downtown which spread its tentacles from Tammany Hall to Tin Pan Alley, Jessie could meet kindly, grey-haired women, heavily jewelled and basking in the luxury of a husband's or a child's success, who would wag their heads and sigh, "You know? Your Auntie Esther made my wedding-dress!"

"Bertha," she said, turning from the mirrors, crisp, chic, poised, a portrait of this day and this moment if one did not see in her face the old memories and old resemblances which Bertha Meyer saw there. "Bertha, do you ever feel as if we were ghosts? Spooks? From a shadow world of our own?— and what are we doing here now?" Her voice was low and muffled, her eyes distrait.

Bertha Meyer pulled her weary body from the chair and said, "My God, I haven't got the time."

Jessie saw a pin sticking upright in the nap of the dove colored carpet. She bent down slowly and picked it up, thinking of the little girl who used to run about with a magnet, collecting spilled pins from the floor of The Place and putting them away in their boxes.

X

Sarah met her at the front door as she came in, saying "Miss Iris is here, Mum. I put her in the library."

"*Miss Iris?*" said Jessie, handing Sarah her furs. "I was not expecting her."

"I know, Mum. She telephoned and whin I said ye'd be in about five, she said she was comin'. She said it was important."

Jessie sighed, "Bring the tea there, please, Sarah." She went

121

into the library, where Iris was sprawled on the couch, reading *The New Yorker*. The room was blue with smoke and the ashtray beside Iris was full already.

"Hi," she drawled. She dropped the magazine on the floor, and did not rise or change her position.

Jessie could have barked at her. There was something about this child which rasped Jessie's nerves to needles. Her long, hatless, blonde hair, hanging below her shoulders, which Iris combed in public wherever she might be; her insolent, empty, staring face; her clawed fingernails painted blackish blood-color; her abominable manners; her incessant, dirty smoking. The abrupt "Hi" which was a crude, if cheerful commonplace from anybody else became an impudence from Iris. Jessie felt so irritated that she could scarcely answer; she gave vent to her twitching annoyance by seizing the brass shovel and hearth-brush from the fireplace and sweeping up the cigarette ashes which Iris had piggishly dropped on the rug, too lazy to aim at the ashtray. If Iris had burned the rug, or the lovely old mahogany table beside the couch, Jessie would have had difficulty restraining the desire to slap her. Such things had happened in the past.

Sarah came in, her face a caricature of Jessie's thoughts. She placed the tilt-top table before Jessie's chair, took away the ashtray from beside Iris as if it were something putrid, put a clean one there, and went to get the tea-tray. It was not, thought Jessie, watching the black-and-white back leave the room, that Sarah was a snob; it was that Iris was a mess. Sarah could take people as she found them, but her mind slammed the door on degeneracy. If Iris was not the complete degeneration of her heredity, Jessie knew nothing.

"How will you have your tea?" she asked. "Sugar—lemon—?"

Iris looked pained. "I——"

"I didn't order drinks," said Jessie tartly. "I'm tired and I want my tea."

(Must you, her mind asked itself, be such a crabbed old crow? Must you be such a stuffed shirt? You know perfectly well that you are only acting like this because the girl annoys you.)

She held out a cup of tea to Iris, coldly waiting for her to heave herself off the couch and come across the room to get it. Irish finally did so, snippy and sullen. Jessie managed to master her temper and give Iris a reasonably human smile.

"Sit down here," she said, indicating a small bench before the fire, "and tell me what's up."

"Oh," said Iris, "I don't know what to do. It's Mother again with her song and dance about coming out and all the rest of that bunk." Iris scowled. "I'm not going to do it!"

"Then—" said Jessie.

"Oh, you can't tell Mother off like that. You know. She's like a drawing of Mary Petty's there." Iris motioned at the magazine that she had flung on the floor. "Mother doesn't even argue with you, she just 'simply doesn't understand'." Iris's words ended in a mocking falsetto, with her blonde eyebrows lifted in sarcastic arches.

Jessie was silent. She knew that Millicent's putting Iris through the paces of an elaborate and anachronistic debut would be an ill-savored farce, but she could scarcely mention to Iris the real reason why Millicent Fielding was immovable in her determination to do the thing. So it became the extreme of cynical debasement for Iris to say, "That's Mother's idea of the way to bottle up the stink about Father and Isabel."

"You call her Isabel?" asked Jessie faintly.

Iris shrugged. "Who doesn't?"

Jessie thought for a time. Iris sat smoking, humped upon the bench, her long legs wound about each other, her feet and ankles coarsened by the flat, spread, shapeless black sandals which Jessie thought so ugly. Evidently it did not make Iris in the least uncomfortable that Jessie should stare at her, not altogether by intent, but with some curiosity and some measuring of Iris against standards which the girl herself would not understand. Jessie was deliberating whether or not it might be constructive in the end to give Iris a good stiff scare right now. At last she said, "Iris, what makes you think that your mother is only worrying about your father and—and—Mrs. Allen?"

Iris blew a long stream of smoke and asked truculently, "What do you mean?"

Jessie picked up a biscuit from the tray and slowly bit into it. Her eyes were lowered.

"I have done my best," she said, "though you may as well know it was against my judgment, to keep any knowledge of your doings and whereabouts from your mother. But you are far too shrewd, you know too much about what goes on, to think that nobody else would ever tell her."

123

"There's not much to tell!" said Iris defiantly. "After all, if Mother's going to go on living in the Nineties you can't expect me to stay there too. She probably does know I go out once in a while—so what? If she ever let on that she knew, and started to raise hell about it, I'd only do it anyway. Then where would she be?"

Jessie realized with an uncharacteristic sense of shock that Iris was undoubtedly right. And in that realization she saw too, the full possibilities of Millicent Fielding's real knowledge and real fears, which had driven her to the despair in which Jessie had seen her yesterday. But Millicent had managed then to conceal from her the truth upon which Jessie had chanced merely as a device just now. Millicent Fielding was not in any way, poor soul, as ingenuous as she seemed. Rather she wore her seeming ignorance of the life led by her daughter and her husband as her only protection from utter ruin.

This threw a very different light on everything, as Jessie thought about it now. She decided to be as bold as possible, bolder than anything Iris could dare; and she said coldly, "Iris, you ought to stop being seen with that man Spanier."

She watched the child closely, and as she had expected, the flat defiance which came down over the curiously blank face did not come quickly enough to hide a flicker of panic in the blue eyes. So it was even worse than Jessie had thought. She was appalled.

Iris said exactly what Jessie had anticipated: "Leave my friends out of this."

"I was not speaking about 'your friends'," said Jessie. "I spoke about a man who has as horrible a reputation as any gangster. A man older than your father. I spoke about a man"—Jessie leaned forward and forced Iris to look into her eyes—"whom I ought not to mention for any reason to a girl of your age. Much less for this reason."

"I don't know what you're talking about," said Iris. Her lids were narrowed, her eyes glittering blue—like Brandon's, Jessie saw.

"Then you might as well go home," said Jessie. "I did not ask you to come here this afternoon."

She got up and walked to the bell across the room and rang for Sarah to take away the tea. Then she went to her desk and began looking through the letters that had come in the afternoon mail. She opened one or two, ignoring Iris who

124

had not risen from her place. Sarah went away, Jessie made a telephone call, and still Iris did not move.

At last, as Jessie had known that she would, Iris said, "Jessie."

"Yes?" Jessie looked up from the letter that she was reading and waited for Iris to go on. The girl made time for herself by taking as long as possible to light a cigarette. Quite aside from her deep disinclination to be involved in this mess which was proving to be a very cancer of spreading and interlocking cells, Jessie was really resentful that Iris should be here in this way now, when Jessie had wanted time to rest and to bathe and dress slowly before dinner tonight. It was almost six o'clock and Mark Dwyer would be here in two hours or less. The thought of him, as Jessie sat at the desk looking at Iris Fielding, was like a great fresh breeze. Jessie might have to go without her rest, but she knew too that the hours she would spend with Mark Dwyer would be more refreshing and more calming than any interval of sleep. So she felt more patient and kindly toward Iris as she said, "I know it's all very unpleasant for you, Iris. But what I said is true. I assure you that Spanier is not a man with whom one's name can be connected without the worst possible implications—and the most possible talk. So——"

"So you think Mother is in a feaz about that?"

"Certainly. And I will tell you that if you were my daughter, I would be in a greater feaz, as you call it, than your mother. Perhaps because I know all about Jack Spanier and your mother probably does not. I'll say that for the sheltered life anyway," she added, forgetting for the moment to whom she was talking.

"There's nothing the matter with Jack Spanier," said Iris, with stubborn resentment.

"If you had the same attitude about some entirely different man with Jack Spanier's background I'd think you were grand," said Jessie. "I want you to get it perfectly clear what my objections about him are. They have nothing to do with his—his origin. They are because he is a cruel, crooked scoundrel, and extremely dangerous besides."

"Oh, Jessie. You sound like a soap opera."

"Iris, it was you who came here to see me. There are things I would far rather be doing than talking to you right now." Jessie rose from the desk and came back to her chair opposite Iris and sat down. "But," she said, "since you came here on the heels of an argument that you have evidently had with your mother, to ask me to persuade her not to make you come out this winter, I can only tell you that your mother in this instance is absolutely right. Even though I think coming out as much hooey as you do. You had better grab this chance while you can, because at the rate you've been going, it's the last one you will have."

"What chance?"

"The chance to extricate yourself from the slime into which Jack Spanier is dragging you and get back among the people where you belong—if they will have you."

"Suppose I don't want to be extricated, as you put it?" Iris's pale face was very sullen.

"Then you are a bigger fool than you've proved yourself already, which is prodigious," said Jessie. "I suppose," she added as a seeming afterthought, very casual, "Spanier has told you you have talent and he will put you in a play he's producing?"

"Why—how do *you* know?"

Jessie thought it would be too obvious to tell Iris the truth, a truth so brutal that it would only make Iris protest the more vehemently. Jessie said, "Instead of believing me, or for that matter, Jack Spanier either, just make a few quietly coldblooded inquiries on your own. You certainly know where to make them, I'm sorry to say. Just ask about—oh—" Jessie looked away vaguely as if she were making an effort to remember. Then she said, "Oh, about Myra Cornhill. And Winnie Blake among others. Leda Thorne."

"*Leda Thorne?* Didn't she—?" Iris's eyes were opened wide now; they were stretched with doubt and fear.

"She killed herself while she was living with Jack Spanier," said Jessie, making her voice as hard and cold as possible.

Iris sat silent and for a moment Jessie wondered if she had been wise. But she could think of no subtler way to deal with Iris, who was a frightening combination of hardness and extreme youth. She was barely eighteen; and though she bore the superficial marks of the life that she had been leading, its habits and mannerisms peppered all through her speech and her bearing, she was helplessly ignorant underneath. She would react only to drastic facts. Presently she said something which Jessie thought shrewd, for her. She said, "If the things you've been saying about Jack are true, why wouldn't Father have flagged me? He sees me around with Jack."

"Probably," replied Jessie slowly, "because your father

belongs to that select group who think that nothing disgusting or scandalous could ever spill out of the sewer where it runs and actually touch them. A sort of 'honi soit' arrangement in terms of people. Or else he may think of you as 'just a little girl' who is so young and pure that no man could possibly have wicked designs on her, to put it as ridiculously as possible."

"Lots of girls I know think Jack is very attractive," said Iris. "They——"

"Oh, yes," said Jessie. "I take that for granted. You would not have gone so far as you have if it hadn't been for the excitement of competition. I suppose it would be too much to expect that you had ever wondered just where all this was going to land you?"

"Why—I——"

"I told you, Iris, that for one play that Jack Spanier actually produces, there will be a dozen that he only talks about. Those are the sucker-bait. Sometimes for the money that he gets from one kind of fool—and sometimes for what he gets out of your kind of fool. You may notice, though, that when he actually puts a play into rehearsal the cast is made up of strictly professionals. Do you know of any beginner or amateur who ever got a part through him?—or a foothold in the theatre?"

Iris shook her head reluctantly.

"Well," said Jessie, "you see how it is. If you really want to learn to be an actress—which I doubt—you may as well get ready for a few years of hard labor, school, and heartbreak. But that isn't what you really want, Iris. You go home and think it over and you'll see what I mean."

Sarah appeared in the doorway and said, "Mrs. Lee on the telephone, Mum."

Jessie rose and went over to the desk, saying, "Run along, now, Iris, I'm going to be late if we talk any more."

In her bath, lying still in the sweet-smelling softened water, Jessie closed her eyes, folding her hands upon her breast and as consciously as possible relaxing, so that her legs and feet turned very light, floating in the water. She wanted to blot Iris and her dreadful little mess from her mind, for while it was not difficult to shunt aside the disagreeable facts that had been forced upon her attention, it was quite another thing to recover her calm after the impressions and responses roused by Iris's cold, strange, blue-eyed personality. For Iris resembled her uncle Brandon Bourne not only with disturbing physical

127

similarity, but in many of the facets of her character. Brandon was not a fool like Iris, since he was first of all spared the ignominy of being a female fool, but he was capable of the same unbelievably wilful mistakes, impelled by the same improbable combination of naïveté and hardness.

The quiet of the warm bathroom was punctured by a long, hideous shriek from the river outside, and Jessie laughed suddenly, thinking how she would hate such a noise if it were not part of something she loved. It was only the whistle of a tugboat, one of the fleet which moved flats of freight cars through the East River; and it must whistle in this shattering way because its tug, hopelessly unwieldy in the treacherous currents, would be deadly in a possible collision. At this time of day, with dusk closing in and night ahead, the unearthly noise was part of a certain mood which meant also the wonderful dark luminous blue of the sky and the river, which came only in certain sorts of clear weather, and lasted only for a fleeting portion of an hour, before the real dark of night should settle, and the curtains be drawn to shut it out.

Jessie thought now, with a small wrench of regret, how many years it had been that she had struggled to make the most of her home and her life with Brandon, within the frame of this loveliest hour of the day. She looked up, from the relaxing depth of the tub, at the beautiful centre window of her bedroom which she could see through the open door, where that rare, vivid dark blue of the early evening sky was framed by the thick rosy curtains; and she remembered, without at all intending to, a small but infinitely familiar disappointment of long ago, which now had no power to disturb her. But in those early years her desire to have Brandon come home from his office at this hour of the day, when their home at its loveliest should, she thought, be most attractive to him, had been repeatedly and doggedly frustrated. That was the hour when he was the most sure to be off about his own concerns, roughly shutting her out of his pursuits and his friendships with the irritable explanation that she did not fit.

Now she was delighted not to have to be bored by the people whom Brandon found congenial, but in the early stages of a marriage entered into from the real but unsound motive of intense romantic love, she had suffered piteously. There had been times when his rebuffs and his abrupt dismissals of her as a factor in his plans had stunned her, leaving her almost insensible with wretchedness, only to find that clearer thinking about it later crushed her with humiliation.

She put her fingertips over her eyes, slowly stroking her lids and her temples, and though she wanted it not to happen, she could somehow not prevent herself from remembering an evening much like this one, when Brandon had said he would be at home early, and instead had rushed in just in time to dress to go out to dinner without her. Instead of leaving him alone she had made the fatal mistake of trying to talk to him; of asking whether he found her an intolerable burden, whether his scowling sullenness, his bursts of savage temper, and his dark secretiveness over a long stretch of months past meant that he was sick of her and wanted to get rid of her.

"Not at all," he had answered coldly, with a condescending touch of surprise.

"But—" she had tried so long, so uselessly, to talk to him, and talk had proved always to be the worst stupidity— "but——"

"But *what?*" he had snapped. She was standing in the doorway between her room and his, wishing with all her soul that she could find the cold sense to go into her own room and shut and even lock the door. Instead, she stood there watching him put into a shirt the black pearl studs that she had given him for Christmas, and to her shame, stooping to the disgusting emotion of feeling sorry for herself. She knew that she must appear, hesitating there in that doorway, the most undignified, most unlovely of creatures; in these circumstances the last thing that she wanted of Brandon was sympathy for her intolerably ignominious situation. She understood also that she was too far gone in self-abasement to evoke anything but irritation from him.

"You—you make me feel so unwanted," she murmured, with stiff lips.

"Well," he said abruptly, "you are."

"Then I had better leave you," she said. "That is what you want, isn't it?"

"No." He was concentrating upon his necktie.

"But you don't make sense, Brandon. In the same breath you say you don't want me, but you don't want me to leave you. How am I supposed to know?"

"Oh——!" With the foulest of oaths he flung his silver hand-mirror across the room and heard it crash on the marble sill of the bathroom floor. Jessie turned weakly aside into her own room and leaned against the door-jamb, swept by a wave of inner trembling and plunged in fear. She moved away when she felt her legs steady enough, and with no plan or purpose went out to the hallway and stood near the top of the stairs. She should not have been there; her own judgment, overcome by paralysis, but still remotely aware, was straining to tell her to go to her own rom and shut herself up there. Yet she stood, doing the one thing that would invite another savage blow, and knowing that this would come.

He came out of his room, dressed, and hurrying towards the stairs.

"What the hell do *you* want?" he asked, on the top step.

"Oh," she said, in a shaking voice which made her wish that she could choke to death then and there, "I suppose—I was just—saying good night."

He looked at her with pure hatred. And suddenly, even though she was too shattered to realize now what she would see clearly an hour later, she knew that his real hatred was not for her at all, but for himself. At his best he would hate a man who could act in this way, who could so horribly assault the feelings of a woman who loved him, who could so ruthlessly jostle her out of his life, leaving her alone night after night, forcing her to be tragic or pathetic or abject when her real capacity was for charm and gaiety and animation.

"God damn it!" he snarled, brushing past her, "don't you ever have anything to do yourself?"

He was down the stairs and into his topcoat before she realized it; she stood there bracing herself for the wild slam of the front door which invariably proclaimed his comings and goings.

Ah, she thought now, opening her eyes and moving her head against the tub to notice that the blue hour was past and that Josephine was drawing the curtains in her bedroom, ah, it is the hideous unimportance, the tininess, the triviality of the things that men and women do to one another which have the hateful capacity to return and to offend one's dignity years and decades later. There is only one reason why these isolated memories of rudeness, cruelty, and selfishness matter at all, and that is the lasting damage wrought by them cumulatively upon the people who perpetrate and who endure them. Perhaps the victims can recover, I am not sure; but the doers surely never. And yet for those who have been through these debasements in any way, there will be scars always. Some part of one's capacity to share life with one's fellow man will remain twisted, crippled, a thing of which to be ashamed, a deformity that one can never completely hide.

And now, she reflected, why should she, anticipating a

happier evening than she had known in years, lie here in this bath and find these images and episodes materializing, when she would have believed that she had forgotten them? Why— she exclaimed aloud, flipping one foot in the water and watching the bubbles bob about, burst, and vanish—why am I allowing this to take place? Ah, well—can I suppose that the substance of the years will dissolve like the salt in this bath, leaving a fresh, empty vessel ready for new experience, ready as if it did not still contain the unriddable residue of all the past? She moved her head slowly from side to side, a tenuous denial, and again closed her eyes.

XI

When Mark Dwyer entered the drawing-room Jessie was seated near the fire in her favorite chair, an old bergère of fruit-wood upholstered in faded apricot-colored silk. She put out her hand and he took it and kissed it lightly; not the back of her hand, the most formal of salutations, but her fingers, near the tips. He sat down in the chair opposite her, and she saw in his face the same appreciation, mingled with something like puzzled disbelief, that she had seen when he looked at her and her house last night.

He was wearing a dinner jacket with a soft piqué shirt.

"How nice you look," said Jessie. "I thought that wasn't allowed."

He shrugged, smiling. "Let's confine the admiration to you. You look edible—at the least."

She was wearing a gown which she had always particularly liked, of pale blue crêpe embroidered with fantasies in charming, unexpected forms and colors; butterflies and small silly beetles and even a lady-bird perched on the draped cowl collar. She loved this sort of gown, which one wore only at dinner in one's own house, because she loved the mood and the occasion for which it was designed.

Sarah gave them cocktails and small piping hot mushrooms with some sort of spicy surprise hidden inside. Mark was especially quiet; for a time he said nothing at all, and the relaxed atmosphere was more welcome to Jessie than any conversation that she could possibly imagine. But presently he said, "How do you make your hair go into that nice shape? It looks so organized."

"It's that kind of hair," she said. "Curly." Her grey eyes looked up at him and went mischievous at the corners. "Just like your own, only you hadn't noticed. Grey too."

"I hadn't noticed that either." He winked.

If she had ever seen eyes more minutely observant than these brown ones of Mark Dwyer's, she did not know when. He was leaning back in his chair, his gaze moving along the cove of the ceiling where the pale pine panelling ended in a dentellated moulding. There was evidently far more in his mind than he would ever put into speech, and Jessie knew too that whatever he did say would always be cleanly economical of words. It must be a combination of nature, long habit at his work, and the recent years when terseness, if not silence, had often been the measure between life and death.

"What did you do all day?" he asked.

"Just about what you would expect an idle woman to do, I'm afraid. A committee luncheon—a fitting——"

"It seems out of character."

"Well, of course, it is. But how queer for you to say so. You don't know me at all."

"No. Not at all. But I know a situation when I see one."

"Situation?"

He let Sarah pour another cocktail for him. When she had gone he said, "Not that you don't fit the framework of your life charmingly. You do. Only it's a framework. Two dimensions——" By a gesture he indicated the absence of a third. "Aren't you bored?"

"Most horribly." She stared at the coals glowing quietly in the grate. "Not in the sense of being jaded, you understand. Not with wanting excitement or pleasure." She made a small rueful face. "But with being useless."

"That's going too far."

"No it's not. I am useless—more perhaps to myself than in the sense of not being useful to somebody or something else. But it doesn't matter what you call it—I don't like it." She sighed.

"But why did you ever stop working?"

Jessie raised her head and let her eyes move slowly about the broad, beautiful room, and then rest upon the great bay window, as if by consulting her friend the river outside, she could find just the right answer. She did not speak at once.

Dwyer also swept the room with his eyes, both a scrutiny and a tribute to what she had made of it.

"You wanted to—to——"

She nodded. "It seemed so important at the time," she murmured, quietly enough so that Dwyer leaned forward to catch her words. He caught too the submerged meaning of what she had said, but he contrived not to let her notice. "And," she said, in a more matter-of-fact tone, "since *The World* was sold just about that time, and since I have no talent that keeps a person at work of itself, it seemed wrong just then to keep a job from somebody who really had to have it." She smiled.

"But there was something you wanted much more anyway."

They both laughed a little, because the meaninglessness of a laugh was an agreeable device just now, and Sarah announced dinner.

Mark held Jessie's chair and then took his place, with an expression of thoughtful curiosity as he looked about the dining-room. It was as much the exquisite order in which the place was kept as its beauty which seemed unreal to him. Heavy gleaming silver, old Derby porcelain, Irish crystal, lace, soft candlelight, the velvety patina of fine mahogany superbly polished—this made no sense.

"Were you here all during the war?" he asked, as they began to eat the soup.

She nodded. "I wanted frightfully to go over and do a job —it was the same feeling that I had had here for years anyway, wanting to get out, get at some reality, where I could work and be necessary. Of course the war simply intensified that."

"But——?"

"But when I looked to see what I might do in London or anywhere abroad, there was nothing that I could do well enough to justify my cluttering up the place. And they sold me a bill of goods about how important I was to a lot of war things here—oh, well, it doesn't matter. Someone had to do it."

"Bourne?" asked Mark. He put a dozen meanings into the quiet monosyllable.

Jessie shrugged. "Nothing," she said.

He let the whole burden of her answer go unnoticed as he had a few minutes before, and presently she asked, "Where are you going back to when you leave?"

"Central Europe. Points East. Pretty much the old stand. Perhaps I'll hardly know from week to week. Prague, mostly. There's not much that I can say about it. I may even make a mess of it." He ate some celery and some more soup. Then he looked up and said, "But I have to try, that's all I know." His face was extremely serious.

"Somebody must," said Jessie. "God knows."

"Well, you see. There isn't anything I can say about it. The minute you start talking, it begins to sound like all the other high-sounding stuff that turned sour and stunk up our so-called victory."

They helped themselves to a *truite au bleu,* curved round on itself in the classic manner, accompanied by a beautiful Hollandaise.

"I hope I never talk about it," he continued, eating. "Any words you can find for thinking you might help the thing only make you sound like a braying ass. At the worst, it's like some chaps I know who never were alive until the war, they had never had a chance to know there was a world, much less the kind of one they got out into. And now they don't want to go back to the stock-brokering business or whatever it was. They don't want to stop being heroes. My God, for all I know, I look like that."

"Don't be silly."

"Well, that's what George Stillman thinks. He keeps jawing at me that the war is over, and then every day he prints an editorial reminding the folks that it's not. So you see—everybody else is crazy too."

Sarah brought in a casserole whose fragrance caused Mark Dwyer to stare, his mouth open.

"I don't believe it," he said, watching Jessie help herself.

She laughed. "I hope you like it."

"Like it!" The casserole held partridges cooked in sauerkraut. The dish was rich and delicate with sour cream, and presently there followed small potato dumplings, brown-crusted.

"The fantastic thing is," said Mark, "that I've just come from the part of the world where all this belongs and most of the poor devils have forgotten that it ever existed."

"Don't they even have *sauerkraut?*" asked Jessie. The commonest, the lowliest form of food, she thought.

He shook his head. "Nor anything else that grows, except potatoes. Oh, it will get better. I'm not given to breast-beating

134

anyway. If you're going to get wrought up about it, don't begin with their bellies. Other things matter much more."

The wine was a Burgundy that Mark did not know, a Clos de la Roche of 1929, grown by a certain Armand Rousseau. It was heavy and full, with a big bouquet, wonderful with the highly flavored birds and their garniture. Jessie smiled wryly when he said so.

"I know," she said. "You just told me that it's useless to think this way, but I still feel utterly miserable in some part of me even when I am enjoying my dinner as much as you are."

"My dear little fool," said Mark, "that is an idiotic sentimentality. It doesn't matter what you do eat and what those others don't—so long as you know that they are there, and what's happening to them, and what you are going to do about it. I mean—" he gestured impatiently as if at his own clumsiness. "I'm not talking about you—as such," he said.

"I understand."

He took a second helping, raising his eyebrows at his own greediness, and said after Sarah had left the room, "Do you mean to tell me that that chap lives here and doesn't enjoy it? My God, between you and that cook——!"

Jessie laughed. "He never knows what he's eating. And I'm no mean cook myself, by the way."

He shook his head, looking at her, and his expression changed suddenly from raillery to entire seriousness.

"Why," he asked, "in the name of God did you do it?"

"Have you ever been married?" she retorted quietly.

"Yes." She started with surprise; she had not expected to hear that at all. "She was beheaded in the Pankrác Prison," said Mark, his voice flat.

"Oh—*Mark!*" Her exclamation was almost a wail. "Oh—I —forgive me."

He shook his head. "No, I don't mind. You might not understand. It was not really a marriage. I mean, they were friends of mine, all her people. I was trying to help them through a bad thing and we thought—oh, I'll tell you some other time. It's a long story."

Jessie was puzzled, but there was nothing that she could say now when she saw that he did not want to talk about it.

When they went back to the drawing-room for their coffee, they both paused as they had last night to enjoy the dramatic beauty of the view. The moon was not yet high, nor so brilliant as last night, but it was rising, a shade smaller on the wane than yesterday. It was a fresh and delicious autumn night, the kind of weather, Jessie said, when it is pleasant to have windows open and a small fire too.

"But," she sighed, as she motioned to Sarah to put the coffee on a table near her in the bay window where she had sat down, "there you are. The same thing, I cannot go on about everything as if I didn't even know it! Imagine—burning coal on a night when it's warm enough to have a window open!"

"Well," said Mark, "I suppose if somebody is going to say it, it makes more sense for you to do so than me. It's second nature for me to think those things, and a bore to harp on them . . . but it's an achievement for you."

"Sugar?" asked Jessie.

He shook his head. He was standing beside the piano, looking at a large and dramatic photograph of Rosa Landau, taken perhaps twenty years ago. It was a picture in the grand manner, in evening dress, the broad beautiful breast and shoulders bare, the face a mask of dignity and serenity which even in this artificial medium, did not conceal the warmth and deep humanity of the great wide eyes.

"She was much more beautiful than you," said Mark slowly, coming to sit near Jessie and take his coffee.

"Of course. And oh, Mark, so much wiser!"

There was a silence.

"Is it as bad as all that?" he asked.

She could interpret the question in any way she chose. She wanted to smile, or laugh aloud, or make some bantering reply. Instead she was astonished to feel the sting of tears in her eyes, and she turned her head, swallowing, to look through the window and let the moment pass in silence. This was the first time in her life that she had ever known a man whose understanding could be more entire, more totally natural with no words at all than the utmost that any other person had ever managed to say. Only Helen Lee, of all the people she knew, had become a part of her inner life in this same way. It was almost devastating to come to this knowledge about a man who, as she had said to herself yesterday and was silently saying again now, was a stranger. A stranger—no stranger at all, ever.

"You know," he said, holding out his cup for more coffee, "there is something I'd like to ask you."

Jessie almost blurted, "Why bother?—you'd know

anyway," because that would have been so accurate a reflection of her thoughts. But looking at him, she was not so sure, and her moment of unreality faded away. Then, just as disturbingly, her throat contracted in the sharp grip of anxiety, almost like an instant of faintness, by which the nerves anticipate something distressing. She was so certain that Mark Dwyer was about to ask her something that would lay open the whole quagmire of her wretched relationship with her husband, that she started with amazement as he said, "Will you tell me what you were doing on *The World* twenty years ago? You certainly didn't have to earn your living."

She burst into peals of laughter, as much from relief as from amusement, for the trend of her thoughts a moment ago had been in a very disquieting direction. Her instinct was right; she would not know Mark Dwyer much longer before he would enter upon the gloomy forbidden ground upon which she had managed to keep the gates locked. She answered him, "That was my mother's doing. She was quite fantastic, you know. She had, as I just said, a great deal more sense than I, but she did things very differently."

Jessie swept a circle in the air with her arm, indicating the full and dramatic sweep of Rosa Landau's approach to life.

"She was the warmest, gentlest woman you could possibly imagine," said Jessie. "I feel like a cold, prickly thing—like a sea-anemone—compared to her. I wish I were like her, but—" she sighed. "But all that warmth and sweetness did not keep her from riding down on something when she was serious about it. She had quite a few perfectly amazing obsessions and one of them was that nobody had a right to exist who could not earn his own living. She had a good deal of money, you know——"

"That was what I couldn't understand."

"She had earned a lot of it herself, but my father left her the rest. So it was quite difficult to bring me up to the idea that I would have to go out and get to work. She tried, terribly hard, but you can't fool a youngster about a thing like that. And then, among her other fascinating qualities, she was inconsistent. She meant every word that she said, but you know——"

"When she said it." They both laughed.

"Oh, I never minded after I was old enough to appreciate her. She was marvellous. She would give me the most frightful scoldings and punishments when I made a mess of my finances, and I always did because I was extravagant. And that made her furious. But then I would come home from school for the Christmas holidays and find my closet full of new dresses from Tappé and Kurzman's—all young girls' clothes used to come from them, you know. And so of course Mother's uproars didn't teach me much."

"Damned confusing, if you ask me," said Mark. He was listening with close attention, watching Jessie's face as she spoke.

"Oh—in a way. But also, you see, she used to say that I was supposed to understand her without becoming confused, I must learn to understand that she would never bother to be consistent just for its own sake. She was always quoting the thing about the hobgoblin."

"And what about *The World?*" asked Mark.

"I was—let me think—eighteen. And Mother decided that the way to teach me about money was to put me on an allowance. But of course she was afraid to make the allowance commensurate with the money that she had spent for me up to then, because it would have looked like millions to me and I would have behaved like a drunken sailor with it. So she made the allowance too small, and of course I went ahead and made the most frightful mess anyway. Really, it was bad. You know—big bills that I couldn't pay, and that sort of thing. Of course Mother found out and she was beside herself. She had a terrible temper, but she had really never lost it with me that I could remember. She lost it then, though. Unforgettably, I assure you."

"What did she do?"

"Now that I look back on it," said Jessie slowly, "it occurs to me that she may have laid a good bit of it on. But the result was that she became completely dramatic and put on the most magnificent scene—I'm sure that if Uncle Dan had seen it he would have had somebody write a play around it and tease her into going back to the theatre. The climax was Mother standing at the top of the stairs pointing her hand down at the front door and telling me to get out. I had disgraced her and could go and shift for myself—or a speech to that effect, anyway."

"I think she was dead wrong," said Mark. His face was stern.

"No she wasn't!" said Jessie quickly. "Her methods with me were drastic, and I don't care what your modern child behaviorists would say about them, either. I loved her then, and I love her memory now, in a way that nobody could even begin to imagine. I tell you, I *know* nobody was ever loved the way I loved her—and I never resented anything she did. Never. I worshipped her."

Jessie's face was intense and suffused; her color was high, her eyes wet. Mark, looking at her, crushed down a sudden overpowering instinct to walk over and take her in his arms. But he kept his face impassive, except for the profound expression of his eyes. Jessie was avoiding them from the knowledge that they would hold if she looked into them more understanding and tenderness than she could bear, having been conditioned for so long to doing with little or none. She stayed silent until she could trust her voice to sound steady and clear again, and then she said, "So that was why I went to work. I went down to see Emmett Connor at *The World* and told him I had to have a job and he told Clyde Pritchard to give me one. Of course I realized soon after that Emmett was such a good friend of Mother's that he would have invented some job if there hadn't really been one. But at the time all he did was give me a little talk about forgetting who I was and making damned sure I earned my sixteen dollars a week. Then Clyde started me out running copy and being a kind of female office-boy; I remember he was very crabby about it and said nobody had ever heard of a girl in such a job. But I had the most wonderful time I ever had in all my life, those three years," she said wistfully.

"You got along all right."

"Oh, yes. They began giving me something to do, little by little, as soon as they saw that I really wanted to work and wasn't just doing a stunt. Finally I fetched up in the dramatic department, I was a kind of third-string assistant to Rex Campion."

"I was almost never in the office then," said Mark, as if to note the fact regretfully, twenty years late.

"I realize it—now," Jessie laughed. "I can't say I noticed it then."

"And what did your mother do?"

"She was thrilled. As soon as she saw that I was serious about the job of course she said, come home, all is forgiven, or something to that effect. At first I was pretty independent and I refused, but after a time I got sick of living in a hole with three other girls, so I went back home to live. Only, Mother had thought that I would give up my job, and I wouldn't. I remember I offered to pay her for my board."

"Did she accept it?"

"Mother? Don't be silly! Of course she did. But that Christmas she gave me a beautiful beaver coat, and when I said I couldn't take it, I would not wear anything that I hadn't bought for myself, she cried and made the most awful fuss."

"So of course you sent the coat back," Mark chuckled.

"Of course—not. I wore it for years."

"And so it was only your mother who was temperamental and inconsistent!"

"She was an artist," said Jessie dryly.

"And you were merely female."

Jessie smiled and motioned toward the silver tray with decanters and ice which Sarah had left in a corner of the room.

"No thanks," said Mark. "Not just now. Do you want a drink?"

"Water, please."

When he brought the glass he stood for a moment looking at her, his eyes intent and at the same time puzzled.

"What a strange small party you are," he said. "If anybody had told me a week ago—" He shut his lips abruptly.

Jessie said nothing. It was so easy to understand his unspoken thoughts that she could complete the cycle of silence by a light sigh. They both smiled and presently he said, "You were very charming last night when you drew all that silly family history out of me."

"It didn't seem silly to me," said Jessie. "It seemed more real and more interesting than anything that I've been involved with since—" she made a gesture which managed to comprise all of her life with Brandon Bourne and a good deal that had gone before.

"But," said Mark, "I reminded you that your own story is probably twice as fantastic as mine. In fact, I knew then that it is—you are not altogether a nonentity, you know." He looked again at the picture of her mother. "She didn't materialize from the ether, after all. She had a perfectly tangible dossier that anybody knows whose business it is to know things."

"I have a cousin," said Jessie abruptly, "who is a detective at Headquarters."

"There. You see? The son of one of your mother's sisters——"

Jessie nodded. "The one who was killed in the Triangle Shirtwaist Fire. Hannah."

"My God," said Mark. "And you gaped at *my* story! But you see what we are, both of us. Like cakes off a griddle. And I go to Teheran with the President and you—" he motioned about the beautiful, serene room, a symbol of Jessie's whole life and identity. "And we like what we have become, you know—it would be the phoniest kind of posing to pretend that we didn't. But we don't want the sensation of being chopped off from our roots, either. There is nothing else left in this world that has any permanence, my dear. That's why I'm going back to Europe, if I have to come to terms with a single reason."

"But—" said Jessie, wincing, yet strangely bold, "but what——" Her face appeared stricken; she looked straight at him.

He bent down and took her face between his hands and kissed her lips gently; not with passion but with the utmost tenderness. She sat perfectly still, her hands in her lap; and if she could ever have thought that this would be his first kiss, she would have known the vastest astonishment.

"Sweet," he said softly, shaking his head, "You cannot tell much in twenty-four hours."

"But it was you," Jessie reminded him, still bold with a sense of panic, "it was you who said, there's never any time . . ."

"I was speaking only of pleasure," he said, and his voice was strained. He turned away and she knew that he did not want her to see his face. "Do you play well?" he asked, standing near the piano.

"Presentably."

"I wish you would."

How strange, she thought, rising. What a queer irrelevancy. And moving across the room she knew that she would not have interrupted the mood and the content of this moment as he had done. But he was feeling for time, and also she realized, as she saw his face when she reached the piano, for peace.

"What do you like?" she asked him.

"Haydn," he said. She was pleased that he had not answered, "Oh—anything—" but his taste was surprising. Without comment she began to play the G minor Sonata, B & H number thirty-four. He walked away and stood by the mantel, listening with a calm, critical expression which revealed to her when she looked up that his approach to music was like her own, disciplined and literate. He turned while she

141

was playing the last movement, and sat down on the couch facing the high bank of windows. Jessie had not felt like playing at first, chiefly because it had seemed such an intrusion upon so fragile a moment, one that she would have wished to guard. But it was satisfying to be able to please him.

"You play better than I expected," he said, when she finished.

She rose and crossed the room toward him, smiling. "My mother again," she said. "It was whaled into me. But I never practise."

He put up his hand and took hers and she dropped down lightly beside him on the couch. It occurred to her that any other man whom she could imagine would move to take her in his arms now, and with any other man she would have turned to stone. But Mark Dwyer was not going to do that, and she knew it, and understood.

He sat looking at her fingers in his as if they had some quite unique quality not to be found in all other fingers; and because she knew better than to look, as if she were seeking for answers, at his face, she kept her eyes on his hands too. He had so greatly interested her in other ways that only now did she realize the unusual beauty of his hands. They were of fine size and strength, square, smooth, and very strongly muscled, with qualities revealing a warm and sensitive nature. The fingers were not too slender, perfectly straight and untapered, the joints even and flexible. The skin of his right hand as it held hers felt fresh and silky, not dry or hardened, and there was no visible hair on the backs of his hands, though his wrists were very masculine. Jessie looked at some fine, thread-like white scars on the outer edge of his right hand, and said softly, "Barbed wire?"

"Not stupid at all, are you?"

"The only thing," she said, "that keeps me from asking you questions about the war is that I know you don't want to talk about it."

"That is probably," said Mark, "the result of twenty-five years of newspapering. Once a thing is past it's past. I have a horror of yesterday's spot news."

"But," said Jessie, "you really cannot imagine how I want to know. It was bad enough all those years to sit here praying that such things must be going on, and never knowing whether they were or not. But now to have the chance to know and not to be told seems tantalizing." She looked at

142

him, sidelong, with her thick eyelashes lowered. "Of course," she added, smiling, "my interest is purely academic. Impersonal. Historical."

"I see," he said, and then, "Where was Bourne in the war?"

Jessie was startled; she did not understand exactly why Mark had asked that question, but she answered, "In the Navy. He had quite a lot of rank and he never stopped hoping he would get sea duty, but they kept him doing about what he does anyway."

"Somebody had to," said Mark with a shrug. He knew little about Brandon Bourne, beyond that he was a member of a firm of wholesale dealers and brokers in paper. "Naturally you would expect them to put a fellow like him in their procurement division. Forty-odd, and knowing his business. It's quite a wonder that they had the sense, instead of having some former candy salesman buy their paper for them. Was he here all the time?"

Jessie shook her head. "In Washington mostly. And at Pearl Harbor. He was ill out there and was sent home and discharged last March."

And from the flat indifference of her voice, which she had not thought quickly enough to hide, Mark Dwyer knew that in the absence of her husband during the war she had learned how profoundly bad her bad marriage was. She must have found in those years alone the first peace that she had ever known, and he could feel now as if she had described it, the dread with which she had anticipated Brandon Bourne's return, and the strain of the effort that she had made in the past months to adjust herself again to life with him. Even if that life had become attenuated to the degree of sharing little more than the same roof, Mark Dwyer knew that it had become insupportable to her, a thing of progressive torment and appalling hopelessness.

Suddenly she realized what she had silently told him, and in mortification that she could so completely have abandoned her own intense reticence, she sat back, quite pale, with one hand laid across her mouth. Above it her grey eyes were wide and strained with alarm. But Mark Dwyer almost at once looked away, with the instinct of wisdom and tact that had already become to her a gentleness symbolic of qualities for which she had for years been starved.

She drew a breath and said, "But when Brandon came home, he might almost have been away on a business trip somewhere. It hadn't been very comfortable, and although he

143

had had a great deal of fun, he had had to work very hard. So his one idea seemed to be to forget it all as quickly as possible and—you know." It seemed too absurd to use a phrase like "get back to normal."

Dwyer nodded, saying nothing.

"And because I could not feel as he did, because my war had been a completely different war, because I was still fighting it, he was very irritable. There were always two wars anyway, in people's minds here. Some of us were fighting your war in our emotions and some fought Brandon's. You know—those people scarcely thought of Europe. The Germans were not their enemy—only the yellow-bellies."

"The Chicago Tribune's war," said Mark coldly.

"I know," said Jessie slowly, "that there was just as much sheer heroism, and far more hell in the Pacific than in Europe. But you feel, I suppose, as you are."

"Unless you are so privileged as to be spared the bother of feeling at all."

"For years," said Jessie, "Brandon was annoyed and impatient and bored because of the way I felt about Hitler—the Nazis, the Austrians, the Czechs, the Jews, the Poles, the whole thing. After the very early part of it he used to get so angry when I had people here who had come from there, who talked about it and who cared and wanted somebody to do something . . ." She paused. "It was very difficult," she said.

There was a silence; she had said nothing that Mark Dwyer had not already realized. At last she added, "The strange thing is that Brandon is a perfectly good human being if he is actually presented with something concrete that has to be done about a mess. But until it comes to that, he is furious at being asked to think about it."

Mark said, with weary bitterness, "Boys will be boys."

Presently she found her hand again in his, and once more she marvelled at a calm so real and so natural that simply to be quiet in this way, to share this small, almost child-like contact, seemed as much as she needed for the moment to content her; she knew all this to be derived from him. For this was good and welcome now; and so too would be other and greater moods with all their accompanying impulses, when he should summon them.

She looked at him and after a silence she said, "So perhaps you see why the things that you did, that happened to you, would seem like considerably more than 'yesterday's spot news' to me."

"I suppose so. It was just chance in the beginning that I had so many reasons for being more deeply involved in it than most Americans. You have to make allowances for that. With my people and all that happened to them——"

"Do you know your relatives over there, Mark? Had you known them before the war?"

"Of course. I hadn't been particularly intimate with them—but if you had been over there in the midst of that thing, watching it happen, year by year, creep up on those people—pounce on them—if your aunts and cousins and nephews had been tortured and hounded, or were all in the Underground, naturally it would have felt pretty much like your own private war to you too."

"And then your wife."

"That was different. That was part of the fight we all put up together, it was not a personal thing. I was already in it, up to the eyes. Her brother was one of my closest friends. He was in their Air Force. He got away in his plane in '39, in March—when the swine invaded Prague. It was Nazi policy to make the most savage reprisals against the families of those fliers who had escaped. Most of them were exterminated. Vlasta was his sister and the last survivor of the lot of them, she was a magnificent woman. And we thought we might get her protected on my passport if I married her."

"So that she could get out?"

"Out! Good God, no! She was one of the keys of the whole Underground. She would never have left. Well—it was too late. They got her anyway."

He sighed, and then shook his head as if somehow to convey that all this talk was not what he wanted, that in some way he disapproved of it. Presently he said so: "You see, if you belong there and are part of the whole story, and feel its relation to the past and the future, then it doesn't seem so—oh, I don't know a more descriptive word than corny—to talk about it. But——" he looked up, about the exquisite, untouched, unreal room, through the windows at a river-front which had never been a prime bombing target, across at the thick-huddled roofs of Queens where the factories had worked in unbelievable, uninterrupted safety, and then back at Jessie, sitting close to him and listening with her eyes fixed intently on his face. She said nothing; but he saw how wholly she was bridging the gap that he could not bridge, how she had indeed lived these years in a physical isolation of safety and ease which had no relation at all to the passion of heart and conviction of mind which would have swept her to any extreme of action had the circumstances been different.

He was struck by her quietness; she sat so still that she was like a child spellbound by a favorite story wonderfully told. Her grey eyes were open wide, the thick lashes framing their glowing intensity instead of veiling their expression as was almost always the case. Mark looked into them, slowly taking her in his arms.

Like every other expression of his, like every word that he had spoken, like the deep tones of his voice, the touch of his hands, the calm sad tenderness in his eyes, his kiss too seemed for Jessie something that she had known always.

Presently he moved his lips from her mouth to her eyelids, to the clear delicate skin where her hair sprang from her temples, to her throat, her cheek, her mouth again. The pressure of his hands about her was deep, warm, calm; again that calm which was more wonderful to her in its depth and firmness than any other resource that his warmth could hold. She looked at him with eyes that told him eloquently that this was so; and an infinity besides.

He turned his head presently, and looked away in that same unconscious gesture which Jessie knew now to be a way of retreating to the habit of solitude which must be woven through every instinct of his nature. Whether it had evolved from choice or from chance, it was there; and she understood it, because it was the texture of her own inner life too, forced upon her at first, but long since her only shelter.

When he spoke, his voice sounded shaken and hoarse; he only said, "My God, how I need to think."

She smiled, holding her handkerchief near her eyes, and groping inwardly for the quiet which she wanted to show. There was nothing that she could say; she had never in this way experienced this sensation of needing to be silent, of knowing that silence was the only possible medium for anything that she felt. She knew exactly what Mark Dwyer was going to do, and presently he did it. He rose to his feet, drew her up by her hands, and kissed her again, holding her against his strong, heavy body in the most perfect balance of strength and lightness. Then he let her go, she felt his lips on her eyes and her forehead and the tip of her nose; she heard him say, "Good night—darling"; she heard him stride across the room, and presently she heard the outer door close.

She went and stood at the windows over the river, staring out at the moving, glittering, strange live thing which held, she thought, as much knowledge of her inmost self as any extreme intimate with whom she might have lived these thousands of days, thousands of nights. Once more she watched upon its surface the motions of incomprehensible forces, the farther side of the queer eddying stream flowing up, the nearer down, the centre a swirl of stubborn, confusing currents.

"Ah," she sighed softly, and she watched the small puffing ferryboat which plied the river from this shore to Welfare Island. As it always must, it moved carefully upstream, off its course, crabwise, in order to let itself be borne down upon its wharf by the powerful currents reversing their direction where the little boat reached midstream.

She sighed again, turning from the window.

III
WEDNESDAY

XII

"Will you lunch with me today?" asked Mark when he telephoned.

"I should love to, except for certain misgivings."

"What are they? My intentions?"

Jessie laughed. "No," she said. "I hope I am quite clear about them." She tried to make her voice seem teasing, but she thought that probably it sounded only idiotically happy.

"Are you?" asked Mark, and his voice went very low.

"I think that women are possibly much bolder than men," she said. "Especially at my age."

"I think you are a trollop."

"And I think——"

"Stop thinking. What are these reservations of yours about lunch?"

"The first is that you may get tired of me before this week is out and I would regret that very much."

"I am a perfectly capable judge of how much I want of what."

"What a charming, subtle compliment!"

"And if that is as intelligent as the rest of your misgivings, we will skip the lot of them. I will call for you at once."

"But," she said, for no reason at all except a curious flurry of shyness, which caused her to seek silly excuses for appearing less accessible to him than she really felt, "but I will not be here."

"Where will you be?"

"My goodness, one has things to do, you know."

"Oh. I suppose you are going to John-Frederics with some hen and sit there and cackle over the hats."

"How attractive you make us all. And you have never seen me wearing a hat, you know, many women don't," she said, deciding to wear for lunch the most beautiful John-Frederics hat in New York.

"Well, then, where are you going?"

"To market," she said meekly.

"Don't be a fool. Doesn't that Empress of Koh-i-noor in your kitchen do her own marketing?"

"Not if I feel like doing it."

There was a silence. Then Mark said, "Well, I'll go along."

Jessie was amazed. But she only said, "What a way to spend a leave."

"I am not on leave, Mrs. B. I am on special orders issued to myself by myself. But since we appear to be snarled up with a passel of celebrities tonight, why pick this morning to go marketing when you won't be home for dinner?"

"Because I have people coming for dinner tomorrow. And they like their orders ahead of time, the butcher and everybody . . ."

"But you're dining with me tomorrow!"

"Oh, Mark. What can I do? I asked these people a week ago—or more. Before—" she swallowed. "But of course you must come," she said, "unless you don't want to."

"I want to be with you," said Mark. "Alone, preferably."

"I—oh!" she breathed. "So do I."

"Darling."

"Mark," she murmured.

"What?"

"N-n-nothing . . ."

"Please," he said, "can't you get rid of them?"

"I would like to, but it would not be wise," she said quietly.

"Very well. But the rest of the week——"

149

"We could take that up at lunch."

"What about the rest of the week?"

"I had told Helen I would go up to the farm with her and Sam on Friday."

"But you're not going."

"No," she said, trying to keep her voice level, and thanking God for Helen Lee, "No, I am not going."

"When do we take off on this domestic expedition?"

"It's too silly. Why don't I just meet you for lunch wherever you say?"

"Where will you be at twelve-thirty?" asked Mark.

"At the greengrocer's."

Mark repeated the address of the place, said something that sounded like "Sweet——" and hung up in the middle of his own words.

Josephine came into the room, carrying a small white envelope. Jessie took it and drew out the visiting-card of her sister-in-law, on which Millicent Fielding had written, "Thank you and love." Every line of the thin, slanting handwriting bespoke the painful effort of its author to override her stifling shyness and her helpless aversion to the expression of any emotion, ever. Jessie was touched, because she realized that Millicent was more grateful that Iris had gone home and consented abruptly to her mother's wishes about the debut, the truth of which Millicent would never know, than because of the check which she had received in yesterday's mail.

"Josephine," said Jessie slowly. "Are the flowers white gladiolus?"

"Yes, Mrs. Bourne, they are. How did you know?"

"I knew." It was inevitable that Millicent Fielding would choose the stiffest and coldest flowers in the world and the only ones which Jessie really disliked. Josephine knew that. If the flowers had been something gracious and warm and fragrant, Josephine would have brought them here.

"You arrange them, or Sarah," said Jessie. "Put them on the tables in the hall. And I will wear my purple wool dress today."

"And the new red hat?" asked Josephine, with a gleam of enthusiasm in her eye.

"Why—yes," said Jessie, as if she had not thought of it before.

She lay back upon her pillows, indulging a short moment of intense laziness. Though she had the best of all reasons for getting up, the prospect of a day full of happiness, she was overcome for an instant by a sense of deep sadness, which expressed itself in physical listlessness that was not natural to her. From her bed she should see a span of drab grey sky; this was the first day in more than a week when the sun had not been brilliant. The greyness outside was not that which presages rain, but that which seems simply to set a mood. The sky was giving off a queer glow; Jessie felt as if it veiled something menacing in its light. When she knew these unusual moments of fleeting dejection she felt a sense of obligation to conquer them at once, and she knew too why she had formed this habit. It was because in her life there was only one real reason for feeling oppressed and that was Brandon and the heavy failure of her relationship with him. In honesty she knew that she blamed him for that failure more than she did herself, but her mind rejected the shabby refuge of blaming him entirely. She too had failed. She seldom thought about him specifically any more, she was far more accustomed to his absence than to his presence, and now when he moved in and out of her orbit he was almost entirely a stranger. Yet she had decided long ago to hold to the outlines of her original responsibility, now that there was nothing else left to which to hold; that gave Brandon the right to assert himself just enough to keep her sense of distress about him alive, just enough to rouse in her the throbbing bubble of fear which had become inseparable from his physical presence. But why all this should suddenly have risen up this morning from the vault where she kept it locked and largely ignored, she did not know.

Lying there staring at the drab sky blocked against the windows, she heard a sudden crisp, ripping noise, and she sat up in a jump crying, "Putzl! You devil!"

She leaned over the side of the bed and looked down towards the foot of it, where she saw the huge black cat calmly sharpening his claws on the silk-serge upholstery. "Putzl!" she cried again, and then she could not help laughing, for the cat was luxuriating so gloriously in his wickedness. His soft spine was braced in a smooth concave arc, and his powerful claws were delicately, precisely hooked into the fabric while he fixed his green eyes insolently on Jessie, looking at her over his left shoulder. She clapped her hands sharply, which was supposed to be the way to make Putzl desist from crime; and with the least possible surrender of his dignity, he began reluctantly to unhook his claws from the foot of the bed. Jessie heard voices in the hall outside, and as Josephine opened the door, Anna waddled in behind her, gasping from her rush up the stairs and bellowing, "Putzl! *Du!* I kill it that—" She made a dive for the cat.

"He must have slipped up here behind Josephine when she brought the card from the flowers," said Jessie.

She hung over the side of the bed, shaking with laughter as Anna, a bulky bundle of outrage, scuttled underneath to catch Putzl who had, of course, escaped there. Anna was too fat to squeeze more than her head and shoulders under the low box spring. Putzl, no fool, leaped up with a mild *priaow* behind Jessie, and sitting down slowly on the embroidered sheet, began to purr.

"Look," said Jessie to Josephine. "He'll fix those white gladiolus too." Putzl had a shred of chewed gladiolus leaf hanging from his neat white bib.

"This is his big day," said Josephine, handing him to Anna who had struggled to her feet, puffing and scarlet.

"Shame!" she scolded, shaking the cat. He ignored her, with a yearning green gaze at Jessie. *"Ach,"* said Anna, "you excuse him, no? He wouldn't done it again."

She bobbled away, with Putzl riding resentfully on her shoulder, and Jessie lay back again on her pillows, laughing. Helen Lee was coming by in a few minutes, that was why she had telephoned yesterday when Jessie had been glad of the excuse to get rid of Iris. Helen had said that she was going to be in the vicinity anyway, and as they would scarcely have a chance to speak to one another tonight, with all the goings-on, Helen wanted just to run in, knowing that Jessie would still be in bed. Indeed, Jessie's sense of time was so acute that she was not surprised now to hear Helen's voice outside in the hall, coming up the stairs and speaking to Josephine. It was exactly half past ten, the hour when Helen had said that she would be here.

Jessie sat up quickly as the door opened, smiling with delight at the sight of Helen Lee.

"Hello, darling," they said in unison, and Helen bent over to squeeze Jessie in a quick hug. She went then and sat down in the soft chair by the windows, dropping her gloves and purse on the rosy carpet beside her. She had, Jessie thought, the most beautiful face in the world, not because of its exquisite features and lovely warm coloring, but because of her inner radiance, which illuminated her fine, deep hazel eyes, her tender mouth, the planes of her forehead and her cheeks; above all because of her quick, sensitive expressiveness. Whatever lines nature and time and wisdom would mark upon her face, to reflect her character and all that she had done with it, she was one of those few extraordinary people who are without any tinge of sullenness or moodiness; so she would always be free of the cruel signs which these marks of self-obsession leave upon the face.

"I'm so glad to see you, I could eat you up," said Jessie, for the Lees had spent the past two weeks at their farm without coming in to town. "How is Sam?"

"Fine. They're ready to go into rehearsal next week—so I suppose we'll close up the house after this week end. You're coming, aren't you?"

Jessie shook her head slowly, allowing a smile to come over her face the meaning of which she knew Helen Lee would understand. "Do you mind, darling?" she said. "I would like to stay in town."

Helen looked at her, reading Jessie's unstated reasons as clearly as she would have understood something in one of her own sons.

"I am really very curious," she said. "But not—you know."

"You couldn't do anything that I would hate," said Jessie. "Don't worry. I may seem to you to be acting like a schoolgirl, but really I am not."

"I can't wait for this evening," said Helen.

"Why?" asked Jessie, with mock innocence. "What has this evening to do with it?"

They both laughed and Helen Lee said, "Sam knows General Dwyer. He says he's pure wool."

"Oh, Sam knows everybody," said Jessie. Sam Lee had been a newspaper man years ago, before he had stumbled upon the career which had given him the completest success that anybody in the theatre could possibly have: universal regard from his colleagues, never-failing hits, millions, an eminence so great that he was able by now to state his own terms not only on Broadway but in Hollywood and throughout the world. His surname was not Lee at all, but Levy. He was the most honest of Jews, precisely careful to state his real name in *Who's Who* and all other compendia of information, so that one wondered why he had ever bothered to drop the syllable from his patronymic. He said he had had nothing to do with it; it had been done by the manager who produced his first play. By the time Sam had caught up with his sudden burst into fame, the name of Lee had become too valuable to drop.

153

Jessie reflected as she spoke that Sam Lee's opinion of Mark Dwyer was probably as fine a compliment as she could ask. Sam was a rare man, loyal and sensitive and full of gentle humor, but he could scarcely be otherwise after nearly twenty years of marriage to Helen Penfield. Their relationship was in Jessie's experience unique and extraordinarily beautiful, and they had long ago enveloped Jessie in its warmth and richness. For years their home had been her great refuge from the cold, the bitter, and the barren, in which so much of her own fate seemed to lie. But her intimacy with Helen Lee was still a different thing, quite separate; the two elements complemented and enhanced each other.

Jessie looked at Helen now, admiring her with a delightful sense of fresh appreciation. Her hair was a rich and odd shade of dark blonde, in which the muted light from the windows picked up the subtle variations of color. She had spent much of the summer in the sun, having the smooth, youthful sort of skin which tans to a pale bronze and never becomes leathery or dry. The striking quality of her beauty lay in this rich monotone of color in her skin and her hair, as dramatic in its way as the contrast between white skin and black hair which made other beautiful women spectacular. But without the deep warmth, the animation, and the tenderness of her face, she could have had twice as much physical beauty and still not have possessed the quality that made her so appealing.

Jessie said, looking at her, "Darling, I think you've gained some weight."

"I have," said Helen, with a nod and a pleased smile which struck Jessie as a little odd, since neither she nor Helen would ordinarily allow her weight to increase by a fraction of a pound.

"But—why?"

"I wondered if you'd notice," said Helen, "but it never occurred to me that if you did, you wouldn't know the reason."

"But—" Jessie's face began to go blank with a mixture of bewilderment and incredulity. Helen Lee watched it and suddenly threw back her head and laughed.

"No!" exclaimed Jessie, in a long, hollow breath.

"I told you I would! I've had it on my mind for a long time."

"But Helen. But . . . I thought you were joking . . ."

Jessie's face was set in the expression of dumb astonishment with which she would have reacted to the most grotesque imaginable statement. Her mouth stood open in a small incredulous "O," and her forehead was ruffled with horizontal puckers. Helen was laughing with a mischievous pleasure which seemed to Jessie even more unbelievable than the fact that her dearest friend, only a year younger than herself, with two sons nearly grown, should be so happy over something which appeared to Jessie's instincts an incredible, disastrous blunder.

"I"—she drew a breath and opened her mouth and shut it again. "I cannot believe you really mean it—meant to do it."

"But of course I did. Darling—" Helen's face turned suddenly serious, and she rose quickly from her chair and went over and sat on the edge of the bed, putting her hands over Jessie's and looking into her eyes. "I know why the whole idea seems so appalling to you. But it's quite different for us, entirely different. I'm not even asking you to make believe that you are pleased for my sake."

"But I am," Jessie assured her. "Sometimes—actually a lot of the time—the nearest I come to being happy is by a kind of reflection from you and Sam. Of course I think you're an idiot to start in on a whole new cycle of responsibility and all that sort of thing. But—" she paused, sighing.

For some reason Helen was staring at Jessie with an expression of great concern, and there were tears standing unshed in her eyes. She knew Jessie Bourne so well that she had anticipated her feeling precisely. She knew that the news of a friend's pregnancy could evoke in Jessie a troubled, indeed an abnormal reaction which Jessie went to great effort to conceal, since she herself realized that it might appear monstrous to other women. But it was the truth that the statement that a woman was expecting a child fell upon Jessie Bourne's ears like a plumb weight dropping into a closed area of dead space. Jessie did not possess the faculty of sharing vicariously the peculiar intense joy with which women who wanted children were able to say that they were producing them, though she was ordinarily very sensitive to important emotions felt by people whom she loved, and above all, to anything that concerned Helen Lee. In this instance, which was of course momentous, she was already beginning to be miserable because she could not feel anything except dull amazement. Once again she faced squarely the knowledge that something within herself was not only atrophied, but dead, stone dead.

155

And this was what Helen Lee knew now; this was the reason for the intense concern in her lovely face, the tears that glistened in her eyes. She bent over and kissed Jessie on her cheek and said, "I know. Don't try to pretend with me. But somehow I have an idea you may become far more reconciled to this than you can possibly believe."

"It is not," said Jessie, shaking her head, "as if you hadn't got Philip and Peter already. They're so wonderful . . ."

"That's just it," said Helen quietly. "I've had a feeling for quite a time that in a year or two or three when they're really men, with lives of their own, the best thing I can do for them is—" she made a gesture with her hands almost as if of dismissal. "You know—let them go. Humanly, I mean, or emotionally, I don't like to use such words anyway. But they will never," she said, with a firmness that was almost stern, and not very characteristic of her, "never find me clinging to their shirttails with any of that wretched passion wrapped up in the word 'Mom'."

"But you still want something to—to———"

Helen nodded. "And why not? Really, darling, I'm not so old. We think we are, but———"

They both laughed. Helen was right, Jessie knew very well. There was nothing too formidable in the idea that a woman should have a child at the age of thirty-eight. It was far more extraordinary, in the circles in which they moved, that she should have made such a magnificent thing of her nineteen years of marriage to Sam Lee, and her two sons now seventeen and eighteen years old.

"What do Sam and the boys think?" asked Jessie, smiling quizzically.

"Oh, they love it. They're all amused and pleased—they remind me of the way they used to act when we promised them a puppy or a kitten. If it's a girl, she'll be the worst-spoiled brat in the world."

Jessie sighed. "No, she won't, not with you there. No wonder you said you wanted to see me this morning. Good God," she added, "suppose I'd had to sit there and guess it suddenly tonight."

"You'll have your mind on other things tonight," said Helen, winking. "I'm no fool. I want all your attention when I want it."

She rose and went to a mirror and began to powder her nose. "I've got to go along and let you get dressed. If I hang around here we'll get nothing done all day, either of us. How long will Brandon be down there among the horses and asses?" she asked.

Jessie moved her shoulders in a slow shrug, at the same time raising her eyebrows with comical indifference.

"Just as well," said Helen sourly. "I wish he'd go native altogether and find some drawling paleface and tell you he wants to marry her."

"Of course," said Jessie, "you are no paleface yourself."

"After twenty years of Sam?" exclaimed Helen. She was the daughter of a Methodist minister in Hornell, New York, and in the most typical, wide-eyed way had come to the city at the age of seventeen, armed with a four-hundred-dollar legacy from an aunt, to make her way in the world. The way had led to a typist's desk in the office of a magazine publisher where Sam Lee had found her. So Helen considered that her own plain background, merged with the tough and lusty strain of Sam, was the utmost possible extreme from the world of what she called "palefaces," the arid, dwindling world of Brandon's family and their kind.

She thought, with far greater detachment than Jessie could possess, of the time when Brandon Bourne had been one of many young men who had embarked on their lives with the intention of stepping over the boundaries of patrician sequestration and of making places for themselves in the fluid, fascinating world of the talented and the famous. They could not have entered this world without making some contribution to it; since it excluded the dead weights of nonentity and dullness, these young men had offered their only possible contribution, names or money, usually both. Some had also brains and charm, but these were outshone by the native gifts of the men and women who wrote the books and plays, acted and sang and danced in the theatres and cinemas, composed and performed the music, painted the pictures, wrote and edited the journals and newspapers, and filled in the details of the realm of art and entertainment and opinion and laughter.

It had been pleasant and it had added a type of roundness and balance, known to the great metropolitan cultures of older worlds, for this bridge between talent and privilege to be formed; naturally a number of marriages had resulted, like that of Jessie Kernan and Brandon Bourne. Jessie herself had never accomplished anything to make her a figure in the creative world, but she was an initiate, she had grown up in the orbit of Rosa Landau whose house had been a hub of its activities; and Brandon Bourne, without the money to give

157

him importance, had nevertheless possessed sufficient charm and, in those days, flexibility and grace of mind. Also he had been one of the handsomest men it could be possible to imagine, indeed he was still spectacular in his good looks. That had made his way easy and had made him confident of his own attractiveness to a degree which Jessie had at last come to find intolerable.

But as, with years, all men and women tend to crystallize in the patterns and associations most intrinsic to them, so Brandon Bourne for a long time had been moving back into his original sphere, or into its residue, since it was rapidly dissolving; and it was among the paraphernalia of that society, the country houses and the horses and dogs and the complacent stricture of mind, that he now felt most at ease. For he had never matured; he was like a fruit which, grafted upon a highly cultivated tree, fails to ripen and to achieve color and juice and substance, but remains small and hard and green and one day drops unnoticed into the orchard grass, while the tree is being harvested of a good normal yield.

So while Jessie expressed mere indifference as to when Brandon might return from Virginia, it was Helen Lee with her complete grasp of life and her much broader prospective, who wished volubly that he would stay there.

She turned from the mirror, kissed Jessie again, and said, "Be at Twenty-One early, darling, seven at the latest."

"So you can have plenty of time to form your opinions," said Jessie laughing. "By the way, who did you get for poor Preston?"

"Hall Peters," said Helen. "Preston will be all right. Poor chap, he doesn't notice where he is, or with whom. The rest of us will have a good time."

"We certainly will," said Jessie. "Really, darling—whatever you think, I'm awfully happy for you. In fact I've been so carried away that I haven't asked you yet how you feel." She looked at Helen closely. "Are you all right?"

"Perfectly wonderful," replied Helen. "After all, I wouldn't have done this if the doctor hadn't said I would breeze through it. Now don't fuss. It's not till next May!"

She waved her hand and left the room. Jessie lay looking after her and thinking, as if she had not done so innumerable times before, what beautiful and embracing warmth and tenderness glowed in Helen Lee, how it illumined Jessie's own life, as well as the very rare relationships that Helen had wrought with her husband and her sons. Jessie did not envy Helen Lee her family and its intense life, she had few tastes that would have fitted her for anything like it. But, she thought, if one were going to have children and all that went with them, Helen had created something far beyond a work of art. Then Jessie's memory reminded her sharply that Helen could never have done it if she had not had a man like Sam. And, though it was quite against her will, that some prodded memory rose from the deep, sealed shaft where Jessie had learned to jail it; and roused by the bitter clang of that little lead plumb it rolled back the curtain which the years had gathered over a small quiet mound of ruins.

XIII

She had been lying quite still in the few moments since Helen Lee had left the room, her hands clasped beneath her head, eyes closed, inviting deliberate physical inertia as a counterpoise to the deep spiritual disquiet which her thoughts had stirred. Now she opened her eyes and looked at the clock with a sense of discouragement; she should probably be up and dressing. But to her surprise it was earlier than she had thought, not yet eleven. She was relieved in a remote way; she had been overcome by a heaviness of mood which made the contemplation of any activity momentarily unbearable. She closed her eyes again, sighing softly; and the happenings of that year long ago, ten years ago, the very worst year of her life, surged forward in a fresh effort to claim her memory.

It had seemed to her ever since, she thought now, that if she allowed herself to recall any single event of that calamitous year, all the other equally dreadful events fell readily into step and marched past her, each bearing the draggled banner of a separate grief and all forming together a haunted, grotesque parade. She had come in this way to believe that the fundamental forces of life have irresistible attraction for one another, like certain physical elements; and that to set one of them in motion or to be moved by it is also to rouse its affinities which grip, or shape, or drive, or ultimately make or break the capacity of the heart to live and to be part of the life of others.

Like the parade of fate which it actually was, that year had opened with the small holiday ceremonies traditional in Brandon's family, following Christmas which for Jessie had always been her mother's special day. But only later, when she had lived the year through, would Jessie have the retrospective vantage to see it within the great tragic frame of her mother's death. It was that last Christmas of Rosa Landau's life, when she had given the beautiful watch to Horace Howland and some of her own most splendid jewels to Jessie, explaining that she had not lately felt equal to any occasion where she would wear them. "I feel so tired," she sighed, with lightness and a gentle mingling of surprise and resignation which Jessie knew her mother did not wish her to remark. But Rosa was already very ill, and it was more terrible for her to hint in this way that she realized it, than it would have been to hear the most dramatic announcement of illness that anybody else could have made.

Rosa was not expecting a great crowd of people that Christmas day, only her closest friends who all understood how very little resistance she had. And Jessie had promised that she and Brandon would come to Sixty-sixth Street by five o'clock in the afternoon at the latest, to take from Rosa all the effort of the party; Rosa would stay on her couch in the drawing-room and a few friends at a time would visit with her there, while Jessie and Brandon kept things going in the other rooms and acted as host and hostess at dinner in case Rosa did not feel well enough to go down. But when Jessie had told Brandon the plan, some days before, he scowled and said, "I can't do that."

"But," said Jessie, astonished to the point of using a word that she had long since dropped in talking to Brandon, "but—why?"

"I can't tie up the whole afternoon and the evening too," he said.

"But it's Christmas," said Jessie. "And we've always been at Mother's anyway—only this year she really needs us. Surely you haven't made some engagement of your own—on *Christmas?*"

"Why not?" he asked. "Do I have to keep nursery Christmas all my life?" His voice had the snap to it that she hated and, hating it, feared.

"Oh, Brandon." Jessie had long thought that he could hardly find a new way to hurt her, but this, striking at her through her concern for her mother, was altogether unbelievable. She looked at him blankly and said, "Brandon, *please*, what is the matter with you? Sometimes I—" she closed her lips and decided to go away out of the room without waiting for his answer. She did not really want an answer anyway; she had so carefully built up a wall of indifference to his doings, out of the raw instinct for self-preservation, that she knew this to be the poorest of times to start tearing it down.

She did leave the room, and on her way upstairs the busy little masons whom she had thought safely and silently employed inside her brain, all began to talk at once and to remind her exactly how many times in the past six months she had been alone with Brandon at home. Not more than four that she could recall. The rest of the time that they were together was either when she had invited friends of his whom he wanted to see, or had accepted invitations from those to whose houses he was willing to go. But more often than not, when she had made some engagement for both of them he simply did not show up.

"Where is Brandon?" people asked, when she found herself forced to appear without him. They asked, she knew, neither because they really cared nor were really curious, but from habit; it was habit to expect a man and his wife to appear together unless they had made it extremely plain that they led frankly separate lives. But against this Jessie had battled with all the strength of her pride and all the stubborn force which insisted upon animating her blind optimism that some day, by some miracle, everything would be different and Brandon would have come to the end of all his convolutions and would be ready really to share a married life with her.

She knew too that a woman would have had to be the world's supreme fool not to sense what people felt when she telephoned them at the last moment before dinner to tell them that Brandon could not come. None of her excuses about his having to work or being called to Glens Falls or Canada on business had ever fooled anybody. Even if they had been fooled, it would not have mitigated the momentary irritation which people felt at having their plans upset, and which left Jessie wretched with fear of being *de trop* by herself. If she was urged to come anyway without Brandon she suffered from the knowledge that some kindly friend pitied her; and if she was allowed to withdraw because the party could not use an extra woman, she had at times felt as if she could murder Brandon with her own hands, for the depth of humiliation into which he flung her.

161

She had given up trying to plead with him, or to explain how she felt when she said to him, "They won't want me without you." All he ever answered was, "Oh, sure they will," because it was the easiest thing to say without thinking. And he did not want to think, and to be taught by his thoughts the agony of doubt, of shyness, of fear, to which he condemned her. The fear of being ridiculous, or pathetic, or a problem to somebody; above all, the fear of feeling unwanted, of being left out. The single clearest mark left upon her by these years was fear, all the other fears, but mostly the fear of Brandon's temper and the physical and emotional disorder into which it plunged her.

And yet—and this she knew to be the deepest humiliation of all—she stayed with him. She not only stayed, but up to now she had stayed on a basis which laid her open to these repeated mortifications, because at brief times in the past she had had snatches of deceptive happiness with him, and she refused to believe that she could never recapture such moods and moments again. She knew that one day she would indeed have to shape some sort of existence for herself that was not socially and humanly dependent upon him, but she was not thinking of that when she went upstairs to telephone her mother that she could not be sure of Brandon for all of the afternoon and evening of Christmas day.

"Never mind, darling," Rosa had said. "Horace will be here and it won't matter about Brandon at all."

Except that Horace would far prefer staying in the drawing-room with Rosa to taking Brandon's place as host elsewhere.

Actually it was past ten o'clock on Christmas night when Brandon strode into his mother-in-law's dining-room, in one of his angriest moods. It was an old habit of his, formed early in his boyhood, to appear before those who had good reason to be annoyed with him, in such an evil temper himself that he froze or flayed or silenced whoever might be near him. Jessie was so bitter that she did not look at him, but Rosa reached up from her place at the head of the table, drew down his scowling face so that he had to kiss her cheek, and said, "Better late than never." She motioned to him to draw up a chair between her and Addison Barnard on her left, for Jessie had told Sarah before dinner to leave Brandon's place off. As he sat down the conversation died; before he appeared a dozen old friends had been warmly and gaily enjoying the loveliest of sentimental occasions together. Now the room turned cold and each person in it could be seen rallying to save something of Rosa's evening. They began to talk again, but the spark was dead.

Brandon was served with the courses which the guests had already finished, but he only snapped a few bits of food from the end of his fork and kept a lighted cigarette in the ashtray close to Rosa, where the smoke drifted straight at her. All her friends knew that tobacco smoke distressed her, and Jessie clenched her fists in her lap, stiff with rage, when she saw her mother's face become very pale, and saw her breathing nervously with her lips tightly closed. Ordinarily Rosa Landau would have thought nothing of asking Brandon to put out his cigarette. The fact that she did not told Jessie of an anger even deeper than her own; her mother would sit there until she fainted before she would say a word to Brandon Bourne that would presume him to be human. Meanwhile Rosa was trying to smile at him with the strange, cynical wit which always left him baffled, and even to talk to him in bursts of teasing, but she was too ill to let herself go.

Jessie knew that Horace Howland from his place must be watching Rosa with the same anxiety as she. So she caught Howland's eye and with a flicker of her eyebrow telegraphed him to tell Addison Barnard opposite him to put out Brandon's cigarette. Barnard did so.

Brandon turned round and glared at Mr. Barnard, his blue eyes flashing.

"Why did you do that!" he snapped. His voice rang, metallic.

Barnard for the briefest moment met the eye of his wife and then looked calmly at Brandon as if he were not there. Immediately the talk rose, a quickening of gay and well-bred voices each determined to help as smoothly as possible. Jessie was so upset that she could not hear a word that was said to her. She fixed her eyes and her mouth in a glazed smile on the face of Philippe Maurel who was visiting from Paris and who had painted fifteen years ago the superb portrait of Rosa at her most beautiful, which hung in the drawing-room upstairs. He had known Jessie since her childhood, he was a really old friend, and when he saw that she had no idea what his last remark had been, he leaned a little closer to her and said, *Même chez nous,* nobody could expect you to endure that *bête,* that savage. Even we concede that marriage has its limits."

Jessie was close to tears and this was no time for a wise old friend to display sympathy. She drank some champagne, sighed, and said, "You are very kind, Philippe. I am really distressed for Mother, that is why I am upset."

"You are upset because you are married to an impossible, foul-mannered ordure and are too serious to have thought of leaving him."

Jessie made a small pleading *moue* to beg Maurel to drop the subject now.

They rose, for the plum-pudding and the fruits and nuts and bonbons had all been served, and Rosa was very pale and tired. She stood at the foot of the stairs with Jessie, letting all the women go up ahead of her. Then she began, holding the stairrail with both hands, with Jessie's arm about her waist, very slowly to climb the stairs. She had never been so visibly ill and feeble as this and Jessie was chilled with grief and despair. Rosa felt her daughter's arm trembling while it supported her; she turned her head and whispered, "Darling, you feel much worse than I do. Buck up." She managed a radiant smile and one of her most mischievous glances, that lovely warm brown light from her wonderful eyes.

"I am not going home with him tonight," said Jessie. "I shall stay here with you."

"Good." They were near the top of the stairs now and Rosa was too exhausted to say another word. Jessie walked into the drawing-room with her and settled her on her couch again. Marguerite Bernard came over and sat beside her for a moment and said, "We are all leaving in a few minutes, Rosa dear. You must be longing to get to bed."

"Not while I can enjoy being with you."

Daisy Barnard smiled and as the other women grouped themselves around Rosa she turned to Jessie and asked if she were staying here with her mother tonight. "She doesn't look well at all," said Mrs. Barnard anxiously.

There was a heavy, unpleasant thud downstairs and Jessie knew what it was. When the men came into the room a few minutes later Brandon was not with them. Horace Howland exchanged a glance with Jessie; as if she had been down there in the front hall beside Howland, she could see Brandon stalking out of the dining-room, taking his hat and overcoat from the hall closet, and slamming the door behind him as he left the house without a word to anybody.

And, she thought late that night, after her mother was asleep and she lay wretched and restless in her old bedroom, if I should ever ask him why he behaved so outrageously tonight he would pretend not to know what I was talking about—unless he lost his temper with me for mentioning the matter at all.

Jessie opened her eyes with a slight start, to find Josephine standing by her bed saying, "Miss Crowe is on the telephone, Mrs. Bourne."

She picked it up to hear the great bass voice booming, "Hello, you lazy slut. Still in bed, I take it?"

"Why not?"

"You've got me there. Want to lunch Thursday?"

"Love to." But even as she said that, there flashed through Jessie's mind a thought of Mark Dwyer, and she knew that she would have put off almost anybody else, to keep the day clear if he should want to be with her. Yet Althea Crowe was different and special. "Have you anything much on your mind?" Jessie asked her.

"Just a rag of vestigial friendship."

"That's flattering. What time?"

"The usual. Daniele's all right?"

"Fine."

Daniele's was a rough and wonderful Italian restaurant in a rackety midtown cross-street not far from Althea Crowe's office. For years Jessie had been eating amazing meals there at Althea's own corner table; and now she realized again, sharply, how often that strong, brusque companionship had been her soundest recourse from just such desolation as that recalled by her present train of thought. It was curious that Althea Crowe had called just now, for she had her place in the pattern of intricate memory which each small happening of this morning seemed determined to force into review.

Jessie stirred once more with concern that she really should get up now, and yet it was odd that the clock had turned contrary, there was still plenty of time until eleven-thirty which was the latest that she could rise and be about her dressing in time to meet Mark Dwyer as she had promised. Get up now, she said to herself silently, get up at once. But instead she only closed her eyes again and surrendered to the distressing sensation of unfinished business which her wilful memory appeared insistent upon completing. She went back to that dreadful Christmas day, and to that night when she had felt as if she could never be in the same house with Brandon Bourne again. She had stayed on with her mother in Sixty-sixth Street, drawing consolation from Rosa Landau's extraordinary faculty for eloquent silence. Any other woman, surely any other mother, would have had something to say about Brandon, or about Jessie's troubles or her marriage or her future or, at worst, would have probed and questioned her intolerably. Rosa Landau did none of that because it was all unnecessary; she knew everything, not only about Jessie's life but about life. She also knew that in the past Brandon Bourne had had the power to keep Jessie in love with him, or to renew Jessie's capacity to be in love with him, and she doubted that he had lost the last of that power even yet. If it survived at all, its evidence now when Jessie was growing resigned and mature, would be the evolution of the tortured relationship into some of the outer forms, all compromises of course, of permanent marriage.

Toward the end of Christmas week, Brandon telephoned and spoke to Jessie as if nothing had ever happened to interrupt the ordinary course of their existence. His voice was its quietest, it had none of the hard staccato twang which roused the sick, throbbing fear in her. A different sort of woman might have refused to speak to him, but Jessie saw no use in that. Either she would continue with the effort or she would give it up, and since she still intended to continue there was no use in being sullen. Indeed she was incapable of it.

Brandon spoke of luncheon on New Year's Day with his family as if he were the last man on earth who would violate a holiday tradition or anybody's sentimental feelings. Even while she was assuring him that she would be at home that morning, and would go to lunch with him, Jessie thought what it would be like if she should say, "I detest your relatives and after your treatment of my mother I shall certainly do nothing to be polite to yours."

But she only asked, quietly, "I suppose you are full of plans for Monday night?" That would be New Year's Eve.

"Well," said Brandon. His voice had the artificial lazy calm which he assumed whenever he wanted to appear particularly conciliatory in the face of something which he knew Jessie would loathe. "Well," he said, "nothing very special. I thought you would probably want to be with your mother . . ."

"Naturally," said Jessie.

"How is she, by the way?" asked Brandon. Jessie stiffened with rage.

"She is better," she said. "But not well at all."

"That's too bad," he said. He was still speaking in that voice which was supposed to keep Jessie off her guard. "Well, then, I'll see you Tuesday."

166

Jessie went upstairs and wept, so wretched that she could not distinguish whether from distress about her mother or despair about Brandon.

Then they were beginning luncheon on New Year's Day. Mrs. Bourne sat at the head of the table, Evander Fielding at the foot. Millicent, and Iris, an ugly little girl of eight, and Jessie and Brandon and Cousin Sophie Daingerfield and the Blaine Illingworths and Aunt Louisa Brandon were all in their usual places, where they had sat at these ceremonial occasions ever since Jessie had known the Bourne family, and long before. Millicent looked nervous and uncomfortable. The household was put to the greatest possible strain by the mere formality of placing Mama at the head of the table on these holidays. The rest of the time she conceded the position of hostess and head of the house to her daughter since it mitigated to some degree the ignominy which they both felt because neither Mrs. Bourne nor Evander Fielding could have afforded to maintain this ménage alone. By combining households they were able to continue in the stuffy style to which they had all been accustomed for generations.

They lived now in a large, dark, depressing apartment, with most of the windows facing a drab vista of dun-colored brick court and the bleak back yards of neighboring brownstone houses like the one from which Mrs. Bourne had had to migrate when she grew too enormously fat and clumsy to climb the stairs any longer. The apartment house had a good address in East Eighty-fourth Street, and was conveniently near to Iris's fashionable school, but the dark inside rooms told the story of tight-lipped and disgruntled economizing.

Jessie had once said to Brandon upon leaving the place, "Do you know, your mother could have the most heavenly apartment on the West Side for much less rent than she pays for that horrible hole. With sunshine and a view of the Park——"

"The *West Side?*" Brandon had repeated, as if Jessie had spoken of Canarsie. His nose looked pinched. "Nobody but you would have such an idea."

"You'd be surprised what beautiful apartments there are on Central Park West, just the same," said Jessie.

"I'm not at all surprised at your taste for them," said Brandon sourly.

Jessie had burst into a peal of laughter which appeared to irritate him. "I don't see what's so funny in that," he said.

"Oh," she said. "I wasn't thinking of anything you said. I

167

was remembering the house on West Eighty-fourth Street where I was born. My father built a whole row of them, perfect horrors, but the people who lived in them——" she broke off and closed her lips tightly. She had thought better of what she was about to say.

But Brandon, waiting for the traffic light to change, looked at her and said, "Frights, weren't they?"

"Good God, no," said Jessie. She decided to say what was on her mind, after all. "On the contrary. I was just thinking how much more fun they all got out of life than your family there in that ghastly apartment across town on the same street."

Brandon's family always put such thoughts into her mind, and she pursued more of them that New Year's Day, sitting between Evander Fielding and Cousin Blaine Illingworth and spooning at the white library paste with ominous grey blobs in it which went in this house by the name of Oyster Soup.

"Oyster Soup," Mrs. Bourne had bumbled as they sat down. She spoke in a queer hooting voice which, though low-pitched as every lady's should be, had a strange resonance that rang authoritatively through all other sounds. She also ran her words together as if she could not be troubled to make herself intelligible by vocal punctuation, like anybody else. She never conversed anyway, but only remarked and pronounced, all her phrases mortared in rigid complacency. "Oyster Soup. We always have oyster soup for holidays."

"Yes indeed," echoed Cousin Sophie Daingerfield. "I have dear Grandmama's receipt for it written in her household account book."

"It is just like my Mama's," said Aunt Louisa Brandon, whose mother had been a sister of Cousin Sophie's dear Grandmama, "except for a pinch of sage. We always used to have Nora put a pinch of sage in it."

"Impossible," said Mrs. Bourne. "Nobody ever heard of sage in oyster soup."

Nobody ever heard of any seasoning in your kitchen, thought Jessie. Every word of the talk about the soup had been precisely repeated at every holiday dinner since Jessie had known the Bournes.

"Mother, may I be excused?" shrilled Iris suddenly.

Millicent Fielding turned to stare at her daughter, angry and shocked.

"Certainly not," she said. "Sit up straight and——"

"You'll be sorry," said Iris, wriggling.

168

Millicent turned scarlet and rose from her chair. She escorted Iris from the room, leaning down over her pale, skinny child and sibilantly saying that which Jessie could have quoted: "Why didn't you attend to that before Mademoiselle went out? You naughty girl."

When they returned, the plates had been changed and the large, sad, over-roasted turkey had been placed before Evander Fielding to be carved. He was a messy carver and thoroughly bored by the entire occasion, besides which he had the most vicious visible hangover that Jessie had ever seen. Brandon was not in much better shape.

Jessie was always conscious of being careful not to watch Mrs. Bourne eat, because the sight was one of those grotesqueries which become insidiously fascinating. Mrs. Bourne was so fat that her arms were like great swollen elongated balloons, so heavy that she could scarcely move them; and from the slight indentations that were her wrists depended two tiny, puffy hands with short, twiddling fingers crusted with old-fashioned rings. These hands manipulated a knife and fork, and carried food to the small, hard, greedy mouth with a flipping kind of busy agility that contrasted utterly with all the rest of the woman's torpid immobility. Mrs. Bourne, in fact, was habituated to two and only two physical actions, eating and talking. But, thought Jessie, she never ate anything worth eating and she never said anything worth saying.

"Until we gave up the house," she said with a resentful glance at the pantry door, "I always had them stay on duty until I went to bed. Absolutely outrageous."

"—traitor to his class," said Cousin Blaine Illingworth. "Can't understand it, unless it's her influence. He was perfectly normal when we were at Groton."

One of the two stony, rawboned maids was pouring wine. Jessie placed her finger over her glass to refuse it.

"Oh, come, come," said Cousin Blaine Illingworth in his special, convivial voice. "You don't mean that. Evander——"

But Jessie smiled and said quietly, "No thank you."

"You must have some, Jess," said Van Fielding. "I opened it especially for you and Bran. Forster Traminer . . . you'll love it."

Jessie tried to turn their attention, but Evander Fielding was in that clouded, stale post-alcoholic state where only the thought of the moment has any urgency, and where repetition becomes important of itself. He insisted again that she drink the wine. Everybody was noticing the matter now and Jessie had decided to let the maid pour the wine and to leave it untouched, when Fielding said, suddenly, "Why? Bran, what's the matter with her?"

Jessie's lips closed tightly. She had become frightened, the matter had got out of hand and she was afraid of what Brandon might say. To her vast relief he only murmured, "Skip it, Van. Jess doesn't want any, that's all."

"Well, why not?" asked Fielding truculently. He was still more drunk than sober and his mood was growing ugly. "Damned rude of her when I was trying to . . ."

"Let it ride, Van," said Brandon. Jessie gave him a look of such appreciation that his cold blue eyes softened in the rarest of kindly expressions, and Jessie felt like a neglected child that has won unusual praise. The others at the table were now murmuring along in their customary way, putting the most serious emphasis on the utmost trivialities, but Van Fielding was unable to let go the obsession upon which his wavering attention had fixed itself.

"Damned rude of her," he repeated. "Look here," he insisted at Brandon, "she makes enough fuss about wine in your house, why does she turn up her nose at mine?"

Jessie's heart began to beat harder, for she saw Brandon's eyes going flat and cold and she knew that he had been pushed to the danger line. And experience had taught her that if Brandon were going to seek an object for his temper, her presence almost infallibly provided what he sought. So it was with emotion much keener than ordinary relief that she watched Brandon stare at his brother-in-law and say with the snap in his voice which was, for once, not directed at her, "Jessie doesn't drink German wine, Van. Now drop it, will you?"

"No!" retorted Fielding. He turned his bloodshot eyes on Jessie and said, "What's the idea? Looks darn fishy to me, drunk lots of Rhine wine in your house, what do you mean anyhow? Why won't you drink my wine?" His voice had the meaningless, nagging rasp of a spoiled child's.

Jessie gave Brandon another eloquent look. On the rare occasions when there was a real current of sympathy running between them, she could communicate a great deal to Brandon without speaking at all. He saw now that she wanted to know whether she must answer; or would he. He flung his napkin on the table with one of the abrupt gestures that she knew, to her sorrow, so well, and turned roughly towards Van Fielding.

"If you had any tact," he said, while the women about the table drew themselves up and clipped their lips together in stiff discomfiture, "you'd have shut up when I told you to. Jessie happens to have made herself a promise not to drink any German wine until Hitler and the Nazis are cleaned out of Germany and I don't blame her one God-damn bit!"

"Brandon!" boomed Mrs. Bourne. Her voice was thick with rage.

"Balderdash!" said Blaine Illingworth.

"—might have expected that!"

"After all, you would think——"

Jessie sat with tears scalding her eyeballs, tense lest they spill over and made a sight of her. She had an impulse to bend her head and look down at her plate, but instead she drew herself up and gave Brandon a grave, proud look of intense appreciation. His family were all manifesting various degrees of distaste, disapproval, and icy snobbery. Brandon had flung down in the middle of their holiday table the horrible, inexplicable mortification around which they had all had to pick their way in pursuing the main course of their otherwise serene complacency about themselves. It had never become less of a disgrace and an irritant to them that Brandon had made this incomprehensible mésalliance; but to have him uphold it now in this shocking way was nearly intolerable.

But when Jessie tried to thank Brandon in the car while they were driving home, he only patted her knee and said, "What else would a fella do? And—look here, Jess." He was manœuvering to pass a crosstown bus and he kept his eyes on the street ahead of him. "I'm sorry I was such a bastard on Christmas."

Ah, God, she thought, as she turned over to try to sleep late that night. Ah, God, if I only knew how to keep the best side of him the real one, the one whom I want when I put out my hand, who walks in when he opens a door, who speaks when he says a kind or loyal or honest thing. Why can I not have that instead of never knowing, never being sure? Will he be there, or the devil incarnate? Brandon whom I want or the brute whom I hate? Please, her mind echoed in the caverns of approaching sleep . . . please . . .

XIV

Josephine appeared again; Doctor Sheldon was calling on the telephone. Jessie smiled, delighted to hear from him.

"Hello, Reath dear!" she said. "How nice."

"How are you?" asked the low, gentle voice. This was not her physician's question, but her old friend's.

"Good—I hope!" she laughed. "What's new?"

"I wondered if you would like to go to the Philharmonic with me next Thursday?"

"Oh, of course, the first concert. I'd love to." Nobody she knew loved music so much as Reath Sheldon, and therefore brought so much to it.

"Fine," he said. "I'll stop for you early—about seven. We'll dine somewhere."

"Why don't you let me meet you? You always work so late, why dash way up here to collect me?"

"Well—if you say so. Voisin's, then? At seven-thirty?"

"Good. Oh, and Reath—" Jessie thought now on impulse, wondering why it had not occurred to her before. "Would you like to dine here tomorrow—just quietly? I have a few people coming, you know them all. And the Blocks. Hulda will play for you, I'm sure."

"Why—that might be fine." Jessie understood perfectly the tentativeness in his voice. He had found almost unbearable the company of strangers or casual acquaintances since the death of his wife last year, and yet he was pathetically lonely. Jessie thought how years ago it had been he in a dreadful passage of her life who had borne the weight of concern for her; now she was aware how much the situation was reversed.

"I take it Brandon will be out," Sheldon was saying.

"He's away," said Jessie.

"For long?"

"I haven't the least idea," she said, allowing a note to color her voice which to him would be the equivalent of a shrug. He laughed. How good it is, she thought, to have this comfortable ease as the consequence of all that troubled past, without it one would never have any peace at all.

"Tomorrow, then," said the doctor.

"Good, I'll be so glad to see you, Reath. Eight o'clock."

"Black tie?"

"Yes—or not, if you're tied up late at the hospital."

She really must get up now, she saw, as she put the telephone down, and crossing the room to her dressing-room and bath she paused to let her eye caress a small French armchair upholstered with needlepoint so fine that her friends were almost incredulous when they were told that it had been worked by Jessie's mother. The petit-point centres of the seat and back must surely, they said, have been done in Paris or Vienna, by some poorly-paid artist drudge, working under a glass. But Jessie remembered now, as she had so many times before, the poignant sight of her mother in the last year of her life, hurrying to finish this beautiful thing, her thick brown fingers plying the needle with astonishing delicacy. Jessie had always loved to watch the charmingly inconsistent sight, even when it wrung her heart intolerably. She put her hand for a moment on the silky surface of the embroidery, and found herself thinking how strange it was that Reath Sheldon had happened to telephone just at that moment on this particular morning, when other flickerings of chance had put in motion that long, ghostly pageant of tragic memories. She would have said that it had done with her for the moment; yet the accident of two or three brief encounters had forced the whole sequence into focus, all dovetailed together in a diabolical master design.

She sighed, turning away from the chair and thinking vividly of her mother on a January day in 1935, just after that dreadful poisoned Christmas. Slowly Jessie dropped her bedjacket and nightdress on a stool, about to step into her bath which had the curious, crisp sparkle which one did not find in water elsewhere; how silly I am, she laughed, to feel pleased with the water in this city as if I could take some kind of credit for it! But it was true, and though she had no idea why, the water in New York really was different; it tasted brisk and fresh, it left one's skin soft, it had none of the unpleasant features of water in other great cities, such as the revolting malodor of the water in Philadelphia, or the exasperating alkalinity of water in European cities, which turned one's skin to sandpaper if one did nothing to prevent it. Why had her mind wandered from ten-year-old memories, needlepoint, her mother, Reath Sheldon, to a fantastic irrelevancy like the water in Europe? Ah yes, she thought, of course; Paris and all that had happened that year. She shook her

173

head sharply, as if to dismiss the persistent fingers of memory which were pushing and sliding all those scattered pieces of a pattern into place. And stepping from her bath, briskly drying her skin with a big Turkish towel, she glanced through the dressing-room window where the sky had suddenly and sharply lightened, and she could look down if she craned her neck, at the river beginning to come out of its earlier sulk, and to reveal itself as very busy indeed of a Wednesday morning. Two small boats shrieked fussily at one another as they passed.

Sitting down at her dressing-table, her mind swung back again to her mother in Paris that year. Reath Sheldon and all the consultants whom he had brought in had come to the end of their resources in Rosa Landau's case; there remained, they said, only the greatest research scientist of them all, now working at the Pasteur Institute in Paris, a refugee from Hitler and Berlin. Rosa Landau, threading a fresh needle, had looked at Jessie and said, "So this gave me a little idea, darling." She had that look of grave tenderness in her face which carried the whole substance of her silent understanding of Jessie's miseries, to which she never referred; and now she only said, "I thought you might like to go to Paris with me."

Jessie jumped up, as quick as her mother to play this part, and said eagerly as if no other purpose than pleasure were involved, "Wonderful!" Her mother's life was not hanging in the balance; she herself was not groping her way through the most desolate wasteland of the heart. She thought briefly of Brandon, who since his Christmas outburst had been treating her with more kindness than for a long time past. It might be a mistake to go away now, but no other consideration was even to be weighed if she could go to Paris with her mother.

"When do we sail?" she asked. "I'm thrilled to my shoes. We haven't been in Europe together for ages."

"I'm afraid this won't be much fun for you," said Rosa doubtfully.

"Fun? Just to sit in a room in Paris with you and laugh will be heaven. Do you remember the pink pig? And Monsieur Dubouchet? And the hats we had one year, with those rolls of ribbon that you called——?"

They began to laugh, with the wonderful capacity for mirth in spite of tragedy that was perhaps Rosa Landau's single most priceless gift to her daughter. They laughed while they telephoned Sheldon and said that they would go to see Otto Wasservogel, and while they telephoned the travel agency to book their cabins, and while Rosa told her maid when to start packing, and even when Reath Sheldon called back to say that he was sending one of his best nurses with them.

But when Jessie left the house to go home at the end of the day, the laughter dropped from her face like a mask unpinned. She knew that the entire undertaking was hopeless and futile. But to give her mother the illusion of relief, the breath of hope, was more worthwhile than anything else in the whole world. That was what she expected Brandon to say, when she told him about it before dinner. He had been so uncharacteristically gentle recently, not tender, not affectionate—he had never shown the least capacity for that—but kindly to a remarkable degree. He must have been moved by the keenest remorse for his behavior on Christmas night. He listened while Jessie told him about the plan to go to Paris, and then he looked at her with an expression which astonished her by reflecting regret and disappointment.

"Of course," he said, "if your mother really needs you——"

Jessie put down her cocktail and stared at Brandon with the utmost surprise. It had not occurred to her that he, for his part, could feel the slightest reluctance for her to go to Europe. He had certainly never shown it before, but had welcomed her annual summer departure with an alacrity which dramatized his chafing at marriage.

She said, "I—it never occurred to me——"

"Oh," he said, "if your mother is depending on you why—" But there was no conviction at all in his voice and Jessie was completely bewildered. Her forehead ruffled and she leaned forward and asked, "Brandon, do you mean you wish I would not go?"

He rose from his chair and put his hands in his pockets and began to pace up and down the room. That compelling physical restlessness could presage almost anything, and had long ago become deeply distressing to Jessie; it was the symbol to her that he was never there, placed, put, solid, when one wanted or needed him. He took one or two turns up and down the room, jingling some coins in his pocket, and visibly feeling for a way to put into words something that was on his mind.

"I was going to tell you anyway," he said. "I've been thinking about something and—" he stopped speaking to light a cigarette. Jessie sat back in her chair and her eyes followed him in his pacing, up and down, up and down. She did not know that she had turned quite pale and he, of course, did not notice it; he was entirely preoccupied with his own concern.

"You see," he said, swinging about abruptly and stopping his pacing to stand by the fire, with his elbow on the mantel, "you see, I've been thinking a good deal about—us."

Jessie kept her lips shut tightly; she was aware of drawing very slow, hollow breaths behind them. She had no idea what he was about to say; being Brandon, he could be on the verge of saying anything. He was groping for words and looking at her as if to invite her to help him; there was nothing for her to do except murmur, "Yes . . . go on."

"Well," he said. "I got to thinking a good deal about all this after—" he hesitated and then blurted like a flustered, defiant schoolboy, "after Christmas. I didn't mean to act like that, Jess—honestly I didn't."

"I know," she said. "You've always been a lot nicer inside than the things you did. I told you—I've forgiven you. I don't even want you to wear a hair shirt about it." She felt an unaccustomed courage and added, suddenly, "I just hope you won't act that way any more."

"I hope so too," he said, widening his strange, oversized eyes and bringing into them a glow which she knew to be reflective of sincerity. She knew too that such a statement from him was almost epochal; it was very far indeed for him to go.

"The thing is," he said, fumbling his way, and keeping his eyes on the rug at his feet, "I—well, this may sound crazy, Jess."

"No it won't," she said quietly. "Please don't be afraid to say it."

"Well," he muttered, "it's not so easy to say. But—well—anyway—I told you I felt like hell about that thing at Christmas. And then when Van——"

"Oh, that was nothing," said Jessie. "You know Van."

"Oh, sure. He's only a birdbrain anyway. But he made me —well, all I can say is, when he squared off at you like that do you know—it made me feel some way I almost never feel."

"How?" asked Jessie, in a whisper.

"Married," said Brandon. "That's what I'm trying to tell you."

Except for the knowledge that she must not show any

emotion, Jessie might have melted then into tears and into every other evidence of profound relief and joy. She was not religious, but if she had ever prayed in her own subconscious way, it had been to hear Brandon say what he had just said. She only looked at him and managed as calm a smile as she could, in spite of the tumult of feeling inside her. She did not speak and she saw that that pleased him.

There was a long silence, and Jessie almost thought that Brandon had come to the end of what he wanted to say. But a moment later he spoke again.

"I wish I had felt like that a lot more than I ever have," he said, "and a long time ago."

She put out her hand over the arm of her chair and said, "But it is not too late now, Brandon."

He touched her fingers and then moved farther away and asked, "Isn't it?"

She shook her head.

"I wanted to find out," he said. "Wanted to make sure. Because——"

"Why?"

"Well—if you're willing to give me the benefit of it—then —" he made a rather comical face, a combination of awkwardness and earnestness. "Then, well, I guess we'd better *be* more married than we were before. I guess we'd better—" now Jessie's ears were pulsating as if she had already heard what she knew with amazement he was about to say—"I guess we'd better have a child."

This was astounding. It was incredible. It was directly contrary to everything for which she had thought she must finally settle. She stared at Brandon and spoke without knowing what she was going to say.

"Have you really been thinking about it?" she asked.

He nodded slowly. "I got to wondering what the hell was the matter with me anyway. I began trying to figure out what made me—well, you know. Anyway, I began to think that maybe if we had a child I wouldn't be so—I wouldn't always be in a kind of war with—well, with you. With the idea of being married."

"But," murmured Jessie, "you were always so positive that you didn't want us to have any children. You made me promise finally never to mention it to you again."

"I couldn't let myself go," he said, in a strange, spreading, helpless way. "I didn't want to get trapped. I wanted to feel—free—oh, we've been all over it before. You know it all."

177

She nodded slowly. She knew it all.

"But these last couple of weeks somehow I've seen it differently. Maybe we ought to fish or cut bait. Maybe it makes no sense for us to stay together unless we—well, are tied together. That way."

She looked at him, still too astonished and too full of emotion to trust herself to speak. He moved from the fire to stand directly before her chair, and looking down at her asked, "Will you do it, Jess?"

There was only one answer and she wanted overwhelmingly to give it at once. She wanted Brandon, she had struggled to win in this battle of their marriage, and now she had evidently got her victory.

"Will you do it, Jess?" he asked.

"You know that I will," she said, looking up at him. "You did not need to ask me. But—when?"

"Oh," he exclaimed, with an almost wild note of impatience which frightened her, "oh, right away. The sooner the better."

I wonder why, she thought, sinking back in her chair again. I wonder why. But she did not need to wonder. It was because he did not trust himself. If he could have the result of his new decision dramatically fast he would feel satisfied. If he must wait, he would begin to lose interest and things would drift backwards to what they had always been. She looked up at him, her feelings so torn and confused that she did not dare to speak at all. She wanted to ask him if he would be good to her. She wanted to ask him if she could depend upon him. She wanted with a sudden rough slash of clarity to tell him that she was mortally afraid to have a child because she did not feel safe in taking his part in the new state of things for granted. At the same time she felt, looking at him, the irresistible force of his physical hold over her, which had been weakened from time to time, but which he still possessed and, more distressingly for her, knew that he possessed. She could not find words to ask him any question reflective of all these anxious and troubled feelings, but she did say, "The only thing I am worrying about is Mother. She——"

Brandon's face presented a quick succession of reactions; he was first annoyed, and Jessie had to suppress the instinct to hate him for that. He had completely forgotten the plan that Jessie should take her mother to Paris. He did his best to conceal his thought, and he spoke slowly and seemingly with careful kindness.

"I know," he said. "I know that makes it all pretty hard. But Jess—" he sighed and looked at Jessie with an expression of such pleading and helplessness in his blue eyes that she felt tied hand and foot. My God, she thought, my God, why must he always find ways to torture me? Why must he choose now, when Mother is dying, to force me to make a choice between him and her? She was unconsciously twisting her hands in her lap, she thought that she was sitting perfectly still and maintaining the quiet façade of acquiescence which was the surest way to keep him on an even keel. But she found suddenly that he was down on one knee before her chair, grasping her tormented hands in his and pressing them hard together, and saying, "Oh, Jess, try and do this for me now. I can't tell you why I think it will make such a difference, but I feel it. Honestly, I do." He looked at her with pleading intensity. "Believe me," he said. "And besides——"

"What?" asked Jessie faintly.

"I have a feeling that if you asked your mother about it she would tell you this is the thing you should do. Even for her sake . . . let alone ours." He remained silent for a time and finally he said, "Don't you think that? Isn't that how she would feel?"

Jessie was so distressed, so uncertain, so torn, yet so clear in knowledge far sounder than Brandon's, that she could only nod her head in slow resignation.

I am afraid, she felt rather than thought, far, deep inside herself. I am afraid, afraid . . . and yet she knew that she would have even more to fear if she should refuse Brandon's wish now. This should have been the happiest and most wonderful hour of my life, she reflected, and instead like everything else it is bitter with sorrow and fear. Now, if she should say that she insisted upon going to Paris with her mother, Rosa would not allow it. Rosa would say that Jessie must stay and do what Brandon asked. There was no use in letting the matter move to that extreme. Jessie bowed her head, and Brandon leaned down over her and kissed her.

She had finished now with her face and her hair, had put on her stockings and her shoes and her underclothes; and she went into her bedroom where Josephine held up the purple wool dress while Jessie slipped into it.

"Oh, Josephine," she said, fastening the small silk strips inside the shoulders of her dress, "go down and ask Anna and Sarah for their lists for tomorrow. I don't know where the morning has gone, but I'm going to market and now I'm late. Find out if Binger's ever sent those crackers I ordered last week . . . such a silly thing not to be able to get."

When she was alone, putting on her earrings and then, carefully, the wonderful red hat, her eye fell on a small framed photograph of Brandon which had stood on a table near the window ever since she could remember. The picture had become so absorbed into the room that she realized now she had not distinctly noticed it for years. And then she made a grimace. Do I have to remember all that too? she asked herself. If I hurry out right now, I will break this maddening chain of unwanted thoughts. Instead and quite involuntarily she walked quickly across the floor and flung open the door between her own room and Brandon's. She stood in the doorway staring at the handsome, comfortable room, unnaturally neat because of Brandon's absence, a room designed to please him and full of possessions reflective of his tastes; and as she looked at them, pictures of his crew and his hockey team, of polo, of some of his relatives, at mementos of ski trips and tennis tournaments and the Navy, she thought with a kind of surprise which denied her ever having thought it before, how total a stranger was the occupant of this room. Perversely and resentfully, she stood there in the doorway and saw herself, those ten years ago, standing farther inside that room, near his desk where he was sitting; she heard his voice and remembered his face, and the whole detestable wreckage came clattering down about her; and she gave a bitter, cynical shrug and folded her arms and stood there, staring, waiting for Josephine to come back with the marketing list.

By February, ten years ago, her mother had been gone some weeks, accompanied by Reath Sheldon's nurse and her maid, and with Horace Howland's promise to join her in Paris before the end of March. Jessie was already pregnant. And a new kind of balance had been struck, between her extreme physical wretchedness and the amazing change in Brandon. She was horribly ill, tortured by constant nausea and faintness, but this different Brandon made it bearable. He came home straight from the office at the end of the day, bringing her flowers, content to have dinner alone with her or with one or two friends; kindly, genial, and manifestly delighted with himself. It was all perfectly extraordinary; and if only she could soon hope to trust herself not to flee from the room or reach in panic for the aromatic spirits, life would be on the way to what she had always longed to make it.

She remembered their disappointment at finding after some six weeks that her stubborn illness did not lessen; she began to worry that Brandon would grow restless and bored; and through the doctor to whom Reath Sheldon had turned her over, there evolved a plan for Brandon to take her to Pinehurst, where the climate was ideal in March. Brandon would get a good golf game every day while Jessie rested. He was enthusiastic, he arranged a week's absence from his office, and they planned to go down on a Friday night train. Not in years had they spent a ten-day holiday together, and Jessie felt as if her cup of fantastic happiness were running over. The one ominous cloud was her intense and deepening anxiety about her mother. Horace Howland had cabled upon reaching Paris the truth which he had promised Jessie before sailing; Rosa did not appear to be better and so far there was nothing hopeful to report from Otto Wasservogel's observations.

Jessie was sitting up in bed, holding that cable in her hand, when Brandon telephoned her from his office about eleven o'clock on Thursday morning, the day before they were to leave.

"How sweet of you to call," she said, making her voice as bright as she could contrive between her grief about her mother and her suspense about her own heaving stomach.

"Well," said Brandon, his voice lazy and low. "I wanted to know how you are."

"Pretty good," she said, trying to laugh. "Three strikes this morning but I'm not out. I refuse to play by the rules."

"That's good," he said. And then, "Say, Jess——"

"Yes?"

"Well—something's come up here. I kind of wondered—" already she knew that he had some disappointment for her. Nothing else would account for the exaggerated, self-conscious drawl in his voice.

"Oh, Brandon!" she exclaimed. "Don't tell me we can't go to Pinehurst!"

"Uh—no," he said slowly. "It's not that. I just thought maybe you wouldn't mind if I shifted things around a little."

"But how?" she asked. "Can't you take next week off after all?"

"Oh, sure," he said, with easy warmth which did not reassure her at all. She knew by now that he was feeling for a way to tell her something unpleasant. "I'll tell you. How would it be if you went down on the train tomorrow night and I joined you there Monday?"

"But—but—" whatever she did, Jessie did not want to sound childish and complaining now. She was tense with distress and bewilderment and the sense of an old, familiar misery coming back to roost. She was silent. Brandon had to say something.

"I kind of forgot that I made this date quite a while ago," he said.

"A *date?*" gasped Jessie. Was her rosy cloud evaporating so soon? My God, she thought, reaching for the aromatic spirits and trying to breathe calmly, oh my God, what shall I do?

"You could," she said, trying to sound reasonable and worldly and casual, "put it off, couldn't you? After all——"

"Well," said Brandon uneasily. "You see I told this—" Jessie's tongue was a sour, rigid ball, and the cold sweat was starting from her skin—"these people that I'd go up to Franconia skiing with them this week end, it's the last good snow of the season and they'd set it all up and——"

"What people?" asked Jessie. Her voice was a blur now.

"Oh—you don't know them. Tex Wilder and his wife and——"

"And—?" said Jessie, forcing out the word. She was beginning now not to be able to distinguish whether she was more ill or more angry.

"And her sister," said Brandon, very casual. "Just a kid, I don't think she's out of school yet."

Forced into the open, thought Jessie. *How long has this been going on.* Oh, *Christ,* her inner self shrieked, stop it, stop it, stop him! She said aloud to Brandon, "I'd hate that. I don't want to be a wet blanket but it seems to me there's a real reason for our trip to Pinehurst and none at all for you to—to——"

"Well I see it differently," he said. His tone was becoming sharp; Jessie knew what was about to happen as clearly as if it had taken place yesterday which, indeed, in innumerable variations, it had. But she felt helpless, utterly powerless to stop the thing, to hold it back, to change its course. Ruin had been put into motion and was gathering momentum irresistibly. Whatever Jessie said now would be something that she would pray tonight never to have said, but she could not stop herself from saying it. Her brain in some way seemed to have been betrayed by the condition of her body, and she was so deathly ill that she felt crazily determined to assert herself before a shattering bout of nausea overcame her.

"I think you're unkind!" she cried. "You know perfectly well I am too ill to go off on a sleeper alone overnight and——"

"Take a nurse with you," said Brandon abruptly.

"Thank you. While you go away on a——a——oh, I can't believe it!" she wailed. "I thought you'd changed. I thought you'd changed. But you are just the same——"

"Only I, of course," snapped Brandon. "Only I was supposed to do all the changing. Of course there's never been anything the matter with you. Nobody had the right to expect you to grow up and stop being a jealous, possessive millstone. If you had the imagination of a moron you'd see why I wanted to do this."

"Would I?" asked Jessie, holding the telephone in both her dripping, shaking hands, and swallowing the bitter gall that flooded her mouth. "Why, then?"

"Because I can't be expected to be a goddam lapdog *all* the time!" he said, almost shouting. "I've had enough of this itsy-bitsy collar and leash stuff for a while—anyway if that's what the rest of my life is going to be, I want a break once in a while. I know I'm never going to have any freedom," he assured her, "but you're a damn fool if you don't give me the illusion of some!"

"Oh," she said. "Oh, God."

There was a silence. She expected him to break the connection but he did not. She heard him striking a match.

"Brandon," she gasped, for she was really very ill now. "You can't mean that. You can't mean you are going with those people."

"You're goddam right I mean I'm going!" he said. "And after this little exhibition from you I'm not coming to Pinehurst at all. Good bye." The telephone clacked and was dead.

It must have been six o'clock that evening when Jessie raised her head from the rumpled pillows which had come to feel like the inside of a hot metal box, and forced open her swollen eyes. Whatever had happened in the black space that had passed, she knew only that she had swung between racking fits of vomiting and still more shattering bouts of retching and sobs. She had heard sounds outside her door but she was too ravaged even to identify them; she had only groaned "Go away," and had dragged the bed linen over her head. But in spite of the perfectly dark room she became aware at last that someone was standing beside her bed. It was only the chambermaid Helga; she said, "Mrs. Sam Lee bane on telephone, Madam. She called already four times today. She say she got speak to you, or she bane coming anyway."

Jessie rolled over, the room or her own head rocking crazily, and felt the telephone being put into her hand.

"Jessie," she heard, in the quiet, warm voice of that nice Helen Lee whom she knew just well enough to be able in the midst of this nightmare to identify.

"Hello," said Jessie. A gasping croak was all that she could get out.

"Your maid says you are very ill," said Mrs. Lee.

"Ugh," said Jessie.

"Don't try to talk to me. But will you mind if I come over for a minute?"

"No."

The telephone fell from her hand and again she was not able to make sense of anything until she felt a cool, fresh, perfumed hand on her forehead, and heard the voice of Helen Lee saying, "Poor lamb. Poor Jess." Helen sat down lightly on the edge of the bed, keeping her hand quietly on Jessie's forehead, and Jessie did not know how much time elapsed before she heard Helen Lee say, "Would you hate it if we try to make you a little more comfortable?"

She was so quiet, so calm, so natural that her presence made Jessie feel like a sick child, obedient and helpless. Jessie felt herself gently moved; felt warm, fragrant water, eau de cologne, bath powder, the slow strokes of a hairbrush, the clean sting of mouthwash. Presently she found herself back in bed, the linen fresh, the pillows welcome and quiet beneath her head instead of fighting one another and her, as they seemed to have done all day. It was extraordinary how silent Helen Lee remained. She had not said a single word. When Jessie opened her heavy, burning eyes Helen smiled and again touched Jessie with her marvellously soothing hand; still she said nothing, which would always remain in Jessie's knowledge of her an evidence of inspiration in human instinct.

Presently Helen Lee took something from Helga at the door, and without any remark Jessie found herself slowly nibbling a dry water-biscuit. It seemed the most delicious thing that she had ever put into her mouth. There began to grow about her the strange sense of suspension in place and

184

time and association which often follows an interval of insensibility. She could look at Helen Lee now, in some way become the only person on earth who had any reality, and accept her presence and the reassurance of her authority in the midst of chaos, as if it had always been part of her life.

"I want you to drink a little brandy," said Helen. "You'll be surprised how good it will make you feel."

Jessie took the small glass, still with the docility of a child, and began to sip the brandy in drops. She knew that she would surely feel better because Helen Lee had said so. From time to time Helen moved about the room, doing some small thing, or going to the door to say something quietly to Helga. Jessie had no concern at all in what went on; this had become Helen Lee's room, or house, or world; Jessie felt like a rag doll suspended in the midst of it.

The weeks dragged by in an evil cloud, of which she now remembered only fragments; horrifying nausea, terrible, strangling asphyxia, the tender, silent concern of Helen Lee, the bluff encouragement of Althea Crowe, the frigid punitive attitude of Brandon, implying that her condition was imaginary or hysterical, going about his own affairs almost as if she did not exist. Some days she saw him not at all; some for a moment in the morning, or when he came home to dress for dinner, for which he was always out. Sometimes the only evidence of his presence was the savage slam of the front door, or, hours past midnight, she would wake from a heavy sick sleep because she had heard the click of the electric switch as he entered his room beyond hers. It was extraordinary how she might sleep through other sounds, but if that switch clicked in the dead of night she would find herself sitting bolt upright in bed, trembling, her hands clammy, her heart pounding with a sensation for which she knew no other name than terror.

The news about her mother in Paris was as terrible as it could be; Rosa wrote short, joking, gallant notes, and Horace Howland wrote the truth. Early in April he wrote that it was now a matter of trying to conserve Rosa's strength so that she could stand the voyage home. She was planning to come, she had reached the point of obsession about it. The unstated truth that she was determined to come home to die, and to see Jessie before she died, was implicit in every word.

Jessie tried to tell this to Brandon, but it seemed to her that life had resolved into an ugly, rigid pattern the parts of which were herself lying in bed a helpless prisoner, with Brandon cold and scowling in the doorway of the room, indifferent that he had so condemned her.

"If I could only get there to Mother!" Jessie lay holding Horace Howland's latest note, her arm across her eyes. She was struggling not to weep, which she understood would only be an irritation to Brandon. She might have saved herself the trouble, for he only said, "You probably could if you wanted to badly enough."

She turned her head away and shivered. She might have reminded him why she was here at all; she might have told him of the endless treatments and expedients which had failed to help her; she might have screamed, "Do you think I do not want to be free of this unspeakable misery, which is all your doing?"; she might have told him of her useless and despairing prayer that she might die instead of her mother. But that would do no good. He would dismiss whatever she said, or go into a rage about it. If she should speak of dying, she could anticipate his saying, "You see? I told you it was all hysteria."

She realized that in his mind there was no child involved in her situation at all. During the first few fantastic weeks, he had referred to the child with considerable excitement and pride, as if his child were to be spectacularly different from any other. But now when she tried to project her own imagination to the birth of the child and beyond, Jessie only became lost in a hopeless fog of troubled emotion about her mother. At her bitterest, alone hour after hour, day after day, and worst of all, during the interminable evenings and nights, she knew only that this crucifying mess into which Brandon had got her was keeping her from her mother. It was not worth it. Nothing that was any shred or part of Brandon Bourne was worth one hour of her mother's life.

She became very frightened at the growing intensity of her hatred for him. Always before when he had slid off into one of these periods, when one by one she had recognized the symptoms of a new affair, the air of cold excitement, the secretiveness, the false casualness about his comings and goings, the telephone conversations behind closed doors, the remote blank stare when she looked at his eyes, she had known first of all the agony of grinding jealousy. She had in the past been driven, helpless and desperate, to fighting her rivals with all the ignominious, ugly tale of weapons in the feminine arsenal. And now she was losing the desire to fight and the power to care. When Helen Lee, whose genius for understanding extended to the instinct of what to seem not to know, and what to treat with cynical realism, deliberately mentioned a second-rate bit actress named Isabel Allen whom Sam had fired during a recent rehearsal, Jessie had only shrugged.

"I know," she said. "She probably can't be bothered working while she's making hay with Brandon."

Helen said quietly, "It will hurt you a lot less if you take it this way."

"Oh," said Jessie, "I'm sure it is all over town. And I don't even know exactly how I know that."

"I didn't think you could be so tough—even in self-defense," said Helen.

"Neither did I," said Jessie. "But it's that or go under. And that isn't even all he is up to——"

"Oh, don't," said Helen. "I don't feel as if I could bear it."

"That is the way I used to talk—to myself," said Jessie dully.

Late that afternoon she had gingerly tried the experiment of getting up and putting on some clothes and going downstairs to the library where she was going to have dinner—alone, as usual—on a tray beside the fire. She was sitting there reading a novel and sipping a glass of sherry when the telephone rang. Evidently there was nobody in the pantry at the moment, the telephone was not immediately answered. So Jessie went over to the desk and picked up the extension herself.

"Hello," said a hard, drawling young voice, a Foxcroft or a Farmington voice. "Is Bran there?"

"I beg your pardon," said Jessie.

"I said is Bran there."

"To whom do you wish to speak?" asked Jessie. Her own voice was frigid, but she could not have changed her tone if she had wanted to.

"Why—I'm calling Bran Bourne," said the girl. "He's supposed to come out to Oyster Bay——"

"This is Mrs. Brandon Bourne," said Jessie, her voice shot with a tremolo of rage. "I have made no engagement in Oyster Bay for Mr. Bourne and myself." She dropped the telephone with no awareness of having said or done anything by volition. The walls were shimmering before her eyes. There was a large framed photograph of Brandon on the desk beside her hand. Suddenly her fingers closed on it; she raised it high above her head with both hands and hurled it at the

187

marble hearth; then she ran across the room and lifting up the skirt of her tea gown, she stamped and stamped on the picture and the shattered glass, grinding them until she broke the heel of her slipper.

Josephine had given her the marketing lists, she was dressed and ready to go out, she had answered a telephone call from the War Fund office, it was past noon, and she must go. But now her mind had come up squarely to face the deep strangeness which runs like a buried brook beneath the whole surface of one's life, gathering to itself other submerged, smaller runnels, each an experience or a personality, to flow into the whole; and all of it at great intervals forcing itself through the surface of intentional forgetfulness, bubbling springs impossible to suppress. Good God, she thought now, why does this thing flow on and on this morning; why do these particular people all happen to have prodded and prodded me in just this way?

For by now it appeared no coincidence at all that Althea Crowe had telephoned her this morning, Althea who since that day ten years ago had never indicated the remotest memory of it. For it was to Althea Crowe that Jessie, in a wild and desperate state, had turned, the morning after she had smashed the picture. Althea had sat right there, in that very chair near Jessie's bed, a calm squatted idol, listening while Jessie said abruptly, "I want to get rid of this child. And I don't know anybody who can help me except you, Althea."

And Althea, wise, cool, cynical, had said, "You can't, my dear."

"Why not? Other women do."

"In the most utterly different circumstances. And not when —" the big square head had tilted from the chin in an encompassing gesture.

Jessie made a hard face. "I would say I had had a miscarriage," she said. "He isn't here enough to notice—or care."

"Your judgment is rotten," said Althea. "I understand why, but that doesn't alter the facts. Can't you see what you would have done if he chose to get tough? And he very probably might."

"No."

"You're not a fool, child. Don't make me use words like 'crime' and that sort of thing."

"Oh, Althea."

"I'm serious. Thank God you asked me about this, and not somebody different. You can't make sense in your present

188

state and I'd like to wring that bastard's neck for it—but I won't let you stick out your own."

Jessie shook her head. "If you won't help me," she said, "I'm going to find somebody who will. I mean it."

"If you try that, I'll tell Reath Sheldon."

Jessie scowled, not understanding. "Reath Sheldon? What do you mean, Reath? Do you know him?"

"Since high school. People have a way of coming from the same small town, you know. Besides, he's my doctor."

"I didn't know you ever saw a doctor. I thought——"

Althea Crowe shrugged. "Diabetes, the hell with it," she said.

"Althea—my *God*——"

"I said, the hell with it. Now look here, Jess. You are not going to do this, and on second thought I'm going to ask Reath anyway to tell you why you can't. I'm a ragged old bag, I can't mix too deep in it."

Jessie began to cry. "I can't go on with it," she sobbed. "I can't."

"I wish to Christ you'd never got into it. But I know what I'm talking about." The look on Althea's face amounted to a statement of harsh past experience. "Reath will be up this afternoon."

"I don't—" Jessie tried to insist that Althea had no right to resort to Reath Sheldon. But in the end she only shrank down among her pillows whimpering, "I can't go on. I won't." She tried again to say that to Sheldon when he came. And now, so many years later, it proved to be not what he had said on that afternoon, but what he had conveyed without remembered words, that had settled into the substructure of life, the masonry beneath all that was visible. One could, thought Jessie, going back into her dressing-room for a final inspection in the long mirrors, go along for years without examining that substructure, but how surely would one's life fall to pieces if it were not there!

She set off on foot to market, walking briskly westward on the double-width crosstown street, noting with her usual satisfaction that all the small personalities and happenings of the neighborhood were about their normal ways this morning. Mamas were airing bedding from the windows; others with their string bags and queerly covered heads were shrewdly selecting, piece by piece, the ingredients that would go into tonight's goulash or *pörkelt* or pungent thick soup; a bus driver and a hackie were having one of the arguments which

189

consist chiefly of "Yeah?" "Yeah!" with outthrust chins and twisted mouths. Jessie believed that she knew the signs and shopfronts of every inch of this bit of Little Hungary; in the window of a certain flat, her eye noted a card, as it had often done before, which conveyed a startling insight into the lives of her neighbors: Horvath Margit, Midwife. And she thought, my God! am I never to stop meeting these pinpricks today, never manage once for all to shut that whole wretched cycle back into the forgotten where it belongs?

Instead, as she made her way those two very long blocks from York Avenue to Second, she gave up the effort to combat the strange insistence of her memory to follow through its will to a conclusion. Perhaps there is a purpose, she mused . . . I cannot know . . . perhaps it is the power and the mystery of death and life juxtaposed . . . I think it had to be then that Mother was to die, if she must die so unnaturally soon. Jessie remembered the cable from Horace Howland, which came during that same tormented week, that he was sailing immediately with Rosa, that she would be taken from the ship on a stretcher. Jessie knew that the gallant battle of pretense was lost at last. Her own sufferings shrank now to their minimal proportion; it became important only to be well enough herself to get to the ship when it arrived, and to have Brandon there with her for the sake of her mother's peace of mind. He saw the point; he agreed at once to meet the ship with Jessie.

It was due at mid-afternoon, but the crossing had been delayed by fog and Jessie was told a day ahead of time that the ship would not dock before ten o'clock at night. On the morning of that day she waited in bed for Brandon to stop in before starting for the office; she had not seen him at all yesterday. He had not come to her room by eleven o'clock, and he had not yet left the house, so Jessie got out of bed, put on a dressing-gown and slippers and went into his room. He was talking on the telephone, tilted back on the rear legs of a chair with his feet on the desk in front of him. He was speaking in a carefully lowered voice so that he could not have been heard from outside the room.

"—by eight anyway," he was saying. "I've reserved——"

Jessie shut the door with deliberate noise, so that he would hear her, and walked over to him, saying carefully, "Brandon —I beg your pardon. Could you——?"

"Hold it," he said into the telephone. He looked up at Jessie with a scowl.

"I'm sorry," she said. "I just wanted to tell you———"

"Well can't it wait?" he asked, covering the mouthpiece of the telephone with his hand.

"It's about Mother's ship," she said. "It is delayed and not docking until ten tonight."

Brandon's eyes went glassy with irritation.

"I was afraid—I didn't know—" said Jessie awkwardly. "Surely," she said with a rush of daring, "you aren't making an engagement for tonight?"

"I've made it," snapped Brandon.

Jessie drew a deep breath to steady herself and said as gently as possible, "Yes, but—perhaps you could make it any other day, Brandon? Would you mind terribly?"

"I certainly would," he said.

Jessie was so conscious of the woman waiting at the other end of the telephone in Brandon's hand that she could not force herself to speak. Indeed she ought not to speak. But she heard her own voice, thin and unnatural, saying to her surprise, "Oh, Brandon. Don't you remember what you promised me? It isn't for my sake, truly." She gripped the edge of the desk with her numb fingers and breathed, "Please, Brandon. Please change your engagement. On account of Mother."

He sat scowling for a moment, running his hand through his hair, his face hardening in its most ominous mould. He said into the telephone, "Look, I've been interrupted, I'll call you back." Then he flung the instrument into place and glared at Jessie.

"I'm sorry about your mother," he said, "but I think you've built up a thing about this . . . you'll be perfectly all right. You said yourself they've arranged to take her straight home. There won't be any waiting around or customs or anything. You don't really need me."

"It was not for my sake," Jessie repeated, struggling to keep the least note of strain or argument out of her voice. "I told you last week, I'm willing to settle for anything if you will just help me to put up this front for Mother. I don't want to repeat it all, Brandon, I know I would only annoy you."

He was hesitating and she thought that she had persuaded him. She tried to smile, she tried to be relaxed and gentle, she tried to avert her eyes from his face because she knew how it would anger him if she looked at him with pleading or anxiety. "I will be so grateful," she said softly.

"Well, I don't see why it's necessary," he said in the barking staccato which hit her ears like hammers.

"Ah," she breathed, with weakness coming over her like a great salt wave, "you did see. You were perfectly sweet about it." She bent her head suddenly, hard down over her breast, to force the blood into it and keep her from collapsing.

"Jesus Christ," she heard him say, rising from his chair and kicking it away, "I'm so goddam fed up."

"You?" she whispered. "Only you?"

"Yes!" he said, making the syllable a whiplash. "No other man I ever heard of is always snarled up in a mess of—see here!" he said. "I told you I've got a date and I've decided to keep it."

"You're quite sure?" she asked. Only the utmost extreme of distress and pain could have brought her voice to this strange, low, throb. She did not recognize the sound herself. "You're quite sure it is worth it? Sure you couldn't go to this same place tomorrow?"

"No I could not," he said. "I'm going there tonight. It's not my fault if the French Line brings their ship in late."

"I see," she said. Walking with what she thought careful steadiness, she turned and went back to her own room.

She was surprised at how calm she felt as the day wore on. It was, to be sure, the calm of death; she said to Helen Lee who came in during the afternoon, "I think I've reached the point now where literally nothing can hurt me." She had not told Helen any part of what had taken place with Brandon. But Helen could judge for herself when she learned that Jessie was going to the pier alone.

"Will you let me go with you?" she asked.

Jessie shook her head. "No thanks, darling. Doctor Sheldon will be there. And for Mother, you understand—" The presence of an outsider would only dramatize Brandon's absence.

It was Reath Sheldon who carried Jessie as well as her mother through that ordeal; who managed through all the uproar of a docking ship and a turbulent pier to bring Rosa down a special gangway and into the waiting ambulance, with such quiet speed that the details would always be blurred in Jessie's mind. It mattered only that she found herself inside the ambulance, holding her mother's hand and looking into her grey, wasted face. Once she could see again her mother's extraordinary eyes, sunken and huge now and black with suffering, and touch again her soft brown hand, curiously light in spite of its heavy bones, everything else lost reality. They sped out of the pier, with the muffled siren whining, and were in Sixty-sixth Street in what seemed an instant.

Reath Seldon's car with Horace Howland was close behind them. It was but a few minutes until Rosa was lying in her own bed, the nurse little in evidence, and Jessie sitting close to her mother, smiling with all the courage that she could muster.

Rosa had of course asked, "How are you feeling, darling?" and other natural questions, but she had not mentioned Brandon nor appeared to notice his absence. How wonderful she was! Jessie thought, and perhaps Brandon is right when he says I am hysterical and making mountains out of molehills. After all, what difference would it have made if he had been with me tonight?

She kept her mother's hand in hers; the contact was like a benediction which held the power to heal every injury and hurt and sorrow of these past months. And yet her mother was so fearfully ill that Jessie dared not let her feel the burden of her need for her. Rosa must have lost twenty-five pounds; she was a frail cage of bones beneath the covers of the bed; her voice was never stronger than a whisper. And Jessie had been warned already not to let her talk. She did not have the strength. For Jessie it was enough to lay her head down on the pillow near her mother's, to hide her face in the pitiful bony angle of the neck and shoulder which had been so gloriously beautiful; and when the faint pressure of her mother's hand said that for which there were no words, pouring into Jessie's heart the only love on earth of which she could be sure, Jessie locked her teeth together and felt the hot pressure of her pulse pounding with the determination not to give way now to what she felt, which could only have harrowed her mother.

It was growing late now, Rosa should long ago have been settled for the night. The nurse stood for a moment in the doorway to signal Jessie that she should leave. She whispered to her mother that she would be there in the morning; she kissed her forehead, pressed her hands for a moment, and straightened up from the bed. Rosa Landau made then an effort so prodigious and so gallant that Jessie's throat felt raw with the struggle to choke back sobs. Rosa opened her beautiful, now tragic eyes as wide as she could, smiled with her lovely warm mouth now pinched with agony and said, visibly straining to make her voice gay and radiant as it used to be, "We'll have fun together still, darling. I even managed to get some lovely clothes for the baby in Paris."

Oh, thought Jessie, fighting not to weep. Oh, the baby, the

193

poor baby that doesn't make any sense, the poor baby . . .
She bent down quickly and kissed her mother again and Rosa
lifted her shadows of hands and took Jessie's face between
them.

"Are you all right, darling?" she asked. Her voice was
warm and clear and to her daughter it was and would remain
forever the sound of human love. "Are you really all right?"

Jessie nodded, forcing a smile to her face, and the motions
of her hands and head and shoulders to be quick and reassuring and gay. She nodded hard, putting her finger over her lips
to tell her mother to be quiet and rest now. Then she turned
and left the room. She started down the stairs, with the sound
of her mother's beloved voice still clear in her ears. Horace
Howland was standing at the foot of the stairs, outside the
drawing-room door, looking up at Jessie and waiting for her.
There was safety in his presence, and calm and sureness and
warmth. The fine clear eyes smiled encouragingly, and he
came towards her holding out his hand. Jessie noticed with
strange special preciseness the heavy seal ring on his finger,
the crisp white cuff with the jewelled link sparkling in the
light from the hall. Dear Horace, to love her mother so, to
have loved her so for all these years. How did one earn such
love, Jessie thought, how did one find it and hold it?

What a long, strange flight of stairs this was, and why had
she so much time to think on the way down? And how many
times had her mother's voice repeated those few precious
words? Jessie moved with one hand on her breast as if to
hold the sound close inside there. "Are you all right, darling?
Are you really all right?" She heard it even above the buzzing
in her ears.

"Horace!" breathed Jessie as she fell. It was not a long fall,
it did not seem anything but a slip almost at the bottom of
the stairs, as he leaped forward not quite in time to catch her.
But that was the night that Jessie lost her child.

XV

The day had cleared after all by one o'clock when Jessie was
walking up Second Avenue with Mark Dwyer, both in the
highest spirits. He had met her as she was standing by the

sidewalk display of fruit and vegetables outside Tommy Pecoraro's market. She picked up a blue plum and handed it to Mark, saying "Good morning. Just occupy yourself with this until I finish here."

"Thanks," said Mark, putting the whole plum into his mouth and talking around it. "Only this isn't the way to eat this and I bet you don't know what is."

"No?" she said, "except that my friend Anna was making those things before you were born. With pot cheese and poppy-seed strewn all over them."

She looked into Mark's eyes, laughing, but in such a way that the glitter of nonsense lay sparkling on the surface of her face. They stood among the celery and beans and beets and onions, with shabby, plodding neighborhood housewives gabbling all around them, trucks roaring past, bystanders gaping at the spectacular woman and the decorated general; and they held such a silent conversation of the eyes, serious behind the glints of playfulness, as only natures perfectly and spontaneously accordant can know.

"You are not," said Mark, "dressed quite suitably for the occasion."

"I'm sorry," she said. "I decided to leave my boudoir cap at home."

"We could buy you one," said Mark, raising an eyebrow at the neighboring store, which had put out on its sidewalk stand a wonderful collection of local necessities: odd crockery, chipped grey agate saucepans, pink glass tumblers, boxes of buttons, darning eggs, spools of thread, toilet paper, scrubbing-brushes, dishmops, knitted hug-me-tights, and many other things in a casual bargain-jumble of hardware and drygoods.

Jessie laughed and turned to Big Tommy in his dirty white apron, who was gazing at Mark Dwyer's decorations with beaming eyes. A small boy ran out of the store and peered from behind Tommy's elbow.

"Jeest, Pop, looka!" said the kid.

"Gwan, scram," said Tommy. "Gimme a box iceboig outa da back."

A spotted kitten scuttled from under the fruit stand and batted excitedly at a dangling paper tag. Jessie bent down and swooped it up, scratching it gently under its chin. It was a pretty kitten, gay and not timid at all, which was one reason why Jessie liked the Pecoraros. All their cats were well-treated and friendly. This one was purring like a small machine.

"Must you?" asked Mark. "You know you will ruin your clothes."

"I can't help it," she said. "I always have to play with cats. I cannot leave them alone."

"Mis' Bourne knows all da cats on da block," said Tommy.

"How are the pears today, Tommy?" asked Jessie. "The last ones tasted like wallpaper."

"You're tellin' me. Green stuff. Don't take none today. Mushrooms is good, dough."

"They ought to be! Ninety cents a pound."

"Moider, ain't it? Watcha gonna do?" He shoved his cap to the back of his head and shrugged. Jessie put down the kitten, brushed her gloves against each other, called good bye to Tommy's wife inside the store, and started up the street with Mark Dwyer. He walked rather slowly, carefully eyeing each shop and sometimes pausing to look thoughtfully through the windows at the people inside.

"It's changed a lot," he said. "But then in other ways it hasn't changed at all. Any of those women waiting at that counter there could be my Ma, or somebody she knew."

"They are good women," said Jessie. "Or at least I think so. Probably I'm a sentimental fool because I don't know them and would have nothing in common with them if I did. But I like to be among them and feel the sense of life that I get from them. Do you know," said she pensively, "sometimes I have a strange idea. I know people who love the country, who say that the sight of trees and meadows and growing things gives them strength, or contentment, or peace . . . you know . . . ?"

Mark nodded, watching her.

". . . that is their contact with Nature and that is real to them. But mine seems to be people like those——" she nodded towards two heavy, swollen-legged, shapeless Mamas dressed in cotton print house-dresses, sagging coats, and worn, misshapen shoes. They were standing by the curbstone gossiping and Jessie said, as she and Mark passed them, "You see, I can't even understand the language they are talking. It could be Sanskrit. But it doesn't matter, I don't need to talk to them. In fact if I had to, there would be very little for us to say."

"They are talking Slovak," said Mark, with a strange solemn look in his eyes.

"Well—it might be anything else, too. Hungarian most probably in this particular block. Or German a few blocks

196

away. Or Italian. Or Yiddish. Or—you know. You know it all better than I do. I'm only trying to say that I get some kind of joy out of being near people like that, out of having some reason for doing anything that they do. That must be why I go to market like this, for of course there is no other reason."

"Poor kid," said Mark, looking down at her with tenderness. "What a long way off base you are."

"And not you?" asked Jessie.

"Certainly, sometimes. But I told you last night——"

"Yes," she said. "I remember."

"And I am much nearer to these people than you," he said. "To me they are just the normal human furniture of the bit of space into which I was born. You are a generation removed, naturally the distance has become a little enchanted. You ought to get a good look inside there."

He pointed to the doorway of a five-story coldwater walk-up, a small dark hole opening on a darker hallway with steep crooked stairs squeezed against a peeling wall.

"I can stand out here in the street," he said, "and describe one of those flats as if I lived in it. I can tell you about everything, all of it from the cracked kitchen oilcloth to the leak under the sink, the chromos on the walls, family groups and confirmations and weddings, and souvenir calendars and a colored landscape of somewhere in the old country. And the embroidered sofa cushions and the dried-up palm from last Palm Sunday and the shabby furniture that's too big for the rooms and the sagging beds and the dark hall toilet where the airshaft never lets any air in. And the way those hallways smell, that mean damp stink even when the tenants keep the house clean as such houses go, and the onions frying, and the rats in the cellar and the cockroaches in the walls. Oh, I know all about it."

"Nevertheless," said Jessie, "to me the people who live there are infinitely more interesting than most of the ones whom we are going to see tonight. And of course I am absolutely inconsistent and ridiculous."

"Absolutely," said Mark.

They came to the door of the butcher shop west of Third Avenue where Jessie and her mother before her and hundreds of old-fashioned, substantial people had dealt for nearly fifty years. There had been a time in the market world when all the best butchers, both wholesale and retail, had come from the solid German-Jewish stratum of the wonderful polyglot layer-cake of Manhattan; names like Loewenstein and Buchsbaum and Schweitzer and Frankenthaler had meant good meat and sound business for generations, as had small, weazened Mr. Hoexter whose rule over this hustling establishment was effected through his two tough, strapping sons while he wandered about in a seeming state of vagueness which did not mean anything at all. He was as smart as a mink, and incorrigibly honest. If he did not like your hat or want your trade, he said so.

"Hullo, dolling!" Jessie was greeted by a rough bass roar.

She smiled and said, "Hello, Walter. Hello, Jack." The girls in the cashier's cage threw in their hellos, the meatcutters in the back of the shop grinned theirs. Jessie said, "This is General Dwyer, boys. He came along because he doesn't believe anybody ever goes to market any more."

"General *Mark* Dwyer?" Walter held out his slab of a hand and they shook. Cigarettes were offered and lighted. The Hoexters accepted the presence of the general, whose identity they appeared to know well, without the slightest *empressement*.

"Have you anything to eat this week?" asked Jessie.

"Fa' you, sweetheart, anything," answered Walter.

"You can't call me that yet," said Jessie, winking.

"And why not?"

"Because," she explained to Mark, "this place is known as the store where they call all the customers 'darling' if they're under forty, and 'sweetheart' if they're over."

"Fa' that hat," said Jack, leaning over from his block and gesturing with a cleaver, "you can choose your own name."

"But not my own steak," said Jessie. "Last week——"

"Neveh mind last week. You wanna run this business, dolling? It's yours."

"Thanks. I only want a pot roast for tomorrow's dinner."

"Is she gonna make pancakes with it?" asked Walter. "I'll be right over."

"She isn't going to make anything unless you come across. I'm so sick of birds I could cackle."

"Ya hear, Pop?"

"I hear," muttered Mr. Hoexter. "She's eating still, no? She should complain."

Jessie laughed.

"They're perfectly right," she said to Mark. "I don't know how they do it, but they always have something to eat. Well, Walter—about eight pounds and lots of suet, all the way around?"

198

"Didja hear about the fat collection?" he asked, chopping off the feet of a chicken at the knee joints.

"If you sent that chicken to my house you'd catch hell for it," said Jessie.

"Sure. Thank God the other customers don't put on so many airs."

"French style, *nebbich*," muttered Mr. Hoexter.

"Good bye," said Jessie, starting towards the door.

"So long, dolling. I'll be up for them potato pancakes."

When they were on Lexington Avenue, looking for a cab, Mark said, "Do you always horse around with those people that way?"

"Of course, that's why I go there. Aside from the good meat. Oh Mark, look."

"What?" He turned his attention from the passing cabs to the direction of her eyes. He saw nothing except everyday people going about their business. But Jessie was looking at a woman who had just passed them; she was watching the woman's back in its neat grey tailored suit, her conservatively dressed hair-colored hair, her modest brown felt hat, the small, correct neckpiece of brown fur, the low-heeled alligator pumps, the prim purposeful walk of a personality who believed in plenty of wholesome fresh air and vigorous family life.

"What in the world is newsworthy about her?" asked Mark.

"Only that she and her kind give me the green crawling creeps. I tell you, I would react with less horror to meeting a python loose in Central Park."

"But why?" An empty cab stopped and Mark helped Jessie into it. "What's wrong with the woman? She looks harmless and all too decent. Go to the Plaza, driver."

"That's just what she is," said Jessie. "Decent. The guardian of all the decencies and conventions and hidden brutalities of her mouse-minded kind against the helpless young. I know her and dozens like her. You can always see them at this time of day on Madison and Lexington Avenues, doing their errands. Their name is always in my mind Robinson or Delano or Potter, whether it really happens to be that or something else. The mothers of the snippy little bitches in the good schools—you know, like Brearley and Chapin and Hewitt's—who gang up on any wretched pariah who happens to be the least bit different, and make her life a broiling hell. I know. I know all about it."

"But you are so violent!" said Mark, astonished.

199

"That is what happens to me when I see one of those women. The whole thing slides through my mind like a train —the whole fixed, rigid pattern, with these terrible women sitting like a court of judgment that you sometimes dream about in a nightmare when you've committed a crime—did you ever have such a dream?"

He nodded, his face intent and very sad.

"There they sit, grimacing at the bars, one side of them that vomitous sick-sweet manner and tone of voice for their own kind, and the other the most slashing, brutal snobbery for everybody else, and particularly the children of anybody else. They run the dancing classes and the subscription dances and the whole geared-up machinery that leads to the debut and the preservation of their own damned life-cycle, which appears to be breaking down at last, thank God. I am sorry to see some of the lovelinesses of the old world go, but not what they are bent on preserving."

"I had no idea you could be so ferocious," said Mark.

"Anybody is who knows the workings of that machine," she said. "My sister-in-law is one of them, or more exactly used to be—but her own husband and daughter have become such a cup of gall that she cannot hold her head up in the line any longer. She goes through some of the motions but—" Jessie shrugged.

And sitting quietly in the cab with Mark Dwyer beside her, she began to wonder that she had let off steam in such a harsh and uncharacteristic way. "I didn't mean to," she said aloud in the midst of her thought, and Mark, taking her gloved hand and holding it for a moment against his cheek said, "Of course you didn't mean to. That's why I'm glad you did."

And so there disappeared the need to say anything more at all, and they fell into one of the brief eloquent silences which served them so well in the intervals of eager and enchanted talk. Jessie sat back in the cab, her hand in Mark's, and stared as they passed at the monument to the Fighting Sixty-ninth in The First World War. New York's Own Regiment, she thought, with a quick sense of warm possessive affection, and then though she had been only a little girl at the time, she remembered the gloriously naïve joy with which the city had welcomed home the victorious Fighting Irish. She had seen that parade, and many another too, from the Fifth Avenue windows of her mother's hairdresser; and so deep runs the love of a parade in the born New Yorker's heart that

Jessie like the rest had gone through life remembering and cherishing the memories of distinct parades . . . indeed, she thought now, and suddenly said aloud to Mark, "That's the only real memory I have of my father. I remember sitting with somebody in a grandstand when he was marching in the Saint Patrick's Day Parade, and how excited and proud I was when he waved to me. I had a green coat and an ermine muff and bonnet."

"How old were you when he died?" asked Mark.

"Less than three. So of course I can't really remember him at all. What I have is not really a memory, just an impression of a big, red-faced, laughing, noisy man who gave off a lot of warmth and filled that funny house on the West Side with uproar and cigar smoke and parties and beer and people. Oddly enough, it was an absolutely different world from anything else that ever touched my mother, but I think she enjoyed it while it was going on. After he died she must have begun to shape up the next phase of her life very quickly, for I can't remember much about the in-between period until we fetched up in Sixty-sixth Street."

"Everybody knew Mat Kernan," said Mark. "In some ways he was better known than your mother. You must have a lot of relatives on his side too."

"Yes, but I've never seen them. I think they must have broken with him when he married Mother—of course it was a terrible thing that he did, in their eyes."

"You were never baptized," said Mark thoughtfully.

"No, that's just the point. I suppose there must have been a dreadful session when my mother refused to have me brought up a Catholic—so of course that would explain their never recognizing that I had even been born."

"Didn't her own family carry on just as much?"

"Well, it was altogether different. If Mother hadn't been herself, and all of them so concentrated on helping her—you know, Mark, such people can be quite extraordinary. One couldn't generalize—but I know dozens of famous people whose backgrounds were just like my mother's, and who have troops of these nice folksy relatives tucked away like that."

"Sure. And not only that special breed either." He laughed.

"I know. But here there are so many more of that kind—of us. And the relationship is quite remarkable. You'd expect more of such tribes to try to hitch onto the successful one's wagon, and some do. But more often they're just nice easy-going people who take Max's or Sadie's success for granted

. . . aren't too impressed . . . and never do anything that would be an intrusion."

"And your mother's sisters, of course———"

"They were like that. They really loved her, so they left her alone and left it to her to keep in touch with them. She did, too, until they died."

"Still, I should have thought her marrying Kernan———"

"But, you see," said Jessie, smiling at the sight of a pinwheel and balloon vendor standing by the Park exactly where she could remember him or his counterpart from her childhood, "with them the religious thing was not so strong. They had the old-fashioned background and they brought the candlesticks and all that to the United States when they came here, but they were all women. And that made the difference. To those people a family is scarcely a family without a husband and father, the whole ritual and tradition revolves around him. That's really all I know about the subject and I regret it very much. I would love to know more—but I've never had an opportunity to learn. There must be millions of people like me," she said, with a sad shadow crossing her face, "who would draw a lot of strength out of their own roots—if they had never been cut off from them." She sighed. "And you can't go back and do an artificial graft years later, either."

"No, I suppose you're right," said Mark. "But it's really fantastic if you stop to think that you have cousins and nephews and relatives all over the place, whom you have never seen."

"Fantastic," she said, "but you'd be amazed to realize how many people are in the same situation. I don't know if it's true of the other great cities of the world, but it certainly is here. If I really begin wondering about it it makes me feel like the telephone company—with invisible connections in obscure little homes all over Brooklyn, the Bronx, and Queens—not to mention Manhattan itself. I told you about my cousin Louis Schwartz down at Headquarters, and I've never seen him in my life."

"Then how do you know him?"

"Only by telephone. When my mother died he called me up. I remember how horrified I was when they told me that some detective from the Homicide Squad was calling, and he just said he was so sorry about her, and wanted to tell me so. I was terribly touched."

They were standing now on the steps of the Plaza, enjoying

for a moment the almost foolishly bewitching charm of the sight before them. Only yesterday it had cast its spell over Jessie as she stood in her chemise waiting for Miss Flora to bring her fittings; but now with Mark Dwyer beside her, the great ornate portico, the statues, the stiffly planted flower-beds, the victorias and hansoms with their scampish coachmen and pathetic horses, the glittering towers across the way, the Park smiling elegantly at their left, made Jessie feel even more bewildered, more disembodied, yet more certain of her own passionate attachment to all of this than she had ever felt before.

"We will lunch at one of those nice window tables in the Café," said Mark, turning to escort her up the steps; and walking beside him Jessie felt as if she were stepping back into that strangest, most frightening of all the strange and frightening passages of her youth. But this time, and she laughed aloud at the thought, she had the most attractive and desirable beau of any girl at the party.

XVI

"I suppose," said Mark that evening as they were bowling down the East River Drive on their way to join the Lees, "we are going to see everybody who is anybody and all that."

"Every pushing, shoving, scrabbling one of them," replied Jessie. She looked out the window of the cab and said, gesturing with her head, "I'd so much rather be doing that. Wouldn't you?"

Mark leaned over and looked past her at a sand barge tied up to the river bulkhead; in the pleasant fall evening, the bargeman was sitting outside his little deck-house, his feet on a barrel, smoking his pipe. A woman sat nearby peeling potatoes into a pot in her lap. Smoke plumed from the crooked tin stovepipe behind them. A dirty white mongrel trotted up and down the deck.

"I bet she's got corned beef simmering on the stove inside there," said Mark.

"And presently she'll go and put those potatoes and the cabbage in with it, and they'll have beer and some——"

"Have a heart. I'm drooling. And we'll be exactly where it's the thing to be. My God."

"I've always wanted to live on a barge like that."

"Just your dish, darling. Who do you suppose we'll see tonight?"

"Why do you care?"

Mark shrugged.

"Faces, they have," said Jessie. "All kinds of faces, and the different kinds of natures that go with them. But they want to be known as Names. So long as they get their names in tomorrow's gossip columns they'll be happy."

"Well, they need to get that question answered," said Mark. The cheap, sad, jangling question of the up-and-up, he thought, quoting, " 'How'm I doin'?' "

"And the odd thing," said Jessie, "is that a great many of them are hard-working and very successful at what they do. Accomplished and important in their way, especially compared to a cipher like me."

"Oh, it's the same everywhere," said Mark.

"I know. But I think it has a special, pitiful garishness here."

"Naturally. Between the way it always was on Broadway and the way the rest of the world is now. But somehow you feel cosier about it over a sawdust sausage in the Savoy Grill."

They were met at the restaurant as the door swung open by the flavor of extra festivity which permeated this place on occasions like tonight. Broad smiles and enthusiastic handshakes greeted Mark Dwyer, admiring welcome surrounded Jessie. She thought, following her old friend Mac up the stairs, that no matter how cynically one might grasp the motives by which an establishment like this must be run, it remained for its old habitués one of the pleasantest places in the world.

Sam Lee rose from the table to welcome them and Helen, looking her loveliest, held up a superbly jewelled hand to Mark Dwyer.

"Hall and Preston are going to be late," she said, "but Sam is ordering for them and they'll have to like it."

Jessie had not glanced at all about the room as she took her place, but she knew perfectly well who was there. She was seated with her back towards a party of four to whom she had nodded on her way in, friends of Brandon's whom she scarcely ever saw.

"I'm so glad to see you!" she said to Sam Lee, patting his hand. "You old philoprogenitor."

"So Helen told you," he said with a smile at his wife. "Pretty fine, no?"

"I was startled at first. But——"

"I'm tickled pink. I hope to God it's a girl."

"Oh, you'll be just as happy with another boy. You're such a darling, Sam." Jessie spoke impulsively, with a rich sense of warmth and sincerity about Sam and Helen Lee, intensified for the moment by the contrast between them and the other personalities with whom the room was crowded. Henry Greenberg was holding forth at his *Stammtisch* in his special corner, and though she could have wished to be dining elsewhere, it would have made no difference; Greenberg would know already that she had spent most of her time with Mark Dwyer since Monday night. Speaking to Sam, she gave a sudden quick giggle.

"What's up?" he asked.

"Nothing. I was just thinking of the contrast between you and him. Between your farm and that high-class house of procurement he runs on Long Island."

Just then Henry Greenberg looked up and caught her eye and she bowed gaily to him and Marge and their party, George and Maureen Stillman and the Irving Laskins, on from Hollywood. As she greeted and dismissed them all in one quick motion, Jessie could not escape the certainty that some quarter of a million dollars in platinum-colored mink and matched emeralds, black pearls, and grape-sized diamonds had come temporarily to roost on the much-profaned body of Dorette Laskin; that the money would presently pass on to another, even more venal transient proprietrix; and that as it moved its stench would intensify, like the stink picked up by a slow summer wind on its way through a particularly noisome slum. And to cap the impression as she turned away, she observed the dark, rat-sharp face of Jack Spanier entering the room and pausing to speak to the Greenberg party in corroboration of the common knowledge of his past involvements, all disreputable, with Laskin financially, with Dorette sexually, and with Henry Greenberg in the evil subtleties of mutual blackmail.

"*No, no*," said Giglio's soft voice at Jessie's shoulder, directing away a waiter with oysters, "*non pella Signora*."

He placed before her a cup of her favorite Créme Sénégale, a magnificent curry soup which Jessie liked hot instead of iced as it was usually served here; and for each person at the table there appeared the precise small consideration for his personal taste which made him feel like a well-petted cat. Buttered hot gluten toast for Helen, English pepper sauce for Sam, another bourbon old-fashioned for Mark Dwyer, celery for Jessie, all effected with smooth, smiling speed and deference to the conversation, since nothing was offered or suggested which would distract a person's attention.

"This girl-friend of yours is a little crazy," Mark was saying to Helen Lee. "Did you know she spent her mornings playing with alley-cats and scraping up acquaintances on Second Avenue?"

"Why of course," said Helen, circling the room with her eye and passing on the collective impression to Mark. "Wouldn't you, as an antidote to most of these?"

Aware that Helen and Mark were talking about her, and warm with the knowledge that she would fare well between them, Jessie turned back to Sam Lee who was watching the progression of Jack Spanier across the room.

"The only reason I can imagine for anyone's speaking to him," said Sam, "is what he must have on them. Thank God he has nothing on me. Look at that poor girl with Joe Kincaid——" and as Spanier turned then to look straight at Sam's table and make what he could of its uncompleted party, Sam Lee stared back without recognition, and began to eat his oysters.

"I'm afraid I am going to have to do something about him and my niece," said Jessie, almost whispering. "I tried to throw the fear of God into her the other day, but——"

Sam Lee shrugged, glanced swiftly at Mark Dwyer, and then again at Jessie. "Let 'em stew in their juice," he said. "You ought to put your attention on something more rewarding."

Jessie laughed, feeling a sense of childlike pleasure in the approval of Sam and Helen Lee for Mark Dwyer and for whatever Mark and Jessie might make of the few days of possible happiness that had fallen their way. She felt as if Sam had deliberately marked out a small safe province for her, over which he would stand guard in any way that he might consider necessary. She gave him a look of poignant appreciation. She thought him the most lovable man she knew, particularly dear to her because of his intense devotion to Helen. Jessie loved his kind, blue-shaved, spectacled face, his wise and sentimental brown eyes, his intellectual head, his big generous ears, his deep voice which sometimes suggested the singsong echo of his early boyhood. Sam's rise from the almost classic origin of the lower East Side had long since merged into the legend of American success, but he could and sometimes did, to this day, make tangibly vivid the cruel and bitter life of hunger and cold and rigor which had been his earliest memories.

"Poor Norman," he said, thinking of Norman Feiner who was known to his colleagues as the worst and the most pitiful firstnight sufferer of them all. "He must be about crazy by now."

"Renée slips luminal into him all day when this is going on," said Jessie, "and naïvely supposes that Norman doesn't know it. Ah, here are Hall and Preston."

"I'm so sorry, Helen," said Hall Peters as she dropped into the chair which Mark Dwyer had risen to draw out for her. "Hello, Sam. Jessie, that's the most beautiful dress I ever saw."

"Six years old," said Jessie, "but thank you. How are you, Preston?"

The newcomer turned his blank, shocked face from Mark Dwyer with whom he had been shaking hands, to give Jessie a meaningless, mechanical smile.

"He's probably as sick as a pup," said Hall Peters, "after listening to that swill at the broadcast where he picked me up. I wouldn't blame him."

"Well," said Sam Lee mildly, "if you will write the number one best-seller . . ."

"Balls," said Hall Peters. "In three months I'll be back on my shelf and left there to rot until the next time something about me is news. I should tell you!"

They all laughed, shrugging at their mutual experience of fame and its ephemeral importunities.

Shaw sat silent and almost immobile, already at his second drink and eating nothing. The plates were being changed and the remainder of the dinner served all at once as Sam Lee had ordered it; thick cuts of prime roast beef, hashed brown potatoes, and coffee in large cups with cream and sugar.

"It may not be elegant," said Helen of the coffee served in this way, "but Sam——"

"Sam takes his coffee seriously," said Jessie.

"And why not?" Sam shook his head at the waiter serving the beef and said, "No, well done for me."

"Sam!" exclaimed Hall Peters. "Why bother to order good beef if you're going to treat it like pot roast?"

"I can't help it," said Sam, with comical pathos. "It's the way you're brought up. We hardly ever had any meat but what we had was kosher——"

"I know," said Hall. "Salted to death and all the life cooked out of it."

"It's too bad you never had my Grandma's boiled beef with farfel. My God, if I knew where to get the same thing now——"

"Darling, can't you learn?" asked Jessie of Helen.

"You'd be so surprised," said Helen. "It's his memories that he keeps on tasting, not his Grandma's cooking."

"Listen," said Sam. "You don't know what a plate of good soup or a cup of coffee really mean unless you've been out with your papers until after the bulldog is on the street, one or two in the morning and ten below zero and you haven't had a meal since breakfast and little enough of that."

"It was the same when I was a kid," said Mark Dwyer. "In lots of ways."

"Well," asked Sam, "and wasn't the coffee the most important thing in the whole damn world?"

Mark nodded solemnly.

"I remember," said Sam, lighting his cigar, "I remember that big grey agate coffee pot on the back of Grandma's stove, down in the kitchen in Allen Street. I used to sleep in the kitchen when I finally got to bed, but most of the night some of us were in there sitting around the table and schmoozing and drinking coffee, we called it 'cawfee'. That kitchen had the only stove in the flat, no wonder we all squeezed in there."

"Who were 'we'?" asked Hall Peters.

"Oh, God, it would take a week to tell you," said Sam. "A lot of *mischpocheh*, aunts and nieces and Grandma. And they'd all come in from work late at night and sit there in that steamy little kitchen with rags and papers stuffed in the cracks of the windows. They'd sit around waiting for the coffee to boil and quarrel their heads off. I can smell it and hear it still. Grandma's coffee couldn't have been as good as I think it was because she could never have afforded to make it as strong as it needs to be to be good. But it tasted grand to us. They'd all sit there hollering at each other in Yiddish and all of a sudden we'd hear a hissing noise on the stove and somebody'd yell, *'Gevalt, the coffee!'* and jump to the stove and grab the pot just before it was about to boil over. Then somebody'd put the pot on the table and Grandma'd pour a few drops of cold water down the spout to settle the coffee and then somebody else'd jump for the milk—it was about to boil over too. We always had boiled milk and maybe that was why the coffee tasted that way."

Jessie was listening with her chin in her hands, intent and captivated. Looking at her Mark Dwyer saw in the solemn and almost awestruck tension of her eyes and her taut mouth that this talk of Sam Lee's was no matter of idle fascination for her, but that it was striking a chord somewhere in her own deep, perhaps originally submerged memory, a chord whose echo was identical. Mark saw too that while Jessie's attention was entirely preempted by Sam Lee, she was also deliberately not allowing her eyes to move and her glance to meet Mark's. If she did, something would be said silently which neither would wish to say in the presence of any other person. Mark Dwyer set his face in a conscious mask, uncommunicative yet interested, but the current running between himself and Jessie Bourne must, he felt, convey its electric vigor to her and more than probably to Helen Lee.

"The way you're drinking that coffee," said Sam to Hall Peters, responding to the warm interest of his guests who were enchanted with his reminiscences, "'the way you're drinking coffee, black and no sugar, nobody'd have touched it down at Grandma's. We used to drink ours in glasses, thick, chipped, squatty glasses, no two ever alike. I suppose Grandma bought them off a pushcart or out of a barrel outside some store. The idea was to keep enough glasses in the house so we'd each have one, full of coffee and boiled milk, and we'd have a lump of sugar on the side. A big square lump, not these fancy flat ones." He flipped over an elegantly wrapped lump of sugar, with the iron-gate trademark of the restaurant smartly engraved upon the paper.

"We'd hold the lump of sugar in our teeth," said Sam, "or bite off a corner of it and take a mouthful of coffee and then swallow it after it had melted the sugar. My God, what on earth made me remember all this. We always sat crowded around the oilcloth, wearing sweaters and shawls, hunched up with our elbows on the table and holding our glass in both hands to warm us, and the lump of sugar in our teeth. We drank tea the same way," he said, "Russian tea made off a tea brick, with lemon and the spoon sticking in your eye . . ."

"Somebody," said Jessie, her voice curiously plangent, "somebody somewhere has the samovar that my grandmother brought when she came here."

"Of course," said Sam, shrugging and matter-of-fact. "Some niece or cousin or somebody. And the candlesticks and a couple of priceless copper pots and probably a Turkish coffee-mill. Everybody brought 'em." He motioned for the check.

"It makes everybody else's background so flat by comparison," said Hall Peters to Mark. "People like Sam are so full of—you know—*juice*. Me and Grand Island, Nebraska—" she sighed.

"We put garlic in our cooking too," said Mark, at which Jessie gave him a swift glance of secret delight and Hall Peters stared completely uncomprehending.

Mark Dwyer laughed, placing Jessie's furs across her shoulders, and observing the small quiet smile that she was exchanging with Helen Lee. He noted too the few words which Giglio addressed to Jessie as he bowed the party away from the table, very correctly meeting the conventions of the superior maître d'hôtel, and also conveying that deep simple Italian wisdom in which utter realism merges with sentimental warmth, to produce such a smile of pure affection as he was turning upon an old friend now. Making his way through the crowded room in the wake of the three women, Mark found himself involuntarily aware, as if from the tips of his nerves, of the astonishing, almost unbelievable diversity of obscure origins from which most of the couple of hundred persons about him had sprung, to merge here into a fluid sparkling mass as insubstantial as a chemist's gases. It was a manifestation of futility, yet nearly everybody in this room, with the passionate self-absorption of the *arriviste*, would consider his presence here tonight of pressing importance to himself and, he would probably say, to others also.

Jessie bowed again to Brandon's friends and murmured a greeting as she passed their table on her way out. They sat looking after her and her party, the women's eyes resting appraisingly on the tall, splendid form of Mark Dwyer in his uniform, the men bored.

"Well," said Nancy Rockwood, "there goes the sauce for Brandon."

"Wouldn't you?" asked Denise Jones. She turned to her husband, a forty-four year old child named Willingdon C. P. F. Jones, and said, "Order me another cognac, Bill."

"You've had three already," said the gallant stroke of Brandon's winning crew.

"And I'll have three more if I like," said his wife.

"She's all right," said Gerald Rockwood.

"You ought to know," said Nancy Rockwood nastily, but she and Denise both laughed. "Darling," she said to Denise, "wouldn't it be a scream if that snooty bitch stubbed her toe on that hunk of brass?"

Willingdon C. P. F. Jones winced visibly. He had never grown used to such language as used by his own wife and all her friends. He said rather pompously, "I don't think Jessie Bourne deserves to be called a name like that. Of course Bran shouldn't have married her, but——"

"He did, and I've always been sorry for him," said Rockwood.

"Me too," said his wife. "I can't stand that woman."

"Why?" asked Denise Jones, as if she could not imagine why.

"She's so damn superior." Nancy Rockwood blew a long chute of smoke from her narrow nostrils and her hard mouth and said, "Who the hell does she think she is? If I were Bran Bourne I'd have chucked it long ago."

"I'd have chucked it if I'd been her," said Denise, who knew something too much of Brandon Bourne. "I don't like her either, though. I know what you mean, Nance. I was in school with her. Considering that she's really a nobody that manner of hers is a hell of a nerve."

"Oh, she probably does it to hide something," said Gerald Rockwood indifferently.

"Well, you know how she runs that apartment of theirs. My God, it's so damn perfect it gives me the jitters. And she's so precise and—and what do you call it——"

"Exacting," said Nancy Rockwood, who was more intelligent than Denise. "She is. And cold as a fish."

"Nuts," said Gerald Rockwood unexpectedly. "When you women start showing what you know about other women you make me snort. That gal is as hot as a stove."

"And who asked you?" asked his wife, with hatred.

"Who's giving this party, anyway?"

"Well, she's been a rotten wife for poor Brandon," said Nancy. "Stiff and selfish as they come, I bet you. If I had to live the way she lays it down, I'd have slept around more than he has."

"She used to be worse than she is now," said Denise Jones,

211

in the manner of one who knew from experience what she was talking about. "Jealous as hell."

"I remember," said Nancy. "And after she got over being that way, she got this way. So goddam high-asted I don't see how he stays in the house with her."

"Well, he doesn't—much."

They all laughed.

"I'd still love to see her fall flat on her pan over this," said Nancy Rockwood, indicating the doorway through which Jessie had passed with Mark Dwyer. "She has it coming to her, for my money."

They ordered more drinks.

In the theatre Mark and Jessie found themselves in the seats which Norman Feiner had given to Mark, separate from the rest of their party. They arrived as the house lights were going down. Jessie sighed with relief that they were to be spared momentarily the ordeal of being scrutinized, tabulated, and forced to exchange greetings with people who measured their smiles and bows, in temperature and readiness, by the celebrity of the recipients. She felt a curious sense of contrariness; just because a good many hundreds of persons considered this the most desirable of all places to be on this particular evening, she wanted to whisper to Mark, "Let's slip out and go home quickly before the curtain goes up."

To her surprise he turned his head and looked at her in the nearly complete dark as if she had spoken aloud. He lifted his eyebrows as a way of saying, "What can we do, we are trapped now." They exchanged a glance in pellucid silence, a glance which began as a smile, and having thus established its warmth and gentleness, changed gradually into a statement of clear, wholly requited passion. As he sat with his arms folded, Mark placed the fingers of his left hand, hidden beneath his right sleeve, in the curve of Jessie's left arm, pressing the delicate skin inside the bend of her elbow to find the strong, accelerating pulse. They sat with their heads stiffly poised, staring straight at the stage, though Jessie would later be able to recall nothing beyond an intense excitement distortedly unrelated to the play upon which the curtain was now going up.

XVII

"Mark," she said, when the first act was ending. She spoke close to his ear in the unsibilant whisper which does not carry beyond its intended bounds. "Mark, how on earth are we to get through the rest of this?"

She had in mind as much the great disappointment of the play as their mood, which was grotesquely out of tune with it. The lights went up and Mark turned to her, his face reassuringly expressionless except for the deep warmth of his eyes. She could say anything, she saw, and no matter how she phrased it he would supply what she might omit or conceal.

"I'm afraid Norman was right," he said, also in a dull whisper. "But I hoped not."

"I always expect so much of him and——"

"Particularly in this character of Jim Tilford. After all—he's just Norman's own convictions—with a very ingenious plot to set them off. This weaving between the front and the people at home ought to come off damn well."

"And it has no impact at all," said Jessie. "Or is it us?"

Mark arched his eyebrows. "We'll probably know better in the next act," he said. "But something tells me that 'A Street in the Village of Bastogne' is going to strike this bunch of cannibals like nothing but last week's news."

Jessie nodded. This audience, even more bloodthirsty and hard to inspire than the usual first-night savages, was restless, bored, and typically ahead of the general public who would wait only to get their boys home before slamming shut the doors of their minds on the war and every shade of its meaning.

"Wherever the fault lies, it's damn tough on Norman," said Mark, and Jessie felt the same, but she felt also a ripple of regret and some sense of guilt that her own tense preoccupation with Mark Dwyer was making her the poorest possible spectator at the play. She had so much wanted it to be a success, and she felt now as if she were wilfully withholding something that it was her part to contribute.

"But I can't help it," she smiled at Mark, lowering her eyes, and then, as the smooth, tough, arrogant crowd poured into the aisles, combing through the knots and pairs of men and women with bold, calculating stares, she said, "You go on out and smoke, Mark. I'm staying here."

"So am I," he said, stretching his legs under the vacant chair in front of him.

He observed that Jessie was already involved in the multifaceted small necessity of balancing her attention between him and the greetings of acquaintances whom it would be an error to ignore. She was unwillingly playing the evening's game, but having begun it, she could not withdraw and make herself conspicuous by proving to be more interested in Mark Dwyer than in the empty roundabout of seeing and being seen.

"Hello, Althea," he heard her say with a warm smile to a great, slow-moving mass which he discerned with surprise to be a woman. And he was more surprised to see that Jessie exchanged a wink with the small eye in the vast pink face, as the monolith moved past her up the aisle.

"My God," murmured Mark.

"One of my very best friends," said Jessie, "and I'm not kidding. You ought to hear her sound off about these charming occasions."

"Then why is she here? God knows not because some chappie invited her." He turned his head just enough to see that Althea Crowe was accompanied by a rail-thin mouse of a faded, middle-aged woman.

"Business," said Jessie. "She's just as cynical about it as she looks. That woman with her is Barbara Straughn—you know, the widow of Desmond Straughn. When he was writing all those hits of his, these people used to flock around him and Barbara and lick the shine off their boots. Now Althea looks out for Barbara when all her so-called friends have forgotten her."

"Give me the stockyards any time," said Mark.

"Of course. That's what I mean."

"You'd think to hear us talk," said Mark, "that there isn't a decent human being under this roof."

"Oh, there are lots," said Jessie. She laughed shortly, rather a bitter small laugh, and added, "Perhaps much decenter than we are."

"Don't you believe it."

"Why not? I may let myself lash out now and then, but I try not to forget my mirror while I'm doing it. Have you ever selected some single, small, special motive of your own, like one particular grape out of a cluster, and deliberately forced

214

yourself to follow every shade and quiver of its way with you, from beginning to end?"

"Look here," said Mark, "are you getting any special pleasure out of this?" He smiled, but there was a flicker of something like pain, or it might be irritation, between the abrupt spacing of his heavy brows. Jessie felt troubled and uncomfortable, almost appalled to find that her contrary wish to be away from here had suddenly grown much stronger and in the growing, had momentarily turned her hard against Mark. She had a quick, disagreeable instant of hating herself and him too and anybody else whose identity crossed her mind, perhaps a natural reaction in the midst of so many flashing and insistent personalities. Mark said, "I think if you don't mind I will have a cigarette after all," and Jessie murmured "Of course."

He rose from his chair and she turned upon him a smile of extreme, meaningless cordiality. She was relieved that their places upon the aisle would make it unnecessary for him to disturb anybody else when he returned, and she bent her head over the program in her hands as if the names of the stage managers and technicians, the house staff, and the firms who had made the scenery, costumes, and accessories were keys to the most critically important store of information that she would ever wish to acquire. She stared blankly at the pages, thinking of the terrible phenomenon of a society which collectively professed the keenest admiration and affection for Norman Feiner, and at the same time could watch with absolute relish and perverse excitement while he endured the humiliation of a public failure.

Why, she thought, as she watched Alexander Lowden escort his wife back to their places with false, courtly pomposity, do they not turn their diseased attentions towards *that?* She knew that somewhere on the other side of the theatre her frog-witted brother-in-law must be sitting with Isabel Allen, in seats that he could not properly afford, but which he had surely been brow-beaten into buying; and indeed it was just then that Mark Dwyer returned to his place to tell her so, with a short laugh as he saw the Lowdens across the aisle.

"You never saw such a catfight," said Mark of the hysterical crush in the lobby. "Everybody but Adam's off ox is here, making sure that all the others know it. And your friend there," he whispered, indicating Serena Lowden with his eyebrows, "is a great lady."

Jessie imagined, because she knew it so well, the calm

proud stare with which Serena Lowden had reduced the presence of Isabel Allen in the crowd to the status of an insect, buzzing outside a screened window. Yet on the other hand, she reflected, if one were to see Isabel Allen in her own peculiar milieu, as hostess of one of her chic, shrewdly devised cocktail parties, one might think her a woman of identity and some charm. Her beauty was inarguable, beyond competition; but again, Jessie remembered having seen it crumble into comparative trash against the cool, sad nobility of faces like Serena Lowden's. Jessie moved her shoulders in something more delicate than a shrug of dismissal and whispered, "You will see, Serena will go home after the theatre and Alec will show up alone at the party and make a fool of himself watching Van with Isabel."

"Isabel?" breathed Mark. "At Bucky Whitelaw's? Why?"

Jessie raised her eyebrows. "Something with Phyllis," she murmured. "She likes her."

And Mark thought, as Jessie had supposed he would, that a liking between two such women as Phyllis Whitelaw and Isabel Allen would most probably have come about through the complexities of what he was mentally terming a dry shave for some poor bastard.

"And yet," said Jessie, reading his mind, "Phyllis is not a bad woman."

"Not exactly," he laughed. "Only according to what map you are travelling by."

His low chuckle cleared the air and restored for Jessie her calm which had been so disagreeably shaken. Then the lights went down and in the darkness, completely overriding her malaise, her sense of troubled disorientation, Mark took her left hand and wove its supple fingers lightly between his own, pressing the dry, silky warmth of his palm against hers. She was taken by surprise almost as keen and delicious as if she had been a young girl, but there followed immediately a surge of intense physical joy in his touch which she knew to be anything but young.

She bent her head, lowering her eyes from the gloomy, unconvincing spectacle on the stage, and pressing tightly Mark's fingers still entwined with her own. The program in her lap slid to the floor, and she sat motionless as Mark bent down, not to pick it up, but to place his lips hard in the palm of her hand, and for one bold instant to force his teeth and the tip of his tongue against her perfumed skin. Then he sat back very straight, and with an odd brisk finality he laid her

216

left hand aside, across the right one holding the handbag in her lap. Jessie swallowed in the effort to clear her ears, which seemed to her to be ringing with some great load of sound, though she knew when she looked at the stage that there was nothing to hear since the characters were at this moment engaged in a pantomime of crawling with their guns through deep snow. She drew a long breath, as deeply as she could fill her lungs, and tried like Mark beside her, to keep her attention on the stage.

When the play was over, Jessie said, "Usually I am the first one out, but——"

"Of course not," said Mark. Like her, he was applauding heartily; so were many of the audience, Norman Feiner's friends and the hard-working theatre professionals who rallied for a loyal moment out of the grim knowledge that this could happen to any of them in turn, and would again as it had before. The critics, their bored faces set and sour, had slid out before the final curtain. And now the showoff spectators began to get to their feet, the fat-jowled balding men who were impatient to be outside where they could light their cigars, and their women instantly identifiable. Some were wives, with complicated arrangements of curled grey hair and faces that were curious mixtures of flint and slop, hard in surface expression and in their greedy eyes, but puddles of sagging over-massaged tissue beneath. Or the women were dolls or babes whose badge of investiture was the most beautiful shade of dyed hair that they could possibly achieve, worn in unbelievable lacquered mountings and turnings known as the upsweep, or in great cascades and falls whose vulgarity was only exceeded by the complacency with which it was displayed. But all the women escorted by all the loud and terrible men were uniformly sheltered from the zephyrs of a mild October night by fur capes and wraps and stoles of the most exaggerated cost; they were all studded with supreme bad taste in the form of too much, too loud, too bulky jewelry; and they all inched up the aisle past Jessie and Mark, clutching the trophies of their hunting in predatory fingers tipped by glittering blood-red claws.

Therese Street and Mart Ferguson were taking a curtain call alone, gravely bowing to the charitable applause which they accepted for the personal tribute that it was. They had worked beyond ordinary exhaustion, their faces beneath their make-up were bone-white, their hands quiet with the stillness which Jessie could see to be stark control. She felt desperately sorry for them, not because the play was a failure—that was the natural hazard of their profession—but because she knew that they really loved Norman Feiner and had only gone through with this crushing experience for his sake, meanwhile refusing offers of other plays which would probably have been successes. She thought now of her own words when she reminded Mark that there were indeed good and decent people in this theatre tonight.

"Do you think we have to go backstage?" asked Mark, when the applause had pattered out, and they were able to rise and begin to move.

Jessie sighed. "I told Helen we would meet them there. But it will be——"

"I know."

"Why don't we wait in the alley? We will see Norman and all the others at the party, and they would probably be grateful to us for not going back now."

"They would probably be more grateful if Buck would call the party off."

"So would I," said Jessie quickly. She moved lightly ahead of Mark and through a row of empty seats, heading for a side exit which opened on the alley by the stage door. Mark followed her, his eyes resting with appreciation on her slender figure, more elegant in the stiff black and gold lamé gown which she had said was six years old, than that of any other woman in sight. They stepped into the dark alley, which Mark was surprised to find quite empty. Evidently nobody was yet ready to leave the theatre from the stage door, and the street end of the alley was blocked by a shuffling, raucous, fluid mob who had come to watch the celebrities at the first night. Just now the horde were pitching about and clawing one another in their struggle to get at some motion-picture star who would almost find the clothes ripped from her back by the time she had fought her way across the pavement to her motor.

"Some more of our charming mores," said Jessie, turning her back upon the spectacle.

Mark had paid no attention. He put out his hand and drew her close to the wall, under the shadow of the balcony fire escape.

"My dear," he said, as if with difficulty. "Look at me."

She moved her head uneasily and murmured, "Oh, that uniform is so conspicuous."

"When my back is turned," he said, with a glance towards the mélée in the street, "I look like any other G I."

She shook her head again as he took her in his arms. But she felt helpless, carried far beyond the resisting thought that this was a preposterous, a dreadful place to find herself being kissed with commanding strength and passion. She felt the rare and lovely sensation of his lifting her outside the limits of her will, though she kept her elbows quite primly at her sides while he shielded her from the sight of the wild strangers in the street. When her lips were free she bent her head until her forehead rested on his chest, and she heard herself breathe, "Oh Mark . . . my . . . I . . ."

"I know," he said. His voice was thick. "I too."

They turned and stood waiting, lifting their faces to the gritty gasoline-laden air which hung over the echoing alley.

Dereliction is the fate of great houses like the Whitelaw palace on upper Fifth Avenue, and tonight it seemed to Jessie that the vast rooms disdained the strange company rattling about in them as old Mrs. Dominick Whitelaw herself would have done had she come back to earth. The house was destined to disappear, it had been sold during the war to a syndicate of apartment-house builders and it would be torn down as soon as new building became possible. Meanwhile it was used sporadically, casually, and inelegantly by Bucky and Phyllis Whitelaw in their passages between half a dozen residences and resorts to which their restless, rootless variations of mood propelled them. Bucky Whitelaw was rich enough to consider the fantastic town house, once called the masterpiece of Stanford White, a joke rather than a headache; he had no love for it and doubted whether any of his family had ever had. The house had been intrinsic to the power pattern, the only imaginable setting for the monstrous twelve-course dinners, the solemn upholstered receptions, the coldly magnificent balls, with which the stamp of multimillions had come down upon Society from its origin in the jungles of railroads, coal, oil, and the bloody battles of the incipient Steel Corporation.

And now in a pair of imposingly overfurnished drawing-rooms (the ballroom floor had been shut up for years) a hundred or more of the new elect of New York moved carelessly about, nearly oblivious of their surroundings, for they were intent upon themselves alone, whether in actual self-concentration or in the mirrors of other personalities. The background of carved seventeenth-century panelling, bloated tapestries, forbidding Jacobean chairs, gimp, gilt, crimson damask and Brobdingnagian chandeliers made no more and no less impression upon them than the mirrored and all-shades-of-white Park Avenue room where they might find themselves tomorrow night or the Hollywood swimming-pool where they might be next week.

Phyllis Whitelaw with her perverse affectation of wilful vulgarity and hardness, her cadaverously pale face, her lank dark hair, her invariable black sheathlike gown, her sullen manner, was a bizarre mistress for this incredible house. Jessie wondered why the Whitelaws used it at all, but she knew too that the answer lay in Phyllis's twisted, hostile personality. She had a sharp taste for distorting her heredity and its accoutrements to the roughest crudities of the contemporary world. She used the Whitelaw house for this purpose, dismissing any thought of running it as its style and size demanded. She kept most of its rooms closed and she had never considered the impossible, the assembling of a staff of servants such as the place required. She could never have found them anyway, she shrugged, and thank God for that. When she gave a party like this she called in enough caterer's help to leave her feeling less responsible for the pleasure of her guests than a total stranger.

"What's the use?" she drawled, lounging with the inevitable cigarette and highball on a couch in the gloomy library. "We're hardly ever here and the only kind of party I can stand is where nobody gives a damn."

Moving away from the dark small huddle of people around Phyllis, whence rose the aroma of sycophancy like mist over a bog, Jessie felt like a small child minding its manners for having sought out the hostess to bid her good evening. Phyllis's attitude conveyed that any such person was far queerer than herself who by normal standards should have been standing in the centre hall greeting her guests at the top of the stairs.

"I guess Bucky's outside somewhere," she said to Jessie. "Poor Norman, how that play stinks . . ."

Henry Greenberg made a remark, intended to be ruefully humorous, to the effect that Bucky would find his losses the most malodorous part of the disappointment; and as she left the room Jessie found herself marvelling as she had before, at the cheapness of the people to whom Oliver Whitelaw had fled in his headlong rush to escape. But now as she saw him standing in the foyer between the drawing-rooms, quiet, pleasant, and in spite of himself a natural complement to the exaggerated setting, she realized that he was as helpless as Gulliver to free himself of the myriad threads which entangled him in his origin. In startlingly different degree, thought Jessie, he was in the same situation as everybody else. And just then she saw Mark, from whom she had purposely wandered away, for she did not intend to spend the whole evening at his side, catching the eye of a waiter who was passing with a tray of glasses of champagne. She saw Mark wink deliberately at the man, she heard a quick, quiet word between them in a totally unintelligible tongue, and she saw a grin of thorough satisfaction cross Mark's face as the waiter went on about his serving. Her curiosity was extreme, but later she found it no surprise for Mark to explain that the man was a boyhood friend, the son of Bohunk neighbors on the block.

"He's doing all right, too," Mark reported with approval. "He's one of the owners of that catering business. When they're short of help these days he just pitches in himself."

The party was in its early, uneasy, unfocussed stage. The guests of honor had not arrived, and Jessie knew that they would put off the ominous moment as long as they could, for to mount the stairs or step out of the elevator into this shifting sand of collective emotions, whether good or bad, loyal or treacherous, pitying or malicious, would be a horrible experience for them. But enough other people were about now to create a sense of fluidity and motion involving some choice of company. The high, nervous, collective chatter of a large party was already under way.

Preston Shaw came towards Jessie, saying, "Don't you want a drink, Jess?" She reflected, while answering with a smile that she did not want one, that there was probably nothing else the poor man could say which would make the slightest sense. She saw some people clustered in the rear drawing-room across the stair-hall; the musical-comedy actress Eva Moorhead, laughing and incredibly pretty with her blonde curls and sparkling beaded dress; her present beau Simon Trumbull who used his millions as fingers with which to probe into every provocative pie; the theatrical producer Laurence Millstein whose vein of golden luck had never failed him yet; Maureen Stillman sharing some unroarious joke with Sam Lee.

"Let's go and see what it's all about," said Jessie, moving

along with Preston Shaw. That knot of people were all friends of his who would absorb his tragic presence effortlessly for a few moments; then somebody would have to carry him on to another momentarily willing prop. The elevator door opened as Jessie went past, and among the chattering people who trooped through it she saw without surprise the chill face of her brother-in-law and the seemingly fragile, floating beauty of Isabel Allen. She exchanged greetings with them in casual monosyllables and as she had anticipated, the pair moved in the opposite direction from her. Isabel Allen was exquisitely dressed in azure chiffon, her figure so delicate, her breasts so perfect that it was only after a purely aesthetic response to their loveliness that one realized the cool wiliness with which they were displayed. There were by now several dozen of the most beautiful women in New York assembled here, but Jessie realized again, as she had before, that none of them had the unbelievable natural perfection of this otherwise ordinary creature. Yet as Isabel Allen passed her, the lights from the massive chandelier slanting directly upon her face, Jessie saw that beneath the strangely stupid lilac eyes there lay uncharacteristic dark smudges; that these had been treated with the most artful possible maquillage; that about the delicately pouting painted mouth there were indications of unmistakable tenseness, and that the smoothness of the doll-like brow was held there by sheer force of will.

Such tale-telling was so unusual in this woman's stock-in-trade of a face that Jessie's curiosity was aroused. Of course Isabel Allen must be bored to despair by Van Fielding, but she would never have allowed that irritation so to jeopardize her looks. After all, it was her business to be bored at times. And certainly she must be pleased to be at this party tonight; it was of signal importance to her to be seen here. No, thought Jessie, she is in trouble, very bad trouble because in Isabel Allen's world nothing short of violence and terror would be recognized as trouble. Mere debt or scandal or the loss of a desirable man would be commonplaces.

And then something struck Jessie as queerly alarming. Perhaps because she was moving slowly across the great stair hall with Preston Shaw, and his tormented silence made it unnecessary for her to make smalltalk with him, her attention roved. She knew that she was nodding and smiling and lightly greeting people as she passed them; but her eyes, quite contrary to what she thought was interesting, were following Isabel Allen into the farther drawing-room, where Jessie had not yet been.

There, half in profile and half in a great Florentine mirror, she saw Alexander Lowden, who had left his wife at home and arrived here even sooner than Jessie would have thought. She watched with sardonic amusement as he greeted Isabel Allen and Van Fielding, a touch of the patronizing in his manner. But then, in total amazement, Jessie saw the elevator door slide open again, and, behind the shoulders of the women who stepped out first, the narrow, nasty face of Jack Spanier. How on earth, she thought, could he have got here! —not even Phyllis with her tastes would invite him.

But here he was. And with his cheap, loathsome way of combing a crowd, his eyes seeming to Jessie to perform the same function as the rows of needle teeth through which the shark strains its prey, he took his time in deciding to whom to speak, just what he wanted to do. Meanwhile, and Jessie was to remember later the abnormal sensation of fear, almost a prickling of the scalp, with which she observed it, Spanier stood with his hands vulgarly in his trousers pockets, his shoulders even more vulgarly slouched against a lozenged oak panel, and with the coolest insolence he stared at the tableau of Isabel Allen and her two pretentious laughingstocks. But Jack Spanier was not laughing. A beautiful red-haired woman gave him the empty high-voiced greeting of "Jack! Darling!" which he answered with a careless monosyllable, all the while keeping his rodent's eyes upon the trio across the room. Except for its permanent eager-greedy alertness, his face was inscrutable. Jessie turned from the sight, swept by disgusted resentment that through Brandon Bourne she should be linked with that ignominious situation because his fool of a brother-in-law was part of it.

Her outraged self-righteousness was short-lived. Preston Shaw had wandered on ahead of her and she was alone, going towards the rear drawing-room, when a voice said "Good evening, Jess," and she found her right hand in that of a tall, heavy man who was looking at her with the lightest possible tinge of irony in his otherwise cordial smile; or so she thought, for this was a person whom she would be profoundly relieved never to have to see. But life was not like that.

"Good evening, Enoch," she said. "How are you?" (Idiot, she damned herself. Is that the scope of your ingenuity?)

"You're looking lovely," said Enoch Starr. "I saw you in the theatre." He meant more precisely that he had watched her in the theatre, and Jessie regretted once again that she had ever embarked upon this evening. She was glad that Mark Dwyer was not beside her at this moment, that she could not see him and did not know just where he was.

"When did you get back, Enoch?" She asked not because she wanted to know but because of her haste to throw the unavoidable moment of conversation upon him and his concerns. Also because she did not want to see him at all, now or ever, she looked straight at him, laughing and consciously coloring her expression with raillery. She knew that they made a pleasant and decorative sight, just the sort of attractive and amusing accessory to such a party that hostesses hope to assemble. Inwardly Jessie felt as if her stomach were poised upon the edge of a cliff, sure to be dumped into space by any current of motion or air.

"Oh, quite a while ago," replied Starr. "End of July. I was stationed in Rome, you know. Over a year."

"I didn't know."

"Have you ever been in Rome?" he asked. He fixed her glance as tightly and wickedly with his twinkling eye as if he had taken her wrist in his hand and twisted it.

"Why—yes. I think so," said Jessie gravely. She could have killed him without a qualm, yet why should he not tease her at this level of precise mischief, had she not laid herself open to it? Actually he had always behaved impeccably, he was altogether a gentleman, not a stuffed and mounted specimen of gentleman either. Jessie hated him now with flashing fury, and in the same instant she knew that it was not he, a charming man, whom she hated, but herself. No, she thought, pursuing the sniping, devilish smalltalk with the same apparent skill as he, no it is not even myself because of whom I am swamped by this flood of hatred, it is Brandon Bourne.

"I used to fly down to Capri for week ends," said Enoch Starr. "Of course Capri was a mess with all those G I trippers, but if you knew Capri well you could still set yourself up pretty nicely."

"And of course you knew Capri well," said Jessie, deliberately laying another twig on the fire because in a moment she meant to extinguish the small flame with one figurative stamp of her foot.

"Of course. It's not the same as it was nine years ago—but I had no trouble recognizing it."

"I'm sure I would not have remembered it," she said, bringing down the foot. "Because I have such an impossibly bad memory, you know."

"I wouldn't know," he said, changing his expression and turning suddenly impersonal, as a spectacularly beautiful, very young woman swept up to them, saying "Oh, there you are, darling! I've been looking—" She was English, and a stranger.

"Jessie, I don't think you have met my wife. Susanne— Mrs. Bourne—" Enoch Starr could not have been more utterly at ease, nor Jessie.

"How do you do?" she murmured, as Mrs. Starr babbled some triviality and it became miraculously simple within a moment to drift away from the couple. But now instead of following her first, unimportant notion of joining Sam Lee, Jessie felt as if the whole concatenation of horrible feelings stirred together inside her in these past few minutes—actually much less than five minutes—was about to explode and make a spectacle of her. She was standing as it happened just at the foot of the great sweeping red-carpeted stairs with their gilded lacework balustrade, and the steps beckoned her upward with the sudden driving realization that she had to be alone. She would move slowly, she would melt so inconspicuously away from this floor of the house where the party was going on that nobody would notice her absence or care. There is a way of moving in a situation like this which is artful in its aimlessness, and Jessie had learned it very long ago.

She began to slide up the staircase in this vague and cloudlike way and as she moved a thought slashed through her mind which made of the party, moving and glittering and chattering below, an utter brawl. I do not care, she told herself contemptuously, I do not care by one nerve, I have not cared for a great many years. But she realized with a fresh surge of hatred that if she should pause now and look behind her, she would see not alone Isabel Allen but a distinct number of other women on account of whom Brandon Bourne had seared and scarred her in the long past before she had lost the capacity to suffer. All these experiences had finally come together into one hideous legacy, the brutal and shameless invasion of her privacy. Everybody else, her reason argued, is in the same situation, such things are only unendurable as they are unique, and this is commonplace. But her encounter with Enoch Starr had roused to fury the ancient smouldering accumulation of her bitterness. Such a thing, she knew, should never have happened to her, it was alien, alien as crime to every fibre of her nature. The episode was comparatively meaningless in this milieu where her life was lived. Yet

225

to her it was the dregs of humiliation, and she had never been able to override that shame by rationalizing that she had only done out of killing despair that to which Brandon Bourne had driven her. I must be alone, she thought now, I do not care what anybody thinks down there, I am suffocating behind this mask of blitheness, I must be alone. She moved on up the stairs.

XVIII

She knew that beyond Phyllis Whitelaw's bathroom, modernized but still a *fin de siècle* parody of pink marble, enormous redundant fixtures, and rampant gold dolphins, there was a queer, old-fashioned dressing-room redolent of the days when magnificence was measured by wasted space. Here were cupboards and dress-closets sixteen feet high, from whose racks maids must use an extension pole to reach down the gowns; not a mere dressing-table stood against twenty feet of mirrored wall, but the whole wall was one continuous installation of built-in dressing-table, with such a superfluity of drawers and compartments that one would need a catalogue in order to put one's hand on a particular object. Jessie knew that there could be nobody in this room except Phyllis's maid, and she had seen the maid downstairs upon arriving at the house, superintending the caterer's women in the ladies' coatroom. So she felt sure of not being intruded upon when she slipped into the dressing-room, far from the stream of the party downstairs. With a sagging sensation of relief she turned the heavy silver door-handle. But as the door moved open Jessie started back, realizing that there was someone in the dark room. She heard a sharp gasp, heard the stir of a person startled and frightened, and heard a high, artificially levelled voice cry out, "Who is it?" The voice was the voice of a woman who had been weeping violently and who was able to speak now only because of panic-stricken urgency.

"I'm so sorry," said Jessie quickly. "I thought—" and she stepped backwards, drawing shut the door. She felt a nerve jumping in her temple.

"Oh," said the woman in the room. "Perhaps—I'm afraid I am in your way."

"No," said Jessie. "No, no. Please. I disturbed you." But before she could entirely shut the door a light was switched on, and she was confronted by the sight of Phyllis's friend Elizabeth Betts, tensely twisted to a sitting position on the edge of the long massage-table in the centre of the room, her thin hands clutching the edge of the pink leather mattress. Jessie could see that she had been lying face downwards and had sprung to this attitude upon being disturbed. She appeared in every visible way a wreck; her blonde hair rough and rumpled, her face puffy, streaked, and shapeless—the woman known to the fashionable world as perhaps its most exquisite, flawlessly perfect ornament. She moved her left hand in a curiously clumsy beckoning motion and said heavily, "Come in. I recognized your voice."

"But," said Jessie, miserably embarrassed. "But—I——"

"You had the same idea I had," said Elizabeth Betts. "You had some reason for wanting to be alone in here. Why not? Hell!" she exclaimed, with savageness of which Jessie would never have believed her capable, nor her sudden profanity either, "how do I know you aren't worse off than I?"

Jessie stood nervously in the doorway, intent upon getting away.

"Now that you're here," said Mrs. Betts, "I wish you'd come in."

"But," said Jessie again, helpless.

"Don't ask me why!" said the distraught woman. "Come in and shut the door!"

Jessie stepped across the marble threshold and silently closed the door behind her.

"If," she said, trying to find a word that would not be intolerably banal, "if there is anything——"

"Anything—!" Elizabeth Betts repeated the word in a shrill, but muffled cry. "Anything you can do? Can you put this whole drunken cockeyed shattered world together again? Can you give me back my—my——"

Jessie had never felt so crushed by inadequacy, dumbness, and helplessness. In all her life she had never had an encounter like this, a brutal shove into the arena of another woman's naked hysteria. I have held too much aloof, she thought now, and kept my mouth shut and my head up with the same stubborn pride as Elizabeth here. And now it is only accident that she has blown up and I have been swept into the wreckage, it could perfectly well have been the other way about. Perhaps it has happened just because she is so nearly a stranger, perhaps there is a design about this into which I am supposed to fit for some reason involving me too. She stared at Elizabeth Betts, whose delicate nose was red, whose fastidious mouth hung slackly open, whose beautiful eyelids were crudely swollen. My God, thought Jessie, my God, shall I keep on trying to think what to say or shall I let her sweep me into her maelstrom? Perhaps that is what she needs, perhaps there is nothing else for me to do. And quite without further deliberating she asked, "Do you really feel so terribly about Philip, Liz?"

"Not Philip," said Elizabeth Betts, with a dry sob, "not exactly Philip. But—" she leaned forward and Jessie saw the veins come up in blue cords on the backs of her hands, "the mess. The thing that's happened to my life. I can't stand it," she said, in a sudden dead, leaden tone, far more distressing than the high pitch of hysteria. "I wasn't made for it. I can't endure it. You have no idea—" she paused.

"But," said Jessie, groping too clumsily for some rationalization, "but you were not happy with Philip."

"Of course not," said Elizabeth Betts. "Happy? Who is happy? In many ways I loathed him. But I had got used to that. And I had a life, do you see what I mean?—there was shape and form so you knew where you were—*who* you were. Do you know what it feels like," she said in a sudden outcry, "not to know who you are? Not to be anybody?" She thrust her chin forward and stared with her ruined eyes at Jessie.

"You know, Liz," said Jessie, her voice as gentle and slow as she could make it, "nothing would make you believe it just now, but that could not be true of you. Not to be anybody. You always were somebody—much more of somebody than Philip. In every way."

"Oh—family perhaps, or money. But that's not what I mean. Just because I was Elizabeth Vanderpool and inherited a lot of money, do you think anybody cares about that? They don't give a damn. I thought we had a lot of friends, Philip and I, I had always taken the—the—you know, the whole shape of existence for granted. And now I'm just another divorced woman, a drug on a glutted market, I haven't four friends who think otherwise about me. It's too God-damn much trouble," she said. "I know. I remember how I used to feel when people got divorced. You meant to be kind to Vera or Claire or whoever she was but it was such a nuisance to fit her in, pretty soon you just naturally sloughed her off."

Jessie sighed. She understood so thoroughly what Elizabeth was trying to explain that she could have begged her to leave it all unsaid; but that was not what she felt that chance had brought her here to do. There was a strange element of compulsion here, it was as if she had been ordered to listen to all this and she was far too shrewd not to sense exactly why. She looked at Elizabeth Betts and tried, though it seemed grotesque, to give her a small smile of encouragement or sympathy; and just then Elizabeth leaned forward sharply on the table again and cried, "Have you got any idea what life turns into when this happens to you? Do you know?"

Jessie would have said earlier that she thought she knew but now she only shook her head weakly.

"Well I'll tell you!" cried Elizabeth. "If you had the happiest marriage in three continents I'd tell you. But you haven't. Your marriage is as bad a mess as mine was—worse, some people say."

She gasped then at her own brutality, but she was far too gone to care. She watched Jessie look at her with utter calm and by her silence, agree.

"I know all about it," said Elizabeth Betts with rasping urgency in her voice which belied everything that Jessie had ever known about her before. "I know so much about it that I'll go stark staring mad if I don't tell somebody what I know. I know what it's like to be so wretched in a marriage that you sit for years on end dreaming about what heaven it would be to get out of the damned thing. And then something happens and you *are* out—all the way out in a howling wilderness that you'd never even suspected before. It springs up around you like—like weeds. Big weeds, miles higher than your head." She gestured with both hands.

"But Liz," said Jessie slowly. "People are devoted to you. Honestly they are. Not so very *many* of them, perhaps, but who has more than two or three real friends in the whole world anyway?"

"I know. The way you feel about Helen Lee. The way I feel about Phyllis. But that's not what I mean. You can't hang your whole existence around some friend's neck like the albatross. And besides," she added, in a queer, insinuating slide of tone, "did you ever hear of pride?"

"Oh—forgive me," said Jessie.

"That's the kind of hell it is. Pride and keeping up a façade and having to tell all the lies and do all the contortions that that means. Having to go back to manipulating the trifles of life the way you did when you were a debutante. Do you remember that little slice of hell?"

"My God," said Jessie. "And you were called the most beautiful and popular girl who ever came out in New York."

"I've been called the most beautiful something or other all my life," said Elizabeth, "but here we are tonight. And as for popularity—you know what that is. Slaving to set up this idiot's delight, this endless chain of something to do, somewhere to go, somebody to be seen with, until you have them all thinking you're practically impossible to reach, and they all start galloping after you. That's not even fun when you're young, but it's comparatively easy. Now I am forty-one years old and I tell you I'm too tired! I'm too old! I can't," she wailed, bursting into a torrent of sobs and flinging herself face down on the table again. "I can't! I can't! I can't!" She wept wildly.

Jessie sat rigid, appalled to horrified silence. Once she looked nervously about the room, as if a glass of water or some aromatic spirits could be of help to Elizabeth, and then she leaned back limply in the low slipper-chair, resigned that there was nothing whatever that she could do. To go and put her arm around the shattered woman on the table and make the motions and speak the words of overt sympathy would be a mistake. Elizabeth Betts even in this dreadful condition was not a woman who invited such demonstrations, and Jessie was not one who could give them, to anyone short of the most intimate possible friend—to no one, in fact, except Helen Lee. And Jessie knew well that it was precisely because they were not intimate friends that Elizabeth Betts had burst this dam tonight. Jessie sat quite still, once raising her eyes and meeting in the mirror-lined room uncountable multiplications of the wretched tableau made by the sobbing woman on the massage-table and herself, pale, her lips pinched, her eyes dark with distress, shrunken together on the small chair.

There was a long silence, during which Elizabeth Betts' sobs gradually faded, and finally subsided into deep, intermittent gasps. At last she raised her rumpled head, looked at Jessie, and said in a low, very controlled voice, "So you see what it is. If I were like a lot of women we know, with a profession or a job to keep me busy, or a family to keep me company—but this way I am honestly afraid I shall go mad. I wasn't prepared for my life to turn into this, nothing had ever led me to expect it. The mere question of *men!*" She made a dreadful grimace as if she had tasted aloes. "You can spell that one out for yourself. Would you pay off for any wretched dinner and evening at the theatre? Or let your friends' husbands—and by the way they are mostly swine—think you wanted *that* badly to be taken out? Would you be driven to combing through all the crackpots and homos who have presentable clothes, just for somebody to take you somewhere or fill a place at a dinner table? And if you couldn't endure any of that, then where are you? Back on the mercy of all the married friends you had before, who think an extra woman a visitation of the devil and I've thought so many a time myself. So then you turn to the other women who are in the same boat as you, and could you spend your evenings dining cosily and playing a little quiet gin with them? My *God!*" cried Elizabeth Betts, driving her jewelled fingers into the wreckage of her lovely hair and shoving it back from her temples.

Jessie had nothing to say, she was still sitting humped uncharacteristically in the least possible amount of space on the seat of her chair, with her hands clasped tightly around one knee.

"That God damn *book!*" said Elizabeth Betts, gritting her teeth. "That engagement book on your desk, with its pages staring at you and staring and staring——"

"But Liz!" Jessie found herself interrupting. "You are always invited somewhere. We meet you everywhere we go."

"And what do you think is involved in that?" replied Elizabeth. "Effort and planning and effort and coping and effort and—there it is. Entertaining without a host—the most nerve-racking damned ordeal. Keeping yourself in circulation. Plotting and thinking and wondering and twisting through a needle's eye to make sure you aren't overlooked. And why do you care? Because the moment they get used to your not being there, that's the end of you. And I can tell you that a string of blank evenings ahead of you on the pages of that horrible book is enough to put you in the madhouse. And the whole thing is false and phony and strained, you must never let anybody think you've nothing to do, they only want you so long as everybody else wants you too. The things you learn. The things you realize. Never, never telephone anybody after dinner in the evening—they might think you're alone with nothing to do. Suppose they thought that! Just suppose!"

The two women fell into a silence so deep, so pervasive, and so expressive that neither could think of another word to add to the torrent that had surged over the dam. Not a syllable of the lesson had been lost on Jessie. The dreadful immediacy and concreteness of Elizabeth Betts' troubles had pushed Jessie's more inchoate distress into remote perspective. She had come here to this queer isolated room to escape ominous vibrations of past and present anxiety; she had not expected to be handed a dossier of facts applicable to a possible future. Though no single statement of Elizabeth's had been a complete surprise, Jessie found herself astonished at the sum of them. She realized now that she had presumed Elizabeth's beauty and money and position and charm to have made her as desirable alone as she had ever been with Philip. The war too had obscured the real problem. Jessie had enjoyed her existence while Brandon was away, but that had been largely a matter of casual companionship with other women whose husbands were also at war, an atypical interval in the stage-managed gladiatorial spectacle which Elizabeth's outburst had proved her stratum of society to be. Jessie had known it all before, in a way; she had always known it. That is why, she thought, I cling to the elements of my life which are alien to the jungle. They may be my only resource some day, they may save me if . . . if . . .

Elizabeth Betts raised her head suddenly. She looked at Jessie with the cool mask and spoke in the clear ripple which were the face and the voice that the world knew: "Now," she said, "I am going to take on the beautiful Mrs. Betts again."

She slid from the massage-table and with a graceful motion swept off her dress, shaking it out and reaching for a hanger on which to place it. She went into the adjoining bathroom, as slender and fresh of body in her fragile single undergarment as an eighteen-year-old girl. Jessie heard her splashing in the shower; then in a nimbus of fragrance she returned to the dressing-room, switched on the banks of theatrical lights around the dressing-table, and sat down to restore the work of art that was her face and hair. She chatted as she worked, touching casually upon this, that, or the other among personalities and happenings, as if no puff of wind had ever disarranged one iota of her poise. Though her skin was astonishing for the age that she had admitted, she loaded it with the cream-colored paste maquillage which accounted for Phyllis Whitelaw's gloomy pallor. The effect on Elizabeth Betts was quite different, she emerged a pearl of subtle lustre. She brushed and shaped her fairy eyebrows, blued and oiled her eyelids, put a drop of some drug in each eye, after which nothing but knowledge before the fact could have betrayed

232

the state in which Jessie had found her. Jessie sat during the whole performance trying not to watch too closely, but tempted to do so by the same naïve wonderment with which she remembered in her earliest childhood watching her mother make up in the theatre. This which Elizabeth Betts was doing involved infinitely more artifice, and in such different degree that Jessie could have shuddered at its implications.

With her dress replaced, as unaccountably unmussed as she herself, Elizabeth Betts sorted out her jewels from the heap in which she had flung them upon the dressing-table, put them on with grave attentiveness, and stood up.

"Let us," she said, slipping her arm through Jessie's, "go and be gay."

The noise of the party had reached the shrill unison key which to unthinking ears meant success, a good party. Jessie was not quite so sure. In any such gathering there were always certain people who drank enough, quickly enough, to prod them to the production of this kind of noise. Their unmirthful laughter, their insincere cries of delight as they greeted one another, their mercurial encounters and partings were so much stage-setting. One responded to it or not according to one's mood or one's capacity for delusion. Jessie had never felt so remote or so indifferent as when she reached the bottom of the stairs and watched Elizabeth Betts melt off into the crowd. Then Mark Dwyer appeared beside her, his eyes full of question and anxiety. She realized that she must have been gone for a long time and she felt immensely glad to see him.

"Hello," she said, smiling reassurance.

"Are you—all right? Are you well?" he asked. His voice was troubled.

"As can be expected. Do you think I might have a little whisky?"

"Food too? There's—" he indicated the stream of decorative traffic flowing in the direction of the dining-room.

"I'm not hungry. But why don't we just—circulate a bit and then——"

"Then by all means," said Mark.

They moved slowly towards the dining-room beyond the rear drawing-room, where a pair of carved oak doors had been thrown open upon a spectacle which Jessie said, "looks like the last scene of *Don Giovanni*, does it not?"

George Stillman breezed up to them holding a plate of food and talking cheerfully around a mouthful.

"Goddam," he said. "Quite a sight, ain't it?" He could be speaking in derision or he could be impressed, though he had seen this room often before. The Sargent portraits of Bucky Whitelaw's parents hung against the crimson damask walls, flanked by less spectacular portraits of old Mr. and Mrs. Dominick Whitelaw, he with his mutton-chops, she with her incrustation of diamonds. Great golden girandoles dripping with baccarat prisms flashed brilliance from every corner of the room. The crystal chandelier when brought from France had been the newspaper sensation of its day. The furniture was overwhelming. The carpet had already been promised to the Metropolitan Museum.

The setting seemed haunted by the heavy-bellied lords of industrial empire and their forbidding wives, and by the ranks of liveried men who had served them terrapin and canvas-backs, haunches of Southdown mutton, giant prize asparagus and grapes and peaches sent down in cottonwool from the family hothouses, architectural extravaganzas from the pastry chef, Lafite of '65 and Romanée of '95 and Cordon Rouge laid down in thousands before the vintage came on the market. And now a handful of hired waiters hurried about, indistinguishable in their black from more than a few of the guests, clearing away discarded plates and glasses and replenishing the dishes and platters on the buffet table where people helped themselves according to their natures, some with picking indifference and some with fervid greed.

"Actually," said Jessie, watching the scene from the corner where they stood, "it is as fascinating a study in anachronism as you will ever see."

"That old pirate would have a stroke," said George, glancing at the portrait of Bucky's grandfather.

"There are probably not ten people in this house whom he would have let in," said Mark.

"Over his dead body," said Jessie. "And as for her—" she indicated the old lady with her eyebrows. "Can you imagine what she would say of Isabel Allen?"

"Isabel hell," said George Stillman between his teeth. "What about her grandson's wives?"

"For that matter," said Jessie demurely, "what about me?"

"You? You are at least semi-acceptable, *Mrs. Bourne*. I bet your mother-in-law thinks the Whitelaws were parvenus."

234

"Oh, she does," said Jessie with a laugh. "But what do you suppose she thinks about me?"

"Well, whatever it is, it hasn't killed her yet," said George, with a wink which Jessie understood too well to dare to notice it.

"You know," said Mark, watching the people at the buffet, "I think Phyllis does these things very well, considering the elements she is balancing."

"Very well indeed," said Jessie quickly. "She might be a little warmer or more gracious if that were her nature, but her idea is sound. Did you ever go to a party in a house like this before the—I almost said before the revolution. Anyway, before the last war? Mother used to tell me all about them when she came home. Supper at little gilt tables, with your long gloves on—oyster patties and chaudfroid of chicken and fancy ices in spun sugar nests. And a string quartet out there on the stair landing. And now look."

They all broke into laughter as they watched the most admired and envied brains and talent and money and fame from a dozen different circles, clamoring, gesturing, waving forks and glasses, reaching past one another to the buffet table, where the great silver platters and footed dishes were set forth full of corned beef hash, baked beans, hot dogs, kosher dill pickles, potato salad, and cold cuts.

"And I hope," said George with a snicker, "that the old girl up there on the wall really appreciates the dessert. I'm going to have some now, how about you, Jess?"

She shook her head, laughing.

"Sure?" asked George. "Goddam, usually when I want Lindy's cheesecake I have to stagger there at three a.m. to get it."

He disappeared into the crowd and Jessie moved away with Mark. How fine it would be, she thought, if we could leave now and why, for that matter, did we come in the first place? But she recognized among the other hard truths revealed by Elizabeth Betts' gashing of the silken curtain of expediency, the familiar sophism of wishing to be included in something for which one had no real taste; indeed which one might hold in contempt or dread. It was all very unpleasant, and she felt tired, helplessly peevish, like a small child dragged by its mother on a shopping tour, who flings itself down in the crowded aisle of a department store and bursts into howls. She became so conscious of the image that she could not help laughing at it, and thus she appeared to be in the best of spirits as they came upon Norman Feiner who stood talking with Bucky Whitelaw and Hall Peters. Mark put his hand upon Norman's shoulder and Jessie pressed his fingers warmly, but neither said anything about the play because they knew that Norman must already be exhausted by the thoughtless weight thrown upon him of hundreds of false assurances that the play was "wonderful," and "sure to be a hit, darling." He looked tired and strained, but not by any means tragedy-stricken, he was far too seasoned in the theatre for that.

"I told you it stank," he said quietly to Jessie and Mark.

"It doesn't," said Mark. "But I think you were bucking something almost hopeless, Norman."

"I've thought of that too," said Norman with quiet sarcasm. "I wouldn't accuse you of escapism, my boy, but just why are you leaving for Europe on Monday?"

"You could leave too," said Mark.

"I could also stay here," said Norman quickly, "and try to keep them remembering what the hell it's all about and incidentally dig myself out of hock. You are better fixed, that's all."

"With exactly what?" asked Mark.

"Too much of something," said Bucky Whitelaw. "What's the good of your job in Europe if people act here the way they did tonight?"

He was speaking of the audience at the theatre, but Jessie saw Mark's eye sweep the crowded dining-room behind them and return to glance at Oliver Whitelaw with deprecation that was almost pitying as a comment upon his confused thinking. In these past days Jessie had not once heard Mark voice an emotion which she knew to be straining always at the brakes of his mind, his revulsion from the greedy, reckless spectacle of life in the United States. He was going back to Europe because he could not help it, because he had to go.

Jessie stood obliquely watching his face which had taken on a forbidding expression that she knew to be unconscious. She had a startling impression of seeming to see this man apart from his identity, without the spectacular decorated uniform, without the periphery of famous and admiring friends, a figure of loneliness and humility, absorbed in something difficult and remote. The notion was gone in a flash and with it a thrust of poignant feeling which, had they been alone, would have swept her into his arms. Instead, she stood making the careful effort to appear oblivious of him, joining in the delighted clamor which followed the announcement by the composer Abel Goodman, Sam Lee's partner, that Jennie Wren was going to sing.

"Ah," said Jessie, leading her small group towards the front drawing-room where two pianos stood with their bends fitted together, "this is where I come in." This was indeed the only development at the party which could have deflected her from her intention to signal Mark that she wanted to leave. But Jennie Wren was a taste as special as pickled herring; one felt it as avid appetite or utter loathing. Jennie Wren was a dark, dumpy, pop-eyed woman with a hoarse, blaring contralto voice and a glorious free vulgarity in the execution of popular songs which had earned her millions of dollars and millions of passionate *afficionados*. Mark looked at Jessie with astonishment as she settled herself on a couch beside Harry Blitzer, a Broadway character who performed some go-between function in the maze which a person outside the theatrical world could never hope to understand. The room was quickly becoming crowded, for the word about Jennie Wren was drawing the whole party to this spot, and Mark dropped down to sit on the floor near Jessie, with many others close about.

"Do you know, Mark," said Jessie, leaning forward, "Harry here was an old friend of my mother's. I have known him—how long, Harry?"

Blitzer took the cigar out of his mouth and winked. "You really want me to tell, Jess?"

Mark felt a sense of the sharpest appreciation of Jessie for the tone of her introduction of Harry Blitzer. With his pot-belly, his sparsely covered bald spot, his fat face, his thick hairy hands inevitably sporting (Mark thought, there is no other word to describe it) a colossal star-sapphire and diamond ring, he was a masterpiece of vulgar ugliness. And yet Jessie had her reasons, which Mark did not know, for being loyal to Blitzer and for showing him that that was so.

"Would it do the slightest good if I didn't want you to tell?" Jessie teased him, her eyes twinkling. "He is one of those people who always knew everybody when," she said to Mark. "Jennie too. As a matter of fact, you got Jennie her first job, didn't you, Harry?"

"In a basement joint in the Village," said Blitzer. He looked up and about the room, making sure that Jennie Wren was not yet ready to sing; then he leaned forward towards Mark Dwyer, his fat thighs straining the cloth of his trousers, and said, with the thick gusto of his kind, "The first time I eveh saw Jennie Resnick she was a dirty little kid playing jacks on the stoop of a tenement in Eldridge Street." He spoke almost in a whisper, but not such a whisper as is used for the communication of secrets. "You know why I noticed her?" he asked Mark.

Mark shrugged.

"Yeh," said Harry Blitzer, chuckling. "I guess we all looked fa' the same thing. She didn't have any pants on. I noticed it because we boys were always in'arested, but anyway she was squatting there on that stoop with her behind up in the air, you couldn't have missed it."

"Somebody told me once," said Jessie, "that poor people's little girls never wear drawers. I was terribly shocked, and my God!—what a prig."

"They never do where I come from," said Mark. "Here or in Europe."

"Well you know," said Harry Blitzer, "once that made me wonder if maybe that was the reason why it was always poor girls you heard of getting in trouble and having babies in tenement hallways and hiding them in shoe boxes under the stairs." He shook his head. "But later I saw it was just because there are so many poor girls. Rich ones get in just as much trouble but there's always somebody to hide everything, with money and taking 'em away on trips and hushing it all up. It had nothing to do with wearing drawers, imagine," he said. And he settled back to listen to Jennie Wren-Resnick with an expression of thoroughly satisfied pride.

It was during one of the spates of applause and shrill babblings of delight for Jennie Wren and Abel Goodman accompanying her in his own music, that Harry Blitzer moved his head closer to Jessie's and spoke to her in the expressionless murmur, lips scarcely moving, which meant that he had something really private to say.

"How much do you know about that damfool niece of yours and him?" he asked, contriving to indicate Jack Spanier in an opposite corner of the room without a glance in his direction.

"The worst, I suppose," breathed Jessie.

"Well, look. You better do something."

Jessie gave Harry Blitzer a glance of shrewd questioning. "You mean you——"

She began to applaud and make herself part of the clamoring audience, to enable Blitzer to speak to her with the most possible privacy.

"Spanier's in for about a quarter of a million," he said. "The Schimmers have it on him cold. He'll have to get the money somewhere."

"But surely," said Jessie, "that couldn't have any bearing on this mess about Iris? She's just—" she made a gesture. "There are always fools like her."

"Yeh." Blitzer gripped his cigar between his teeth. "But I'm warning *you*."

"Me? Why, Harry?"

Almost imperceptibly Blitzer rubbed his thumb against the tips of two fingers. Jessie tried to steady herself against a shudder.

"But—but that seems impossible," she whispered.

Blitzer shrugged. "I'm warning you," he said. "The bastard's desperate. Look a' that." Without indicating what he meant, he caused Jessie to look quickly at Jack Spanier, who then turned his head to avoid her glance; and Jessie saw Spanier squinting at a corner where Alexander Lowden was talking to Phyllis Whitelaw, who had at last emerged from her retreat to join her own party.

"He could scarcely blackmail a man for something that everybody knows anyway," said Jessie. "Besides, Alec has not a penny of his own. It all belongs to Serena."

"Neveh mind the details. That's a cornered rat and he isn't going to be so fancy whose place he stinks up. Sure," he said suddenly aloud, very loud, lifting his head towards Jennie Wren, "you gotta sing *Honeybee*. Come on, Baby!"

In a short time Jessie signalled Mark and rose from the couch, bidding Harry Blitzer a warm good bye. He grinned up at her, saying "Remembeh what I told you, honey," and Jessie nodded, turning away. Only a moment later, as she and Mark were about to start downstairs, she encountered her brother-in-law carrying two glasses of whisky-and-soda across the hall. She contrived to let Mark go ahead of her and then she said, "Van. Just a moment."

Fielding stopped and looked at her with dull surprise. He was so accustomed to the cynical, tacit understanding by which his relatives conducted the fiction of not seeing him when he was escorting Isabel Allen, that he had quite forgotten he was not in the usual public place with Isabel Allen beside him. He was only carrying a drink to her, but he had

239

had so many drinks himself that it was difficult for him to switch his habit-signals to the normal mien with which he should speak to his sister-in-law in the house of mutual friends. Nobody could say, thought Jessie, watching the narrow, blank face, the uneasy eye, that Evander Fielding was out of place here, but she could have laughed at his bewilderment upon being confronted by her.

He looked about distractedly, and just as Jessie was expecting him to blurt, "Well, what do you want?," he pulled himself together, smiled idiotically, and said, "Good party, isn't it?"

"Yes," she said. "Wonderful. Van, can you find time to come in and see me tomorrow? Or as soon as possible? There's something I want to—" she paused, feeling for a phrase that would not antagonize him, for it was clear that he would be resentful and suspicious of anything that a member of his family might ask to speak to him about. "I ought to tell you something," she said, hoping for the best.

But he scowled anyway, the weakness in his face making petulance of the expression instead of determination. He made it clear that he supposed Jessie could have nothing to say to him except some tiresome protest concerning Isabel Allen, which would be none of Jessie's business; he confessed a thoroughly clumsy guilt by shifting his glance down the hall and through the room where Isabel Allen sat, among a group of four men and one woman, Mrs. Irving Laskin, whose husband was planted beside her with all the subtlety of a mameluke at the gate of a harem.

Jessie watched Evander Fielding's jellylike eye narrow and harden, though she could not read the least strength in the glance, only a disgraceful kind of consternation as he saw Jack Spanier materialize behind Isabel Allen, lean over her—making of her incredible barely veiled breasts an indiscriminate lubricity—and speak to her with the hard-lipped secrecy typical of his kind. How unbelievably disgusting, said an observing nerve in Jessie's mind, and fascinated by the sheer scurrility of the scene, she stood beside Evander Fielding and saw Isabel Allen raise to the man behind her the face famed for its enamelled expressionless beauty, across which, almost faster than Jessie could believe, there flashed a break as violent as the smashing of a tray of crockery. Jessie could not remember ever having seen a human action of such lightning speed; it had happened far too quickly for her to interpret anything. She turned aside, alarmed by what she had seen and what she sensed of its hideous inner workings, and found herself thinking with sudden icy concern of Serena Lowden. That is strange, she thought then, because at least that fool of a husband of hers appears to have gone home. And surely it is no business of mine.

Evander Fielding spoke suddenly in his irritable, polished drawl. "Well," he said, "I suppose—" He was still nervously watching the group at the end of the long room, and he was too patently anxious to get away from Jessie.

"I have to speak to you about Iris," said Jessie quickly. "Nothing—else."

"Iris?"

"Yes. I cannot tell you anything here. Will you call me tomorrow?"

Fielding's blond brows twitched and he looked at the glass in his right hand.

"What's on your mind about Iris?" he asked.

"I just told you, Van, it would be impossible to speak about it here. But somebody must do something about her. I think it should be you."

"Oh, all right," he said with truculence. "I'll call you some time tomorrow."

Jessie moved past him and down the stairs, certain that he would have forgotten all about the matter by tomorrow, and even more certain how fervently she would thank God for any miracle that would remove the entire Bourne and Fielding connection and all its ramifications from her life. Mark was waiting for her at the foot of the stairs, but before she could join him she found herself blocked by Henry Greenberg, on his way up, whose presence at this particular moment was the final straw in an intolerable load.

"Leaving, Jess?" he smiled, in his most affectionate manner. "Why, the party's just getting good."

"I know, Henry," she laughed. She wished that there were a way of signalling Mark Dwyer to disappear from sight. "But Sam and Helen are waiting . . ."

"Sam and Helen left an hour ago, tchk, tchk," said Henry Greenberg with a wink for which she could have put his eye out. "You won't change your mind about the week end, Jess? Come on out, the Porters are coming and Joe and Mack, and Dinko's plane will be in from London. And bring anybody you like," he said, as broadly as if he were pasting up a billboard.

241

"Thanks, Henry, you're a dear. I'm going down to Virginia . . . another week . . . yes, wasn't it . . ."

And joining Mark in the hall she cursed the eyes in the back of Henry Greenberg's head, mounting the stairs.

In the taxi Jessie turned to Mark with a low sigh. In one soft, exhausted sound she confessed more than she would have permitted any words to say. He leaned forward, finding her for the first time not only yielding but entreating as he took her in his arms, feeling her deliberately put aside the gentle stiffness which had been her way of admitting, up to now, all that at the same time she abjured. Her left hand went up suddenly and around his neck, her right arm lay limp between them as he bent over to hold her hard against the swaying of the cab, and to find that his mouth upon hers met sudden, complete response. He had not realized until this moment how very great had been her reserve, though he had also never been mistaken that that reserve was coldness. The discovery moved him to a hoarse exclamation almost as if of pain, and for what time they did not know, they remained lost in their first step together. When Mark released her lips, Jessie clung as closely to him, and presently whispered, "I think—I suppose—not even now—if you were not going away."

He did not answer, overcome with the sense that there was nothing to say; but Jessie uttered suddenly a hard, smothered cry and buried her face against his chest. He held her very tightly, his face against her hair, his closed lips upon her temple. It must be, he understood, a prodigious surrender of her guard that he could feel her slight body shaken by sobs, though she managed to make no sound at all. He said after a moment, "Darling, try to be calm, try not to cry—" and when she raised her head he kissed her eyes and the upper corners of her cheeks with marvellous tenderness. He drew her head to his shoulder, aware that she must wish him not see her struggle to compose herself. Almost until the cab reached her door he held her, one hand with the most delicate lightness caressing her hair, and in the last few moments he said softly, "You are very tired, darling. If I could, I would come with you and hold you in my arms all night. But it is nearly three o'clock now. To be with you for an hour or so and then——"

"You are right," she said, against his coat.

"That is not what I want for you—that is not—not——"

242

"I know."

"Tomorrow?" he asked, turning up her face towards his and looking into her eyes. "Will you spend the day with me tomorrow?"

She nodded slowly, looking straight at him, as plainly allowing him to see all that her face could say as she had asked him, also without speaking, to take her in his arms.

The cab stopped and the driver sat waiting for them to get out. Jessie drew apart from Mark, torn between the knowledge that it would be, as he had said, altogether a mistake for him to come into her house with her at such an hour, and the childish desire to cry out to him not to leave her. Then she saw in a rush of gratitude that he had prevented her from committing in her helplessness an unfastidious blunder which she would eventually have loathed; and that whatever lay ahead for her and Mark to share, he would bring to it a delicacy of taste and judgment which would keep it a lovely thing, "lovely enough," he had said a little while ago, "for you."

He put his hands on either side of her face, his sad dark eyes intent but warm with the tenderness for which she felt a craving hunger; and he said with such simple authority that she could not help smiling weakly, "Now you are to go to sleep, my darling." He kissed her lips lightly. "To sleep. Will you do that?"

She nodded, conscious with sharpest relief of the luxury of meeting this small exaction of his will. It feels, she thought, like playing at being a child, but what is wrong with sensing oneself a child beside a thorough man?

He stepped out of the cab and helped her out and walked with her to the door where they stood waiting for the night man to answer their ring.

"I will telephone you before noon," said Mark. "But not too soon before. You are to sleep until then, and I don't want to hear about any engagements that you have made, all day long."

"I will cancel them," she said meekly, "if there are any. I can't remember."

The man opened the door and Mark kissed her hand and left her.

IV
THURSDAY

XIX

Jessie had slept heavily for a time after going to bed, but she was awake in the early morning, with the bludgeoned sensation of having slept too little. Nothing was more distressing to her than this, to wake unrested with black dullness in her head, with thoughts as rude and confused as the dreams which they had succeeded, dreams from which one wakes frightened or upset or resentful, with no tangible memory of their content. Then she fell into a brief period of almost weeping petulance, than a moment of feeling crazily sorry for herself because she had had the misfortune to wake so soon. Then came the inevitable petty battle between her intention to look at the clock and her wish not to know what time it was. At last she turned over and examined the crystal clock on the night-table, its luminous dial glowing in the artificial dark of the curtained room, and she saw that it said a quarter past seven.

"Oh my God, my God," she groaned, rolling over with an

uncharacteristic roughness of action, and burying her head under one of the pillows. "Oh damn damn damn . . ."

It seemed cruel to her that this had happened when she needed so badly to sleep. She felt much too dull and distrait to clear her mind purposely to the anticipation of what the day was to hold, but she knew that she had hoped to meet this day fresher, calmer, more rested and serene than she had ever been in her life. She dare not give up the struggle and admit that she could not sleep any more; she must sleep at least three hours longer or her day would be ruined.

She tried to lie as quiet, as liquidly relaxed as she could make herself, and in the knowledge that unless she gave her mind some lovely and caressing thought to hold it would turn on her and become a snake's nest of anxieties, she brought to it the image of Mark, and to her lips the sound of his name, which she whispered against the back of her hand. She drew long and regular breaths, inviting the conscious dream of his presence to come and take possession of her and enclose her in the extraordinary sense of strength which she drew from his voice or the touch of his hand. This, she found, was good; she was quite able to mould this mood to her desire, and she could feel the quietude travel as if from some central source farther and farther outwards, to her skin, to the nerves of her closed eyelids, to the tips of her fingers and her toes. The thought materialized slowly that this was to be the day that she had promised to Mark, and in time she discovered that she had so well succeeded in using the idea of his gentleness to calm herself that she could lie here really resting and think, not of the splendor which she knew his lovemaking would be, but of his heavenly tenderness while she rested beside him when all time had been abandoned. She remained in this way increasingly content, motionless in a degree of relaxation which took from her light body any sense of contact with the bed upon which it lay. She might be floating. She might be drifting through air in which, if she listened, she could hear his calm admonition that she go to sleep again. Go to sleep, she thought, in unison with what she heard, go to sleep again, to sleep.

When she came awake again it was past ten o'clock and she felt perfectly calm. She rang for Josephine, pursuing her usual habits of the morning. She took a strange and surprised satisfaction in proceeding with the small routines of mail and household memoranda and details about the evening's dinner-party, which she would so thankfully have cancelled. But, she thought, I shall have had the whole day with Mark, I shall have travelled thousands of miles away from all this into a lovely place which will seem like my native land and from which I have all my life been exiled.

It was now that she realized how subtle and keen had been his instinct not to come into this house with her last night. Though she had for so many years been saturated in solitude here, it had been a solitude not of identity, but of force. This was the house where she was Mrs. Brandon Bourne, and no faintest element of her feeling for Mark Dwyer partook of the cynical contriving of a love-affair, which was exactly what all her detestable acquaintances must either be saying of it already, or would say before long. She could not prevent that, but she felt a sense of stature in the knowledge that such gabble did not really matter, and could not hurt though it would repel her. Brandon Bourne had no more bearing upon this day and its event than a total stranger, and if he should know about it, she thought, he would care less than anybody on earth. But the depth of Mark Dwyer's concern for her reassured and warmed her wonderfully.

She had promised to cancel all her engagements for the day, and when she looked at her blue book she was relieved to see that she could free herself easily. There was only her lunch with Althea Crowe, afterwards the coiffeur, and then a cocktail party at an art gallery where the proceeds of the *vernissage* were to go to one of Patty Duncan's charities. She telephoned Althea Crowe at her office.

"Hell, no," roared Miss Crowe, when Jessie asked if she would mind changing their luncheon engagement. "You could try giving me some bull about your husband's maiden aunt descending on you from Chappaqua but I'm too smart for that and so are you! Go ahead and have a good time."

"It's not—" began Jessie a little lamely, but she was drowned out by a peal of brassy laughter. She could not help laughing herself. "All right, Althea," she said. "Next Tuesday, then. You're a darling."

"Tell that to sweetie," said Althea Crowe, and rang off.

Jessie put off the coiffeur until next week, but arranged to have Miss Stella here tomorrow morning to do her nails. She wrote a note of apology to Patty Duncan, enclosing a contribution for her charity, and then she realized that she had better plan the seating of her dinner-table now, for she might not have a chance later, and in any case would feel even less like putting her mind to it. She sat looking at the list

246

of names on today's page of her book, wondering helplessly how she had come to let herself in for this, which had seemed so pleasant an idea when she had planned it and which now had lost every vestige of meaning, although she was fond of the friends whom she had invited. Sam and Helen Lee were coming, thank God, and the Clyde Pritchards whom she saw rarely, because they bored Brandon and she had given up ever bringing them together; and Jerome Block the economist whom Brandon dismissed as one of Roosevelt's crackpots, with his wife Hulda, an extraordinarily fine pianist; and now also Reath Sheldon, that sort of really dear friend, she thought, whom in this queer life that we lead here we so seldom see.

A few others might come in after dinner, including Myron Waite, who had been a correspondent with the Third Army and who would have much in common with Mark Dwyer— and suddenly Jessie sat up tense with the thought that by this evening that name, that identity, would have become so transformed in her eyes, and she herself would have traversed such illimitable distances, that she might find herself in uncharted territory. Oh, she thought, I am not at all sure that I want Mark to be here for dinner, I think I shall tell him it would be better not to come . . . but how do I know what I shall think by then, how can I tell? And while she was sitting there groping for some reflex of instinct or judgment by which to guide herself, Mark called her on the telephone.

It was then at the sound of his voice that all the strange calm of the morning vanished in one unmistakable thrust, and she held the telephone in a shaking hand, trying to make her voice something other than a helpless gasp.

"Have you slept?" asked Mark, with the same grave quiet in which he had spoken on leaving her last night.

"Yes. Well. Very well." (Oh, she thought, oh, I did not know, in spite of everything, how could I not have known!)

"And you are still in bed?"

"Yes, but I was just about to get up." She could hear her own voice unnaturally low and blurred, she could not have forced herself to change its tone, because something had overriden her control and was straining to tell Mark what she wanted him to know now; at once, she thought, right now.

"Then suppose I stop for you in an hour."

"Mark," she said, without any forethought at all, "Mark, I think I would rather come—" she hesitated and still could barely say above a whisper, "come and meet you."

He understood, better than she herself, for she had not anticipated her own impulse.

"Very well," he said. "I see, darling. Come when you are ready."

He gave her the number of his apartment in the hotel and just as Jessie thought he was about to ring off he said in his characteristic, abrupt way, "Are you sure you want to come, darling? Would you rather——"

"Oh," she said, again without the least power to decide her own words, "Oh, Mark. I have never been so sure of anything before."

"I'll be waiting," he said; she heard his deep voice turn thin and roughen. She put down the telephone and sat still in her bed, her face in her hands, thinking not about the helpless tumult which was rioting inside her still form, but about the knowledge which had broken the shackles of half a lifetime and forged to the peak of her brain commanding to be recognized.

She had her bath, precisely performing all the small acts of habit by which women make themselves desirable, thinking so concretely about Mark that at one moment the strain of cynical humor imbedded in her personality roused itself to accuse her of physical coquetry or even wantonness. That, she replied, in the silent dialogue which an imaginative and solitary person typically holds within himself, is not the point. My wish to give pleasure wholly and as nearly perfectly as I can is but the outermost symbol of the force which is carrying me forward now. Once more there rose in her mind the knowledge, amazing, yet profoundly a matter of course, that her relationship to Mark Dwyer was not discovery but recognition, the acknowledgement of an intense natural intimacy established infinitely long ago.

She sat down at her dressing-table to "do"—she smiled at the thought—her face and her hair. Inevitably she remembered Elizabeth Betts the night before, and again she wondered at the need in such a naturally beautiful woman to assume so much artifice. I thought I was the most timid of women, she mused, but whatever my fears may be, they do not seem to take the form of obsession with pots and jars. Even while she noted that her skin was not particularly young, and that the grey highlights in her hair would soon be less 'amusing' than revealing, she took a strange satisfaction in the intention to let Mark Dwyer know her precisely as she was; not without the subtle gratifications of delicacy and daintiness and fragrance and allurement to touch, but altogether without the kind of illusion which holds the imminent fear of some disappointing discovery.

She had finished with the simple matters of lotion and a bit of color and powder for her face, and was brushing her eyebrows, dipping the silly doll's brush into a vial of scent, sweeping the dark silk of her brows upwards and then down, when her nerves jumped and plunged with frightful violence, because she heard the shattering slam of the front door downstairs. The small bottle slid from her left hand and crashed on the marble floor. She sat gaping at her mirror. Brandon. While her heart began to pound with the fear which his every unannounced appearance had for years past touched off, she sat staring at her reflection, saying half aloud, "But it does not matter. What does it matter? Why do you care? He never says when he is coming or going. You are silly, you are a fool . . ."

But Mark, said the silent voice within her mind, but Mark.

"But it does not matter," she insisted again, forming the words with her lips. "It makes no difference whatsoever . . ."

Josephine came into the dressing-room, taking a negligée from the rack where it hung, and holding it for Jessie to put on. "Mr. Bourne has just come in," she said impassively. "He is on his way upstairs."

Jessie rose and allowed herself to be put into the dressing-gown. She was cold with suspense and despair and the beating physical fear which the anticipation of seeing Brandon invariably roused, no matter how quickly thereafter she might regain possession of herself and appear to be wholly poised and normal of manner in his presence. By the time he had entered her bedroom she had seated herself again at the dressing-table, kicked the broken bottle out of sight, and taken up her hairbrush. He appeared at the door of her dressing-room, calling "Jess?"

"Why, Brandon," she said, rather surprised at the calm coolness of her own voice. "I didn't know you were coming."

He made no motion towards a kiss of greeting or any salutation that might be conventional after an absence; Jessie felt casual relief at that. She had no wish to look at his face but she had not much choice; it was the only thing to do. So she turned to him with a formal smile, her hairbrush poised, and was astonished to find him drawn, tense, and obviously in the grip of some great alarm. "Why——" she said involuntarily, taking her cue from the anxious stare in his hard blue eyes, "why—what——"

Even while her whole reason was assuring her that this strange bearing of his could have nothing to do with her, the vibrations of her initial terror at his appearance had not quieted altogether; she was desperately uneasy. But he said, his hard voice heightened by anxiety, "It's Van. Van is in a terrible jam, Jess."

"Van?" She would know in an instant what more there was to know; just now she was deeply relieved that she had so accurately judged the impossibility of Brandon's concern having anything to do with her. "What has happened?" she asked. "I saw him only a few hours ago."

"Isabel," said Brandon. He looked over his shoulder into the bedroom to make sure that Josephine had left the room. "Isabel is dead."

Jessie saw in the mirror her mouth drop agape and the hairbrush slither to the dressing-table from her hand.

"But——" she said. "But——"

She rose and walked past Brandon into her bedroom. He followed her and they stood near the windows, talking. Jessie's brow was stitched with perplexity.

"But," she said again, "that—why that can't be possible, Brandon. I tell you I saw them——"

"I know," he said. "It happened early this morning. Van telephoned me at six o'clock——"

"Yes, I was going to ask how on earth you——"

"Chet Claymore flew me up to Washington in his plane and I caught the—never mind. We've got to do something about Van now, Jess. This is serious."

"You mean—he—no!"

Brandon raised his eyebrows and put his lips together with the pursed expression of extreme doubt. "Van did not—Jesus, I can't get used to even using the words—Van had nothing to do with it," he said. "But he was there. And——"

"Where?" asked Jessie.

"In Isabel's apartment."

"And where is he now?"

"Downstairs in the library," said Brandon. "He met me at LaGuardia and I made what I could of his story on the way in. But he's so——" Brandon moved his long hands helplessly. "You never heard of such a mess," he said.

Jessie wondered whether or not she had ever heard of such a mess; she could have reminded Brandon of some that had been less terrible only in degree.

"I don't know what to do," said Brandon, abruptly. Jessie could almost see him slinging down the thing at her feet. "It's going to be a damned nasty business and—well——"

He looked at Jessie with the plain statement in his face that he took her unquestioning help in this for granted. Though she knew nothing as yet, she saw that she had already been rallied to the support of Brandon's family, that she was committed absolutely to protecting them whether that might be her own will or not. Standing there in the window, looking at this detested stranger who was fear and sorrow personified, she felt, with an abrupt tumbling inner sense of collapse, how utterly without choice she was. I wonder why, she thought, I wonder why I surrender to this blow now, why it is my responsibility, why do I know that I shall be hours or days or weeks at the beck and call of these savages . . . oh, she could have wailed, standing there staring at Brandon Bourne's arrogant, coldly moulded face, oh, Mark, Mark, Mark. To-day, tomorrow, Saturday, Sunday—was it too much to ask? Am I not to live, not to live at all? She knew as she looked at Brandon that she betrayed nothing; perhaps, she thought, I shall be able to salvage something for myself, even a fragment of happiness; after all, I am so used to not having any.

She turned her head and looked at the clock with wretchedness which Brandon, if he noticed her action at all, probably mistook for concern about him. Trying as if from perverseness to make herself feel that this man standing here was her husband, which seemed an insane unreality, she said quietly, "Go down and tell Van I will be there in a moment. And ask Sarah to take him in some black coffee, and see that he drinks it."

She stood waiting for Brandon to close the door with his usual roughness, which he did; and when she had recovered from that, she went to the telephone, flicked the switch which cut it off from the other extensions in the house, and called Mark. She found then that she could scarcely speak.

"Darling," he said, his voice strained with sudden fear, but trying to comfort her, "what is it? What's happened?"

She tried to tell him, but beyond the fragments that she knew, there was nothing to say except, "I cannot come. Oh, Mark!" She wept helplessly, making a tangle of piteous

251

sounds, and then she said, "If I had left the house ten minutes ago . . . if I had only been gone, they would not have been able to find me all day."

He was glad that she could not see his wry smile caused by these childish words. If some such thing had to happen, he thought, thank God that nobody had had to go searching for her all over town.

"Darling," he said, and she wept again because she was so far from the comfort of his voice, "darling, it may not be as bad as you think now. And anyway," he said slowly; and then he was silent.

"What?" asked Jessie, with a sense of fear.

"Nothing, darling," he said, regretting his thought, which he had managed not to convey to her. "Nothing. You don't know yet, do you," he asked slowly, "just what the details are? How—in just what way Fielding is involved?"

"No," she said. "Only that he—oh, my God."

"The newspapers," said Mark.

"Yes." In a spasm of misery she felt herself stiffen with resentment that this unspeakable thing had happened, that the fragile loveliness of her mood and the paradise of anticipation in which she had enjoyed it, had been smashed in this way, for such a reason, so soon.

"There may be some way that I can help," said Mark.

"You're so good," replied Jessie. "I have to go and talk to them now and find out all about it." She spoke with a resigned control of voice which reassured him at least that she would be the calmest and sanest element in the mess.

"Will you let me know when you can?" he asked.

"Of course—but Mark, please don't stay there and wait for me to call. It might be—I can't tell how long."

"Just call when you can," he said. "And darling——"

"Yes?"

He did not speak at once and she waited. She sensed what he might say and then she felt the presentiment that he would not permit himself to say it. This was not the first such moment, there had been others. He had had his reasons, amid the warm intimacy of all their talk, for leaving unsaid the thing that a different sort of man might have said quite lightly.

"I am so afraid," said Jessie, whispering. "So afraid that we will not—that——"

"Of course we will!" said Mark's voice, full-throated, almost a shout of reassurance. "Stop worrying. Call me when

252

you can." And breaking the connection in his usual brisk way, she thought she heard him say something that she had surely never heard before; it was only while she was hurrying into her dress that she realized he had spoken in a language that she did not know.

XX

She found Evander Fielding seated in a stiff armchair in the library, and Brandon pacing up and down the room, jingling the keys or the coins in his trousers pocket. She shrank from the pacing and the jingling, trifles of themselves, but reflective of destructive and hateful qualities which she had learned to dread. She would find a way in a moment to stop that. First she had to accustom herself to the sight of Evander Fielding, whose face showed her the spectacle of a man in the grip of extreme panic and fear. He was a sick yellowish clay-color; his eyes, always pale and vaguely focussed, appeared to have been cut off from contact with their controlling nerves, simply to roll loose in his face. His greying sandy hair had been thinning from his narrow forehead for years, but now Jessie received the preposterous illusion that he had become suddenly bald.

She closed the door behind her and crossed the room to a chair near Fielding, saying, "Brandon, come over here and sit on the couch—we can speak more quietly."

Then she said to Fielding, "Van, Brandon has not told me anything except—except about your finding Isabel, and—" good God, she thought, is this all to be put in this way upon me? What am I doing here! She turned sharply to Brandon and made a gesture enjoining him to take over. But Brandon only said, "I think you ought to tell Jess the whole thing—if you can, Van. I mean, both of us. Maybe," he said, "the three of us together will be able to figure out what you ought to do."

Fielding made a despairing sound, looking from Jessie to Brandon and back to Jessie again, and by his silence indicating that Brandon might as probably be right as not. He shook his head as Jessie started to pour some coffee for him, saying, "No thanks, I've had all I want."

He was in the trembling funk which resulted from having

been violently and instantaneously sobered by shock. He made one attempt to hold and smoke a cigarette which Brandon lighted for him, but his hand shook so wildly that he could not manage it; presently Jessie took a paper-knife from the desk and crushed out the stub in the ash-tray.

"You know, Van," she said quietly, "it's really very hard to start making sense when one doesn't know any facts. What actually happened to Isabel?"

"It was Spanier," said Fielding, his mouth twitching.

"Jack Spanier! You mean he killed her?" Jessie spoke in such spontaneous amazement, inextricable for the moment from relief, that to Brandon she sounded insanely gay. "Then——"

"No," said Fielding. "He didn't kill her. Oh, God." He dropped his face into his shaking hands.

Jessie stared at Brandon, her eyebrows lifted in bewildered peaks. She shook her head as they both sat watching Fielding. Brandon leaned forward and touched him on the shoulder.

"Van," he said. "Why don't you try to start at the beginning of what happened and simply tell us, just as you remember it? I couldn't get it straight in the taxi. And we've got to do something, you know, damn fast. About Isa—about the——" Jessie saw his mouth form a soundless 'Jesus Christ!' as he took the handkerchief from his breast pocket and mopped his forehead. Again she asked him a silent question, this time horrified, and Brandon shook his head with a grimace. Jessie sat back against her chair. Fielding raised his head, swinging it like an animal, and said, "I'd better have a drink."

"He had, at that," said Jessie. Brandon brought a pony of whisky and Fielding gulped it off, shuddering, as Jessie, who was trying not to watch, had grotesquely expected that he would. Then he moved as if to straighten himself, gripped the fragile, turned arms of his chair and said, "Maybe I can't remember what happened exactly, it gets harder to remember all the time." He paused to try to think, and Jessie said, "Put it any way that it comes to you, Van, but is it the case that nobody—that Isabel—I mean is she still there? In her apartment?"

"You mean do the police know yet?" asked Fielding in a sudden streak of lucidity as shocking as if he had begun to gibber. "No, they don't. At least they didn't an hour ago and nobody would have gone there since."

"How about Alec Lowden?" asked Jessie in a tone of which she felt in some way ashamed.

"He never went there in the morning," said Fielding, revealing the whole cynical, sordid pattern of which he was a part. "You know."

They did know, thought Jessie; everybody did who was familiar with the scared, pompous hypocrisy of Alexander Lowden's existence. For twenty-five years he had been at his desk at *The Press* punctually at nine-thirty every morning, "to set an example to the staff," to make of the indefensible fatuity which was his life "an open book."

"But he may—soon," said Brandon, glancing at the small clock on the desk. It was twenty-five minutes before twelve. "Or try to telephone."

"I know," said Fielding. He made a vast visible effort to order his senses and his wits, and he began suddenly to talk.

"The size of it is," he said, "Isabel is lying dead there in her apartment and so far, nobody knows it but Jack Spanier and me. But somebody has to know and—don't you see!", he exclaimed wildly, "as soon as anybody finds her of course they will call the police. Isn't there some way of—of—what *happens* in a thing like this, Bran? Don't you know?"

"Hasn't Isabel got a maid?" asked Jessie slowly.

"No, not now. She did. I mean she never had one who lived there, just women who came in. And she hasn't had one for a week or more—she was always in a mess like that."

Once again Jessie tried to make Fielding begin at the beginning, and in answer to her question about when he had left the Whitelaws' party, he said, "About four o'clock. I took it for granted that I would take Isabel home, I had brought her to the party, and—you see. It was that way."

He meant that Alexander Lowden had purposely left the Whitelaw party early and alone, not expecting to see Isabel Allen again that night.

"But when we were in the taxi Isabel acted very queer. As a matter of fact she had been jumpy and nervous all evening."

"I know," said Jessie. "I saw her." She remembered now every detail of the impression made upon her by Isabel Allen's damaged looks and harassed manner.

"She told me she didn't want me to come up to the apartment with her," said Fielding. "She tried to make me leave her in the hall downstairs. Jesus!" he groaned, "if I only had!" But then he shook his head wretchedly and said, "But it probably wouldn't have made any difference. I told her I was damn well going upstairs with her."

255

Brandon leaned forward sharply and said, "Say, Van. By the way. Has Isabel moved? Since—lately, anyway."

"No," said Fielding, not understanding. "Why?"

Brandon did not answer him, but he did turn to Jessie. "I was worried about a doorman or elevator man," he explained.

"Oh, no," she said. "Not Isabel."

How utterly mad this is, she thought, that I should have reason to care that Isabel Allen lived in a remodelled private house with an automatic elevator. Fielding seemed not to notice that he had been interrupted. Started upon his story, he went on talking doggedly, repeating himself.

"I told her I was going upstairs with her," he said. "I can't see now why I had that fool idea. It wasn't as if——"

Jessie and Brandon exchanged a glance which was almost the equivalent of a shrug. When Evander Fielding was drunk he was sure to be seized by some such stubborn obsession.

"Anyway," he said, with a horrible sweeping gesture of admission that the thing was sordid beyond their worst conclusions, "after I found out she wasn't expecting Lowden I insisted on going up to her apartment with her. I can't remember how long it was exactly, but we had a drink and Isabel got more and more jittery. Now I see why, but of course I didn't know then. You know how it is when you're tight— you always get so—so——"

You do, thought Jessie. He went on talking.

"All of a sudden we heard the noise of the elevator outside Isabel's apartment. She nearly had a fit. The doorbell rang and I guess I got pretty rough about it and she said she was expecting somebody on business and hadn't she told me not to come up with her anyway. I said what the hell kind of business did she have at five o'clock in the morning but by that time she was in a real panic. She shoved me into her bedroom and shut the door. I guess she didn't know what she was doing, she couldn't have thought it out." Fielding clutched his head between his hands. "If she had, she'd have shoved me into the kitchen and I'd have gone out the service exit. But there is no way out of that bedroom except through the living-room."

Jessie thought, barely avoiding a shudder, of the evil symbolism of those few words.

"So you heard everything that happened after that," she said.

Fielding nodded, his face if possible more nearly green than before.

"And—" he choked over the thought—"and saw it too, finally. Because they got so—it was so——"

"It was Spanier who came in?"

"Yes. When I heard his voice through the door I could hardly believe my ears. The way she talked to him. My God!" He turned his hagridden face questioningly to Brandon. There was silence for a moment while Jessie looked from one man to the other, weighing the monstrosities of knowledge suspended between them, and fitting into place the shocking thing which she had seen flash across Isabel Allen's face last night. She stared at her husband with so flat and cold a reminder of his own past history in respect to Isabel Allen that Brandon gave a sudden, sharp shrug, turned to Evander Fielding, and said, "Didn't you *know* about Isabel and Jack Spanier?" He spoke in such a tone as to heap deprecation and scorn upon the befuddled stupidity of Fielding; as if to rub his nose in the raw fact that if he had gone adventuring in such a quagmire he should at least have provided himself with maps and charts before setting forth.

"No!" said Fielding, in defiance that rang with hysteria. Jessie saw at once the reason for the voluntary fog in which he must purposely have obscured the identity of Jack Spanier, but they would get to Iris's place in this nightmare soon enough. Jessie was herself without the pivotal fact which would explain what Brandon was projecting now, and she listened in dull amazement as he said, "Isabel was absolutely blind, crazy, mad about Jack Spanier. Nuts about him."

"You mean," asked Jessie, knowing that she sounded like an idiot, "she was in love with him?"

"What did you think I meant?" asked Brandon. "She certainly never gave a hoot in hell about anybody else." His unmistakable inclusion of himself in the catalogue of Isabel Allen's connections was to Jessie almost unbearable. "For years—fifteen years, maybe—Isabel was in love with Jack Spanier in the way I guess only a woman like that can be." Jessie suppressed a shudder. "He kicked her around and dragged her through hell—" Brandon broke off and looked with sharp anxiety at the clock and then at Evander Fielding. "Look here," he said, "for God's sake let's get to the end of this. It's late."

"Well," said Fielding, hopelessly, "you see. That explains it. He came there to get money. An awful lot of money," he said, in the incredulous tone of a person reading a ghost story aloud. "She didn't have it and she tried to tell him—she didn't see how she could get it."

"From Alexander Lowden?" asked Jessie.

"Who else?" replied Fielding with a hoarse sigh. "And the fight they had was something I never—oh, Christ!" His voice slid abruptly upward to a screech and in the collapse of his control they saw and heard more than any words could have told them. They sat in silence, Jessie so overcome by disgust and shame that she could scarcely see the two men in front of her; she had a sharp sense that the only one of her faculties which was functioning was her hearing, because the ticking of the desk clock seemed so insanely loud and she realized that ordinarily one did not hear this little timepiece at all.

"Well," said Brandon's voice, after what seemed a long time, "just exactly what did you see, Van? How did you come to see it?"

"They had this fight," said Fielding, trying to speak coherently. "Spanier raised such hell threatening her that I was damn near beside myself—" He turned on Brandon a look which struck Jessie as intolerably tragic; it held the wreckage of all the decency and gentility in the man's heredity. "You'd have felt you had to protect a—I don't know—an animal, even, from that. And then she cried and pleaded and carried on and tried to get him to—to—" he clawed at his forehead with his twitching hands and Jessie breathed, "Oh, don't say it, Van. Never mind."

"She only made him madder. I can't remember what either of them said, there was such hell going on, but finally she screamed just 'Jack' in such a way I guess I thought he was really going to beat her up, and that was when I opened the bedroom door just enough to see through it. They were standing near the fireplace and she was trying to put her arms around his neck and he was looking at her—" Fielding stopped speaking and just as Jessie was bracing herself for another explosion of hysteria, he leaned forward slowly and spoke with heavy, horrible clarity. "I have never seen anything as cruel and beastly as the look on that man's face. It was angry, God knows—but cold. Not excited, not excited enough for him to have struck her a blow that would kill her. He just pushed her, gave her a shove with the heel of his hand that made her lose her balance. She fell and struck her head on the brass fender of the fireplace. And Spanier—" Evander Fielding paused and looked at Jessie and Brandon with eyes which appeared at last to have regained the capacity to focus, but which to Jessie seemed to be trained upon the utmost possible horror, visible only to Fielding.

"What did Spanier do?" asked Brandon.

"He put his hands in his pockets," said Fielding, "and—and—he *shrugged*." Fielding's forehead was laddered with lines of horrified bewilderment.

"Do you suppose he knew she was dead?"

"I don't know," replied Fielding, "whether he knew it then. He said something or other, I've forgotten what, and then all of a sudden he seemed to get angry all over again. He was just turning away, he hadn't bent over her or touched her or even really looked at her, and I could see him stiffen up the way he had been, ugly mad. He kicked the—the thing like that." Fielding pointed at the rack of fire-tools which stood by the hearth on the other side of the room. "He gave it a terrific kick, and knocked the whole thing over and it fell down and those brass things hit Isabel on the head. Then Spanier just turned away and picked up his hat off the couch and walked out. He even slammed the door."

"Did he," asked Brandon very slowly, "still have his hands in his pockets?"

"I don't know," said Fielding, mumbling a little. He stared at Brandon with his mouth open. "I couldn't see the front foyer. But I bet he did."

"And you?" asked Jessie. "What did you do, Van?"

"That," said Brandon, rather gently for him, "is just the trouble."

So Jessie understood that Evander Fielding had done what any normal human being would have done—rushed to Isabel Allen, touched her, moved the things around her, acted in spontaneous concern and fright without the least thought of criminal involvement.

"But when I realized that she was dead," he said, "I—you know, it must have been quite a long time that I just stood there feeling paralyzed with no idea what to do. Then of course it began to occur to me that somebody had to be told, something had to happen. Would *you* know what to do in such a spot?" he blurted at Jessie, swinging round towards her.

"I—" she spoke with difficulty—"I suppose—the police——"

"That's what he says he thought," said Brandon, as Fielding clutched his head in his hands again. "He thought he would just tell them the truth about Spanier and then he

259

realized—" Brandon turned his right hand over, palm up, a gesture which said more than enough about fingerprints. "All over the place, you see," he said, shaking his head. "I tell you, it's a damn bad mess. Because no matter how it might come out in the end——"

"I see," said Jessie. They did not need now to go into the horrors of an inquest, an investigation, and all that must follow, about which none of them understood anything at all. "So—what *did* you do, Van?" she asked.

He raised his head, trying so hard to breathe deeply enough to continue speaking that they could see his nostrils pinch and flatten. "I went to Jack Spanier," he said.

"Oh," said Jessie. And then with what seemed to her the utmost stupidity she asked, "Why?"

"To dump it on him," replied Brandon, glancing again at the clock, for nearly half an hour had passed and they had come to no decision about anything. "Van told Spanier Isabel was dead and that he had seen the whole thing and asked Spanier what he intended to do about it."

"And——?"

"Spanier told me," said Fielding, "that the bead was on me. He said I could call in the police if I wanted to but when he —when he—" Fielding paused and the enormity of the case against him slid, all its components complete, through Jessie's mind.

"Spanier told me," said Fielding again, his voice thick in the back of his throat, "that he didn't give a damn what I did. But—but that after I thought it over he was betting I would find a way to hush the whole thing up unless—" he stopped, apparently unable to say any more. They sat for a moment but Jessie, nervous about the time, leaned forward and asked, "What, Van? Unless what?"

"Unless I didn't care anything about Iris," he muttered.

"I see," said Jessie, sinking back against her chair.

"Oh God," said Fielding, covering his face with his hands again and mumbling from behind them. "The things he said about Iris." He turned roughly in his chair, put his arms across the back of it, and laying down his head broke into sobs. Jessie rose from her chair, unable to endure the spectacle, and went to stand at the window, gazing down at the blue brilliant river and the utterly lovely day in the midst of which the stinking shame of these happenings seemed so wildly unbelievable. It might be a year since the time less than an hour ago when she had felt so perfectly part of all that freshness and radiance. Behind her, Brandon said, "It was after that that Van telephoned me and I told him to go home and change his clothes and meet me at the field."

There was a brief silence and then Jessie walked across to the desk and picked up the telephone.

"What are you going to do?" cried Fielding in terror, and Brandon exclaimed, "Wait!"

Jessie went on dialling a number. "I am telephoning to Horace Howland," she said. "Can you think of a better person to ask what to do?"

She said in a moment to Howland, "Horace, something perfectly terrible has happened and I—we—have no idea what to do."

To her astonishment Howland did not ask her what the trouble was. He said, "I see. Where are you, my dear?"

"At home," she said. "With Brandon and his—our—brother-in-law. Could you possibly come here right away?"

"Jessie," said Horace Howland's cool, beautifully articulated voice, "I gather it must be the same thing. Serena Lowden telephoned me a few minutes ago. She is in great trouble."

"Oh," said Jessie, in a flat sag of tone. "Already?"

Fielding and Brandon, listening, exchanged a look of fear and Fielding started from his chair. "What do you mean?" he shrilled, " 'already'? The police? The newspapers?"

Jessie was saying to Horace Howland, "Not so far as we know. But it's so late, Horace, anything could——"

"I will be there as soon as I can," said Howland. "You caught me just leaving the office, because I am on my way to Serena's."

"But—" said Jessie nervously, "I hate to say this, but I'm afraid our—we have to do something even faster than Serena. You see, Van Fielding was *there*."

Howland was silent for an instant. He said, "Suppose you telephone Serena now and tell her you have spoken to me and ask if she could manage to go to your house and meet me there. With Alexander." He paused again. "They are all going to have to face it together anyway," he said.

Jessie put down the telephone and turned to Brandon, who was once again pacing the end of the room, running his hand through his hair; and Fielding, leaning over the back of a chair, his eyes senselessly hanging upon Jessie.

"The Lowdens know," she said.

"How?" asked Brandon, which Jessie ignored.

"That means——" mumbled Fielding, clutching the chair.

"Anything," said Jessie, picking up the telephone again. "We will hear soon enough now."

XXI

"Either," said Horace Howland to the circle of faces hanging upon each of his words, "a doctor signs a certificate of death from natural causes, giving the direct reason; or, death of any other sort—accidental, violent, anything that could happen to a person—must be reported to the police. And from there on——" his quiet gesture indicated the automatic procedure by which detectives, medical inspector, homicide squad, the whole machinery of the law, would move into action within a few moments. Jessie sat thinking: but this is insane, obscene, impossible, this cannot be us, that cannot be Horace, talking to us about such a thing. Not Horace Howland! In the pause which felt to her a bottomless hell of frightened silence, she turned her head and looked at Serena Lowden. The lovely remote profile with its deep-lidded eyes and delicate mouth had the look of a clay mask; Jessie imagined it to be hardening in proportion to the inward anguish which it must conceal.

She had learned in a few murmured words upon the Lowdens' arrival what had happened to them this morning. Jack Spanier had gone to Alexander Lowden and had demanded two hundred and fifty thousand dollars, on the threat of tipping off the police and all the newspapers about Isabel Allen.

"Alexander as much as told the man that he refused, for of course he had nothing to do with her death," Serena had said to Jessie. "But then he realized that that would make no difference. He told the——that man——that he would speak to him again by two o'clock. Alexander" said Mrs. Lowden, "could not——his position could not——survive the scandal. Nor——" with a glance so fleeting that Jessie was just aware of it, Serena Lowden had indicated Evander Fielding. It was an unbearable, grotesque injustice, but Serena Lowden had made clear her acceptance of the urgency of protecting the Fielding

262

family together with her own. It seemed to Jessie the depth of abomination that two such men as Lowden and Fielding might escape the direct consequence of their acts through the intervention of a woman like Serena Lowden.

"But Serena," Jessie had said, "even if you should—" she swallowed nervously and bit her lips, for only to seek the words to discuss such a thing with Serena was torment, "if you should give—pay—the money, you could never be sure that that would be the end of it."

"I know," said Serena Lowden. "That is perhaps the vilest part."

"But what will you *do?* Pay the money and then——?"

"I don't know, my dear. It is not the money as money that I care about, it is the—whether that man—you understand."

"Oh, surely Horace will find a way. He must."

Serena Lowden had only shaken her head faintly and sighed. And now with the time racing on, a little before one o'clock already, they were still sitting here in Jessie's quiet sunny library listening to Horace Howland, the unlikeliest person in the world, discuss what they ought to do about a disreputable woman lying dead in a grubby apartment whose nastiness of soiled furniture and curtains, sticky glasses, reeking ashtrays and bad air Jessie was envisioning with disgust.

"Therefore," continued Horace Howland, "there is no choice except to find a physician who is willing to sign a certificate of death from some natural cause. That is not an easy thing to do—it could very well be impossible."

Jessie stared at him, conscious of what it was that people meant when they used the phrase, "to look through the wrong end of a telescope." More clearly than any part of what she saw here, she could picture scenes of ten or twenty years ago when this wise and gentle man had been integral with treasured memories of her mother, and with poignant passages of her own life. This, she thought, is too fantastic to be borne; and turning her head she encountered the sight of Alexander Lowden, sitting panic-stricken, the rags of his false self-importance clinging about him like straws to a clod emerging from a haystack. If he had not been the precipitant of so much danger, he would have been supremely ridiculous. His queer turtle-like eyes which had always suggested his faculty for duplicity and evasiveness were now slanted downwards in his intent not to look directly at anybody; Jessie could also see his glance slide nervously towards the clock when Lowden thought he was unobserved. Nothing could so have drama-

263

tized the hollowness of the man's bombast about his "position" as this admission that it could, like Cinderella's joys, vanish on the stroke of an appointed hour. But that is what Serena will prevent, thought Jessie, and she could not help but ponder why . . . why . . . as if you do not know! she rebuked herself. As if we are not all committed to this wretched venture in equal helpless acquiescence. Self-preservation, yes, she thought, and all that can mean, but responsibility also, this iron collar which Serena has worn for so many years, and I too in different degree.

She looked about the room again, observing the paralysis in which Howland's last words had left each of these people. Somebody had to say what all of them were thinking, but what none could bring himself to say. Jessie spoke at last, with a sense of fearing the sound of her own voice.

"Does any of us," she asked slowly, "know a doctor who would do such a thing—take such a risk—for his sake?"

There was another silence. Then Brandon said, "Of course there are lots of doctors who skate around the fringe—there must be some who do this sort of thing as a—a——"

"A sideline?" asked Jessie, with scorn in her voice which she wished she could have concealed.

Horace Howland said quickly, "I think that is precisely the sort of character that we do not want to bring in. Is it not enough," he asked, with a frankly baleful look first at Lowden and then at Fielding, "to be at the mercy of a man like Spanier?"

"Yes," said Brandon, "but a doctor who has broken the law or connived at a—at something, is so vulnerable himself that——"

"Brandon, we had better leave this to Mr. Howland," said Serena Lowden sharply. Jessie felt the blood surging to her face; she turned and looked miserably away through the window.

"As a matter of fact," said Horace Howland, "this does not begin and end with the doctor alone. What we are really facing is the need to make a plan around the entire matter, which will take every aspect of it into account. You realize, of course, that you are not going to keep Mrs. Allen's death out of the newspapers altogether." He watched the faces of the three men fall into appalled consternation. Fielding's mouth hung open. "You cannot; and if you tried you would precipitate exactly the hue and cry that you want to avoid. The woman is sufficiently conspicuous so that she cannot die without the usual newspaper notices appearing in the normal way. To suppose anything else would be insanity. You," he said, looking at Alexander Lowden, "realize that, do you not?"

Lowden nodded, with shame as repellent as his former pomposity at its boldest. He was far too experienced a newspaperman not to have known what Howland had pointed out, but Jessie realized that his whole terrified preoccupation had been with the danger to himself and his fear that all the rival newspapers of *The Press* would break out with the full scandal while he was trying to suppress it.

Howland waited as if for someone else to make a suggestion, but since nobody did, he continued. "So it seems to me that some very simple consecutive story must be decided upon as being what happened to Mrs. Allen from the time she reached home last night—or this morning, more exactly —and the time it will be reported as vaguely as possible, that she died today."

There appeared now in Evander Fielding's distraught face the semblance of some effort at thought. He was following Horace Howland's words with painful, scowling attention. Brandon Bourne, sprawled in his chair, his feet twisted in the same ugly disposition as Jessie remembered Iris Fielding's a day or two ago, smoked assiduously and gazed at the ceiling. Jessie realized that he wished not to look at Horace Howland. It cannot be, she thought, because he knows that Horace has no use for him; it would not occur to Brandon that anybody could feel so about him. She remembered instances of suffering because of some rash or cruel or angry act of Brandon's, when she had suppressed the urge to scream, "What makes you think you can do this thing and go scot-free! I will make you see how others hate you too!" But she never had. Now she could sit here as coldly disdainful as Serena Lowden, and look at the well-shaped planes of Brandon Bourne's face, and wonder with acid curiosity how she could so helplessly have loved this man and struggled so long to hold him. All the while she sat with her hands folded in her lap, her face intent upon Horace Howland, her mind the only one in the room which was working together with his, disciplined to the execution of a detestable necessity because there was nothing else to do.

Horace Howland was revealing by everything that he said how far he could go in forcing himself to acute, precise thinking in a range that was absolutely alien to his instincts.

Horace! thought Jessie, Horace who will not touch a case which has the slightest human ill-savor, and here he is descending to this unendurable beastliness to protect Serena and me. She listened as Howland said slowly, "I believe that if we follow this plan, this hypothesis of stating what happened fictitiously, so to speak, we will then fit in the necessary identities, if we can find them, to make the picture complete." He leaned back in his chair, braced by his elbows, with his hands placed palms together, and said, "Let us say that for some weeks or months past, Mrs. Allen had been under the care of a well-known specialist in some type of serious illness which, in the nature of her activities, she was extremely anxious to conceal. Something which could terminate fatally, quite suddenly. Let us say that she had been warned not to overdo, that her physician had ordered special treatments and rest and no late hours, which she had disobeyed. You realize," said Howland, with a resigned sigh, "that everybody close to Mrs. Allen must have this clearly in mind, because—" he shrugged delicately as the swiftest way to dismiss what they all nervously understood, the flurry of gossip which would briefly follow tomorrow morning's news, until the next sensation came along to supersede it.

"Upon reaching home from the Whitelaw party she felt very ill and, naturally, she became panicky. She was afraid to be alone; that was what she told some woman friend to whom she telephoned, asking her to come at once. Now we must decide just who that woman friend could have been."

Howland looked about the room, as if inviting each person to make a suggestion. But the faces remained as blank as before, some of them even more baffled, for the roster of Isabel Allen's women friends was bizarre at best, and, as Howland now pointed out, the friend must not be a woman like Isabel herself; such personalities were too vulnerable to scandal.

"Phyllis?" asked Jessie of Serena, raising her eyebrows.

Mrs. Lowden shook her head. "Not at all," she said. "Besides, I do not think we should drag Oliver into this."

"No," said Howland. "Some older woman, with a far less well-known name. A plain, capable sort of woman, remote enough from the rest of Mrs. Allen's acquaintance to be outside the spotlight. I think it safe to say," he added, "that all conspicuous or—eh—notorious people have such connections. I think we have all had experience of that."

Jessie bit her lip, for an idea was beginning to form in her mind. A plain, older woman, vigorously not of Isabel Allen's definition, and necessarily, no fool. A woman shrewd and wise and somebody who would have a motive for willingness to do this dangerous and disagreeable thing.

"The friend," continued Horace Howland, "arrived as quickly as possible, was admitted by Mrs. Allen, and helped her to go to bed. It was then, say, about five o'clock this morning. The friend did not realize the seriousness of Mrs. Allen's symptoms. But after sleeping for a length of time, Mrs. Allen appeared to be, late this morning, in a state of acute illness. Her friend then telephoned for her physician. He arrived about noon, to find Mrs. Allen in very grave condition, and he remained with her until she died. Naturally, the friend——"

Alexander Lowden raised his white head, its handsome arrogance all collapsed, and asked, "I don't exactly see why all this about the friend——"

"Because," replied Howland, with tartness so crisp that it became almost visible contempt, "because there is a time element of speculation as to who might have been with Mrs. Allen during the night, or what remained of it; or whether anybody was with her at all. If she was as ill as she must presumably have been she could probably not have telephoned to the doctor herself, or admitted him to her apartment so close to the time when she supposedly died. And also——" Howland's expression became even grimmer——"because I am coming to the real point of just exactly what is to be done—now. You remember. The—ah—Mrs. Allen is still lying there in that flat."

Lowden's head went down between his humped shoulders, and his eyes to the floor. Fielding and Brandon Bourne exchanged a look.

"We have no choice now," said Howland, "except to throw ourselves upon somebody's mercy, and such a woman as I have described is the safest sort of person to choose. Obviously none of you can be the woman who has been in Mrs. Allen's apartment since five o'clock this morning."

Jessie made a quiet exclamation, rather to her own surprise. Howland looked at her in question. She stared back with meaning more cogent to him than if she had spoken.

"Can she go immediately to that apartment?" asked Howland as if they had had a detailed conversation about the person in Jessie's mind. "And does she know the doctor who will join her there?"

267

The three other men and Serena Lowden sat stupid with amazement and suspense, watching Jessie and Howland.

"She knows him very well," said Jessie. She felt as if she must be talking in her sleep; no part of this idea seemed to be her own, or within her own power to arrange. "I will telephone her now."

She rose to leave the room. Lowden looked up at her with dumb anxiety as to what she meant to do, but without the courage to inquire. Fielding jumped forward as he had when Jessie had telephoned Horace Howland, but Jessie ignored him. On her way upstairs to her own room where she could telephone privately, she realized that Althea Crowe must be out at lunch. But suddenly the heavy voice boomed "Hello!" and Jessie said, almost hoarse with relief, "Oh, I was so afraid you would be out."

"What the hell," said Althea Crowe. "When you stood me up I decided to have a sandwich and a beer at my desk and do a day's work for a change. But why aren't you out with dreamboat?"

Jessie told her.

"Is that so?" was Althea Crowe's comment, spoken slowly and with extraordinarily little surprise. "Right in the groove, isn't it?"

"How amazing you are, Althea." It was indeed typical of her that she should see this thing panoramically; if one surveyed life as objectively as Althea Crowe, one must lose the capacity to be surprised when women like Isabel Allen met violent deaths. They met them all the time, reflected Jessie; they committed suicide by jumping from high windows and inhaling carbon monoxide in automobiles and taking lethal quantities of sedative drugs; or they died like Isabel, in shadows which the convergence of public and private influence, taste, and expediency found it wiser not to penetrate too deeply. With her blue blade of a mind Althea Crowe cut across Jessie's troubled and hesitant preliminaries and said, "I see." There was a pause while Jessie knew her to be weighing the possibility of success in carrying through the ruse, for Althea Crowe would not undertake any venture unless she felt—she would say—mathematically sure of succeeding. Jessie held the telephone, staring meanwhile at her reflection in a mirror across the room. She looked at her own face with a sense of crazy unreality, feeling that she had lost the power to know through which of several different lenses her mind's eye could discern her real self. Then Althea Crowe said, "All right, Jess. I'll do it."

Jessie knew that this was no moment, either in time or mood, to try to thank Althea Crowe. Instead she made her own voice as precise as possible and she asked, "What about Reath, Althea? Shall I speak to him now, or you?"

"I will," said Althea. "You stay out of his corner in this. He may have some way of—anyway, leave it to us. I want a key, right away."

"I'll send Josephine with it. Where do you want her?"

"My office. She'll be on her way while I'm talking to Reath. Good bye, Jess."

Downstairs again Jessie opened the library door and called Alexander Lowden out to the hall. He came, stooped, shuffling, looking a raddled old man.

"I want the key to Isabel's apartment," said Jessie brusquely.

Lowden opened his mouth, an uneasy glimmer in his eyes. Jessie said, "Please don't waste time proposing you haven't got the key. If it is not in your pocket, where is it?"

Lowden swallowed and drew a gold key-chain from his pocket. With fumbling fingers he detached a Yale key and handed it to Jessie.

"Does this open both doors?" asked Jessie. "The street door and the apartment upstairs?"

Lowden nodded. Jessie motioned him back to the library and took the key to her room. When Josephine had left with it Jessie sank into the low chair near the bedside table and heard herself, with surprise, utter a strange, weary sound, neither a groan nor a wail, but resembling both. She bent her head, pressing her temples hard between the thumb and fingers of her right hand, holding her eyes closed as if that could help to shut out the hideousness through which she had been struggling and must still further make her way. After a moment she opened her eyes and looked at her bed, made up for the day now, closed, beautiful, discreet, the rough rosy silk of the coverlet falling in sculptured folds to the carpet. She tried to make herself believe that less than three hours ago she had been lying in that bed, alight with the supremest joy, talking to Mark Dwyer who had been transcendently important to her. And now this beastliness had pushed him aside as a hooligan elbows a person in a crowd.

"Oh my God," said Jessie aloud. "My God, my God." Her sense of unreality had become so great in the midst of this morning's nightmare, that Mark Dwyer too had lost identity. She sat frowning, confused and shaken, trying to recapture the mood which had enclosed the beginning of the morning, with all its magic anticipation. But she only found herself dully disbelieving that it could have been true.

"Oh, yes," she said finally, half aloud. "I did say I would let him know." At least, she thought, as she dialled the number of the Ritz, I can prevent his wasting any more of the day, when he has so little time in New York.

His voice brought warmth to her chilled, shocked nerves. But it is only comforting, she thought, as she listened to him asking how he could help; only consolation, not enchantment, not anything that was coming into bloom until this brutal thing crushed it off this morning.

"No," she said quietly. "I'm so grateful to you, Mark, and if there were anything you could do I wouldn't hesitate to ask you."

"Would you mind," asked Mark very slowly, "would it seem too intruding if I asked you a question or two?"

"No," she said, "except that this——"

"I see." She was quite right in her reluctance to talk through a hotel switchboard. "I only had the newspapers in mind," he said. "I think I could help there."

"Could you?" asked Jessie. He took that almost as permission to go ahead and do what he could. "But not before——"

"I understand. I think you can leave that to me."

"Thank you," she murmured, because she could think of nothing else to say. At this point some part of her mind was blankly inquiring just who this man was, after all, and precisely why she should confide in him.

"Can I reach you later in the afternoon if I telephone?", he asked.

"Why not?"

"I won't keep you now, then. Bless you, my dear."

As she reentered the library Jessie thought first of the time. It was just short of half past one. The Lowdens and Fielding and Brandon were sitting as she had left them, all silent, all turning their eyes from Horace Howland, who was at the desk concluding a telephone conversation, to Jessie, shutting the door.

Tacit questions lay in each face, some that must be answered, some which deserved only to be ignored. Jessie conveyed silently to Howland that Althea Crowe had taken her assignment in hand, and Howland said, "My office has been in touch with——" his face showed disgust at having to pronounce the name—"the man Spanier. I have delayed giving him his answer at two o'clock by arranging that he come here. But he will be here before three."

"Here?" Jessie felt as if it had been suggested to bring something fœtid into her house. "And how did he consent——"

"My dear, I did not ask him here from choice." Howland spoke so distantly that Jessie winced for having forced him. "I believe that he will find himself at the greatest possible disadvantage here and——"

"But surely he knows that himself. And also that time is on our side."

"Certainly. But, you see, he also knows that he is guilty of manslaughter. It makes no difference that Fielding here did not realize it—nor the rest of you. Naturally Spanier was not going to point it out."

"Then——" Jessie's hands went up in a gesture of vast, relieved dismissal. At the same moment she saw that nobody else reflected such feelings, and Horace Howland said, "Not quite, my dear. It is not quite so simple. Spanier does not get convicted of manslaughter without an inquest, an indictment, and a trial. We are as much committed as ever to preventing that. Fielding and Lowden would both be dragged through it and, worse, their families. No, Spanier remains as dangerous as ever, and now we have to use his tactics too. He is gambling that he gets what he has demanded, and we must gamble at his level. There is no defense against a blackmailer except to hold some knowledge over him as ruinous as his over his victim—worse, if possible. And it must be knowledge about something in which one is totally uninvolved oneself—that is the weakness in the matter of Mrs. Allen's death, and you may be sure that Spanier knows it. But I tend to think—" and Howland paused.

"This town is full of people who know enough to jail Spanier," said Brandon, coming down with a thump on the front legs of his chair. "Say, Jess," he added, "can you have them fix something to eat?"

"I've asked for some sandwiches and coffee to be brought in."

"Well, Okay," said Brandon. "Who do we know who has the works on Spanier?"

Jessie's mind stirred with dislike for Brandon's way of speaking; it was meaningless slang, but its flippancy at a time like this was disturbing. As if for corroboration when she had need of it, she turned and met the glance of Serena Lowden. Mrs. Lowden's face was if possible more frozen than before, but the heaviness of her eyes proved her despairing concern with every word that was said. Jessie watched her as she turned about and levelled her gaze at Evander Fielding.

"I think," she said, her voice falling like drops of ice-water in their ears, "your daughter may be such a person, Evander."

Fielding's putty-colored face turned a dull, shamed red as they watched him. His head came up as if to defy the slur upon his daughter, and then went slowly down between his shoulders again. It was, thought Jessie, the most ignoble of sights. There was a troubled silence, during which Sarah brought in a coffee tray and a dish of sandwiches and arranged them on the tea-table in the corner. When she had left the room Jessie said, "Please help yourselves if you wish something to eat." She queried Serena Lowden silently, who shook her head, and then Jessie said, "I agree with Serena. I think, actually, that Iris is too—ingenuous—to understand much of the truth about Spanier, but I think she should be here, anyway—and Millicent too. Iris had better learn once for all just what he has been mixed up in. And," Jessie added ruthlessly, "what it has cost her father and the rest of us."

"That still leaves us looking for somebody who really has the dirt," said Brandon.

It was Lowden then who looked up with a sigh, and for the first time appeared to dare to speak at all.

"I should think Henry Greenberg is the man," he said, and fell to eyeing the floor again.

The cold distaste which colored Horace Howland's face seemed to Jessie the least surprising of sights. Yet she knew that Howland would weigh the usefulness of Greenberg, completely dominating his feelings with his reason. She said, "I think we all realize that Henry is a dangerous man but——"

"He is less dangerous than Spanier in this situation," said Howland.

From the corner where he was pouring a cup of coffee Brandon said, "You can't stop to be so particular now. Henry fishes in this kind of muck all the time and he may haul something up for us."

"That is perfectly true," said Horace Howland.

"On the other hand," said Jessie, thinking carefully as she spoke, "Henry will do nothing without his pound of flesh."

272

"Whose noose would you rather be in?" asked Brandon with his mouth full.

"Brandon is right, my dear," said Horace Howland. He examined his watch doubtfully. "But Greenberg is not likely to be in his office now. He must be out at lunch."

Brandon was at the desk, about to telephone for Henry Greenberg. "Then he's at Twenty-One," he said. "He's never out of reach of a telephone. Here," he said, beckoning to Lowden, "you talk to him."

"You may as well send for Iris, Evander," said Serena Lowden.

Jessie crossed the room and bent over Horace Howland's shoulder. The speculation about Greenberg had thrown her mind back for the moment to last night's party, which the happenings of the morning had obliterated. How very curious, she thought, that only now am I remembering Harry Blitzer's warnings. I am becoming an imbecile. Why didn't I think of this right in the beginning? She told Howland now what Harry Blitzer had said.

"Let's get him here at once, by all means, then. He's all right, that man."

"Oh," said Jessie. "I forgot that you knew him."

"I? But for years, child."

"Of course," she said. She put her hand to her forehead. "I must be losing my wits, Horace."

"I should say that the provocation was extreme," he murmured.

"I'll go and try to reach Harry Blitzer," she whispered to Howland. She went again to her own room.

His office told her that Blitzer was still at home, and Jessie remembered thankfully his queer Broadway habits; he spent the night in circulation, wound up with a weird meal at Lindy's, and went to bed at seven o'clock in the morning. His voice when he answered the telephone was thick with sleep and the coarse morning roughness of the heavy cigar-smoker. But he reacted so fast to Jessie's few words about Jack Spanier that she could almost imagine she heard his brains click into action. He promised to come as quickly as possible. She put down the telephone and sat back to try once more to regather her senses from the wilderness in which it seemed to her that they were scattered. The telephone buzzed and Jessie jumped so sharply at the noise that she felt ill with the rawness of her nerves. Althea Crowe said "Jess?"

273

"Yes," said Jessie. She looked to make sure that the switch-off key was down. "What—how——"

"So far so good," said Althea. "The bus is on its way over."

"Oh, God," said Jessie, feeling a faint unnatural moisture spring to her forehead and the palms of her hands. There flashed then through her mind, in precise tandem form, two thoughts: how she would never in her life be able to compensate Althea Crowe for this unbelievable service, and how miserably undeserving of it its beneficiaries were.

"Has—are—" she scarcely knew what she wanted to ask Althea, but she realized too that any questions would be dangerous. She paused.

"There's a sister in Wapwallopen, Pennsylvania," said Althea. "She's——"

"What?" cried Jessie, in a snap of hysteria which sent a mad laugh into the telephone. "Where did you say?"

"Only what I found in the desk while I was cleaning house," said Althea drily. She paused to give the fullest possible import to what she had said, and then she continued while Jessie listened in a haze of relief mingled with awe at her boldness.

"Apparently our dolly came from there," said Althea. "I called up the sister. She will reach town this evening and take baby home with her. She's as sore as a boil. Says dolly has never been anything but a pain in the neck to them and I should please—" Althea gave an equine snicker—"keep her out of the papers."

"Oh, God," said Jessie again.

"So I'll meet Mrs. Katzenschwanz——"

"What?" shrieked Jessie, surrendering to idiocy at last.

"Look," said Althea. "I didn't make it up, I could have done better. I will meet Mrs. Katzenschwanz at the Penn Station and by God she won't be out of my sight until she's back on the train with dolly."

"Oh, Althea."

"I don't mind. By the way, how are you making out at your end?"

Jessie explained.

"Anh." The noise through the wire was a type of grunt; Althea Crowe was thinking. "You can always ask that bastard a question or two about that Thorne girl, you know."

"You mean—really? Did he, was he——?"

"Well," said Althea Crowe thoughtfully. "Who is to say,
274

Jess? Who is going to say three years from now exactly what happened about all this today?"

"Why, yes," said Jessie. She felt extraordinarily naïve. "Why of course."

"That's just what we are doing now," said Althea. "When we are through we will have made some useful confusion. People will talk—but they will be talking mostly through their hats. We're buying the hats, right now."

"But—the Thorne girl. You knew her, didn't you?"

"Sure. She worked for me for a while. She was a flyweight. Drifted around and got into some show or other and fetched up with Spanier. The usual thing with that kind. I hadn't seen her for a long time, but I did see her a day or two before she died."

"You did?"

"Jessie, my dear, don't get so melodramatic about this. Just —try to see it for what it was, the same thing that happens every day. The kid was in the usual jam and she came and asked me what to do. So I told her and the next thing I knew she was dead. But that wasn't necessarily enough to make her commit suicide, my God if it were, the town would be strewn with female corpses every morning! She probably asked him for the three hundred dollars or whatever she needed and he probably pushed her in the face. But one of you can tell him——"

And Jessie listened carefully to Althea Crowe.

XXII

It is true, thought Jessie, that when the unbelievable happens, the utterly grotesque, one sits in the midst of it and finds it familiar in the same way that the most horrible bad dream is never novel; one has dreamt it often before. Not in the wildest imaginable nightmare could I have contrived to bring together in such a way, for such reasons, all of the people in this room. Yet now that they are here I am without surprise, I feel as if I had been through it on some occasion before. She turned her head slowly and examined one by one the faces ranged about her; and when she came to Jack Spanier,

275

though she averted her eyes to suppress visible evidence of her disgust, she could still not achieve that sense of astonishment at his presence here which would have relieved her, like a great draught of fresh air.

They were now suspended in a heavy, tangible silence which had followed the last words that they had heard, a slow and thoughtful admonition from Horace Howland to Spanier to consider well the meaning of the presence of each individual here. Iris Fielding and her mother were isolated in a corner, seated side by side upon a small settee, curiously erased in personality; they were one-dimensional, it seemed to Jessie, as if they had been squashed flat by a steam-roller like the idiotic clowns' turn in the circus, where nothing remains but a great paper doll.

Harry Blitzer, gross and crude and blue-jowled, his clever pop-eyes moving from warmest devotion for Jessie to shrewd peril for Spanier, belied in character everything that his physical presence proclaimed. And Henry Greenberg over there, Jessie realized, is the precise opposite—kindly, easygoing Henry with those steel-rimmed spectacles and that benign, soothing manner—think what lies behind it! In some way the two men had contrived to place Jack Spanier, cocky and vinegar-sharp, upon a small hard chair between them. His dark beads of eyes switched constantly from one face to the next, boldly roving round and round the room. Horace Howland, seated at Jessie's desk with his frail hands quietly folded before him, created the grave impression of sitting in judgment, which Jessie knew, for all his fineness, to be no accident. If he must deal, she thought, in the cheap stuff of charlatanry he will carry off a better show than those who make a trade of it. She watched Henry Greenberg's face, aware that for such a personality, driven by a perverted craving to hold power over others, it must be insufferable to see a man like Howland calmly assume the mastery of this situation. Yet Henry is so clever, Jessie knew, that he concedes he could not possibly have done so dramatic a thing so well. And he is utterly overjoyed to be here, to be in on this. He will never let Alec Lowden forget it for one breath, all the rest of his life. But what other prices Henry Greenberg might exact for his cooperation now, Jessie had not the courage to weigh.

Serena Lowden sat near her husband, her head raised and poised with the majestic remoteness of a queen, her eyes fixed upon Howland, directed icily past Spanier. Evander Fielding had succeeded almost in obliterating himself; he was shrunken and silent in a chair, his chin in one hand, his eyes lowered. And Brandon—Jessie sighed. Perhaps it was as well, it lent a variety of mood to the grotesque gathering, at least. Brandon had sat as long as he could; his physical restlessness had reached the peak of compelling impatience where he could no longer remain in a chair, and he was standing by the fireplace, one arm on the mantel, crossing and recrossing his feet as he shifted his weight from time to time. There stood upon the mantel a pair of very old miniature girandoles which had belonged to Rosa Landau, small blossoms of prismed brilliance, and each time that Brandon in his kinetic inquietude abruptly moved his elbow, Jessie locked her teeth against the urge to tell him to be careful. Ah well, she told herself, you should have learned to bear that by now, you have far more critical things to worry about. And she turned to listen to Horace Howland.

He was speaking, in manner and voice so much the classic image of a great judge upon the bench that he compelled the eyes, the mind, and the will of every person in the room. He said, "To sum this matter up, Mr. Spanier, I will now review exactly what your situation is in relation to each person present here, and to others with whom they are connected.

"First, in respect to the death of Mrs. Isabel Allen. Mr. Evander Fielding is prepared if necessary to testify and to describe exactly what he witnessed, which resulted in the death of Mrs. Allen. You hold nothing over Mr. Fielding. You not only have, by your own admission to him early this morning, no personal evidence that he was in Mrs. Allen's apartment when she died; there is no circumstantial evidence whatever that he was present there, innocent as that presence was."

(Oh, thought Jessie, God bless Althea Crowe; and for an hysterical instant she faced the incredible image of that trumpeting elephant of a woman, grimly scrubbing down that evil place. She composed her face with care.)

"On the subject," continued Horace Howland, keeping his fine eyes coldly upon Jack Spanier, "on the subject of your character and your habits, which would be inextricable from the issue should it ever receive public hearing, there is the word of Miss Iris Fielding, who is prepared if necessary to repeat in court those statements about you which she has made here during the past hour."

Sitting with her head bent to avoid the sight of Iris and

Millicent, Jessie heard the loud uneasy breathing of all the others, burdened with shame for the girl and for a father who could have dragged her into this. Howland continued speaking.

"You have brought into this matter certain questions relating to Mr. Alexander Lowden and to his friendship with Mrs. Allen over a period of several years past. You have heard Mr. Lowden admit, and Mrs. Lowden agree, that that friendship has been a matter of such general knowledge that there is no way in which you could embarrass Mr. and Mrs. Lowden by threats of public exposure of it at this time, or ever.

"Pursuing the all-important matter of your personal and professional record, which, I repeat, would be cited in any open issue brought in these connections, you have heard Mr. Harry Blitzer declare that he can produce evidence by which you could be proved liable to prosecution for certain specific financial improbities and dishonesties in connection with theatrical undertakings. Mr. Blitzer has knowledge of your collusive dishonesty together with a Mrs. Emily Sanders, in connection with falsified accounts of funds raised at two large theatrical benefits for war philanthropies during the past year. I believe that these facts in Mr. Blitzer's possession have made clear the uselessness of your attempting to give information to any newspaper about any element of this afternoon's discussion, and particularly to *The New York Record* where I understand Mrs. Emily Sanders is now employed."

Jessie looked up suddenly to meet a cold blue stare from Brandon; and as if correcting herself, she bent her head again, not wanting to read his mind. She listened carefully to Howland.

"Again," he said, "in respect to your own reputation: you have heard Mr. Henry Greenberg cite three specific instances of dealings that he has had with you, or in which he has represented as counsel those who have had dealings with you, any one of which is sufficient to make you liable to various processes of law.

"Finally, you have heard Mrs. Brandon Bourne, in the presence of these witnesses, declare her knowledge of the existence of a letter, which would be produced should you make it necessary. The letter was written by a certain Miss Leda Thorne on the day before she was found dead, presumably a suicide. The contents of the letter are such as to furnish proof which any court would find incontrovertible, that Miss Thorne was in dire and mortal fear because of threats and compulsion by you; that this fear was directly involved with her violent death; that these proofs would be sufficient to reopen the medical examiner's verdict of suicide; all of which, I may add, would come, at this time, well within the statute of limitations."

Horace Howland paused, gazing sternly across the desk at the ten faces ranged opposite him. Of them all, only Serena Lowden and Jessie Bourne met his eyes squarely, although Henry Greenberg was gazing in his direction with a mild, quizzical expression which might mean anything, but which Jessie interpreted as wondering, if reluctant, admiration. Harry Blitzer was looking at Jack Spanier with the rough, final disgust that might have marked his knocking out a mug in a brawl. Brandon Bourne, lighting a cigarette, remained peculiarly impassive which was unusual, since the hard, open planes of his face had never enabled him successfully to veil his reactions, had he found it important to do so. It was part of his strange, intent arrogance that he had never bothered.

All the rest sat with their eyes downcast, forcing upon Howland the cynical knowledge that, escaped or not, they felt intolerably their disgrace and guilt, in a degree of shame of which Jack Spanier was proving himself incapable. He sat, still raking the room and the people with insolent eyes; upon his pointed, weasel face he wore a snide grin. Howland shut out the sight by a faint motion of his deep eyelids; even more deliberately than before, he said, "Therefore, upon the strength of the combined knowledge of facts and circum-stances concerning you which I have just reviewed, you will kindly sign this waiver of claims and threats against all the concerned persons whose names are appended, and against all members of their families and their associates who are in-cluded."

And he pushed across to the front of the desk the papers which he and Henry Greenberg had hastily put together, while waiting for the arrival of Spanier. Greenberg had ex-pressed doubt as to their legal validity and Howland had echoed that they were, indeed, probably worthless, but both men had agreed that their psychological effect upon Spanier would be the only result that mattered. Spanier shrugged, lifted himself vulgarly from his chair, ambled to the desk and, taking a fountain pen from his pocket, signed the papers spread before him, after so cursory a glance down the sheets as to dismiss them contemptuously. Gravely Horace Howland and Henry Greenberg affixed their signatures as witnesses, and Howland said, scarcely permitting a moment to intervene, "Brandon, will you please show Mr. Spanier out?"

As the library door shut loudly behind them—in her relief Jessie felt that for once in her life she was grateful to Brandon for slamming a door—Harry Blitzer said something to Henry Greenberg in words which nobody else understood, but which elicited a thick snicker from Greenberg. Jessie's one idea now was to stir the group up, get them moving, get them out. This was no time either to thank those who had so amazingly been of help, or to excoriate those who had dragged them all into this cesspool. They were getting to their feet now, making uncertain motions in the direction of breaking away, for this had been so fantastic an experience that there was no precedent for extricating oneself from it.

Harry Blitzer was standing in the window embrasure, talking to Horace Howland, and Jessie moved over to join them for a moment. She smiled at both men with feeling so deep that they saw the tears standing unshed in her eyes, and Blitzer, squeezing her hand, said, "She looks more like Rosie all the time, heh?"

"I told her so just the other day," said Horace Howland with a tender smile. "You've been splendid, Harry. Just—" he gestured. "Just as I'd have said you would be."

Blitzer nodded and smiled warmly. "And why not? Never mind how I hate that slob, to me Jess is another Rosie. Well," he said, extending his pudgy, jewelled, hairy hand, "I gotta run. That was a smooth job." He made that gesture, thumb and forefinger joined in a circle, the hand flipped from a stiff wrist, which marks the special approval of his peculiar world; and Jessie accompanied him out to the hall.

"You're such a darling, Harry," she said, as they stood waiting for the elevator.

"Nah. It all shook down, that's all. What a prince, that Howland," he said, wagging his head. "A real prince."

"You've known him a long time," Jessie mused.

"And how. My God, since he began going with your mama. Jeez, that's a long time ago."

"It seems funny in a way, that you and he became friends."

"*Nu?*" shrugged Blitzer. "Should I hate him on account of Rosie? No, I should love him. So—" He made a sign of wonder at the years that had fled.

"It's good," said Jessie. "A good thing, to have known people that way, all your life. Where did you first see him?"

Blitzer squinted. "Lemme see. Maybe—no—wait, I got it.

280

On a Staten Island ferryboat, one Sunday afternoon. Well—" he grinned. "So long, honey."

She stood at the door, shaken by fatigue, by her thoughts, by the great vibrating arc of memory, by the discovery of iron strength in old, forgotten links, by glimpses into a buried, tightly-knitted world which seemed a safer and a better place than this in which her visible life was lived. But it is wonderful, she thought, it is beyond belief that by turning back to all that, to the people in it, I can find safety. "Don't forget, honey," Harry Blitzer had said on his way out, "you still got an ace up your sleeve if that bastard eveh lets out another yip."

She had had no idea what he meant, and in some surprise he had explained, "Why, Louis. Your cousin Louis Schwartz. He's a big shot in the Department, didn't you know?"

"I did know," she said slowly. "In a way. But I've never— it sounds crazy to you, Harry, I know———"

"Listen," he said. "Nothing sounds crazy to me. I neveh see anything but nuts."

"Well—since I've never seen Louis, I wouldn't like to turn to him suddenly for the first time when I am in trouble. That's not—you know, Harry."

"Sure I know. But look, people like Louis don't want to know you just because—" he gestured to indicate the world and all its accoutrements to which Rosa Landau had risen and carried her daughter with her. "You'd be surprised. People's folks take what happens to them for granted. You get rich, you get famous, okay so you get rich and famous. Maybe you fall on your pan, too. They're used to everything."

Jessie had listened with fascinated appreciation. "So if you got any more trouble, you give me a buzz and I'll tell Louis," Blitzer had said. That was when he had rung for the elevator and Jessie had stood there waiting with him, talking about Horace Howland. After the elevator door closed upon him she had turned back into the foyer of her apartment, and she was standing there, leaning back upon the closed front door with her hands clasped behind her, groping inwardly for a moment's peace, when Brandon came out of the library, escorting Henry Greenberg to the door. Jessie was immensely grateful that Greenberg made a quick departure; she thanked him as fervently as she knew would please him and, indeed, as he really deserved.

Then Brandon said, leading her into the empty drawing-room, "Jess, I think we ought to—well, you know, sort of

281

anticipate the kind of talk that will start tomorrow when the papers come out with Isabel. You know what I mean. Kind of sew up Van and Alec in——"

"Oh, Brandon," she sighed. She sank into a chair and leaned her head back, and felt the weakness of utter exhaustion flickering up and down her limbs and her spine. "I am so tired." Her voice broke a little.

"I know," he said, in an unusually sympathetic way. "It's a hell of a note. Personally I'd like to get royally plastered to forget the goddam mess. But we're in this so deep already——"

"I suppose you're right. What do you suggest?"

"What's going on tonight?"

It was like him to speak as if he took it for granted, like other husbands, that his wife would have made plans for both of them; it seemed not to occur to him that she might be engaged quite differently in view of their peculiar situation of his own making.

"I have some people coming for dinner."

"Who?" asked Brandon quickly, in a sharper tone.

"Friends of my own, I'm afraid," said Jessie wearily. "People you don't care for much. Sam and Helen and the Blocks and——"

"Damn," she heard him mutter. She could so easily have lost her temper that she pretended not to notice him, as the only way of saving herself.

"You can be out," she said indifferently. "They all think you are in Virginia anyway."

"No, I have to be here," he said with irritation. "That's what I'm trying to set up. Any more of your friends?"

"The Pritchards," she said.

He raised his eyebrows. "That might not be so bad. Anybody from any other paper . . . well, I think it would be a good idea if we had the Lowdens here and Van and Millie."

"Oh my God," said Jessie.

"Do you think this is my idea of a pleasant evening?"

"I'm sorry. You're perfectly right. Well——"

Brandon was counting names on his fingers. "That's twelve," he said. "It might be——"

"No," said Jessie. "Thirteen. Reath Sheldon is coming too. You forget you were away." She had decided hours ago not to let Mark Dwyer come, and she saw in view of Brandon's idea how fortunate it was that she had asked Reath Sheldon here. Only she and Horace Howland and Althea Crowe knew now what Sheldon had done today, but tomorrow's newspapers would name him as Isabel Allen's physician; and since he brought the most august of reputations to a very wide practice including many celebrities, it would not occur to anybody to raise a question.

"Hell," said Brandon. "Well, who's another woman?"

Jessie looked at him as if to remind him how many women he knew, and he glared, pacing up and down. "Can't you think of another woman?" he said. "Somebody who's kind of talky and gets around?"

She could. Tired as she was, and feeling as if she never wanted to see a human face again, she knew exactly the person: Elizabeth Betts. But how can I put it to her, she thought. After last night, she will think I am taking advantage of what she said, acting as if she might be free for dinner at the last moment. Oh, rot, she rebuked herself. After all that has happened today, can you waste the strength to care about such a thing?

"I will get Elizabeth Betts," she said to Brandon. She had not decided what story to tell Elizabeth, but she would think of something drastic enough to make Elizabeth feel that she was desperate in a small social way.

They returned to the library, where Jessie had a quiet word with Serena Lowden while Brandon spoke to his sister. Eight o'clock, they agreed; and Jessie, bidding Horace Howland good bye, expressed to him with her eyes more than an infinity of words could have conveyed. She stood near the door feeling as if she had turned into a human clock ticking off the seconds until the last of these people should be gone. She meant after that to send in Sarah and Josephine to turn out the room as if it had not been housecleaned for weeks. Though she had had the windows open, and all day long had emptied ash trays and kept order in small ways, the room seemed to her an infected and befouled place.

They should go; they must go; why on earth had they not already gone? She turned from the door and looked once more at the three Fieldings and the two Lowdens, and Brandon waiting uneasily to escort them out. What was their delay, why were they lingering? Jessie was aware suddenly that in her fatigue she had ceased to notice the play and interplay of glances, the ways in which fearful and nervous people balanced themselves on one foot or the other foot or uneasily upon their heels; the strange, guiltlike hesitation with which they lighted cigarettes; the elaborations of their mannerisms with match stubs, with their rings, their neckties, their eyeglasses. Then she saw why they were hesitating, and, apparently, waiting. They were compelled by the fact that Serena Lowden, risen from her chair, had walked across the room and placed herself with intentional precision before the fireplace, and that she was looking at them all with an expression which amounted to command. She let them wait until the air had become tense with question, and then she began to speak.

"Before I leave this room," she said, her limpid voice like crystal, "and before you leave it, I am going to say something which none of you might otherwise ever hear."

She looked at Evander Fielding; she turned her fine dark eyes upon her shamed and despicable husband; her glance rested upon the blighted paleness of Millicent Fielding and her daughter, failing to control the shifting of their light, uneasy eyes.

"The lot of you," she said, "are equally to blame. And all of you are more contemptible than anybody with whom we have been forced to deal because of what you have done. Those people began life in the gutter; it is not unrealistic to expect some of them to have remained there. All of you knew better. *You knew better*. That is unforgivable."

She looked at Millicent Fielding, who could not look at her, and so she said, "Millicent!" The woman raised her head. Serena Lowden stared at her and spoke again. "I have known you all your life. I suppose you have made some effort to drag Iris back from the filth in which she was determined to wallow, but you have failed because your own motives were shabby and trivial. Even though my own mother thought your mother the same kind of fool that you are, you should have known better. I could understand how a woman like that wretched dead creature could make of her daughter what you have made of Iris. But not you. You are riddled with fear and cowardice, for twenty years your life has been a mean thing. Most recently your cowardice has taken the form of seeming not to know. I," said Serena Lowden, turning a tragic and terrible face upon her husband, "I am the woman who knows what that means, seeming not to know. It is one thing to be driven to that on account of a husband." She paused. "It is quite another to descend to it in dealing with one's child."

Jessie found herself clasping her ice-cold hands together; she felt the sharp staccato of her heightened pulse. Where, her thoughts raced, where shall I look? What shall I do? She pressed her lips together and raised her head and kept her eyes upon the face of Serena Lowden, who turned now to Iris Fielding.

"As for you," she said, "after I have made every allowance for the failure of your parents to live so that you would know good conduct from bad—even after that, I see you as a degenerate—a betrayer of the world into which we were born. It was a world, which is better than the ruin that you and your kind are making. It produced fine people, not always people born in it either, but shaped by it, people like your aunt here. To me you are more vicious than the Mrs. Allen and the Miss Thorne about whom we have talked today. I have no reason to expect that your future will be different from theirs, but there will be less excuse for you, and more people will suffer. I am saying all this because I want you to understand that what we have done today was not done to save you from the consequences of your acts. What you have seen today probably looked to your mind like a clever battle of wits, with the smarter people winning out. What you have seen," said Serena Lowden, "was a tragedy in the lesson of responsibility."

Jessie tottered to the kitchen. On her way through the pantry, where Sarah was counting out silver for tonight, she said, "Come here, Sarah. Listen to this." And throwing herself with absurdly unnatural heaviness into a kitchen chair, she clutched her head in her hands over the marble table, and said, "We have to be fourteen for dinner. Big dinner. Horrible, lace-pants, stuffed-shirt dinner party. Oh my God, I want to die."

She gazed up at the two women, who were exchanging the inevitable look. Anna shrugged; Sarah's face set in the way that it did when anything was precipitated by Brandon Bourne. They all consulted the clock. It was past four. Sarah said, "Well, Mum, there's still time to get Delia Reardon if she ain't servin' some place else."

"Bribe her if she is," said Jessie. "Offer her twenty dollars —twenty-five dollars. I don't care. You and Josephine will need her."

"We'll manage," said Sarah bitterly.

"Oh, you angel. Sarah!" exclaimed Jessie. "Give me a cup of tea. Your tea, in a kitchen cup, right here. I am dying."

"Ye look it," said Sarah, pouring the tea from her own brown earthenware pot. It was dark, red Irish tea, scalding, strong as liquor. Jessie clutched the thick crockery cup in

285

both hands and gulped, wincing. Sarah went away, her stiff back eloquent.

"Oh, Anna," said Jessie. "What will you do?" She looked at the covered iron pot on the back of the range.

Anna shrugged. "Soup I got," she said. "I leave out the *Lebernockerl*, I make it some foolishness. Fancy custard, couple truffle. Fish gives quick, I make I guess filets, stuff mit crabmeat. Béchamel sauce."

"And pot roast with potato pancakes after that," moaned Jessie.

"Nein, I call butcher quick. I make it slobs—"

A shriek of crazy laughter burst from Jessie. The relief was dizzying. In twenty-five years Anna had not learned to pronounce that word. "Oh, Anna," she howled, rocking back and forth over her teacup. "Oh, Anna, if you only knew!"

"Braised slobs," said Anna, waddling to the telephone. "Nice, *bisserl* wild rice und mushrooms, *ja? Du! Putzl! Geh' weg!*" He had leaped to the table and was licking butter from the tip of Jessie's finger, his eyes sensuously closed.

"Ja!", shouted Anna into the telephone. "Und quick! You want I come?" she bellowed, a terrible threat. "So," she continued, coming back to Jessie, "so maybe a salat, I got couple elevator pear—"

Jessie buried her head in her arms and laughed until her stomach cramped.

"Und dessert?" asked Anna. "Mine *Aufgezogenes* wouldn't do, such *Trottls*."

"I'll call Sherry's," said Jessie. "Ice cream will do for them."

Anna shrugged. "Okay. You get me maybe mould mokka ice cream, I make it *Praliné gedeckt*, make nice rum sauce, few cherries, few mandels. So all right, you go now, lay down. So tired, like dead, you."

At half past one in the morning Brandon shut the front door behind the last of the guests, and turned to Jessie. He put his hand on her shoulder. "Jess, you were wonderful," he said. "God knows how you managed it, but the damn thing worked."

"You were wonderful yourself," she answered. He had been; he could be the most charming of hosts when he chose. Between them they had carried off brilliantly an almost impossible feat. The dinner party had been from the first moment a sparkling success in the wildly unpredictable way that dinner parties often prove the opposite of what is expected of

286

them. Jessie wondered now that so much collective apprehension could have been converted to so surprising a result. "Of course we had a lot of help," she said, wandering back into the drawing-room. "Helen and Serena were on the job every minute, and Hulda was an angel. How she played! But my God, poor Serena . . ."

She lay down flat on her back on the Aubusson carpet, stretched the curve of her spine hard down against the floor. "I am so tired," she said, with a shaky laugh, "that I wouldn't feel it if you burnt the soles of my feet with matches." She gazed dully at the ceiling.

Brandon sprawled in an armchair with a whisky and soda. "Carrying Van and Millie," he said, shaking his head. "This has been the god-damnedest day I ever remember."

"I felt so foolish, with Alec and Van at the same party, I was terrified that somebody would notice how grotesque it really was."

"We've done such wild things already today, that part of it was comparatively easy."

We have done wilder things than you know, Jessie reflected; wilder than you will ever know, or than I knew while I was doing them. She remembered again her last telephone conversation with Althea Crowe, while she was dressing for dinner. She had asked Althea what she should do if it should ever be necessary to produce the letter from the Thorne girl, and Althea, invoking a holy suffering God, had snorted, "There is no letter, you innocent, there never was."

"But—you let me think so," Jessie had said blankly.

"Of course I let you think so, you babe in arms! If I hadn't, you'd never have had the nerve to bluff it through!"

Now she realized that that was the merest sample of the grotesqueness of which this day had been compounded, one total incredibility piled upon the next, to build a rickety pyramid upon whose apex a dozen people would precariously teeter, holding their breath, and weighing their every syllable and every glance until the last echo of remark upon Isabel Allen's death should have faded away. If all went well and typically, oblivion would close over Isabel Allen and over people's connections with her, as quickly and quietly as the surface of a pond swallows a tossed stone. But Jessie would carry for years the dead weight of what she had learned today. She had a sense of its literally pressing her now, down, down hard against the floor. She closed her eyes and groaned softly.

"That was a brilliant idea of yours, getting Liz Betts," said Brandon. "By the time everybody's read the morning papers she will have laid it down like a course of bricks. She was here, dining with you know who, and she is going to make the most of it."

"Clyde Pritchard will actually be much more useful," said Jessie. She wished heavily that she had the energy to pick herself up and go to bed, but she knew that she was too overwrought to sleep; and she remained here from inertia. "I really think Alec Lowden the most appalling man I ever saw," she said. "Can you imagine what Serena's life has been, all these years? Why could she ever have married him?"

"He didn't develop these pretty ways until after Old Man Forbes died."

"Yes, I suppose . . . he always acts out this farce of attentiveness to Serena in public, but tonight——!"

"Van was the one that got me down. He doesn't know how to put on that act with Millie, and watching him try was too god-awful. He was so shot that he had no idea what anybody was talking about. Thank God he didn't make any breaks."

Jessie thought it as well not to tell Brandon how she had briefed Helen Lee before dinner, and how Helen, seated next to Evander Fielding, had been the principal insurance against his making the breaks that Brandon had dreaded. But she did say, "Can you imagine what it would have been like if every person here tonight had talked about what was really on his mind?"

"Jesus Christ," said Brandon, "haven't we had enough trouble today?"

Jessie was thinking then of Reath Sheldon, who had gone through the evening without so much as the flutter of an eyebrow to mark the acknowledgment of the secret that they shared. Knowing him as she did, she knew that it might be months or even years before he would refer to Althea Crowe in speaking to Jessie, and there was no possibility at all that he would ever mention Isabel Allen. He had been calm, gracious, gentle; he had conversed charmingly at dinner, and afterwards he had listened with his special intense kind of appreciation to the beautiful playing of Hulda Block. His personality would rule out absolutely the merest breath of comment, after tomorrow morning's newspapers appeared, that he should have been Isabel Allen's physician.

"And the funny thing is that if you had asked Jerome

288

Block to talk about something just to hold such an ill-assorted lot together, you could not have succeeded better."

"I never had any use for the feller," said Brandon, "but I see what you mean."

For the talk, just before Jessie had taken the women away for their coffee, had become a round-table, somebody having tossed up in conversation the strange and eternally fascinating glass bubble of identity in New York, and the ways in which it made men and women differ from others anywhere else. Jerome Block had talked, with the indefinable inflection of the superbly educated, self-made, Columbia University Jew, and though Jessie had been a little nervous for a moment, she had relaxed when she saw how he had held everybody's interest.

"That business of wondering who somebody was to begin with," he had said, "is a different thing here from anywhere else. All metropolitan places are full of people who rose from nowhere, but here there is a special kind of fraternity to which they—we—belong. We are all about the same, a few removes from the old Fourth Ward or the old Tenth Ward."

Several heads had nodded and Clyde Pritchard's wife had laughed; she was the granddaughter of Danny Monahan, perhaps the most spectacularly corrupt Tammany boss that had ever run the Fourth Ward.

"Maybe it was we," Jerome Block went on, "but more probably our parents, maybe even our grandparents, who made the break from the East Side. By the time we get our names brushed up and recognized (and they are usually a good deal different from the names we first had), and by the time we've got handsome apartments with English furniture and Fifty-seventh Street lamp-shades and antique Sheffield plate, by the time we've got a good address that's not in the telephone book but might be in the Social Register, nobody remembers just who made the break and when."

"Does it really matter much?" asked Reath Sheldon.

"No—not really," said Block. "But among ourselves it has a queer twist; simply that people seldom mention it. By then we've been through the middle period when there's often been a little jumbling of certain details, and we feel pretty sure-footed. And then it's very smart to come right out flat with the original facts. We put them in *Who's Who*, and we've become so sure of ourselves that we know it's smart to say we are guttersnipes born and bred. But we might not have said that twenty years earlier. And that makes our city belong to us in a way that it never can belong to anybody else, not even to people like you," he had nodded at Brandon Bourne and then at Serena Lowden, "who were also born here." There had been a round of laughter at his conceding the right of the old aristocracy of New York to claim it as their birthplace. "There are two kinds of people born in New York," he had added. "The privileged ones who never had to take it in the raw. So they can put it on or take it off like a coat. And then there are the rest of us. To us it is our skin. You stay in that."

"You certainly do," Sam Lee had said, "and you better had." That had marked a convenient moment for Jessie to collect her women and retire.

But she had wondered while she was pouring coffee for them what turn that conversation might have taken had Mark Dwyer been there to add to it the color of a still different Manhattan nativity, which none of the others knew. Perhaps, she thought, those bright, contrasting threads which run through the main texture of this thick brocade are the most fascinating part of it all, those people in the neighborhoods, the transplanted villages, whom we scarcely ever know. She remembered the life of his childhood which Mark Dwyer had described; and that forced her mind to review an infinity in an instant, all that had happened up to the shining threshold of this morning, from which violence had snatched her back, slamming the door in her face. Now that the people were all gone she felt as if it stood in giant's boots upon her supine body, an exhaustion so crushing that she was unable to disentangle the snarl of horrors of which this day had been compounded. Yes, she had told Mark Dwyer, she would see him tomorrow, but now she felt unable to care whether or not tomorrow ever came at all. She opened her eyes, and when she had rallied enough cohesion to interpret what she saw, she recognized upon Brandon's face a cogitating expression. She had not realized that he was speaking, but now she made an effort and she heard him say, "I suppose we ought to be setting up something pretty definite around tomorrow and the week end. We'll have to——"

"Oh, don't," said Jessie. If I sound tired enough, she thought, and incapable of following him, he will just drop it. And neither of us can possibly make sense now if we talk about anything. "This day," she mumbled "has been the one that the Lord was talking about. Sufficient unto."

"And how."

"Where is it, in Matthew?"

"How should I know?"

"I just thought you might. After all those years of chapel."

"I have an order for enough India paper to print three million Bibles," said Brandon. "And no dice."

"You can read one eventually." Jessie sat up slowly, inch by inch, gathering her skirt about her ankles, and then drawing herself to her feet.

"I'm going to try to get upstairs now," she said. "I could drop dead on the way. In fact I hope I do."

"Please. Must you?"

"Oh," she said, "I'm all mixed up. I forgot for the moment how inconvenient dead women are."

They both laughed, utterly meaninglessly. Jessie said, "Good night, Brandon," and began to move towards the hall with an uncharacteristic, weaving walk. Flipping his hand by way of answer, Brandon buried his nose in his glass.

V

FRIDAY

XXIII

Miss Stella's dark head was bent over Jessie's hand propped upon a cushion, and her brush swept the bright lacquer deftly over the spread finger tips.

"My," she said, "isn't that too bad about poor Mrs. Allen. Real sudden, wasn't it?"

Jessie stared over Miss Stella's head at the grey sky framed in the windows. "I'm afraid I've been shamefully lazy this morning," she said. "I only woke up a little while before you came. I just glanced at the papers while I was drinking my coffee."

"Well, you could have knocked me over with a feather. She was in the place Wednesday having her hair done and everything. Pauline did her manicure, she says she looked all right."

"Oh, I believe she had been ill for a long time," said Jessie. "Heart or something."

"Must have been. Isn't it funny what you don't realize, a thing like that, going on right under your nose. Such a young woman too."

"Ah, well," said Jessie.

There was a silence; Jessie had never found Miss Stella garrulous or gossiping, but a piece of news like the death of Isabel Allen would draw remark this morning from anybody who had ever seen her. Miss Stella was given to minding her own business at least as much as the pressure of her trade allowed; or so Jessie believed. But, she thought, it is more likely that she talks to whatever degree her clients prod her. That is all part of the game. Jessie closed her eyes, heavy still with yesterday's exhaustion.

The telephone buzzed and Jessie caught herself just short of a start which would have ruined Miss Stella's handiwork and, far worse, betrayed the state of her nerves. Most probably Mark Dwyer was calling, but it might be Helen Lee or Althea Crowe or Horace Howland, somebody to whom she could not talk in Miss Stella's presence. She did not wait for Josephine to answer and tell her who was calling, she picked up the telephone herself. It was Mark. Jessie was queerly surprised to hear the dull impassive tone of her own voice, and to feel her reaction to Mark as strangely leaden. He gathered at once that she was not alone, and he asked merely if she would lunch with him, adding, "and we'll see if you feel like doing anything afterwards."

"I don't know," said Jessie. "But we can lunch."

"At one," said Mark briskly. "Here." He was gone.

Jessie gave Miss Stella her other hand, and lay holding up the finished one in the air, waiting for the lacquer to dry. She heard Brandon in his room beyond the closed door, and she found herself wondering whether her sense of perturbation could communicate itself by some faint vibration through her fingers to Miss Stella. She hoped not, but, as in every other instance of facing a thought or a fact this morning, she could not really care. She had not seen Brandon today, and she had held some idle hope of getting out of the house without seeing him, but that would be stupid in the circumstances; she would simply move through any encounter with him, as calm and as remote as she could manage to be.

"Thank you, Miss Stella," she said, when the girl had finished.

"Thank *you*, Mrs. Bourne." There was always a particularly generous tip when one went out to a client's house to work. "Be careful now and don't smear your nails."

Jessie lay quiet for a time, wishing that she had not promised to go and join Mark Dwyer. She could not feel the

293

slightest desire to see him or any other person on earth; her head ached blackly, and in every way she felt as dark of mood as the ugly metallic sky lowering through the windows. This was evidently one of those ominous days when oncoming November jumps the calendar, to warn that the sharp blue wonder of October is transient like every other definable joy. It seemed inevitable then that the door from Brandon's room should open and that he should come in, a cigarette in one hand, the other hooked around a bundle of newspapers under his arm. Jessie wanted so sharply to exclaim, "Do please put out that cigarette!" that she shut her lips implacably upon the impulse. Oh, she growled silently to herself, you are becoming a disgusting bore! And she gave Brandon as much of a smile as her very real headache would allow her to contrive.

"Doesn't look too bad," said Brandon, flopping into her low armchair and dumping the newspapers on the floor beside him. "Somebody's done some damn slick footwork." He paused. "I didn't realize just what you were up to, with all your telephone calls yesterday."

"Nothing much."

"Go on. I never would have had the nerve to ask Reath Sheldon to——"

"I did not ask Reath," said Jessie. "Really, that is true. In fact, the truth is one of those things nobody would believe." She had decided suddenly to tell Brandon a monstrous lie, something so involuntary that she felt as if she were acting under hypnotism. She neither could nor would weigh her words; she simply opened her mouth and said, "Isabel was a patient of Reath's."

"Ah, Jess. You expect me to believe a rigged thing like that?"

"It's all the same to me," she shrugged, still asking herself why on earth she should have said such a thing. I am glad I did it, she thought then, with a quick sense of perverseness which felt excellently stimulating. Even her head was pounding less. Why, she thought, I feel quite well. Why did I have that impulse to tell Brandon such a lie?

"Anyway," he said, "the papers toss it off pretty smoothly. Even the tabloids. Of course Serena must have put George on the job yesterday afternoon, and he would know how to set it all up."

Jessie thought then of Mark Dwyer. There seemed today, at this gashed distance, more things about him that she did not know than there had been on the very first evening that they had spent together. But least of all, she knew, will I ever be told exactly what he did around the newspapers yesterday afternoon.

"I hope this is the end of it," she said, gingerly touching one of her fingernails to see if it was dry.

"Well—I'd gamble that it is, so far as the papers are concerned. But I think we've got to be awfully cagey about—oh, everything—people, places, anything around town. For quite a while still."

"Charming."

"Yes." Brandon made a face. "Just my idea of a hell of a good time."

"What do you suggest?"

"Well, first I think we'd better take Van and Millie out tonight. Take 'em to Twenty-One for dinner and then to the theatre and then to the Stork, you know, the works . . ."

"That's too bad," said Jessie, "because I'm not free."

"What do you mean?" He looked at her with the flat cold stare, suddenly hardening his blue eyes, which meant the rousing of rage at having his wishes contravened.

"Why, I am dining out."

"Where?"

If you lose your temper now, Jessie admonished herself, or make a false step, you are a fool.

"With General Dwyer," she said quietly. She wanted to snap, "none of your business!"

"Who?"

Jessie's impulse to clench her fists in irritation was checked by concern for her fresh manicure, and the whole sequence was so ridiculous that she laughed.

"Brandon, what's the difference? An old friend of mine who is on leave from Europe for a few days and I've said I would dine with him."

"Well, for God's sake, Jess, you can break a date if you have to."

"But I don't have to," she said, her voice as light as she could make it. "I'm willing to help out about this mess of Van's, but not to the extent of——"

"God, you're unreasonable. I suppose I'm delighted to have my vacation all mucked up!"

"Millie is your sister, my dear."

"Damn it! I never heard of such a selfish——"

Oh, yes you did, thought Jessie. Dozens of instances

whisked through her mind, when a suggestion that Brandon change an engagement of his had set off shattering fireworks. If she should remind him of such things now he would only turn ugly and add to the burdens of the week the preposterous element of opposition to her doing what she wished, about which she knew that he did not personally care a hair. He wanted her presence now for strong public reasons, and even while she was hardening in her decision not to let him interfere with her plans, she felt a wave of bitterness over his motives. But this was no time to touch off Brandon's temper. She spoke easily, with a small laugh, and said, "Oh, it can't matter that much whether I'm along, if you are taking out Van and Millie. The important thing is to have them seen, I agree with you about that. In fact, you really ought to have Iris for the fourth in my place. She needs rehabilitating even worse than Van does."

Brandon raised his eyebrows, reluctantly conceding that Jessie had made a point. But he was still angry, his native obstinacy had been roused and merely because he wanted his own way he said, "You certainly pick a fine time to get stubborn about some date of your own. Besides—" he scowled sharply as Jessie watched a new idea darken his face with temper.

"Why, what?" she asked. She was afraid at once that her tone sounded so sweet as to suggest irony. But then she saw what was troubling Brandon; the last thought in the world that would trouble him except for his uncharacteristic concern with this caricature of family solidarity in the face of crisis. Again she laughed, stretching her arms over her head and speaking in the most bantering possible way, for she knew well that nothing would so quickly enrage Brandon as her insisting seriously upon having her own way.

"Oh, none of it really matters," she said. "I could as well dine out any other night, but this is a friend who is only here for a day or two and there it is." She waved her hand carelessly, aware that the gesture was a contradiction of her real thoughts, which had already jumped ahead to tomorrow and Sunday, when she meant to be with Mark Dwyer as much as she could. And yet it is perfectly mad, she told herself; a quarter of an hour ago I was sorry that I had even told Mark I would lunch with him today. Now just because Brandon is acting like a spoiled brat he is making me feel like one too. But I will not fall into that trap. I will not give him an excuse now for being a nuisance tomorrow. She said, "Don't worry, Brandon. I assure you I shall not do anything conspicuous this evening while you are out with your family. As a matter of fact, if we want to carry this thing off really well, we'll avoid overdoing it. It will be a nine days' wonder for Van and Millie to be seen together—it might be too much if you and I burst forth upon the town in a family cabinet portrait. We had better let something about us just be the way people are used to it."

She was right, and Brandon knew it. He shrugged sullenly and Jessie became acutely eager for him to leave the room and put his mind upon something else before it occurred to him to open up the question of Saturday. Out of sheer contentiousness he would be sure to make an issue of that, and Jessie meant to deal with it at her own convenience, not at his.

"Now go along and stop fussing," she said lazily. "You've been perfectly extraordinary about this whole thing, far more than Van deserves. What are you going to take them to see tonight?"

"I haven't thought. Probably can't get four seats for anything worth seeing."

"Oh yes you can. Joey Gold can do anything, especially for us." She began to dial the number of the theatre-ticket broker, saying to Brandon, "You ought to take them to see *Fools' Paradise*."

"He'll never have seats for tonight," said Brandon. "It's a terrific smash."

"Hello!" rattled a machine-gun voice in the telephone.

"Hello, Joey. This is Mrs. Bourne."

"Mrs. *Brandon* Bourne?" asked Joey with caution. These were days when one had no wares to waste upon strangers.

"Who else? Joey, you have to do something impossible for me."

"Fa' you? Why not?"

"That's nice. We need four seats for tonight for *Fools' Paradise*."

"Ouch."

"Well?"

"That's a toughie."

"Good ones, Joey, you know."

There was a silence while Joey barked a question at somebody in his place. Then he said, "Okay, you got 'em, dolling."

"Good ones, Joey?"

"Say, don't you trust me?" The voice was plaintive. "Thoid row centre. That good enough?"

"I beg your pardon. You're wonderful."

"You bet I am. Box-office, your name. G'bye."

"They will probably cost a million dollars apiece," said Jessie, yawning. "But what can you do?" She looked at the clock and pressed the bell for Josephine. "I have a War Fund meeting at one o'clock," she lied, smiling at Brandon. "Imagine."

When he had left the room, she sat up straight in bed and seized her head between her hands. What am I doing, she asked herself half aloud. What in the world am I doing?

XXIV

The door of Mark's rooms swung open as soon as she had rung the bell, and Jessie found her face against his tweed jacket, his arms holding her tightly, before she had had a chance to look at him. This was good enough for the moment, it felt to her the first honest sensation that she had recognized in more than twenty-four hours. He did not kiss her. That too was good, for she needed far more the strength which she drew simply from standing inside the fortification of his arms. After a time he put one hand under her chin, tilted her face upwards and said, "Why, you look like a plucked chicken!" He kissed the tip of her nose and they moved across the room.

She had chosen the dullest clothes she owned, without thinking why; she wore a severe oxford grey cloth dress with a matching coat, a small coq-feathered beret, plain black pumps and gloves. No furs, no jewels except a brooch at her shoulder, of gold basketwork set with moonstones, which had belonged to her mother. She let Mark take the coat from her shoulders. She said, "I feel like a squashed bug. But you look nice. I like you, out of uniform."

"Tut," said Mark.

They dropped into chairs and Jessie leaned her head back, turning her face to him and saying, "Thank you for what you did yesterday."

"I did nothing, and unless you need to get it off your chest, it would be a fine idea to forget all about yesterday."

"Yes, I know. If I could."

They sat silent, quietly looking at each other. I feel nothing, Jessie thought, almost nothing at all. It is good to see him, it is especially wonderful to hear his voice. But all I can feel is nothing. I wonder if he feels the same. Mark was sitting with the graceful repose of body which she found so welcome, looking at her with an expression in his brown eyes that she could not quite fathom. It seemed puzzled, weighing; some element of decision had come into his thinking, about which she did not know. She folded her hands in her lap and raised her grey eyes to his, and tried deliberately to recall the sensations of Wednesday night, which had been and still were the reasons for her being here now. But it was no use; she only shook her head, an almost imperceptible motion, and sighed. But he saw. He said, "Won't you have a cocktail before they bring our lunch? It would do you good."

"I suppose so. Of course I don't feel like eating anything either."

"I ordered you a chop and some salad and coffee. You can manage that. Anyway," he said, bringing her the cocktail, "you are going to manage it, so we can drop the subject." He put his hand on the back of her neck, just under the line where the short curls sprang briskly upward, and she turned her head to rub her cheek catwise upon the sleeve of his coat. If he leans down now and kisses me, perhaps it will be better, she thought; but after leaving his hand quiet on her neck for a moment he went back to his chair and sat down.

They were silent for a time. Jessie sat, sipping the excellent martini that he had mixed, staring at the chic, discreetly anonymous hotel sitting-room, the pale flattering colors of the decor, the grey-enamelled imitation French furniture, the elaborately swagged draperies and upholstery. Through the closed windows she heard the snores of the buses and the yaps of the taxicabs on Madison Avenue. She turned her head and looked at the simulated coals in the make-believe fireplace, and thought heavily that such a mock-up was the very setting for this mood. The day was so gloomy that Mark had the lamps lighted, and the soft spots of rosy illumination about the room were the only relief in the sense of deadness. Presently Jessie turned in her chair, drawing herself up, and she said, "Mark, I really should not have come today. Forgive me." She heard her own voice, rather edged.

"Did you think," he said slowly, "that I expected you to be in any other frame of mind?"

She looked into his eyes and felt through her arms and fingers the weakness, the yielding, almost dragging weight of intense tenderness for him.

The bell burred outside the door, and while Mark concerned himself with the waiter and with having things placed where he wanted them, Jessie sat with her chin propped upon her folded hands, her mind going round in a dark blank. She had no wish at all to eat lunch, left alone she would not have thought of eating all day; but when Mark seated her at the table and gave her with his chin and his eyes such a silent admonition to be a good girl as one would give to a child, she began meekly to eat her chop. In a few moments she said, "Of course you're right, you always seem to be right. This is a good idea."

The strong coffee, piping hot from the thermos pot, was relaxing too, and before she knew it she was telling Mark the more burlesque parts of yesterday's happenings. Whether or not the element of hysteria was the propulsive factor, nobody could have helped laughing at the thought of Mrs. Katzenschwanz of Wapwallopen, Pennsylvania, being met and taken in hand by Althea Crowe.

"Can you imagine what Althea must have looked like to her?"

"Can you imagine what she must have looked like to Althea? I bet I could draw a picture of her, concrete bottom and all."

"And Althea—you know, Mark, she has really done something perfectly appalling. Why, she has——"

"She can take care of herself," said Mark. "You don't think this is the first such thing she has been mixed up in, do you?"

"But you had no idea who she was on Wednesday night."

"Am I supposed not to have learned anything since Wednesday night?"

"Oh," said Jessie.

"For a very clever small party, you can sometimes be so damn naïve," said Mark, and he called "Come in!" to the waiter who had come to remove the lunch table. Instantly the man had gone, Jessie felt gripped by a sense of panic. She looked about her, sweeping the superficial elegance of the room with her eyes, blanking out the sight of the closed door to the bedroom, fighting down the ugliest possible thoughts in the world, the crude, nameless identities of countless men and women who had used these rooms; and when; and how; and why. She went to stand at the window because there seemed no other place to fix her gaze that would not drive her to overt revulsion, and she was staring down at Madison Avenue when she heard Mark say softly behind her, "Darling, don't you know that I understand? There has never been anything to explain, there is not now."

She turned quickly about and looked at him and burst into tears. "Oh, Mark!" she cried, flinging herself against him. She gripped the lapels of his jacket in her hands. "I don't know what to do. I wanted you so. You knew that, you knew it, didn't you?"

He answered but his words were not important; his face was hidden in her hair.

"And now they have poisoned everything. They have taken the very things we felt, the very same feelings and impulses and words and used them to—to—" She wept in his arms.

"I told you I knew, darling," he whispered. "I told you, you mustn't worry about explaining."

"But I wanted you so! I want you still. But I can't, Mark. I can't. I am afraid, oh, not of you!" she cried, fearing her own words. "Not of you. But of them, of their poison, of their ways, their places. Even of here." She swung her arm towards the room. "They have been here, they have been everywhere that I ever go. And this—we would only be doing what they do . . . oh, what am I saying!" She put her hand over her mouth and turned her head and tried to raise it, to free it so that she could see his face. Presently she stood looking at him, probing the darkness of his eyes for understanding. She put her fingers upon his crisp, short grey hair which she realized queerly that she had never touched before, and holding his head between her hands she said, "Is there anything we can have that they have never had? Is there anything to turn to that they have not touched? That is why I—" she paused and he saw her cheeks slowly pale; he saw her halt in the phrase that she was about to say, and murmur after drawing a breath, "That is what I wish you could find for us."

Poor child, he thought, looking into her eyes which were still heavy from yesterday's exhaustion, and suffused with tears. She was tired in the way that makes a woman's skin refuse the transformation of cosmetics and appear dead, leathery, sallow, no matter what she may have done to disguise it. She looked, in short, quite plain, and she had accentuated that by wearing this queerly trying costume. He had never felt so drawn to her, so tender, so warm. But he was baffled for the moment at seeking a way through the wreckage, by which to reach her and draw her to some refuge where she could take comfort. For the moment there was nothing he could say; he stood caressing her cheek with his warm, fine hand, pressing his closed lips to her eyelids, and straining inwardly for the word or the thought which would be the answer. He felt her stiffen in his arms, at which he held her a little away and looked at her. Her eyes were intent, half closed and seemingly focussed at some great distance.

"Mark," she said slowly. Her voice was low and strangely vibrant. "Whoever you are—whatever you are that is not *them*—that's what I want. That person, that—" she stopped speaking and he watched a glow of amazement come suddenly into her face. "Mark!" she cried. "Take me to see your people! The ones up there—in the neighborhood, where you were born. Please! Oh, really, I'm not crazy. I mean it. Please take me."

"Darling girl," he said, shaking his head a little, "of course you aren't crazy. But you don't know what you are talking about. I see why you feel the way you do—but that would not be the answer."

"But why not? I tell you I must get out of this—this——"

"Yes," he said, kissing her again, "of course you must. But you won't find your answer up there in Uncle Aleš's pork store! They are good, plain Bohunk working people—but you don't know what you're talking about, my darling."

"Do you ever see them?" asked Jessie slowly.

His face grew serious, visibly more remote from her. "Yes," he said. "Once in a great while. Not since—the war of course." Now his expression was more than serious; it was grim. Whatever his thoughts, they were for the moment not primarily of her. "I have not been here."

"And would you not have gone to see them?" she asked. She sensed that her persistence might be untactful now, but she was too wrought up to care.

He moved his head slowly, as if to relieve some sort of pain, and then he looked down at her and she was astonished to see tears in his eyes. "If I had had the courage," he answered. His mouth twitched.

"But Mark!"

"They will have a lot to ask me about," he said, "and some

of it will hurt like hell. It will hurt them to hear it and me to tell it. But," he said, with a sudden startling break and change of mood, "if you insist on seeing my relatives, and probably hearing more than you bargained for, we are off for Vaníček's." He picked her up as if she had been a doll and dumped her into an armchair. "You wait here while I change my clothes."

"Oh," she said. "Do you have to put on your uniform?"

"No," he said, disappearing into the bedroom. "I don't have to. But they will love it!"

When the taxi stopped on the east side of First Avenue, Jessie recognized the shop and realized that she must have passed it hundreds of times in the years that she had lived nearby. Crossing the pavement beside Mark, she wondered now why she had never thought to explore here or in other shops like this one. Evidently one must have some motive stronger than mere curiosity, she thought, to experiment so radically; she would have had no idea how to ask for any of the fascinating strange things hanging in the window, except stupidly or shyly to point to it. And probably, she admitted, I would not have known what to do with it if I had bought it. But Anna would have known! What a fool I am.

They stood in the street for a moment looking at the shop window.

"Not much for sale," said Mark, "compared with a normal Friday. But my God, look inside."

The small place was crammed with women, patiently standing in line, such fat and homely women as Jessie had pointed out on Wednesday morning. They were not only not impatient at having to wait; from their nodding heads, smiling faces, and clattering tongues it was plain that this was an important part of the social texture of their lives, a comfortable opportunity for a gossip with friendly neighbors whose interests were precisely their own. Several of them held small dogs on short leashes; fat, folksy mongrel dogs, vaguely tinged with poodle, spitz, and spaniel persuasions. All had sharp snoots, bright eyes, and gay plumes of tails; many communicated with one another in the same secure congeniality which also bound their mistresses.

"I have never seen anything so incredibly clean," said Jessie, examining the symmetrical display in the window. "Each thing in it looks like a scrubbed baby."

Mark grinned. "Too bad there aren't any hams," he said.

"You can't buy any kind of ham for love or money."

"Well—why should you be able to? Haven't you got enough to eat here?"

"Look," said Jessie, pointing to a row of shiny, red-brown smoked hocks, "what do you call those in—in——"

"*Kolenko*," said Mark. "And you see those—?" he indicated small squares of spare-ribs, also smoked and neatly arranged. "*Řebirka*. Jesus, it makes me drool. And you see that?" They were standing now with their noses almost touching the glass, like children outside a candy store. He pointed to a tray of small vermilion rectangles, dusty all over with paprika.

"Oh, they have those in the Hungarian stores up the street too," said Jessie.

Mark's heavy eyebrows bent upon her in a mock scowl.

"Madame," he said, "you will kindly remember that Hungarian meat is our poison. And if you ever hear anybody call that *Paprika-Speck*, you are to spit promptly in his eye."

"What do you call it?" asked Jessie meekly.

"That is *slanina*," said Mark, "and the next time you go to some goddam dinner like the one where I met you on Monday, and they give you canapés of peanut-butter and horse-feathers, just remember this. Try it in your palazzo some time, you'll knock 'em dead."

"How do you cook it?"

"*Cook* it? Oh, Christ! You don't cook it, my darling, you eat it raw, I mean it is cooked already, enough for the likes of us. You slice it in small squares and put them on thin pieces of black bread and eat them with your cocktails and you stink to heaven and feel like a king."

"Garlic?" asked Jessie, sniffing towards the open door of the shop.

"On wheels," said Mark.

"Come on!" she said, hurrying forward.

"Only we mustn't shove in ahead of your mamas," said Mark, entering the crowded shop. "We can wait our——"

Jessie was wrinkling her nose with delight, almost twitching with pleasure at the sharp, clean smells of wood-smoke, spices, garlic, and the pungent slash of sauerkraut, quite forgetting that Mark would tower over the heads of the dumpy mamas, and that the brisk bull of a man cleaving pigs' trotters at the chopping-block would look up, stop his work, and roar *"Mirko!"* in such a way that the whole place blew up in a whoop. The cleaver clanked on the block, the women all

304

babbled at once, asking one another in their motley lingo who this was, Jessie tried to efface herself behind them, and the square, heavy, grizzled butcher rushed from behind the counter, to seize Mark by the shoulders, kiss him on the cheeks, and repeat "Mirko, Mirko," in a rich bass voice, wagging his broad grey head and beaming all over.

"Hello, *strýčku*," said Mark, clapping his shoulders. "Hello. *Nazdar.*"

"When you come? Where you come? Mine God, you look so fine! *Pane Generale!*"

"How are you?" asked Mark. "How's *tetička?*"

"Fine, fine, mine God, how I finish work today?" Mark's uncle looked about, spreading his hands, nodding and motioning to some of the women, his square red face alight and gleaming. "My boy, my sister's boy," he said, as if any explanation were needed, for the women were all clucking and gabbling with pleased excitement. Things like this did not happen every day or, indeed, at all. This was big news. They were eyeing Mark's insignia and decorations with delight.

"We go now," said Uncle Aleš, "we go home, I leave that Karel finish here." He began to untie his apron. "Karle!" he roared, looking about. "Where's that *trouba?*"

The helper's long, black face appeared in the cellar hatchway, carrying two containers of kraut.

"Don't hurry, *strýčku*," said Mark. "There's plenty of time. I've brought a——"

"*Ne, ne, pojd'me,*" said Uncle Aleš. "What you think, this happens every day? I go now," he said to the crowd of women. "Karel takes care of everybody, so long lasts the meat, I don't know. Karle, you do everything, *yoh?* I go now, come on, Mirko, we go home."

"Wait," said Mark. "Wait, I brought a friend, a lady." He stretched his long arm past the women and plucked Jessie out of the crowd, drawing her forward. Uncle Aleš stood hesitating, plainly nonplussed; and Jessie saw on his broad face a flicker of disappointment that he was not to have his nephew to himself; but the expression vanished in a cordial grin and he took her hand in his tremendous, rock-hard one, pumping it cheerfully.

"Fine," he said, "pleased to meet you, hello."

"This is Mrs. Bourne," said Mark.

"Oh, American lady, sure," said Uncle Aleš. "Fine. Hello."

Jessie wondered whether he might for a moment have expected her to be the woman whom Mark had married in

305

Prague, the woman killed by the Germans, for she had no way of telling how recently his relatives had had any news of Mark; but she could not tell what the man was thinking except that he conveyed to her an immediate sense of acceptance because Mark had brought her with him. Uncle Aleš's attention had returned entirely to Mark, and Jessie relaxed at once in the easy sense of being ignored because she was already taken for granted.

Uncle Aleš had removed his white apron and butcher's coat, hung them on a peg, put on his jacket, taken his hat, and was counting the waiting customers with a practised eye.

"You close it the door now," he said to his helper. "Afterwards you wait on customers here, only enough stuff for these anyhow, then you lock up place, go home, *yoh?*"

They made their way out of the shop, past the gabbling women who smiled and nodded their heads as Mark went by, the collective impression a sunburst of gleaming eyes, gold teeth, and good humor. They started down the street, Uncle Aleš walking with a firm, toed-out tread which fairly echoed solid substance and delighted pride, Mark striding along in step, and Jessie, trotting to keep up with them, almost pinching herself in disbelief that this could suddenly have come about in half an hour.

They crossed First Avenue and turned a corner, and came to a neat new-looking block which Jessie saw to be remodelled from former coldwater flats. Uncle Aleš reached for his keys as they started to climb the stairs, Jessie noting with sharp interest that this place was tight and scrubbed and clean, a total transformation from the tenement hallways that Mark had described on Wednesday. But it was an old building, like the thousands which line the miles of humble avenues and the hundred or more cross streets feeding them east and west which are the real bulk and complexion of the city. Smells there were, but not the damp and foul odors of poverty and desuetude, for this was not such a place; but the smells of cooking and baking and coffee and soup, the smells of life as simple people live it, which are good smells for the reason that an unshaven man or an unpainted woman can also be at certain times a good sight to see.

On the third-floor landing they stopped climbing and Uncle Aleš made to unlock the door while saying to Mark, "Maminka, your *tetička*, she will be so happy—" but before he could fit his key into the lock the door flew open, and a

306

woman said, *"Tato!* What you doing, why you home now?"

"Tetičko," said Mark softly.

"Mirko!" cried the woman. *"Bože muj, Mirko, Mirko jde!"* She flung her pudding of a body towards Mark, and her arms around his neck.

"Come," said Uncle Aleš, shooing them all forward like chickens. "Come, go inside, such a noise you make, what everybody thinks . . ."

"And you? You don't holler when you see Mirko?" Mark's aunt flapped her hands. "Where you find him, where?"

Jessie felt again the instinct to efface herself as she had in the shop; she was almost hidden behind Uncle Aleš. Aunt Olga stood under the droplight in the narrow hall, holding Mark off by the shoulders and examining him with ecstasy in her shining round face. She was short and round and, Jessie thought, shiny all over, like a small bird covered with gleaming plumage. Her face shone, her grey hair was brushed to a polish and swept up to a shining topknot, held in place by studded combs. Her clothes were so neat that they seemed enamelled, finished at the neck and wrists with starched white lace ruffles which Jessie knew she had made herself. On her breast was a large silver brooch, a crowned lion rampant, facing left, claws at attack, an emblem which Jessie would see many times again while she was in this house. They moved down the hall to the parlor, Aunt Olga happily clutching Mark's arm, Jessie with Uncle Aleš who was trying to introduce her to his wife. Presently he succeeded; Mark's aunt turned about, full of apologies and, like her husband, sweeping away her first hesitating instant of question in a rush of cordiality. She beamed at Jessie, took her coat, seated her in the best chair, and then turned to Mark again.

"Tell me," she said, "tell me quick. You come from home?"

Mark nodded, putting his arm round his aunt's shoulder. Jessie had a sudden instinct that she should not look at him now, or listen, but the thought passed.

"And Jaro?" asked Aunt Olga. "Bohuš? The children? Zdenka? You know? You tell us?"

That look which Jessie had seen before came into Mark's face, that slow revelation of deep and terrible things, which made of here and now such frightening triviality. He put his arms around the short, heavy body of his aunt and looked down at her with sorrow in his brown eyes, while his uncle watched minutely, and Mark said, "Yes, I know, *tetíčko*, I know it all. Give me a little time before I tell you. Will you?" He bent his head, and Jessie turned and stared through the ruffled curtains out the window.

XXV

"You see, *strýčku*, it is so hard to think of people singly, and of what happened to them. No matter how much they meant to you. When you mention one person's name you remind me then of the particular thing that happened to him or her—but in my mind, no matter how frightful that thing was and how close the person was to us, it seems to me like—like—" Mark looked up, raising his head from the position in which he had held it braced upon his hands, and sought for an object to illustrate what he meant. "Like that," he said. He pointed to the tablecloth, which his aunt had embroidered. He put his forefinger upon it and traced a part of the pattern. He spoke very slowly, feeling for words to make a difficult thought clear. "You see? Here is a line in red silk, it winds round and round, and makes these knots and those dots, and finally comes to a point here where it seems to stop. But it doesn't stop, it goes on to make more of the same, over and over again. And on the way it crosses and twines with all these other lines in other colors and every time it does that and the others all do their part too, they make the design complete. But the red line just by itself doesn't prove much of anything. You see what I mean?"

They all nodded their heads, their faces very attentive and grave. They had been sitting here around the table in the small, squeezed dining-room for well over an hour, Mark and Jessie and the Vaníčeks and the four others who had joined them when Aunt Olga had telephoned and told them to come over at once if they wanted to see Mirko while he was here. Jessie had their identities fairly clear, and the fact that they were all related to Mark, either through his parents, of the Mráček and Vaníček families, or through Aunt Olga who had been born Bartoš and was evidently a member of a tremendous clan, one of a dozen brothers and sisters. Some had long since died in New York and Chicago, leaving prolific descendants, but just as many had remained in the old country, spread all over the vicinity of Sedlec and Tábor and, Aunt Olga had explained, down the nearby valley to the confluence of the rivers Vltava and Lužnice.

She had shown Jessie the photograph album full of pictures of heavenly countryside, storybook villages, smiling faces, weddings, christenings, harvest and sokol festivals, lusty people in incredibly picturesque national costumes which would have made the book seem like a tourist circular except for Aunt Olga's sturdy finger pointing out each face by name, that one because of a new baby at the time the picture was taken, another for the prizes he had won at the University, Jožka in his new automobile, Mařenka because she was a fool like her mother and all the Jindras, whom no Bartoš in his right mind ought to have married. But the book stopped abruptly like a road at the edge of a cliff, with the year 1938, and as she closed it upon the last blank pages Aunt Olga looked at Mark with a face full of question and solemnity.

Her instinct had been sound, to make the past hour resemble any impromptu family gathering, and to fill the people round the table with delicious coffee and her famous, amazingly varied repertoire of small cakes whose names were incomprehensible to Jessie, but whose lightness and richness of pastry, plum and apricot jam, nuts, poppyseed, caraway, chocolate, and spices she had found irresistible in spite of thinking that she had no appetite.

But that had served its purpose now, and Jessie saw in Mark's face that his people had given him as much grace as he was going to receive. They wanted something of him which she knew he had to give them, and Jessie realized that under no other imaginable circumstances would she ever have seen him do it. His family were already informed, to the fullest extent possible from the news that had come out of the occupied country during the war, and a great deal of it had; but they held it their right now to know what part their own flesh and blood had played, what Mark had been doing all those years, and what had really happened to their relatives of whom they knew only that many were dead.

Uncle Aleš had filled and lighted his pipe, and was leaning back in his armchair with the natural command of the habitual paterfamilias who is most comfortable at the head of a table surrounded by his clan. I suppose, thought Jessie, looking at him, that if I had seen him just as the butcher in that shop of his, I would have thought him a hard, dour sort of man, crude and in no way the person he is here. I would never have thought of his home as what it is, nor his wife, nor these people here. She looked at Mark's cousin Růža Mráčková, known at the nearby Webster Branch of the Public Library as Miss Rose Marsh, by those people who could not pronounce her name. She was a middle-aged spinster with a gentle, intellectual face and wincing, strained eyes; somehow it had been no surprise to be told that she was the librarian of the largest collection of Czechoslovak books in the United States. She sat beside a younger woman who was the widow of a Chicago nephew of Aunt Olga's who had been killed at Guadalcanal, "but Katka belongs in the family too," Uncle Aleš had explained carefully, saying that Katka was the daughter of his closest friend Přihoda who had married his second cousin Božena Nováková on a wonderful summer holiday that they had all taken together years ago at home. Jessie felt at first painfully confused by all the strange names and by the way in which they sometimes referred to a woman by one name and sometimes by another. They had laughingly explained that when they thought or spoke among themselves, or of peoople at home, they always put the feminine terminal on a woman's surname, but when they "spoke American" they usually left it off.

"And why," Jessie had asked, with a perceptiveness which apparently pleased them, for they had exchanged amused looks, "do you keep changing people's names all the time while you talk to them or about them?"

"Haw!" Mark had roared, winking at his uncle. "You would come along on this expedition, would you? And we've been talking English for your benefit, too."

"Oh," she said. "Please don't bother."

"We talk it because we like," said Aunt Olga, frowning at Mark. She had her own idea of polite manners. "Olinko," she said, speaking to her daughter, "go bring me fresh coffee, I left it pot all ready on stove."

This was the only daughter of the Vaníčeks, a vigorous woman of about forty, who had come hurrying in last of all, with her husband Joe, whose last name Jessie never did hear. Mark told her that he had known Joe all his life, since they had played in the same mud-puddle together, and that Joe was probably the best electronics technician in New York, "but," said Mark inconsequently from closed lips, "I never liked him." He had refused the cigar that Joe had offered, and sat now smoking a cigarette and staring about the room, which was full of mementos of the old world, the old ways, the old country. The pictures on the walls, the dishes on the table, the way in which the furniture was arranged, the attitudes that these people bore to one another; it was as if they had never left the land of their forefathers at all. And yet of them all only three had been born "on the other side," in the universal phrase of the quondam greenhorn; they were emphatically, consciously American in a sense that Jessie and her world scarcely ever knew, but the intensity of their feeling for their own people and the physical strength of their attachment to the old country were visible, tangible, tactile. Jessie had never seen stronger and simpler personalities, with a directness about their manner which invited one flatly to take them or leave them. Their warmth and their hospitality were completely natural, they accepted this stranger unreservedly because of their feeling for Mark; she could equally well imagine their being stonily indifferent if they had no reason to act otherwise.

"So, Mirko," Aunt Olga had said, closing the album and looking up at him; and they had all settled down to listen.

"You can see for yourselves," he said, "that it's very hard for me to talk about myself and what I did. Hell, if it hadn't been me it would have been somebody else. And if it hadn't been our Frantík who got shot for blowing up a train, it would have been somebody else's Frantík. Your cousin Ota Veselý died under torture in the Petschek," he said, turning to Růža Mráčková, "but so did thousands of others, for the same reasons."

Miss Mráčková nodded; nobody spoke; they sat grave and waiting.

"When I saw Helenka three months ago," Mark turned to his aunt, "I went to meet the train in which she was repatriated from Ravensbruck—together with four hundred other women who had all had the same dose. Helenka's legs are so scarred and crippled that she can never wear a dress above her ankles again. Helenka," he explained to Jessie, "was one of the best ballerinas in Europe. And when little Štěpán Bartoš was shot and captured parachuting into Zlín from England, 'way back in '41, he might have been any of twenty others who also had brothers who were doctors in hospitals and who did what his brother Tomáš did."

"What was it?" asked one of the women, after a long pause.

"I didn't realize you didn't know. Štěpán was one of the Czech Army men who volunteered for a parachute mission, they were practically always killed, but there were ten volunteers in London for each one who got to go. This was right after Heydrich took over at home because Neurath had been too easy, and the sabotage was going to beat hell. So a mission went in with orders and maybe other things from London. Štěpán was horribly shot up by the Germans before he landed but they didn't kill him, they wanted to try to get information. And the hospital where they put him was the one where Tomáš was the surgeon."

"But—" Aunt Olga interrupted with a puzzled frown. "You mean our Tomáš, he worked in hospital for *Germans?*"

"What could he do? Refuse? The bastards had to use Czech doctors, especially after they shipped all the Jewish ones east. But they never trusted them. And when Tomáš saw Štěpán, he didn't bat an eye. Then the Gestapo lined up the hospital staff for examination and told them on pain of death that if they knew Štěpán or the other three parachutists who had dropped, they had to squeal and make the wounded boys squeal. Nobody said a word of course, especially Tomáš. But in spite of Štěpán's having no identification and refusing to give a name, they smelled a rat. Maybe the boys looked alike. Anyway they took Tomáš down to the torture room and gave him the business, while they had Štěpán lying there on a stretcher, making him watch. They tortured Tomáš—and one thing I will not tell you is just what they did, because if you could stand it, I could not, any more—they tortured him for thirty-six hours and he never said a word. So they took him out and shot him and came back inside and started the business on Štěpán himself, but the poor kid was so far gone already that he died quickly, by the mercy of God," said Mark, bending his head and crossing himself, to Jessie's intense amazement. The gesture was as natural and spontaneous as the flick of an eyelid, but somehow incredible in Mark.

"So you see what I mean," he said after a silence. "Every one of them, including some who didn't behave any too well, in case you think we are any better than anybody else, was some little part of a thing that is still too big to understand. Nobody understands it entirely, and don't let them kid you that they do. The world is still in a hell of a mess." He ran his fingers heavily into his cropped grey curls and slowly shook his head. There was quiet for a time, for he had made it difficult for anybody else to speak. But then he looked up at them all and said, "So I understand what you want me to tell you about, but I keep feeling for a way to try to give you the whole picture—" he made a circling motion over the embroidered tablecloth—"and what it has to go on to, if it is ever to make any sense, instead of just those isolated little parts of the design—what happened to this one and what became of that one."

Finally Uncle Aleš laid his pipe down carefully upon the table and leaned forward on his elbows. He said, "Mirko, you should mybee tell us where you been. Only where you been, one time, next time. But *pořádně*—in order, *yoh*?"

"Yes," said Mark slowly, "that might be the simplest. Some of it just seems now like a lot of accident. But I suppose it wasn't, really. You know I hadn't spent much time in Praha while I was working in Europe all those years before the war. Oh, I could drop in every six months or so, naturally it was fun because I knew so many people and I used to like to drive down to the country and poke around among the relatives, but you know me." He looked round the table and grinned, as much as to remind them that his very deep attachment to all of them had always been counterbalanced by the obsession for independence which had caused him to run away and go on his own as a boy, instead of letting Uncle Aleš adopt him. Some of them smiled back, but Aunt Olga sighed.

"But by the time of Munich, I was beginning to feel pretty tough about it. Any dope could see what would be happening after that, I can't take credit for understanding it, or anything else that happened, a bit better than anybody else. So I decided to stay in Praha, instead of the way it had been before, roving all over the place. And of course you know that between Munich and March, the foundations for the whole resistance were very thoroughly laid. And you also know that all my closest friends were up to their necks in it. Especially chaps like Jiří Horák and a lot of others who became fliers. Jiří was really too old to be a combat pilot but he didn't give a damn, he learned anyway and was a heller."

"Your wife's brother," said Aunt Olga.

"Yes. He was killed finally over Germany—fighter escort. A brave, wonderful guy, the closest friend I ever had. And now it's all so queer, the way time jumps or stands still when you look back on it. Your mind feels tricked by the way you waited for some things you thought would never happen, and then others up and socked you all in a minute. Anyway, back there at the beginning it was people like the Horáks and that crowd who were the spark plugs, not all young by any means, but people who were used to doing things with their heads. You know—" they all nodded—"lawyers and editors and writers and university people, though the other kind of resistance was getting stronger all the time, sabotage and industrial stuff, and the peasants all over the country were terrific. All those people were self-starters, they were raising hell, with their backs up, long before the London government got organized and began sending overall directions by the bedspring radio. But after that started in '40, it was up to my buddies to get it circulated, first just by getting around and whispering, but pretty soon they got the newspaper going. *V Boj*—maybe you've seen copies of it. That was one of the things that Vlasta did. Of course it meant the business if you were caught."

The forbidding expression upon Mark's face silenced the murmurs of grief because Vlasta had been caught, and Jessie knew that Mark's family did not know the impersonal facts about his marriage, nor would he ever wish to explain them.

"So," he continued, "I decided I was going to stay there—for as far ahead as I could see then—and do whatever there was to do that would help. There was plenty to do, too. We all went about it on pretty much the same basis, you put whatever you had to contribute into a kind of pool. Most of what I had was accident—but lucky. I was American and I had a lot of newspaper tie-ups and was used to getting around. And—I had other papers, too."

"What do you mean, papers?"

Mark smiled and shrugged. "It sounds so corny now and it was so damned secret then that I've got the habit of never even thinking about it. But what the hell, it doesn't matter any more. Oh, phony passports and things like that."

"Why—Mark!" Jessie had not meant to speak a word during all this, but the exclamation slipped out. He shrugged again, by way of admitting that if this interested them he had no further reason to hide it, and he said, "I had quite a little collection. Spanish and Portuguese stuff—both kinds of Spanish, from the civil war, when you need to cross lines at my age you try and find the de luxe way to do it."

"Boloney," said Joe. "Were you in the Lincoln Brigade?"

"Why, sure. Name of Sinsabaugh."

"Why you pick such a name?" asked Uncle Aleš, frowning.

"To gum things up. Also it happened to belong to a friend

314

of mine who got killed. You think we wasted papers we could use?"

Jessie stared, open-mouthed.

"You see that's just the kind of thing I mean. I start out to tell you about home, and all of a sudden we're in Spain. Well, there were plenty of other things like that too. And they were all useful in Praha. In the beginning the big job was running the men out who wanted to get around to France and join our army there. The Germans made it very tough, but we had our ways. Jiří Horák of course skipped in his plane like the rest of the Air Force. But most of the fellows just had to dodge it. You know," said Mark, "it used to make me feel like a damn sentimental ass when I'd see them leave and realize that most of them were sons of men who had done the same thing in '17, like Uncle Jaro and all that crowd from home. From all over, in fact."

Aunt Olga squared her shoulders. "Matěj did that this time?" she asked.

"Sure. He went to Russia, not France. I'll get to Matěj later. And the other boys, too. Anyway, for a while there I was quite neatly settled down in Praha, I had a very respectable identity as a kind of absent-minded scholar working at Strahov on a religious thesis about the——"

"Mirko!" His cousin Růža the librarian interrupted softly, but with such curious drama in her worn face that they all turned their heads and looked at her. "I know," she said slowly. "You were that mysterious American who stayed there and gave English lessons to—to——"

Mark looked at her, his eyes twinkling. "Just as smart as ever, eh, Rosie? How the hell did you hear about that?"

His cousin raised her eyebrows. "We heard things, most of the time. But I don't see now why I didn't know it was you."

"Who you gave English lessons?" asked Uncle Aleš.

"To the Germans, strýčku," said Mark with a laugh. He slapped his knee. "What the hell. Don't forget, they were getting ready to conquer England and they all had to know English. Oh, I had charming pupils, Army officers and Gestapo—" he made a face as if to spit. "I didn't do it for long, only through the winter of the phony war. Because things started to get hot in the spring of '40, and I began to fade as much as I could."

"Where did you fade to?" asked Joe. There was curious skepticism in his manner.

Mark shrugged and answered the question mostly with his eyebrows.

"But how you—how you did things, if you hiding all time?" asked Uncle Aleš.

Mark smiled. "It's not as hard to operate that way as you might think, *strýčku*," he said. "It sounds a lot harder from outside than it is. When you're in the middle of a set-up where everybody is living some kind of a lie or a crime or a bribe or a finaigle or a bluff, either on the right side or the wrong, you'd be surprised how many little chinks and corners you can find to fit yourself into. You'd be surprised how much mobility you have, for instance. They make rules that you can't go here and there or do this and that, and then you do it all twice as much as you otherwise would—only in different ways. The only thing you really live in deadly fear of is doing something that might trip one of your own people. And many a time somebody deliberately stuck his neck out and let the Gestapo put the bead on him, just to keep me out of it, because I was more mobile and I guess they thought I could operate over more territory than most of them. Anyway, that was how it worked. Before the end of '40 we had set up a regular line of communication all the way to Bratislava. Of course that cr—excuse me, girls—hooey about 'independent' Slovakia was just a set-up for us. They had a quisling government, all right, and plenty of collaborators, but I never even bothered to find out what part of the Slovaks collaborated. I only know how many of them didn't. Sometimes I wonder still how the Germans could have been such fools. When they are really dumb they beat the world at it."

"So do a lot of Slovaks," said Joe.

"Listen," said Mark. "I can tell you a few bedtime stories about some Czechs we needn't be too proud of, either. Don't be so goddam black and white, Joe, it has the queerest way of turning into scrambled eggs instead of giving you something to go by."

Mark moved his shoulders in what Jessie knew to be a confession of irritation which he would rather have concealed, and he turned to his uncle, saying, "*Strýčku,* sooner or later I'll have to have a beer, *yoh?* You keep me talking like this I'll dry up."

"Mine God!" exclaimed Uncle Aleš. "Oličko, why you let me not think!"

"Because I want to listen," said Aunt Olga drily, rising

from her chair. "Mirko, you wait I bring beer, you don't talk now."

They all laughed, and Uncle Aleš called after his wife in Czech as she went to the kitchen. Mark winked at Jessie and said, "Now you'll get some of that slanina and salami from the store, and you eat it, see?"

"Why, it's barely five o'clock," she said.

"What's that got to do with it? *Strýčku,*" he laughed, "what time of day are you supposed to eat *slaninu?*"

"What time?" Uncle Aleš wrinkled his big forehead. "Mine God, when you hangry!" He spread his hands.

Katka went to help Aunt Olga and they put a large tray in the middle of the table, loaded with bottles of cold beer, tall delicate flute-shaped beer-glasses, sliced black bread, and the famous, pungent meats from the store.

"These I brought last time from home," said Aunt Olga, handing Jessie one of the beautiful diamonded beer-glasses, full to the brim.

"Too bad it hasn't got the right kind of beer in it," said Mark. "But they haven't got it over there either, not yet."

"So," said Růža Mráčková thoughtfully, when they had all settled down again, "you were really an underground courier between Praha and Bratislava."

Mark shrugged. "It was a team," he said. "We all did lots of things. So many got knocked off, you see, everybody had to be ready for anything. There were always two or three to step into each dead person's shoes. That's the beauty of a little country, of course. People know one another and their families, and nearly everybody in every town has a raft of relatives down in the country somewhere that he can depend on. That's how most people ate, for instance. We needed smart, tough country people with guts, and plenty of places to hide things, including us." Everybody nodded, thinking of their own family.

"And ours were—just what you'd think they would be. The line went from Praha to Jihlava to Brno to Hodonín to Bratislava—roughly, of course. Very roughly. Naturally we spread ourselves thin and used our contacts all over the place, wherever they were. I saw more of our folks that year than I ever have before or since. They had the country around Tábor organized like a drill squad."

He paused because he knew that his aunt was going to speak and what she would say. She said it: "And my brother Jaromír? You saw your uncle Jaro?"

317

"Sure," said Mark. "All the time. That year."

His aunt moved her head with a queer jerk, as if to comment upon Mark's sudden taciturnity when he had been voluble enough up to now.

"You tell me now how they kill him," she said.

"It was later," said Mark, his voice pitched lower. "I wasn't there then. He had always been watched by the Gestapo, like all the old Legionaires who were on the list. He was old, then, *tetičko*, really an old man, but my God! he was tough."

"Seventy-seven years old," said Aunt Olga. "Eleven years more than me."

"Well, you wouldn't have thought he was much over sixty. He had about five big irons in the fire and a lot of little ones. After all, just by spotting the whole family around where he thought they would be the most use, he had pretty near a brigade all his own. He was terribly sore about the Jews, too. I don't think he had really thought much about them before, you don't have much contact with them down in the country. But he used to go to Jihlava and Brno on business, at least he called it business, that was before all the Jews had been shipped to Poland. But they were in a hell of a mess, chewed up in those stinking Nuremberg laws and kicked around like dogs, you know it all, there's no story in any of that any more. But Uncle Jaro used to walk up the street in a town and whenever he saw some Jew creeping by in the gutter, with a yellow armband, he'd stop him and shake hands and make a fuss over him and pull a *salam* or a loaf of bread out of his pocket and give it to the poor devil . . . it sounds silly to tell about a thing like that now. But not when you remember that it was a crime to be seen talking to a Jew, and a lot of people got shot for it," Mark sighed.

"You mean they shoot him for *that*?" asked Aunt Olga, her mouth trembling.

"Oh, no," answered Mark. "That was just—a little thing, in its way. What he really did was hide and divert the produce from his farm—not only his; he had the whole tribe, and for that matter the whole district organized and doing the same thing. He just wasn't raising any food for Germans. He used to give most of what he hid to the Underground, because that was the only way we could feed the families of men and women who had been caught and executed. They had to drop out of sight, and not be identified through ration cards or any other papers, otherwise they would have been picked up too. That's where we had many of our most valuable people. And

318

the rest of the stuff, Uncle Jaro and the farmers like him used to sell in the black market and give the money to the Underground because we had to have cash too. By the end of '41 the Gestapo were really hot about this. The more laws they made about it the more the people told 'em to shove it. So they started arresting and executing the worst offenders, and that was what they did to Uncle Jaro."

"You knew then?" asked Aunt Olga.

"Not until about a year later. As soon as I got back."

"From—where?" Again Jessie spoke without intending to.

"Here. Never mind that now. When Heydrich's terror began, they set out to make an example of certain families, the ring-leaders in the most troublesome places. Well," he said, "that meant the Bartošes, that's all."

"But how many?" asked Aunt Olga. "Who?"

The others all sat silent, staring at Mark. He picked up his glass and looked at it as if to measure something, either the empty space left by the beer he had drunk, or the quantity of beer still remaining in the glass. It was a curious, questioning gesture. Then he put down the glass abruptly on the table and looked up and said, almost curtly, "All of them, see? Everybody who hadn't escaped somewhere else."

Nobody spoke. Yet there seemed to Jessie to be resonant sound in the room, which she realized must be the slow and strained breathing of the people about her. She sat with her head bent, looking at her hands folded in her lap, and feeling that under no circumstances should she so intrude upon any of these men and women as to raise her head and watch their faces now. She knew that whatever more they were about to be told, they would hear it in stoic silence; and if they were to deny themselves the release even of a wordless remark, their faces would show a degree of suffering which they would not want observed.

"Some had gone," said Mark, as if to give them momentary comfort. "Like Matěj, and the twins, and Zorka with the Army in England, and Jožka driving a tank in Egypt. But even with all the boys gone who were anywhere near military age, and some girls, the rest of them made quite a quorum by the time they had rounded up the Tábor contingent too— Mihal's family, they ran to books and schools and being doctors and teachers, you know more about them than I do, tetičko. Anyway, they collected the whole works at Brno after combing the countryside for weeks, and they had what they called a mass trial in the so-called People's Court. Then they took them out in the yard and lined them up against the wall. Teta Zdenka walked out and stood up beside Uncle Jaro and when one of the bastards came along to tie her hands she spit in his face. The fellow hit her with a gun-butt, it knocked her eye out and she stood there with her eye hanging out of the socket. Seventy-three years old. Actually there were more women than men in the lot of them—because of the boys who were gone, fighting. Your Mařenka Jindrová who you said was a fool walked out to the line-up carrying her baby, it was a few months old. When they tried to take it away from her she struggled, so they grabbed it by the heels and swung its brains out against the wall. She didn't move a muscle. She and Uncle Jaro and Aunt Zdenka and Bohuš and his wife were shot first."

Mark paused. "After that," he said, "they shot the rest of them, in bunches of five or six. But before Uncle Jaro died, he saw how they were going to do it and he asked the rat in command to let him go last, so the ones who went first would see him there waiting. Of course all he got was a crack in the face for that. And over in the corner of the prison yard there were four Jews tied together like animals. They had been made to dig the mass-grave for the whole crowd, including themselves. Uncle Jaro spoke to them when he was marched past them, and thanked them, and they all yelled 'Pravda Vítězí!' together—and of course got kicked in the—they got kicked and beaten up. Seventeen people went in that lot that day, all, except the Jews, related to us."

He had spoken more and more coldly, with what they all felt as the greatest possible will to be tough himself and to make them be tough also. But they had not expected the staggering surprise of having him bring down his fist upon the table with a crash that set the glasses ringing, and lean forward half out of his chair, and look round the whole circle of faces and say, with the harshness of a man on the brink of tears, "But God damn it, don't stop and sit down and hug this story to your chests and think that's all there was to it. Sure, you care the most about what happens to your own flesh and blood, but this was clean—*clean*—do you understand what I'm trying to say?—compared with most of what happened. With the ones who spent years, two, three, four years under torture, some of them such choice spoils that they were never allowed the relief of dying. Or the ones who got shipped in the transports, ninety thousand of them from our country alone. To Terezín and Oswiecim and even some to

Maidanek. I saw those places, one by one, when they were busted open, I was there. Look," he said, in such a tone that they all raised their heads and stared at him, "it was less than a year ago, some of it only six months ago, and you have goddam imbeciles in this country here saying they don't believe it, it's propaganda . . . Jesus Christ," he said, "if I could open a bottle in the faces of some of those apes, a bottle full of the stink of four thousand gassed corpses that they hadn't even had a chance to burn. If I could park them on their fat asses among the bones in those ovens and let them sit there and think things over. If they could see men and women we know, people with more brains and talent and personality and importance than anybody I ever see around here—coming back to Praha from Germany with faces like skulls, and scars and sores all over them that you'd vomit at the sight of, half of them so punch-drunk from what they've been through that they'll never make sense again. Ladies, women like you—" he thrust his chin at Jessie—"all stamped on the left forearm with a blue tattooed number from the prison or camp or brothel where they've been for four years. Boys and girls fifteen, sixteen years old who've been used for —oh, holy suffering Christ!", he snarled, and rising from his chair he shoved it roughly aside and walked out of the room.

XXVI

Surely, she thought, there must be a way that I can leave. I must leave, it is barbarous for me to stay here, a stranger intruding upon these people at such a time. I should never have insisted upon coming, I should never have done so selfish and blundering a thing to Mark. She had not moved at all, she was still sitting with her head bent, unconsciously seeking at least by her bearing to efface herself; but she had a sense of being more realistically effaced by the supreme, tragic stature of the matters which she now knew to be the real concerns of Mark. She turned her left hand slowly over in her lap, looking at the white piqué piping at her wrist which was freshly sewn in place every time she wore this dress; and she thought of the perfumed skin beneath it, to which nothing had ever happened, nothing that made her feel entitled now to own a whole unbroken body, untouched, unviolated, fed, washed, clean, safe, why?; her mind revolved slowly and shamedly round the thought, why? why? She had never known so overwhelming a sense of shame, not only for her own involuntary security, but for the whole substance of her life, which seemed to her now not to hold one thought, one aim, one wish, one act for which there was the slightest justification.

It was extraordinary that there was no sound in the room. She was sharply conscious of the presence of the men and women around her, indeed she felt it as if it were a cold, very heavy weight, a block of chilled lead square upon her shoulders and the back of her neck. I wish it would crush me altogether, she thought, I wish it could obliterate me, for I am useless in the face of this, there is no way in which the fact of my existence can be tolerated in the light of what I have heard. She sat for a length of time which she had no way at all of measuring, for any such commonplace had disappeared from the content of her thoughts; and after a while she felt a gentle pressure on her right arm. She looked up slowly and saw the squat body of Mark's aunt standing beside her, one hand upon her arm. Jessie stared at her, entirely unconscious of tears that were sliding down her own face. She said, "Forgive me—please. I should never have come here at such a time."

"No," said Mrs. Vaníček heavily. "Better you heard. Better everybody knows."

Jessie pressed her hand and then looked quickly about. "I'm going to slip out now," she whispered, rising from her chair. "Let me slip away while Mark is not here."

"No," said Mrs. Vaníček. She looked hard at Jessie; her brown eyes were anxious and intent. Suddenly she shrugged, as if to dismiss other reticences among the sweeping revelations of the hour. She said, "You like Mirko, no?"

Jessie pressed her hand hard and turned to make her way as quietly as possible from the room. But Mark was just coming through the doorway. He was smoking a cigarette and the cheerful vigorous grin upon his face, though quite artificial, was a feat of will power that one could not ignore.

"*Tetičko*," he said, "why don't we stir around a little? Go in the parlor and spread out?"

"Sure," said Uncle Aleš, rising. "*Pojd'me.* You bring along your beer, Mirko?"

"Sure," said Mark, reaching for it. "All my encumbrances." He winked at Jessie and with his head, in his characteristic way, he told her silently to come on.

"But," she murmured to him, "I think—Mark, I ought to——"

"Nuts," he said, so that nobody else could hear him. Then he said aloud, "What's the idea, you got me started on my show, are you going to walk my audience out on me?"

Jessie was surprised. Knowing as she did how close to intolerable it was to Mark to talk as he had been talking, she decided that he must now have some very strong motive for wanting to continue when he could have stopped. She understood better when they were all spread out about the small parlor, in the chairs with the hand-crocheted tidies, among the embroidered sofa-cushions and the bright glass and pottery ornaments from home, under the colored landscapes of scenes in the countryside and the beautiful mezzotint of Prague which covered half a wall, a view of the Charles Bridge from the foreground of the river, with the Hradčany, and the Cathedral raising its exquisite spires beyond. Uncle Aleš explained the landmarks slowly and lovingly, pointing out each detail with the stem of his pipe. Jessie was a little amused that they should take it for granted that she had never been there, which was not the case at all. She had been there, in past fantastically unreal days, the days of blissful summer vacations, driving one's car across the smiling lovelinesses of Europe in what seemed in retrospect a state of imbecile fatuity. Most fatuous of all, she thought, would be to say now that she had seen this beautiful place from the superficial viewpoint of the happy tourist; at the moment she felt that one's only right to an acquaintance with this country would be to possess a means of being of some use to it. And that I cannot do, she thought wretchedly, I am blankly, utterly useless, and I hate the sensation with every fibre of my body and soul. She stood looking at the picture and listening to Uncle Aleš talking against the bizarre obbligato of trucks thundering up and down First Avenue around the corner; and once when she tried to throw her mind backwards to yesterday or forwards to tomorrow, in the impossible effort to orient herself to existence as it must be presumed to be reality for her, she found nothing but confusion.

She turned her head and looked at the people about the room, who in their own way were displaying a kind of poise

323

and presence which she would have found remarkable in the most sophisticated men and women; they were talking quietly, the heavy calm of their manner the measure of control which they had brought to emotions almost intolerably painful. Aunt Olga and her daughter came in from the kitchen, where Jessie knew that they had been washing up cups and glasses in a retreat to a moment's tragic privacy. Aunt Olga sat down on the couch and motioned to Jessie to come and sit beside her, picking up her knitting from the table and beginning to work with such speed that Jessie could scarcely see her fingers move. She was making a child's sock. "I make usually pair a day," she nodded at Jessie; she never glanced down at the work in her hands. "We send every week big box from church."

Mark was talking to his cousin Růža the librarian who, Jessie realized, knew now and had known all through the war far more of the inside story than the other people here. Jessie wondered how. Miss Mráček nodded at something that Mark was telling her; then she said, looking up, "You really ought to tell everybody, Mirko. It's so interesting, and just what nobody who was outside at that time can imagine for himself." She explained, "Mirko was saying how the people felt after the Germans attacked Russia."

"The whole second half of '41," said Mark. "When the Nazis invaded Russia it was a terrific shot in the arm to our people. You can't oversimplify it, of course—nobody jumped up and said hooray, the end was in sight—but you felt the abscess getting hot and you knew that it would take a long time coming to a head but it would positively burst. As a matter of fact that was the beginning of the very blackest year of all, the year that culminated in Lidice and Ležáky."

"*That* year," said Aunt Olga.

"Yes, that year. But you should have seen the hell our people raised when they had the concrete objective of sabotaging German supplies and communications to the Russian front. I remember once a whole trainload of shells and ammunition left Zbrojovka sealed by the Gestapo, with German guards on the train, and when it was opened at the front there was nothing in it but rocks and scrap and junk. Nobody knows yet how it was done.

"Then six months later came Pearl Harbor and they really felt that the grinders had gone into high gear. Again they had no way of knowing anything, or how long it would be . . . you knew here that the U S had been caught with its pants down, but in there they couldn't know. All they read in the papers was lies and the London radio wasn't telling them any more bad news than it could help. So they began to feel that something was really happening, that they were supported from right and left as well as top and bottom. A difference in a dead weight like that can't be very much at first, but the least glimmer of hope in such a spot looks like a beacon."

"It was then," said Růža, as if to point out what he would not bring up himself, "that Mark came back here to join the Army."

"How the hell did you get out?" asked Joe. "In fact, why did you bother?"

"Liaison," said Mark, shrugging. "At least that's the fancy name for it. We had such a set-up there in Bratislava—we called it Flora—that it was practically a channel to outside, a very tricky channel, of course. But it was really funny—the Tiso government were so noisy about their fine Nazi cooperation that they were a good cover-up for a lot of what we did." He laughed. "My God, some fellows must have been so mixed up about who they really worked for, it's a wonder they didn't go crazy. Most of the London broadcasts were beamed to Slovakia and in one way or another they got our orders to us. We had to do the spadework for stuff that didn't actually begin to happen until two and three years later. But things look so simple after the fact and they are so damn snarled before.

"Anyway, the time had come for us to lay lines from outside in as well as inside out. The Underground was going along, people were caught all the time but there were always others to step into their places. Even Vlasta, I would have thought she was irreplaceable, but after she was—" he stopped and scowled and Jessie saw that he had wished he had not mentioned that. But the force of unspoken questions in the room was so great that he sighed and said, "She was caught in the hullabaloo over the killing of Heydrich. I wasn't there then, in fact it was about the same time as Uncle Jaro and the family in Brno. But you can see what they thought of Vlasta's importance, because after they had tortured her in the Petschek for three months, she was moved to the Pankrác and condemned by their so-called highest court and given the extraordinary honor of execution by guillotine. The counts against her were the gravest possible even without the Underground—her brother was in the R A F and she had married an American."

"They would have killed her sooner or later just on account of her brother," said Růža.

"You're telling me. They set out deliberately to exterminate the families of the Czech fliers, I guess it was as systematic as anything they did. They finished up the job during the heaviest bombings of Germany, that made them the most savage of anything. And just—oh, less than two months ago, when the Air Force came home—" He stopped speaking and slowly shook his head, sitting with his hands clasped between his knees and his head bowed over them.

"What?" Uncle Aleš did not want Mark to stop talking.

"I think," said Mark, "in a certain way it was the most tragic thing I saw during the whole war. It was when the fliers came home from England, just now, in August. The squadrons were arriving every day, in fact every few hours, for about a week. I was out at Ruzýn a good deal and on the way there, every day you would see the whole damn road black with people, packed solid all the way out from town. You know how far it is—four miles at least. And the transportation is still pretty scrambled, the trolleys and buses are all over the place. So they walked. They never knew who was arriving or when, and you realize that almost without exception every immediate relative of every single man had been murdered . . . so it wasn't a case of meeting their own boy. They just went out there every morning, thousands and thousands of people, and stood there all day at the gates and watched the men come home, and at the end of the day they walked all the way back to town again. And seeing those chaps drop out of those Lancasters and Stirlings, most of them with nothing on the face of God's earth to call their own, just some little bag or bundle of stuff in one hand. And the uniform on their backs. And they'd look at these mobs of people standing there waving and cheering, and you saw that they knew there wouldn't be a soul there who belonged to them. Not a goddam soul. And these chaps would smile and wave and let themselves be made a fuss over—and when you looked at their eyes you wanted to lie down and die."

Jessie turned her bent head to keep her tears from being noticed. But by now she need not have bothered. The other women in the room were in the same state. There was silence for a time, then Aunt Olga began to knit almost violently, saying, "Well, Mirko, so now you tell where you went next."

"Texas," said Mark.

"Texas!"

"Sure, Air Force."

"Why you join Air Force?" Uncle Aleš. "You can't fly, old man like you."

They all laughed. Mark said, "No, *strýčku*, for this kind of job you go where it fits the set-up. Sometimes two or three places, one fellow I know was a Captain in the Navy and a Lieutenant in the Chemical Corps, besides a couple of other sets of clothes and hardware he had."

"But you not pretending General now!" Uncle Aleš was pouting like a child whose toy is about to be taken away. Mark leaned back and shouted with laughter.

"No," he said, catching his breath. "I don't know for how much longer, but I am bona-fide. You can relax."

"And I suppose," said Joe slowly, "you were also in the OSS and the CID and G 2 and everything else but the FBI."

"Oh," said Mark, "The FBI too, bud. Everything. It damn near broke my heart to give up some of my aliases. I never realized what fun you can have."

"When you went back to war?" asked Uncle Aleš.

"November. North Africa. That was when you really began to see how the pieces would fit—if they ever were going to fit. I often thought they never would. But the big plans and the history were not my business, I had little fish to fry."

"In a small way at Teheran, I suppose," said Růža drily.

"I'm not going into all that, for God's sake," said Mark. "Have a heart. This can't go on all night."

He went to the dining-room and came back with an open bottle of beer in each hand and walked around the room filling glasses and talking.

"We had an air shuttle between London and North Africa that was practically a Cook's tour after what I'd been used to. In fact, if you want to know the grim truth, I had a very good time during most of 1943. For one thing, Americans are fun in a war. They have damn little idea why they're in it, but they do know what to do in a fight. And all that kidding and horsing-around and plenty of stuff to do things with was such a change from what I'd been used to that I got a big kick out of it. After all, I hadn't been in the U S except for flying trips for almost twenty years, and this was a hell of a good way to get reintroduced to it. Only—"

"What?"

"Nothing."

Jessie wondered if anybody else had so clearly understood what Mark had left unsaid. The question was left alone because Joe leaned forward, lighting a fresh cigar, and saying, "What's all this got to do with Teheran? You were there, weren't you?"

Mark shrugged. "Rosie seems to think so."

"Nuts. It was in all the papers."

"Then why ask me?" Mark winked. "Somebody had to be there whose bailiwick our neck of the woods was. Where do you think all the big plans were made? Why do you think the bases at Foggia and Bari were set up? Well, it's seven shelves of history books that aren't written yet, so we needn't start the documenting this evening. My assignment sounded simple then and it sounds simpler now, but there were sixteen months in between that were the damnedest razzle-dazzle anybody ever dreamed up. In fact," he said, "when I look back on it now I don't really believe it ever happened. You could write pulp thrillers about stuff like that, but when you come to say it was all true, you can't believe yourself."

"But," said Joe, "where did you go after Teheran?"

"Why back home, of course. To Slovakia. Early in '44."

"How?"

"Oh, in a train, kid. In a deluxe wagon-lit with a valet and a———"

"Mirko!" said Uncle Aleš. "Why you make it joke now?"

"He parachuted," said Růža Mráčkova.

"How *you* know?"

Mark and his cousin exchanged a smile.

"You got hurt?" asked Aunt Olga.

"Not much. The main thing is I didn't get caught."

"Where this was?"

"Near Zvoleň. The partisans were very hot around there. They worked down from their headquarters at Baňská Bystrica and way beyond. And they had guts! You realize that practically each thing we tried was a flop in the beginning. Like the OSS team that went in during the summer, and the whole outfit was nabbed. Jesus, we were sunk. They were bringing us radio equipment and stuff that we'd been waiting for for nearly six months—and then *fut!* But by that time the Russians were actually in Carpathia and there was no holding our boys. They went ahead and pushed for the uprising that fall, even though the odds were hopeless. We had so many irons in the fire, it was really fantastic when you look back on it. Hiding all the time and mooching around under three or four different sets of whiskers, and weaving all these different things together—I wouldn't have missed it for anything."

328

"You were in contact with the Russians by then, I suppose," said Růža.

"Oh, sure. I was dropped by the Russians when I went in. They were dug in around Miškovec. They dropped most of the guns and stuff to our people. And then our boys from Foggia and Bari were laying eggs east of there, I was in contact with the Twelfth and Fifteenth Air Forces all the time. Some of their fellows had to bail out right around our territory and the way the people took care of them was wonderful. There was one woman named Pribojová who was the coolest customer I ever saw. She had a farm near Velká Lúka, and she got wind of these boys, hidden in different people's houses down around Zvoleň. So she went there and pointed out that she was all alone and didn't give a damn if something happened to her anyway, and she collected all the Americans and took them to her place. She looked after them for months, but incidentally the place was a kind of traffic centre for Germans. She used to play the Germans with one hand, trade them food and stuff she raised on the farm for cigarettes and candy, and then give those to the Americans she was hiding. About half a dozen neighbors were in the deal with her, but she was the baby, all right. The boys were having a nice time there but they kept plaguing me to get them the hell out and our radio communications couldn't have been much worse. But by then this fantastic fellow George Kraigher had his ACRU operation working all over the Balkans and I finally got word to him in Bari through London for Chrissake to come up our way and get these chaps out."

"ACRU? I never heard that one before."

"Air Crew Rescue Unit. They used to go in all over Yugoslavia and Bulgaria and Rumania—everywhere our men had crashed or bailed out—right under the noses of the Germans, practically always at night. The partisans who had saved and hidden the men would take them to the fields, very often fighting a skirmish then and there to get the damn field from the Germans just for the night, and Kraigher's planes would whiz in, collect the boys, and scram. So finally, after sweating out bum radio and weather and everything else you can think of, they came in to Tri Duby on the seventeenth of September. Jesus God, I guess it was the finest sight I ever saw. Two B 17's and an escort of forty-one P 51's. Our people nearly went crazy. I can't think of a way to tell you what it was like. But there was no time for all the welcoming and hullabaloo, they were gone before you could sneeze. And they brought in a bunch of stuff that was manna from Heaven—guns, ammunition, supplies, medicine, two whole radio stations that we'd been praying for all that year. But that's how it was, you see. A big lift about a thing like that—and the Bystrica uprising crushed just about the same time. You couldn't really begin to feel the parts come together and the whole thing go into high gear until after Christmas. Then the Red Army really got rolling in Slovakia and for the first time, from where we were, we could feel the punch from the West. After we crossed the Rhine there was no holding anybody."

"Must be wonderful," said Aunt Olga. She was knitting more slowly now; Jessie had noticed that though she never stopped, the tempo of her work varied according to the intensity of her feelings. When Mark had told about Mrs. Pribojová the sock had grown a noticeable half-inch.

"So you never went outside the country again, until the end," said Růža.

Mark shook his head. "No need to. And by the spring, there was so much to do it was like living ten years in ten days. Because of course the Germans felt the crunch just the way we did, there was a combination of crumpling up and savagery that was a queer thing to deal with. It all happened the way anybody knew it must—with the tide rolling from both sides and us in the middle, of course we had to be their last stand. I'd been so wrapped up in the outside fights for over a year that I'd almost lost touch with the resistance inside—oh, of course, we worked with them—but it was a different kind of thing by the end. Political, and damned clear about what it was shooting at."

"And no good!" exclaimed Uncle Aleš angrily.

"Now wait a minute, *strýčku*. Keep your shirt on."

"What for? I should holler hooray for Stalin? Hooray for Red Army? Hooray for Communist? Hooray for Národní Výbor?"

"Why shouldn't you? You holler hooray for Patton. Hooray for the U S. Well—you don't know what you're hollering for if you don't see with two eyes, not just one. You might not like it but——"

"I don't like." Uncle Aleš's mouth was hard.

"That's too bad," said Mark slowly. There was something almost like sarcasm in his tone. "I'm sorry you couldn't have seen Matěj when his outfit rolled into Praha. You'd have understood better."

"He was in Red Army?"

"Sure. He was a Colonel in the First Czech Brigade. And by the time he had fought his way home over two thousand miles and three years and after what had happened to the family and everybody else, he was in no political confusion at all. Which is more than I can say for a lot of—others."

"He is Communist?" asked Aunt Olga coldly.

"You're damn right he's a Communist! Why wouldn't he be? Now look here," said Mark. "This thing that's about to bust right out here in the middle of the carpet is exactly why I feel like a blathering jackass for all the talking you've made me do today. Sure, it was a fine victory, a wonderful victory. God was on our side. We were wonderful. We were big heroes. So now it's over. And what are we going to do?—sit here and preen ourselves about what fine brave soldiers we were, and tell each other horror stories, or do we make the goddam thing *mean* something? Is anybody going to make it stick? Not by shutting your mind like a trapdoor and saying, 'I don't like.' Excuse me, *strýčku.*" He lit a cigarette with a rough gesture.

There was a silence. Then Aunt Olga said slowly, "Mirko. Are *you* Communist?"

Mark clutched his head. "God in heaven, no! Why should I be? I don't need to be! I happen to be an American and a citizen of the last country that can afford political luxury. I didn't say liberty, mind you, I said luxury."

"Don't tell me there's liberty in Czecho now," said Joe, sneering.

"I certainly will tell you. I'm telling you."

"Nuts."

Mark turned pale. Jessie saw rising in his face an anger different from any rage that she could identify, and she thought, this is an old, old thing. I wonder what it is. Mark's nostrils flared and he said in a tone which Jessie could scarcely recognize, "If you'd get up off your fat can and take your electric knowhow over there and pitch in and help them get a few factories going, you'd see for yourself how much liberty there is."

My God, thought Jessie in the frightened silence. But Uncle Aleš, in the most casual of tones, said, "Boys, shame on you." Katka giggled nervously. Jessie realized that this was an old story and that they had always been used to it.

"I'm sorry, *tetičko,*" said Mark. "I get sore as a boil when they start that kind of talk."

"But it looks like true," said Aunt Olga mildly, shaking her head. "Is not like before. And now such a *hrůza,* Russians all over country, what we hear they doing! You will see, they don't leave. Never."

"Yes they will," said Mark patiently. He looked quickly at his watch.

"How you know? Who told you?"

"President Beneš."

Aunt Olga's eyebrows moved doubtfully, and she shook her head again, and again said, "Is not like before."

Mark sighed. He leaned forward, clasping his hands loosely between his knees and said quietly, "Of course it's not like before, *tetičko.* That's exactly what I'm trying to say. And it never will be, it can't be. You see, things happened to the people in those seven years of hell. You're a wise woman," he said gently. "You know a lot about human nature. Do you think the people could take that terror all those years, coming on top of Munich, and not have anything happen to them? Not change? The wonder is that they haven't changed more."

"They don't have to change to—all this," said Aunt Olga.

Mark shook his head, discouraged at his own inability to make them understand. When he spoke again his voice was slow and thoughtful; conciliatory. He said, "I'm not pretending that all the changes are wonderful. For one thing, there hasn't been time yet since last May to give them a chance. But when Uncle Aleš says 'I don't like,' and wants me to tell him that everything should go right back to 1935 and be lovely, I can't. Nothing will ever go back like that again. What you've got now is a—a—" Mark looked up uneasily, frowning and feeling for a way to express himself. "History, I guess," he said. "You feel it when you're there, you feel it like a rip-tide. You feel it because you feel the reasons for it. That's why it's hard to understand here. Nothing happened here. But that force moving there—you like it, you don't like it. I can't help that. Nobody can help it. But are you going to buck it? Or be smashed by it? Or are you going to find a way to ride it? That's what I'm betting on our people to do."

He looked up again, frowning a little and feeling for words, and he said, "Some of them are tired and some are awfully shot and some are puzzled. But they all realize what it is they've got to do, in this sense I am speaking of. History. Maybe destiny."

"Sounds to me like a lot of bull," said Joe.

Jessie held her breath, anticipating another outburst from Mark. But to her surprise he only looked mildly at Joe and said, "I know it does. It's too much words, you're right. But when you try to boil the whole thing down that's what happens, you get gummed up in words. And yet," he said, turning to the others, "it seems to me that people can find themselves in a certain spot—" he sighed. Jessie could see that this was not easy for him. "Find themselves instruments of whatever you call it—history—destiny—fate—without necessarily liking every bit of the part they have been chosen to play. But if they recognize this, and go ahead and take this part, they are alive. My God, our people are alive! And if they shrink from it, they are dying, like the French. And if you want to see what happens when they won't bend or ride with the tide, but just get violent, look at Poland and Yugoslavia. Or the poor Greeks. At two opposite ends of the squeeze—with terror and chaos in the middle."

—"And what you think you can do about it?" asked Uncle Aleš, with a queer note in his bass voice which almost suggested ridicule. His face was quite sullen.

"That's what I'm going to know more about as time goes on," said Mark. "If I really tried to answer your question, I'd use a lot more long words and start talking about some things I don't know too much about myself. But I'm damned if I think the way to make the war mean something is come back here to a fat job and stick out my tongue at the Czechs because I don't like Communists and Socialism, or I don't want the industries nationalized, or I think they are naughty boys to make an alliance with Russia. God damn it, I broke into the Pankrác when there were still corpses stuck on meathooks on a trolley all around the room where they chopped off my wife's head. When you have a nation of people to whom things like that happened every day for seven years, precisely because their Western allies dumped them, what do you expect them to do? And the amazing thing is that they are setting out to do it the way Czechs have always done things, the way you and I do things—reasonably. Sanely. And they need help. I'm not talking about food or goods or material things. But something from the U S that will steady them, help them be what they and nobody else can be—in that part of the world."

"What?"

"Stable. Solid. Sense-making. Sounds so simple. Where will

you be without it, and where the hell else can you find it, there where it matters more than anywhere on the face of the earth?"

Uncle Aleš shrugged doubtfully.

"Oh, I wasn't even trying to convince you," said Mark wearily. Jessie had begun to notice how tired he was. "You asked me a raft of questions and maybe I was a fool to answer them. Anyway," he said, getting to his feet, "it really was wonderful to see you all." He went over and put his arm around his aunt and hugged her.

"Oh, you don't go now, Mirko!" She looked up at him ruefully. "You stay for supper, you and Mrs. Brno."

Mark laughed. "Did you hear your new name?" he asked Jessie. "No, tetičko, I'm sorry, it would be fun to stay, but I have to go to Washington tonight." Jessie, speaking to his cousin Růža, pretended not to have heard. They were all standing now, moving about in the preliminaries to saying good bye.

"When you go back, Mirko?" asked his uncle.

"Monday. Jeez, it really was good to see you." Mark slapped the chunky man on the back.

"And you staying in Army?" asked Uncle Aleš. "Or what you do? Who you work for, Government?"

"Oh—this and that," said Mark evasively. "It's American, simon-pure, if that answers your question." He grinned and Jessie understood much more than she had before. The farewells were demonstrative to Mark, beamingly cordial to Jessie.

"You come see us again," said Mrs. Vaníček. "Next time Mirko comes back he brings you again."

"I should love to," said Jessie, squeezing her hand. "I can't thank you enough. Really." She looked into Mrs. Vaníček's bright brown eyes and saw that her words had been accepted as sincerely as she meant them. The whole family followed them out to the stair-landing and continued to call "Good bye!" until the street door closed behind them.

"Jesus!" said Mark, in a groan. He was almost shuffling up the street. "I have never been so tired since I was born, and that goes for all the spinach you heard up there, too. You scheming little bitch, to let me in for that."

"I never had such a wonderful time," said Jessie quietly. "It was the single most interesting day of my life. And the loveliest people."

"For God's sake don't start comparing it with yesterday," said Mark. "I might lose face."

"Are you really going to Washington tonight?" she asked, as they reached the corner of First Avenue.

"Of course not. It was just the easiest way to break away. Hey, taxi!"

He popped her into the cab and got in and shut the door. "Just go some place," he said to the driver. "Start downtown." He turned to Jessie and took her in his arms.

XXVII

Because they knew that it would be quiet and effortless and because they were not in the mood for a crowded restaurant, they went back to Mark's hotel and dined in his apartment.

"Perhaps you'd rather not——" he hesitated, remembering Jessie's feeling of the morning.

"Oh no. Not at all." She looked at him with a smile. "Like everything else, that is relative. You've carried me far enough away from yesterday and the effect of all those horrible people so that I feel quite differently. After all——rooms are only rooms."

She took off her hat, standing before the mantel mirror and making a face at herself. "I'm a sight," she said.

Mark, telephoning to room service, waved at the bedroom door. "Make yourself comfortable," he said. "Hello? hello? I want——"

In the bathroom Jessie turned back her white cuffs, thinking again the thoughts that had overcome her this afternoon. She scrubbed her face and put fresh powder and lipstick on it, suspended for the moment in the strange blankness of mind which the process often involves. She threw a towel around her shoulders, ran through her hair with the small comb from her purse, and then from force of habit she paused to look for the brush with which at home she whipped up the short curls at the back of her neck. She laughed suddenly, realizing where she was. Then her eye fell upon Mark's brushes and his other toilet articles, ranged with the precisest neatness upon the glass shelf over the basin. She stood staring at them, quite as if she were making some original and altogether unique discovery; but she was not thinking at all. Slowly she put out her hand and picked up one of the small, stiff English brushes, with the silver monogram set into the polished wood back, and with it she brushed her hair, up at the nape of her neck, sharply away from her forehead and her temples. Then she stood looking at the brush in her hand, turning it over and marvelling that this commonplace object should have fixed her attention and turned her thoughts in such a way that some span of time or space seemed to have been leaped in the process. She put the brush back in place, and when she looked at the mirror just before switching off the light, she was surprised to see the flush of unusual color in her face.

They sat quiet and relaxed in two armchairs, each with a whisky and soda. "We're about quits now," said Mark, "when it comes to being tired. After what you went through yesterday I almost think you let me in for this beating on purpose, just to get even with fate."

"Why of course. I was trying to be as mean as possible."

"You are so nice," said Mark.

"No, you are nice. Nice and warm."

"Fat and lazy."

"I like that. Your lean and nervous men—" she shuddered faintly. Mark pretended not to notice.

"We ought to set up in a mud hut somewhere," he said, "and communicate in grunts."

"Ideal," she said, thinking of the immaculate, fastidious order in which she had just seen his personal possessions. "Just your dish."

"Yours too. You are such a rotten housekeeper."

"You are such a barbarian. No taste, no perception . . ."

He smiled in an understated way, twitching the corners of his mouth. Jessie felt the sense of pleasure in her wrists and her finger tips.

"Do you think," asked Mark, "that I shall make love to you?"

"Yes I do." She had never heard or answered anything with less surprise.

"I have no plans about it. But I seem to take it for granted."

"I don't even wonder. Particularly," she said, "after what I heard this afternoon. I'm glad I heard it. That may sound selfish but there could be no other way to understand you."

"Oh, a very complicated bastard," jeered Mark quietly.

"Full of neuroses and complexes and compulsions—rot, my darling."

"Oh, really? I thought you were just a boy. Just what I like."

"I like you. You fascinate me. You attract me more than any woman I ever saw. Sometimes I want to smack you a little—just a very small, careful smack——"

"Why?"

"Oh, you get brittle at the edges."

"I know," she said, looking ashamed. "Always about some trifle, too."

"There's a reason," said Mark, making owl's eyes.

"But no excuse."

"Anyway, you're no bore. Sometimes," he said, his manner softening suddenly, "you seem to me like a bouquet. One of those neat little bunches of different kinds of flowers, all mixed together. Not only one or two kinds that I enjoy, but many. And some so very different from the others."

"That's sweet of you," she said. "Of course you seem very much the same to me."

"Well—you couldn't draw a picture of it, all in plain black strokes on neat white paper. What would you have if you tried? Nothing. That's what bothers me so around here, the blackness and whiteness. What about this picture of us? In black and white you will never get two people who fall in love, marry, and live happily ever after. And if you made a work of art out of it, you would get a puzzle in greys, mingled with the colors of that bouquet I was talking about."

"A very private work of art. Too subtle for anyone else to understand."

"Ah, I said I liked you. Here's our dinner."

While they were eating, Mark said, "What are we going to do tomorrow?"

Jessie sighed. "In a way I was putting off thinking about that. It seems so unjust that after years of nobody caring a fig where I am, these miserable people should make a reason now why Brandon wants to make use of my presence."

"How do you feel about it?"

"You mean—do I agree with Brandon? Perhaps I might in the superficial sense of taking my place in a situation that concerns his family—except that," she raised her eyes to Mark's and looked at him for a moment without speaking, "I want to be with you."

"I want to be with you."

337

"Considering that I have not wanted forty-eight hours to myself in this way in all the years that Brandon has not cared or thought where I was, or why——"

"Are you sure of that?" asked Mark slowly.

"How can I be anything but sure? One doesn't need words or endearments to feel that one is wanted or appreciated or even loved—but a vacuum is a vacuum, Mark. When you have nothing—" she put out her hand, palm up, and looked into it—"you know it."

"That kind of man can be a very queer dick," he said.

"I know. The point is that it doesn't matter how queer he may still prove to be, I've put up with so much queerness before that I'm used to it. You know," she said slowly, "I must be a very old-fashioned person, stuffy or Victorian or something like that. It's extremely difficult for me to talk about this."

"You are a lady," said Mark abruptly.

"Well—you see. That is an old-fashioned term of itself. If," she said, "there were the slightest chance of my leaving Brandon Bourne or ditching this incubus after all these years, I might not be so determined to have this little space of time to myself. But as it is—" she paused and looked absently into her wineglass.

"You hate him, which is very sad in view of your determination not to leave him."

"I—" she shut her lips. She had been about to say that she feared Brandon Bourne which was of course integral with hating him, but muddier. Clear hatred, just hatred, could be a hot and cutting emotion; fear such as she knew, the quaking fear of his violence and his temper and his disorder and his touch—suddenly she realized, staring at Mark Dwyer, that the thought of Brandon Bourne's touching her had made her hands and her body damp with cold moisture. Mark was speaking but at the moment she could not comprehend his words, because she was thinking with heavy relief how many years it had been since Brandon Bourne had touched her, made love to her. And that is nothing that I would ever discuss with you, she thought of Mark, looking at him, and then she said involuntarily, "I beg your pardon, Mark, what did you say?"

He smiled sadly. "I knew you weren't listening. It doesn't matter, I only said I admire your seriousness."

"You ought to know my friend Serena Lowden better."

338

"One scarcely needs to. You remember what I said in the theatre the other night."

They were silent while the waiter took away the dinner table and left them with their coffee.

"But Mark," said Jessie suddenly, looking up from a long stare into the bottom of her empty cup, "but surely, life—surely one ought to—how can I say it—find a way to put more into it than just that? Just behaving well in bad situations. Let alone getting anything out of it."

"Frankly, I don't see how such women do stand it. You or Serena Lowden or any of you—the good ones or the bad."

"Neither do I," she said, in a small voice. "That's exactly what is driving me and gnawing at me all the time now—I believe I said something about it on Tuesday. I'm no use. I was no use in the war when I might have seized the opportunity and now—" she broke off, her eyes distended in an expression almost of fear, "now there aren't even the opportunities."

"Don't you believe it," said Mark quite brusquely. Jessie stared at him, reacting to the changed tone of his voice with a twinge of reminiscence, and wondering why. But almost at once she found that she knew where and when he had spoken in that way; only this afternoon to his cousin's husband Joe. She continued to look at him with a sharper understanding of his way of conveying his most cogent thoughts without speaking at all.

"Even," she said at last, very slowly, "even if I could not find a *real* thing to do—or be—I would still know I shall have to break out of this pattern somehow. I—I am too old for it."

"Yes," he said, "and more to the point, the world is too old for it—or too changed. But you'll have to go and find that out for yourself. You weren't talking about your private life, God knows."

"No," she said. "Not at all. That's just a treadmill. It used to seem charming and important—but now I know better."

"Well," he said, sharply changing the subject, "what about tomorrow?"

"One thing we could do," she said, without understanding exactly why the thought had occurred to her, "is plan to go up to Helen and Sam Lee's." Mark raised his eyebrows. "That doesn't necessarily mean we would have to go there."

"Well—if you think so. Where is it?"

339

"Not so far. Connecticut. Near Litchfield. They have a big farm. I was planning to go there for the week end anyway before——" she laughed. "Before anything happened—or everything."

"I see."

"Only—I just remembered. My car is still in dead storage. I would have gone with them today."

"I can borrow a car from Buck."

"Possibly," said Jessie, looking straight at him, "we will not use it."

"Possibly. Shall I call for you with the car in the morning?"

"No," she said calmly. "I will meet you here."

"I'm going to take you home now. I might as well wind up this fantastic day by being quite gallant and telling you that you look like hell."

They laughed. "I know it," she said. "But it was so wonderful to meet those relatives of yours. They were like fresh air, like fresh fruit, I can't tell you how I liked them. I wonder if I shall ever see them after you've left?"

"That's up to you," he said. "They——"

"What?"

"I think you know without my saying. They've got answers to some of your questions—or hints of answers, anyway."

"Yes, I know that."

"But they don't know it themselves."

"I see." She smiled. But her eyes were heavy. "And if I should see them it would be because—because——"

Mark nodded. "That's it. The closer you come to—how would you say it—necessity? Somebody's necessity, anyway."

"I understand."

He held her coat and dropped it about her shoulders, clasping them gently in his hands and turning her around to kiss her. Standing so in his arms she felt her knees tremble, and the feeling of weakness, which would otherwise be frightening, only made her more glad that he was there. "Oh," she breathed, resting her forehead against his chest, "you are so—so——"

"Sh-h—" he whispered, covering her eyelids with light caresses of his lips. She put her fingers upon his cheek, softly touching the line of the bone under the eye-socket, and the heavy black brow above it, feathering off into the strong temple.

"I think," she said, wishing that she could stop herself, "I could die for one moment of tenderness."

340

"Darling—" He did not let her hear the rest of what he said.

She turned away quickly, because her sense of exhaustion had suddenly become so extreme that she knew she would be in tears in another moment, and that was out of the question. Walking down the corridor towards the elevator she said, "I'm not going to ask you up for a drink, Mark."

"I should hope not! The idea is for you to go to sleep at once."

Indeed, she thought, it is; the idea is for me to be shut in my room, asleep, when Brandon comes in, obviating any possibility of my seeing him tonight. As for the thought of his coming in and joining Mark and me for a drink in the library —she grimaced. She sat quietly in the cab on the way home, her hand in Mark's, and her thoughts such that once, when their glance met in the light of a street lamp, they both smiled as if putting the final bit of punctuation upon a long, explicit paragraph.

Glancing at her watch as she unlocked the front door, she saw that it was quite early, it was barely half past eleven. The thought of crawling into bed and lying there, flat and still in the dark, in the fresh cool linen, under the light silk coverlet, with the damp foggy air blowing off the river through the opened windows, made her weak with knowledge that it would only be a few minutes until she need no longer brace herself against this overpowering fatigue. She found herself thinking, my God I must really be unbelievably tired if I long to be upstairs in bed in this way more than I can want even to be with Mark. She pushed open the heavy front door and walked forward and then stood, her mouth dry, her hands icy, the pulse in her throat beating against the high collar of her dress. Every light in every room was burning. Every door upon the central foyer was open, the drawing-room, the dining-room, the library. Every lamp was turned on, every girandole; not a fixture that was not lighted. Brandon. She bit her lips. He had a way of doing this, of forcing the whole house into a meaningless blaze of light, even in rooms which were not at the moment in use, sometimes in broad daylight, very often when she had deliberately set just such an amount of lighting, with candles and understated lamps, as she felt was gracious and beautiful. It was one of his ways of destroying repose. She stood in the foyer clenching her gloved fists; then she walked quickly to the nearest switch-plate and began to turn off the lights. She went then to the dining-room—of all places to do such a thing!—then across the foyer again to the drawing-room. Brandon's voice said sharply from the library, "Jess?"

She stopped, rigid. The fear, the plunging, phobic abhorrence swept up inside her like a bubbling scum; her mouth was bitter. She stood, stretching her spine and her neck to force control upon herself, drawing a stomach-deep breath to get air. Then she walked slowly to the library doorway, saying "Oh. How come you are here? What happened to your party?" Her voice was leaden and bored.

"I came back from the theatre," said Brandon, snapping. "I want to talk to you."

"Oh," she said, forcing a weak laugh. "Not tonight. I am tired. Really tired. I'm going to bed."

"Well, you'll have to stay up awhile. I told you I wanted to talk to you."

Jessie looked at him with a surprised frown.

"I'm sorry, Brandon," she said quietly, "but it has been a good many years since matters between us have been such as to give you any right to speak to me like that. Good night." She turned away.

She heard a crack and a gurgle and she knew that he had slammed down his highball upon a table so roughly that he had broken the glass. She would not give him the satisfaction of turning around and looking at the mess. Let it ruin the table or the chair or the rug. She began to walk across the hall towards the stairs and she heard Brandon come to the door of the library.

She kept on moving but at the same time she was thinking, oh, what is the use of feeding his beastly temper? Opposition, silent or overt, would only stimulate him to be as she most detested him, and as he could most upset her. It was easier to blot him out by seeming but contemptuous pliancy. She heard his hard, high voice say, "I want to talk to you about this fellow Dwyer."

She was so shocked and so angry that she felt it as a chill running all over her skin. She turned slowly about at the foot of the stairs and looked at Brandon standing in the library doorway, at the ugly lines of obduracy in his face, at his staring eyes like illuminated blue globes. She said, "This is the most extraordinary thing you have ever done. Have you lost your mind?"

"No more than you, apparently. Who the hell is this man?"

"There is no reason in the world why I feel obliged to

answer any question you ask me. But if you expect to stay on common speaking terms with me, just be careful."

"Well. Since you're so holier-than-thou about Van and Alec and the mess they're in, do you know you have the whole goddam town talking about you and this General Dwyer?"

Jessie shrugged. "I daresay I've been most indiscreet, dining with a lot of friends and going to parties and the theatre. Invariably accompanied by General Dwyer. But so far as you are concerned, you may as well know right now that I shall do precisely as I please, with whom I please, when and where I please, and that you have no more right to question what I do than the utmost stranger. You have not had the right for —you know how many years."

"That's not the point," snapped Brandon. "Do you have to make a public spectacle of yourself? Especially at a time like this?—when we're—when we've got to——"

"I can't be bothered being a sneak," said Jessie. "I have nothing to conceal—except possibly what I think of you. If I had let that get the upper hand of me I would have left you years ago."

"You didn't, though!"

There was something almost jeering in his manner, which was unholy. Did he think, she wondered, that merely to be his wife constituted a position which she had been unwilling to relinquish?

"It's so remarkable that you of all people do not seem to understand my reasons," she said. She thought of the brief moment when she had touched on this painful subject in talking with Mark at dinner, and with Horace Howland last Monday in his office. "But another five minutes of this will induce me to tell you why I regret them. You will really not like it if I begin to talk."

"Look here," he said, changing his tactics suddenly, in the same abrupt way that he moved and spoke. "You've got a right to be sore at me. You've got a case. I know it as well as you do."

"Well," she said. She raised her eyebrows and left the comment unstated.

"But this mess we're in now, all snarled up with everybody in town—I come back and find those stink-bombs all over the place and everybody talking about you besides. Do I have to take that?"

My God, she thought. My God, is it possible? I thought I knew the most egomaniac things that he could do, but this

343

caps them all. And once again she realized that one of the basic props of his existence had been the Caesar's wife quality of her own; not, she knew well, because of the least moral superiority on her part, but sheerly because of the accident that she had not until now seen anybody on account of whom she would have thought it worth while to make herself vulnerable. This type of man, she reminded herself, looking coldly at Brandon, actually prefers to pursue his gyrations from the platform of the most conventional marriage, it is the ideal set-up to provide for his eating his cake and having it too. And now he feels the platform shaking and he is outraged. She stood, one foot upon the bottom step, one hand on the newel-post, looking at his obsessed face and allowing a swift, sharp sequence of devastating memories to ride through her brain. After all these, she thought, and a thousand others too commonplace to remember, he rears up in the guise of the outraged husband. Oh, my God! She opened her mouth and told him so.

He stalked angrily up and down the foyer, kicking at the edge of a rug each time he passed it. There was a glaring scowl on his face. Jessie started to move up the stairs. He looked at her and said, "Wait a minute. Since it happens that you haven't left me up to now, and since you started out yesterday to stand by my—ah—family during this mess, you may as well know that I expect you to finish the job."

"And what does that involve?"

"The afternoon and dinner tomorrow out at the Lowdens', and Sunday lunch with Mother."

"I am going to Helen Lee's for the week end."

"Is that man going too?" barked Brandon, swinging round on his heels.

"I consider that none of your business. The only reason I would answer you is to remind you that I literally will not bother with deception. It is a long time since you have paid me the compliment of doing so."

"Well, you can't do this! I tell you I need to have you appear with me for a damned important reason, and all of a sudden you get up and crack me with a lot of grudges fifteen years old. Why the hell can't you wait till next week—or some other time?"

"Because I don't want to."

"Well, you'll have to! I won't stand for it."

"Don't, my dear. I am not sure what your not standing for it would consist of, but really I don't care."

"What's the matter with you?" he asked, his voice rasping. "You behaved well enough all day yesterday, you were goddam good, in fact, and now you take the bit in your teeth and turn as stubborn as a—a——"

"No," said Jessie quietly. "I have simply come to the end. The end of my patience, the end of sitting quiet and taking it, the end of a great many things. If you want, the end of you too—the whole thing." She stared at him.

"I don't want that, Jess!" Now he looked at her with a queer mixture of arrogance and fear and pleading.

"Well then," she said, "be careful not to drive me to it. I used to wonder years ago why you insisted that you wanted me to stay with you in spite of the way you treated me, but now I'm so old that I understand. But I feel just the other way. I made up my mind that I was going to stick this out because—oh, I don't know. Because that's me, I suppose, and not somebody else. And I still mean to, Brandon." She stood on the steps a little above him, looking down into his queer hard eyes. She was so tired that though she wanted to stand still and be very composed, she thought she felt herself swaying from the ankles; but she was not sure. "I still mean to. I have no intention of leaving you, unless you put on any more scenes like this one tonight. Then you will drive me to a break. But short of that you cannot force me or frighten me or browbeat me. If you want me to leave you, say so. If you don't want me to leave you, just put yourself in my place for a change, and keep still. Good night. Oh, by the way, I will come in from Helen's on Sunday morning in time to lunch at your mother's. It's ridiculous, but I am willing to play it through."

VI
SATURDAY

XXVIII

"Josephine," said Jessie, when she had finished her coffee, "I shall be going up to Mrs. Lee's for the night. Just put some overnight things into my big suede shoulder bag. I am going in the train and a suitcase would be a nuisance, there are no Pullmans."

"What about a dinner gown, Mrs. Bourne? And slippers?"

"I shall borrow something of Mrs. Lee's."

"Oh, yes, of course, you're both the same size." Josephine took the breakfast tray and went away.

Jessie lay still, holding the palms of her hands flat across her eyes. If this tearing-apart process does not stop soon, she thought, I shall go mad. I wonder if it is possible for one's mind to become black-and-blue like a great bruise on one's body. That is the way I feel. It seemed too as if she could scarcely remember what it felt like to wake rested in the morning. How long has it been since I did, she thought. She remembered slowly backwards, beginning with the cold rage in which she had gone to bed last night, through the astonishing experience of yesterday with its revelations of sweetness and of horror, back through another roll of the cylinder of time to the crushing disgust of Thursday, back to the strange burlesqued mélange of Wednesday night . . . this is preposterous, she said nearly aloud. All this does not happen in a week, none of it real, none of it possible. But just beyond the bounds of her doubt lay the thought of Mark, which she had not squarely faced this morning, but which, when she did, would be the only clear and solid certainty outside the whole unbelievable maze. And before I leave the house, she thought, there are some things I must do, because whether or not I succeeded in cutting all these tangled skeins behind me, there are a few attached to certain people whom I do not want to fail. She picked up the telephone and called Althea Crowe.

"I suppose you're in bed, all cozied up in ruffles," said Althea.

"I am ruffled, which is another thing altogether. How are you, Althea?"

"Fine. Splendid. Full of hell."

"I wonder when I'm going to begin to find a way of thanking you."

"For God's sake don't. Skip it."

"Is there anything I can do?"

"You mean is all the trash swept up? Oh, sure. Sister Katzenschwanz was a bird. She didn't blink or show a sign, positive or negative, until she opened the closet and got a load of dolly's clothes. Oh, boy, have those pussies found a home."

Jessie shook with laughter. "You mean she can wear them? I got the idea she is a—a——"

"Go on, say it. Built like me. Well, just a *leetle* mite daintier. But you ought to have seen those eyes glittering behind the rimless glasses, when she took in the mink coat and the broadtail coat and the foxes and the weasels and the rest of the zoo."

"It's really awfully funny."

"Sure it's funny. If you think of the saps who bought the stuff and look who's wearing them now!"

"Oh, Althea, you are so grand."

"Oh, sure. How's dreamboat?"

"Why, Miss Crowe."

"Oh. So that's the way it is. Well, I'll see you Tuesday, unless——"

347

"Unless nothing whatsoever. How would you like to make it dinner instead of lunch? We'd have more time."

"For what?"

"I don't know. Just time."

"Why not? Same place?"

"Yes, I love it."

"Okay, infant. Have fun."

Once again Jessie realized that some hatefulness of life were compensated for by one's few real friends. She telephoned to Serena Lowden in the country and asked her frankly whether it would put her out if she did not come with Brandon.

"No," said Serena, "of course not. I understand perfectly."

"I feel horribly selfish," said Jessie. "There is something that I want very much to do, I had planned it before you spoke to Brandon."

"By all means, dear. I would really rather you did it."

"But I'm letting you down," said Jessie, feeling all wrong.

"No. Under the circumstances, if I felt that you should come, I would say so."

"You're so good about it. The point is," said Jessie quietly, "it's not something I have to do, only something I want."

"I told you I understood. I wish I—" Mrs. Lowden checked herself. "Don't worry, my dear. You've been wonderful. Good bye."

Jessie sighed, she could still not throw off the uneasy sense of having failed Serena Lowden, but the crystallization of her will about all this had gone so far beyond anything that she could explain or understand that hesitation seemed to have been ruled out by some superior hand. She telephoned to Helen Lee, and in a very few oblique words conveyed what she had to say.

"All right, darling," said Helen. "Leave it that way. Maybe yes, maybe no. There's nobody else here anyway. The house is half closed."

"You're sure it's not inconvenient?"

"How could it be?"

"Well. How are you, darling, how do you feel?"

"Wonderful," said Helen. "Except about you. I mean——"

Only from the moment that they had snatched before dinner on Thursday, and from her own intuition, could Helen Lee sense much of what had been happening. But they had always conveyed as much to one another without words as

348

with them. Helen wasted none now. She said, "I shan't expect to hear from you. Just—as it falls."

"I wish I could see you this minute!" said Jessie on an impulse.

"Are you all right?" asked Helen quickly.

"Yes." Jessie was surprised to hear her own voice quaver.

"I'm worried about you."

"Oh, no! On the contrary. Are you coming down on Monday?"

"We have to."

"I'll be glad. If I don't see you today, I will then. Come here for lunch?"

"Yes," said Helen. "Of course."

"Good bye, darling."

While she was dressing Jessie found that she had come to a decision not to see Brandon before she left the house. She disliked the thought of doing so brusque and evasive a thing, which was typical of him rather than of her; she shrank too from the retaliative flavor of it; but she was reduced to considerations of self-preservation. If she should let him disturb her in any way today she would be unable to recapture enough poise to make it possible to see Mark at all. She felt herself already far too near the edge of a frightening precipice at the bottom of which there seemed to her to lie a deep pool of pure poison.

In a sense, she thought, I am not sure what I am doing, but I have made up my mind to do it. So far as she knew, Brandon was still asleep, she had heard no sounds from beyond the door to his room, which she had with deliberate contempt not locked last night, knowing the symbolic banality of the gesture to be unnecessary; he would not have dared come into her room. But he well might this morning, in a savage frame of mind, determined to ruin for her what he could not prevent. She realized that in rare, icy anger she had made an extreme, terminal threat, altogether out of character, or of what she would have thought her character to be. Yet now she stood beside the door, no longer angry, weighing the possible consequences of her words, and realizing with amazement that, spontaneous as they had been, she had meant them then and she meant them now. She asked Josephine whether Mr. Bourne was up yet, and Josephine came back to say no, Sarah said that he had not rung for breakfast. Jessie finished dressing quickly; she took her bag and gloves and furs from

Josephine, and said, "I shall be back about twelve-thirty tomorrow, we are going to Mrs. Bourne's for lunch. Tell Sarah and Anna that there are no plans for today or tomorrow. We are out."

She walked lightly from her room, observed that the hall door to Brandon's room was also closed, went downstairs, and left the house, all in a tense and uneasy state of nerves which she resented with every fibre of her nature. To have set about the pursuit of the shoddiest intrigue could not have made her feel more detestable than this, when she had had her hand forced in such a brutal way. Justice has nothing to do with it, she thought in the taxi, or reason or equivocation of any kind. It is as it is. And I have no idea what is going to happen, either.

She sat watching the river as the cab ground down the drive, noting with quick pleasure the bloodcurdling scream of a tugboat whistle, a dreadful noise to which she had become attached through habit; and keeping her mind occupied with small tangible sights and sounds so that she would not begin to think. The cab left the drive at Fifty-third Street and started west. Jessie looked out at the ugly peripheral street full of warehouses, trucks backing and turning, and battered, snarling cabs. The whole mess had come to a dead halt, a jumble in which the driver of each vehicle was leaning out of his window, sneering, cursing, or resignedly resorting to a cigarette. Presently the inevitable happened; there rose a chorus of honks, barks, and blats from all the horns, all raising hell in futile unison and wild defiance of the city ordinance against such noise. Jessie burst into a laugh and her driver turned around, shrugging, to look at her.

"Would you believe it," she said, "if somebody told you that the jackass who built that Highway deliberately put an exit on this street?"

"Gawd, no," said the man. "Looka da dopes."

"Furniture factories, a parking lot, Saks's warehouse, a two-way street, and a highway exit—all in the same block," she said.

The cab started again and she leaned back in her seat, tipping her head at a certain angle so that she could see the bright blue October sky, completely recovered from its sulking-fit of yesterday. Why, she thought suddenly, perhaps that is a good sign; perhaps everything will be all right. At the same moment her mind mocked the thought, but she was

350

smiling when she stopped at Mark's door, to find him flinging it open before she had had a chance to ring the bell.

He put his fingers under her chin as they stood near the windows, and looked at her face with sharp discernment, almost with anxiety.

"Smile!" she said, making a small face.

"Is everything all right? Are you all right?"

"Oh, superb," she said. "Splendid. Everything."

"Like hell it is."

"Neither snow nor rain nor heat nor gloom of night nor your ominous suspicions can stay this courier from her appointed rounds."

"You left out 'swift completion.'"

"Oh, so I did. Anyway, I mean to have a lovely day today and I had more or less counted on your company."

"Are we going to the country to the Lees'?"

"Are we?"

"Not if you put it up to me. But if you say so, I go along."

"I am not going to make a decision about anything whatsoever," she said. "I am going to enjoy a little luxury."

"This is very luxurious," said Mark, dropping into a chair with her in his arms. He began to kiss her, covering her face with small, tender, nibbling kisses, as if to explore as carefully as possible the fine variations of texture in the skin of her eyelids, her cheekbones, the corners of her mouth, the delicate rounded angle where the line of her jaw melted into the hollow below the lobe of her ear.

"I could purr," she murmured.

"Please do. It would go with that. I *like* that." He touched the stiff bow in which her white silk blouse was tied under her chin.

They were quiet for a long time. Jessie, with her eyes closed, thought of opening them to give herself the added pleasure of looking at Mark's face; but she felt so content that she sighed and stayed as she was. She felt his hand move upwards across her jaw and towards her lips and she turned her head a little and kissed the smooth tips of his fingers. Presently she opened her eyes and said, "This is so pleasant. Have we any other important plans?"

"We might go to bed," suggested Mark, making hopeful arcs of his eyebrows.

"Yes," she said thoughtfully. "We might. But it is so early in the day."

"Nice, Very nice. Of course eleven-thirty is dawn to you——"

"I don't seem to feel in a hurry. You know—like saving something——"

"Oh, I wouldn't hurry a lady. I never hurry ladies."

"Beast. You are supposed to make me feel as if I were the only——"

"You are supposed to—stop talking." He brought his mouth down on hers and they clung together. Presently he moved her away, holding her against his shoulder and looking at her face. "I think," he said, noting the delicate shadow of anxiety about her eyes, and the pulse flicking at her temple, which she did not know that he could see, "I think we will go out somewhere and get some fresh air."

"Are you joking?"

"No. Why?" He smiled at her. "We have all day, haven't we, darling?"

"And——"

"And."

"Where are we going?" she asked, as they settled themselves in the small car which Mark had borrowed from Bucky Whitelaw.

"Somewhere silly. Somewhere——"

"Folksy," she said. "You know."

"I know exactly. We will put the car on the ferry and go across the Bay to Staten Island."

"Oh, Mark!" she cried. Her voice was full of delight. "How delicious. What made you think of that?"

He shrugged, heading for the West Side Highway. "Your extremely snobbish, limited tastes, I suppose."

"I'm so glad you aren't wearing that uniform. It always makes me feel so conspicuous."

"Of course that's the only reason I wear it. Only to annoy."

"Will you be through with it in—in any particular length of time?"

"Depends, on what they want me to do."

"Who, Mark? The Army?"

"Partly. You know there isn't much I can say about it. But there's a lot of unfinished business over there. You don't just lick the bastards and pull out—at least I hope not."

"And," asked Jessie, "is that really why you are going back to Europe?"

352

He looked at her sidelong, keeping one eye on the car that he was about to pass.

"In a way. But also, if you have to make me spit it out, I can't stand it here. I could dress up my reasons in politics or ethics or hot air—but the truth is I hate everything that's going on in the U S now." He drove faster. "I can't feel the slightest interest in anything they are interested in. The stock market makes me see red, the fat living makes me wild, the spending makes me sick."

"I suppose everything is all on a great high moral plane in Europe," she said rather bitterly.

"You do make me sound like an ass," he said, with a quick smile. "But I'm not being a zealot or a martyr or a hero. In one way I suppose I would like to settle down here with a nice fat job like George's, and act my age. But in another I just know this is no time to do that. Not now. You heard me sound off too much yesterday, so you know . . . It's as if everything about a personal life is just up over a bend somewhere and I can't stop what's more important to try to get there and pay attention to it now. I somehow cannot care, nobody can care that much about everything."

"I know."

"I can't even feel as if I had the right to care. Nobody else who matters to me has been given the choice."

"I know," she said again. "I wouldn't have understood so well if it hadn't been for yesterday."

"Here we are," said Mark, coming out on the Battery and heading for the Staten Island slip. "This is going to be nice. Look at that water."

The bay was almost arrogant in its magnificence today, a brilliant, whistling cobalt blue crested with skipping whitecaps, clean and spicy to the nostrils. Mark ran the car onto the ferryboat, cut off the engine, and helped Jessie out. They climbed to the upper deck and stood at the forward rail, where the glorious salt wind began to spank their faces as the ferry pulled out of its slip. Jessie stood almost on tiptoe with excitement, one hand on Mark's arm.

"Oh," she cried, "I am such a fool. I miss so much! I never come down here and do anything like this."

"One wouldn't be likely to do it alone."

"Look! Do you realize I haven't seen her since 1939? I'm ashamed of myself." Jessie pointed to the Statue of Liberty.

"Poor old girl. She's kind of banged up, and corny too. But

I never fail to feel something when I see her there—and I lost track long ago how many times that is."

"Imagine what she must have looked like to your parents when they arrived here!"

"Or yours?"

"My mother. She was a very small child, but she remembered it vividly. And do you know, Mark, when she was a girl, they used to take this ferry trip on Sundays, it was their favorite outing, she and her friends from downtown there. Most of the girls worked for dressmakers, but my mother——"

And leaning on the rail, watching the ferry swim like an overweight duck towards its slip, Jessie told Mark the story that Horace Howland had told her last Monday morning. Mark listened closely, with fascinated interest, and when Jessie explained that Harry Blitzer had been one of the gaudy, raucous, singing young men in the party with her mother, Mark's jaw fell open.

"That's the most wonderful story," he said. "No wonder he's known you all your life."

"Of course," said Jessie, nodding. "He got my mother her first job. He was a friend of the family, and he was so terrified of my Auntie Esther that he obeyed her orders to the letter. For years he never left Mother alone with anybody, ever, in the theatre. He used to call for her and take her home after the play, and turn her over to Auntie Esther on the doorstep."

"When did your aunt die?"

"About a year before Mother—eleven years ago. She was—" Jessie stopped speaking and clutched Mark's arm. "Listen!" she said.

They both smiled as they stood looking at the Bay, listening to the ridiculous, half-comic, half-mournful sound of a wheezy accordion.

"By God," murmured Mark, "I'd forgotten all about those."

The sound came nearer; the accordion-player was circling the deck.

"Boys and girls together," Jessie sang softly. "Me and Mamie O'Rorke . . ."

"Tripped the light fantastic," Mark hummed.

"On the sidewalks—" they sang together, and by now the accordion-player was right behind them. Mark gave the man a coin and he grinned, showing all his white teeth in his brown Italian face.

"You just can't believe it," said Jessie. "Of course it's all hooey and set up for suckers but—" she stopped and Mark smiled as he saw tears in her eyes. "I'm a fool," she said. "But I love it so."

"I too. You only feel like this when you're here or in the subway or on Election Day or at a ball game or——"

"I know."

They watched the ferry bump and squirm into its slip, with horrible groans and screeches. Then they drove off, Jessie asking, "Where are we going?"

"I don't know. Staten Island isn't much of a place for *tourisme*, but this seems like a great exploration to me. We'll just poke around and if we see any place we want to stop, we'll stop, and if not, we'll go back. Shall we take the Goethals Bridge or the ferry again?"

"Oh, the ferry," said Jessie. "We were so preoccupied on the way over that we never even looked over our shoulders at the skyline."

"Rubberneck!"

"I like the ferry."

"I like you. In fact, it is possible that I love you—in a small way."

"Many things are possible."

They drove without speaking for a time and then Jessie said, "It's too ridiculous. This is New York City. Look at it. Why doesn't one live here?" She waved at a white cottage with chickens in the back yard.

"Stop wondering about the other half," he said, "and see if Madame feels like considering some lunch."

"Well—yes. Now that you speak of it. Where?"

"The choice is dazzling," said Mark. "White Tower. Joe's Bar and Grill. Meisner's Delicatessen. The——"

"Look!" said Jessie, pointing. "I love them."

"Well," he said, approaching the diner-wagon that Jessie had selected. "Some of them are not so bad. This one looks quite superior."

"May we eat here?"

"If you are a nice child."

They climbed onto stools at the counter and Jessie sniffed with pleasure. "I really love these places," she said. "I want yankee bean soup."

"Oh, God," said Mark.

"Why, what's the matter?"

355

"Nothing, darling. You weren't in the Army. Two bean soup, bud."

"It's wonderful," said Jessie. "Hot as hell and beans in it. What more can you ask?"

"What are you going to have afterwards?"

"I don't know."

"No hamburgers," said Mark, frowning.

"Why?"

He ignored her. "Two fried egg sandwiches," he told the man.

"Bacon?"

"Sure, if you got it. I didn't think you had any, or ham."

The man shrugged and turned to his griddle. "How you want 'em?" he asked over his shoulder.

"Turned over. Coffee."

"You seem to know what I want," said Jessie.

"I know what's good for you. You'll eat it and like it."

"Certainly I'll like it."

They ate the sandwiches and drank the coffee from thick white mugs. They had a second cup of coffee, but Jessie shook her head with a laugh when Mark asked if she wanted a piece of terrifying pie, such as the man next to them was eating. It was bright yellow and bright white and bristling with ominous whiskers of cocoanut.

"I haven't had such a delightful lunch in years," she said, as they got into the car again. "I haven't had such fun in years, either."

Mark kissed the end of her nose, before starting the car. "You are so easy to please," he said.

"You are so mistaken."

They drove over half of Staten Island before they fetched up again at the ferry slip.

"I didn't realize it was so built up," said Jessie. "I thought it was still all country and space. It's not a bit what I expected."

"What is?"

"You." She looked at him with queer seriousness, for they had been laughing almost steadily for an hour.

He smiled, rather sadly, she thought, steering the car onto the ferry again. This time they stood on the upper deck facing Manhattan, watching the Wall Street towers sparkling in the sun.

"They are beautiful," said Jessie, "but the only time I ever really feel thrilled by the skyline is around the Plaza and Central Park, at dusk. Or driving downtown through the Park and watching the towers all sparkling with light against that violet sky. I love that."

"My taste in towers is a little different," said Mark, his eyes on the horizon.

"I know," she said.

"Do you?"

She nodded, making a point of her two forefingers and a gesture to indicate the soaring, needle-tipped spires about which he was thinking. "These," she said, tipping her chin at the Manhattan skyscrapers, "always remind you that they were built by men. Those others——" she stopped, because there was no way to complete the thought which did not seem absurdly rhetorical.

"You think nicely," said Mark, turning his head upon his hands, and looking at her. Suddenly it was out of the question to talk any more. They stood leaning on the rail, silent and urgently absorbed in a conversation of the eyes. The small boy who had circled the deck several times came up and yapped at Mark, "Shine, Mister? Shine?" But they did not hear him, they did not hear anything except the quality of their own silence.

"What will you have?" asked Mark when they had returned to the hotel. "Tea or a drink?"

"I think a little whisky, no?"

"I think."

They had said very little in the past hour, and the mood weighed still upon Jessie. She sat quiet on the couch, drawing intense contentment from looking at Mark nearby, but at the same time she felt, like a buried substance working its way to the surface, a profound and troubling uneasiness. I wonder what it is, she thought, I wonder what it can be. Looking at Mark and responding to the sheer physical pleasure of watching his face, his hands, the solid, relaxed lines of his body, she thought without surprise or shyness or coquetry that presently they would go into the other room and go to bed together, which had become the most direct and necessary of conclusions to everything that they had shared up to now. But when Mark, reading her face, rose slowly from his chair and walked over and dropped beside her on the couch, and took her in his arms, a kind of command in his hands and his mouth which she had not felt before, she was appalled to find

357

herself turning stiff in his embrace. Her hands moved from their eager clasp of his head to brace themselves against his chest and to her horror she felt herself pushing him away; she heard herself burst into tears, and she saw Mark jump up, stride across the room, and stand there with his back turned.

"Oh Mark," she said, struggling to speak at all. "Oh, what is the matter with me? I am so sorry." She wept and struggled again with herself and again said, "So sorry. I don't know . . ."

He turned and looked at her; for an instant his face was very cold.

"I—" she braced her lips and tried to breathe calmly and she said, "I—you know I have not been flirting with you. Oh, don't you know that, Mark?" The expression of her face was piteous. "What is the matter with me?", she cried. "I want you—very much. More than you know. But I can't." She dropped her face into her hands and sat, her shoulders shaking. From behind her hands she said again, "I can't. I want to —and I can't."

There was a silence. Then she heard him cross the room, and she felt his hands upon hers, drawing them downwards, away from her face. She looked at him and saw that he had dropped down on the floor before her and was holding her hands tightly in his; and all the coldness was gone from his face and instead she saw there the profoundest tenderness upon which her eyes had ever rested. She sat with tears running down her cheeks, looking at him. He shook his head a little, very slowly, and then he spoke, and his voice was darker and heavier than she had ever heard it.

"Don't you know?" he said, his brown eyes soft and deep with shadows. "Don't you know, darling?"

She shook her head.

"You are going to leave Brandon Bourne," he said slowly. "It has nothing at all to do with this, it would come about anyway. That's why you feel as you do now. I see what you are like, I saw right in the beginning. You have a very straight mind, a great sense of responsibility."

She listened almost without breathing.

"You are afraid of confusing yourself," said Mark. "You are incapable of leaving a husband when you feel anything about another man. If you had not subconsciously decided to leave him, you would make love with me without any hesitation at all."

"Oh," said Jessie slowly, feeling stunned with amazement. "Oh my God."

Mark bent his head and kissed her hands gently.

"I—I—cannot believe it," she said, hesitating. "The wish is there, you are right about that. But I told him only last night that I still do not intend to leave him."

"Ah," said Mark. "So that was what happened last night. You really told him what I have just told you."

"But—but——"

"I know. It has nothing to do with me. And I've tried my best not to confuse you. I'm pretty selfish, as a matter of fact, in making sure that I don't confuse myself. You understand —there is no question of—marriage."

"I understand perfectly."

"It's not you, darling. We have fallen in love, there's no doubt about that. But love and marriage are infinitely different things—they are not necessarily inclusive at all. And so far as I know I have no more wish to be married than I ever had, and I doubt if I am apt to change. I am just as serious about marriage as you are, which is why you are going through such hell now. And why I cannot imagine being married. It's a kind of responsibility that cannot be fitted to the life I have to lead and the things I have to do. I think you understood that right in the beginning."

"Yes I did."

"But also you are so serious that you will not have a lover without caring for him very much. *Very* much. That makes things tough and sometimes tragic for a woman. I wish to God I could spare you that," he said, his voice cracking.

"You are extraordinary," she whispered when she was able to speak.

He shook his head. "No. But you are. You know and I know that if you leave Bourne—or when you leave him—it will have nothing to do with me. But some part of your conscience will try to disbelieve that. It might refuse to turn you free of Bourne—if it nagged you eventually into thinking that you had precipitated the break because of anything to do with another man. You are not a woman to do that. And frankly," he added, speaking with difficulty, "I don't want to be that man. The whole concept is alien to your nature and to mine."

They were silent; Jessie made no effort any longer to restrain her tears. At last Mark said, "Besides, we scarcely know each other."

"Oh," said Jessie, "no."

Mark shook his head sadly, smiling a little. "It feels as if we did," he said. "Lovers always feel that way. It is even possible to be madly in love and almost complete strangers."

"We are not that!"

"No indeed. But you don't know what my life really consists of, and if you did, I think you would dislike a great deal of it."

"But since it wouldn't be mine to share——"

"Well, that's rational of you. But I only mean that what we have—had—has been——" he sighed. "It's hard to talk, darling. I mean this holiday of mine, and a good deal of pleasure that has been nearly ideal—there again. It would look awfully superficial to you in the light of breaking with Bourne."

"But it would have nothing to do with it!" exclaimed Jessie, almost with passion.

"I told you I know that. We both know it. But you asked me what is the matter . . ."

They sat very still, Mark on the floor by Jessie's knees, clasping her hands in his; Jessie stiff upon the couch. After a time she looked down at him and said, "Mark, will you ever be able to forgive me? I feel—utterly hateful and trifling and selfish. I've ruined your holiday and——"

"Hush," he said, bending his face over her hands.

"I can't say good bye," she said. "It's going to be so hard to get up from this couch and pick up my things over there and walk out of this room without saying good bye. But that is the only way to do it."

"I know."

She waited for a time, thinking how she had never realized before that one's heart could really hurt, a keen, piercing pain, no figure of speech at all. Then she leaned forward and said, "Go and sit in that chair over there and pretend not to look at me. You must not see me out or take me home or anything like that. Just——"

He reached up and took her face between his hands and kissed her lips; and she kissed him, more gently and at the same time more passionately than she ever had before. He rose and went and sat in the chair, and she stood up. She did as she had said, she picked up her furs and her bag and her gloves without looking at him again and she walked across the room to the door and put her hand upon the door knob. And then, without thinking, without knowing at all that it was going to happen, she heard her own voice, harsh and shrill, cry, "Mark! I cannot leave you now." She turned and stared at him, her face white.

He crossed the room in a stride and seized her in his arms and the things that she was holding in her hands fell to the floor.

VII
SUNDAY

XXIX

The breakfast table stood between the two beds, and Mark grinned at her across it.

"You look much more presentable now," he said. "There in that prim single bed, all by yourself."

"Have you felt so very crowded?" she asked, bending her face over her orange juice and blushing.

"I never saw you blush before," he said. "It's charming."

"Oh, you weren't looking."

"Why of course. That would explain it. Do you know," he said, "you are nothing to look at at all. Not when there is something else to do with you."

"Well, I am more discriminating than you. My eyes give me a great deal of pleasure."

"I like the way your hair goes into those rough little whiskers when it's mussed, like a Scotty's fur."

"It is *not* mussed and I am not——"

"It was."

They smiled, with a warm, deep gleam in their eyes, the communication of a secret.

"Oh, I *like* you so much," she said, putting down the glass in her hand because her fingers felt suddenly too lax to hold it.

"That's good," said Mark. "Excellent. Of course it's what got us into this extremely agreeable situation. I like you too—that's quite important. To me."

"You mean to me."

"Must I really disentangle myself from this North American trap which is a unique way of breakfasting, just to come around there and give myself the pleasure of touching you?"

"I can wait," said Jessie meekly.

"Just for that, you shan't." He sprang from the farther side of his bed and came around to the farther side of hers, and sat on the edge of it, close to her, and put his hands on the tops of her shoulders, along the curve of her neck, and moved his fingers lightly, under the fine lace, and looked at her face with emotion in his own. Suddenly she buried her head against his chest and his arms went round her and he heard her muffled voice say, "But we were supposed just to be gay and composed now, and all that about breakfast. You made a whole speech about breakfast."

"My God," said Mark, "you shouldn't rely so on your memory."

In a moment he went back to his place and poured her coffee for her. "Hot milk," he said, "and no sugar."

"How did you know? You're quite a good hostess."

"Has it occurred to you," he asked, "that we might have been going on in this way together for a long time past?"

"Do you mean we have wasted most of this week?"

"You know damn well what I mean."

"But that's part of what I am not going to allow myself to think about."

"No," he said. "Don't make that mistake. Don't start quoting Alice Meynell to yourself."

They drank their coffee in silence, and presently Mark said, "What time will you be through with your luncheon?"

Jessie grimaced. "Must you remind me now?"

He smiled. "I'm sorry, darling. I only wanted to know how quickly I can have you back."

"By four at the latest," she said. "Shall I—I mean what time in the morning do you go?"

"Too damned early," he said. "I have to be at the field at six. That means leaving here at—you see."

She nodded. "But I'll come back as quickly as I can this afternoon."

They had finished their coffee, and they lay back on the pillows, their heads turned toward each other, nothing whatever to say. Jessie stretched her right hand across the table and Mark took it and looked at her and she felt his fingers tighten slowly about her wrist.

"I'll get rid of this," he said, moving to dispense with the breakfast table. He wheeled it into the sitting-room and shut and locked the door. Then he came back and stood for a moment looking down at her. She put up her arms and he waited a little while; she saw that he wanted to watch her in that attitude.

"My love," she said, smiling, but her eyes were wet.

He made a quiet sound and bent and touched her face, and lay down beside her.

Here they all were; and just as Jessie had known that he would, Cousin Blaine Illingworth said so.

"Well, well. Here we are. It seems almost like Thanksgiving." That would have been the next traditional occasion to bring them all together here, and Jessie thought grotesquely that thanks to Isabel Allen, they had jumped the gun by six weeks. But, she hoped, unfolding her serviette, maybe, just maybe, possibly, we will not have Oyster Soup, because it is not a holiday.

She looked round the dark, ugly dining-room with the glowering family portraits on the walls, the lace-curtained windows which neither concealed the dreary apartment-house court outside nor embellished the interior of the room; the heavy, oversized, overornamented furniture, about which she had often speculated, for the continuity of family about which Mrs. Bourne had always been redundantly insistent was reflected in her possessions. Since Jessie could find no evidence of Mrs. Bourne's or her forefathers' ever having got rid of anything, she had wondered idly what could have happened to whatever earlier furniture these Victorian monstrosities had displaced. Then she looked last of all at the sight that she wanted least to see: the faces ranged about the elaborate table.

I wish I did not hate them, she thought, consciously tightening the mask of indifference which veiled her face. My hating them is far more unpleasant for me than for them; they probably do not know, and more certainly do not care if they do know.

She said, "Yes, yes indeed," in agreement with some platitude of Cousin Blaine Illingworth's, which she had not heard; and she found herself looking across the table at Iris. The girl was pale and miserable as blue-white skim milk; she wore none of the usual dark lipstick or other exaggerations which she usually affected. She looked at Jessie with an expression in her washed-out eyes which seemed almost pathetic or beseeching, and a little confused; Jessie felt suddenly the sense of cause-and-effect interlocking in her brain. From the crushing weight of the room and the people in it she recoiled almost as if into the mind of the girl, thinking, why, of course! you poor little thing, all this would drive you to become what you are. She smiled at Iris, feeling as if she held concealed within herself a rich enough store of new tenderness to have some to share with the child; and she saw the pale blue eyes fill with tears, the girl's mouth tremble. She looked away, herself close to tears, realizing with horror that nobody had ever smiled at the girl in such a way before.

"It must be an afternoon reception." She heard the strange hooting voice of Mrs. Bourne, making her pronunciamento upon the subject of Iris's coming debut. "We always have an afternoon reception first and then——"

Jessie kept her eyes lowered for fear of showing her disaffection if she should look at Mrs. Bourne. Fruit cocktails had appeared, hacked-up bits of oranges and apples and sour grapefruit from which the bitter white rind had not been entirely cut away, and pieces of diced banana whose odor caused Jessie to grit her teeth against a surge of loathing, for bananas were the one food about which she had such an idiosyncrasy. The maraschino cherry on top of the mess leered up at her and she turned almost hysterically to Cousin Sophie Daingerfield on her left, to ask how her garden out at Chappaqua had done during the summer. Inwardly she prayed that nobody would notice her not eating, and though she saw Brandon's cold, angry eyes rest once upon her, the plates were changed without remark.

"Couldn't it be a tea dance, Grandmama?" asked Iris, making what Jessie recognized as a really courageous effort to take part in this conversation which was supposed to concern her; even to show some preference about the thing, which she wanted not to take place at all.

"Certainly not," said Mrs. Bourne, and Jessie marvelled at the didactic passion that still inhabited the old woman's torpid body. "Millicent, you remember your reception . . . of course it is too trying not to have the house any more, how can one entertain properly in a——"

"But surely you have not room enough here," said Cousin Blaine Illingworth, implying the same contempt for this commonplace multiple dwelling that embittered Mrs. Bourne's existence.

Evander Fielding was struggling with the carving of a weary leg of lamb; family tradition required that he perform this invariable rite, instead of leaving it to the cook, and that they all converse assiduously in the tormented interval while he hacked and sawed and swore under his breath, and the meat on the plates grew cold in the uneasy lapse before the rest of the course could be served. Jessie ignored the small slab of brown leather which was placed before her, and listened with bright, false interest while they discussed the details of Iris's debut.

"I thought the Club would be best for the reception," said Millicent mildly, "and the evening party at the Ritz." She would, thought Jessie, say the Ritz.

The carving implements sagged in Fielding's hands and he shot his wife a glance of mingled fury and panic. Jessie wondered idly how Millicent intended to manœuvre him through the tricky matter of the money that was to be spent on this, but she surmised that after the events of Thursday Millicent would never again worry about his opinions or wishes; she would lay down laws when she chose.

"And of course," said Cousin Sophie Daingerfield, baring all her dentures in an enthusiastic smile, "Jessie will give one of her lovely dinners for Iris before the dancing party, won't you, dear?"

"Of course," said Jessie, refusing the mint sauce. "Naturally." She raised her eyes and looked at Brandon as if for corroboration of her promise, and what she saw in his face made this whole performance, all in an instant, dissolve into travesty. She realized that Brandon had not said a word since they had sat down; and, she thought, there must be a limit to which his behavior can go if he does not want to break to pieces this occasion which he himself insisted upon putting together. But she should have known that by now he was irrational with frustrated rage, and it became quickly a matter of dire necessity to play the remaining cards in this nightmare of a hand, and get away from here without incident. She had not seen him this morning until she had been at home for most of an hour, had dressed and was ready at one o'clock to leave the house with him. And she had realized then that only his fear of her refusing to come here had checked an outburst of some kind. She thought with a retrospective shiver of the moment in the taxi on the short ride here when she had said something about his possibly returning to Virginia next week, and he had answered, "I might, but I'm fed up with visiting people in the country. I want a place of my own."

There was a silence and then he added, "Of course if you were different——"

She sighed. It was quite true; to him she must seem brutally selfish, now that she was about to receive her property outright, not to offer to buy such a place in Virginia as she knew he wanted. She was selfish, she knew it with a dark sense of shame. She thought bitterly of long ago when she had wanted only what would have made complete her life with him, and of the reasons why she had utterly changed.

But I dare not think about that now, she told herself, listening to his family while they talked and talked about lists and names and music and dresses and flowers and the motor car, and she herself, to her own amazement, participated quite volubly; I cannot think about him or anything else that may lie beyond the end of this hour except that I must get safely back to Mark.

The undrinkable coffee had been served in the drawing-room, and the sullen biddy had planked down a tray of glasses of water, and performed the other duties concluding the service of a meal, which were encroaching upon part of her Sunday Afternoon. Jessie caught a look in Millicent's eye which presaged her despairing knowledge that tomorrow morning would see the end of this waitress like all the dozens of her predecessors. Mrs. Bourne, enthroned upon the peculiar chair of her preference, which had a very high back to enhance her majesty, and very short legs because of her fantastic dumpiness which, in a higher chair, would have left her tiny feet dangling from their ballooning ankles, was prating along about the only possible methods and procedures for Iris's debut. The others were all grouped in their most characteristic attitudes, wearing their coats of complacency, patience, arrogance, or submission. And Jessie rose quietly from her chair and crossed the room to bid her mother-in-law good bye; she had given Brandon no signal of eye or attitude that it was her intention to leave now. He must therefore either stay as if he had expected her to leave by herself; or depart with her as if they were going on together somewhere as a matter of course. He could not, without extreme awkwardness, question her decision; she had chosen a perfectly suitable moment to leave.

They stood on the corner of Park Avenue and Eighty-fourth Street, waiting for an empty cab to come along. It occurred to Jessie that her sensation of wild distress would be reflected in a galloping pulse, if she should be such a fool as to feel for it; her mouth felt puckered, her knees unsure. Brandon was still silent and menacing of mood; she was tense with futile protest that he had come along here with her. She had no sense of guilt because of her intention to go and join Mark now, only the most violent irritation at Brandon for his stubborn, clumsy presence here; and a weight of dreadful confusion in mind and emotion caused by her inability to feel her way between what she had said to Brandon on Friday night and what Mark had said to her yesterday. All she really knew was the inflexible determination to go to Mark at once and to stay with him until it was time to leave him; after that she would be ready to deal with everything that lay on the other side of that chasm.

No cab was in sight, almost inevitably of a Sunday mid-afternoon, and Brandon said sullenly, "Well, let's walk, or start to; it wouldn't hurt us."

"You go along," she said. "I'll find a cab."

"What do you mean?" he said, with the slash in his voice.

She shrugged. "I'm going on." She found herself wishing that he were dead.

"Aren't you going home?"

"No."

In his face she saw the savage struggle, which she recognized with mingled shame and pity, between jealous rage, now entirely crystallized, and the fear of her threat of Friday night. She felt her veins heavy, turgid, as if poison were flowing in them, the poison of unnatural hatred more perhaps for herself now than even for him. She was doing something for which she detested herself—not for going to Mark because that was no deception anyway and it remained high above this hatefulness an untouched loveliness, soaring and free—but in acting with such brutal harshness. Brandon deserves it, she thought, he is actually inviting it; but that made it no more endurable within herself.

"I'll see you later," she said, as gently as she could.

"Look here!" Brandon burst out, about to turn savage.

She shook her head quietly. "Please, Brandon. This is no time or place to start anything like that. It would be absolutely useless. I assure you it would."

"Do you know what you are doing?" he asked, with a glare almost mad in his hard blue eyes.

"I know precisely," she said. "I would rather be more subtle but as I said before, if you force my hand you leave me no choice." (Can this be I? she thought wretchedly. I am no fairer, no kinder, no gentler than he. But she felt utterly, irrevocably hard.)

"I'll see you later," she said again, and turned to watch the flow of traffic for a cab.

"What time?" asked Brandon sharply.

"I don't know exactly," she said. "Later."

The moment that she was with Mark, every other thought and concern disappeared from her mind. She had walked swiftly into his arms, revelling in a feeling of naturalness which seemed the most extraordinary luxury that she had ever known.

"It's so wonderful," she said. "So fantastic actually, because here I am feeling this delicious ease, this sense of always having been—and yet I'm so surprised about it."

She had swept the rooms with a quick glance at which he smiled, with his warm expression of knowing what she was thinking. She was relieved because there was no luggage in sight, no sign of packing and departure. As usual, the apartment was meticulously neat.

"When are you going to pack?" she asked.

He began to kiss her, and she him; there was a certain sort of small, precise kiss quickly and many times repeated, which gave them very great pleasure; a conversational sort of kiss which was quite different from greater and more portentous ones.

"You could," he said, between these kisses, "mind your own business."

"You have such appalling manners."

"You would pick a feller from the tenements."

"I love it. I *love* it."

"You do? Let's do something about it, then."

"You are confusing your pronouns," she murmured.

"I? Hah! Will you extricate yourself from that extraordinary costume or shall I rip it off you?"

She was wearing a black silk dress of the type which is so intricately cut that it fits, glovelike and all of a piece, without any sign of how it is put on; the high cowl collar flowed into the bodice, and the panels of the skirt into the waistline, without a visible seam.

"It is this," she said, in a small voice, turning her back. "There's a place between the shoulders where I can't reach it myself." There was a fine slide fastener up the whole spine of the dress, which Mark had not seen.

"This is fun," he said, playing with the fastener, and caressing her bare back with his lips as he pushed the zipper slowly down.

She bent her head and put her cheek against his left hand which lay across her breast. "It is more fun for me than for you," she said, but her voice broke.

"Darling! My darling, what is it?" He turned her around and lifted her off her feet, the dress falling from her shoulders, and sat down holding her in his arms. He looked at her face, picking up the tears in the corners of her eyes with his lips. "What is it?"

"Oh," she said, hiding her face, "you know. You know so much better than I. I have never had anyone to play with, and I am so happy now."

He took a dressing-gown of his own from the cupboard and put it around her when he had calmly and attentively removed a few exquisite bits of clothing that she wore under the black dress.

"I am very prudish," he said. "For some reason I want you to be all covered up."

"Now that you've made sure what is in the package you're doing it all up again. Like sneaking a look at a Christmas present the day before."

"I knew what I was going to get for Christmas," he said over his shoulder. He had thrown back the coverlet from the bed in which they had slept last night, and he came to her across the room and took her in his arms.

"Why is it necessary," she said softly after a time, "for me to say that I love you? You know it, you know all about it, but somehow I have to tell you."

"For the same reason," he answered, "that I must look at your face now." His voice was low and strained.

A long time later she stirred in his arms and she heard him say, "You've been asleep for hours, darling."

She opened her eyes and saw that the room was dark.

"Oh," she said, "but I didn't want to waste our time sleeping . . ." Yet she put her head back in the curve of his shoulder and closed her eyes again. "I love it here," she sighed.

"None of our time was wasted," he said. He put out his right hand and switched on the light, pushing it away to keep the beam from her eyes. She felt for the hand and drew it back across her breast and shoulder and fell into that wilful langour which is in a way heavier than real sleep.

"What time is it?" she mumbled, her lips against his chin.

"It doesn't matter. But I think I'll send for some food."

Suddenly she opened her eyes, wide awake, and pulled herself up on her elbow and looked at his face. "Mark!" she cried. "Darling, it isn't *very* late? Not nearly time for——"

He wagged a forefinger at her. "Be a good girl. Surely I shan't have to give you a briefing tonight?"

She shook her head, smiling. "No. Let me go now. I'm going to go and make an elaborate toilette for dinner."

Mark lay and watched her rise, and smiled lazily at the small tableau of her making up her mind what to do about his dressing-gown, which trailed on the floor about her and completely swallowed up her hands. "But I want you to wear that for dinner," he said. "You look so silly in it that it's just the picture of you I want to carry away with me."

"Oh—*Mark!* How can you be such an utterly wonderful, gentle, tender lover and then turn around and make fun of me?" She was standing near him, her face contorted with mock complaint. He put up his hands and snatched her down against his chest and ran his fingers all through her hair, and spanked her bottom, and kissed her as hard and as quickly in as many places as he could reach, and with another spank and a roar of laughter he put her back on her feet again.

"Now go and make the best of it," he said, picking up the telephone.

While they were eating in the sitting-room she said, "Of course you know it is going to be perfectly dreadful without you."

"Of course. But that's the kind of thing that comes in this package."

"You are very brave, Mark." She thought of the two scars that she had seen on his body, one striping his left leg, the other across his upper back and his right shoulder. "I know I would never have your physical courage. As for the rest——"

"Darling, you will have just what you need to call upon

371

yourself for. You will be goddam lonely, and then you will remember that the actual inner truth of most lives is a measure of overwhelming loneliness. It goes in waves . . . cycles . . . we don't force it. We wait and see."

"Where do I—how do I—" she paused. It was perfectly astonishing that the only question she had ever found herself unable to ask him was how she could reach him after he had gone away.

"I don't know right now," he said. And then he looked at her in such a way, with such an extreme contradiction of expressions in his face, that she sat back in her chair, staring at him, and understanding far more than she had the courage to admit. For the surface of his face was queerly and uncharacteristically hard, perhaps tough, she thought, by way of telling her almost ruthlessly that when they parted tonight it would be good bye in the most definite sense of the word. It was as if he were warning her that he was going to give her pain, and that he expected her to endure it stoically. But beneath those grave and hardened muscles about his mouth and his forehead, she sensed the quality of a tenderness even more profound than that which he had shown her up to now. There was too, against the appearance of almost didactic command in his manner and his voice, a wordless, lovely compassion which would be her comfort tomorrow after he had gone and for as long as tomorrow might last. Part of her brain seemed to be trying to cry out in question and protest and fear, for an endless tomorrow could become a drearier waste than all her life had been up to now. And the other part admonished her to be still and patient and wise and above all to learn not to ask, never to ask; for the only complete knowledge that one could possess was that which came without asking anything at all. Suddenly she felt sure that the answer would come eventually of itself.

She looked at him with much of this in her face, and he nodded a little, as if agreeing about the conclusion of a long conversation. Their fingers were linked quietly across the white cloth; she moved her forefinger from the little cluster, and with the tip of it gently stroked the outside edge of his hand, where the fine, nearly invisible hairs disappeared among the threadlike white scars. We have so much to say most of the time, she thought, but now we will not talk any more. But I can look at him. She raised her eyes from the table to his face, and sat looking at him in the deep, enclosed quiet of the thickly curtained room. It is going to be more endurable

372

than I thought, she knew, because although her heart felt as if it were shackled in sorrow, she had begun to recognize the amazing fact that she was without panic. I may be very sad, she thought, and for a long time empty and bereft. And I may never see him again. Just then he smiled as if again to contradict that, but she had found sudden strength in the astounding knowledge that even if her last painful thought should prove to be true, he would have become in her life a great, sound, healthy core of strength, he would have built within her a fine, balanced vessel filled with self-renewing fortitude.

He said, finally, "I want just to hold you quietly in my arms for a little while, and then I am going to take you home."

When they were about to leave his rooms, he took her in his arms and kissed her forehead, her eyes, her cheeks, her throat, her mouth: but not with passion. No force that she could summon could have driven the words, "good bye" to her lips, but with their eyes they said it, recognizing everything in every sense that it could mean.

XXX

It was almost one o'clock when she let herself into the house, and she knew before she unlocked the door that Brandon would be there waiting. Feeling thus prepared she walked without surprise into the library, where he was standing with one elbow on the mantel, a drink in his hand, scowling and sullen. Brandon was no drunkard, and though she had had other occasions in the past to count this as one of her few blessings where he was concerned, she was more grateful for it now than she had ever been. Perhaps, she thought, dropping easily into a chair and taking off her hat, I can steer him through a few minutes once over lightly, and by tomorrow—she sighed. She said, "Give me a little whisky too, Brandon, just a drop; and soda."

He brought it. She saw that he had been building up in his mind a self-conscious dramaturgy which she could only puncture by this casual and relaxed attitude; she wondered for how many hours he had been at it.

"Wasn't it ghastly at your mother's today?" she said.

"I don't see why," he said. "Of course the way *you* feel about my family——"

"I wasn't naughty, was I?"

He shrugged. They were silent; once or twice he lifted his head and stared at her with a savage, accusing glare which made her feel, along with her inner contemptuous indifference, that it was a brutal thing she had done to him, whether he deserved it or not. The thing to do now was to make a bit of the easiest possible smalltalk, but as she sat sipping her whisky, her eyes on the carpet before her, she realized with consternation that henceforward that would be extremely difficult with Brandon. If we had no superficial interests in common before, she thought, how much less of that material have I to work with now! She watched him open his mouth once or twice, about to blurt out things that he was afraid to say, and in the strangely objective frame of mind in which she found herself, she reflected that it was as well that Mark was leaving now; she could not have kept Brandon on a keel through one more such day. But she was reassuring herself too soon; he swung his head at her again and said, "I think you have turned into the worst bitch I ever heard of."

She looked up at him and sighed again. "Brandon, if you will only just calm down and not give us any reasons for mutual name-calling right now, we will make our way much better. I wish you would realize that I have neither intended nor tried to retaliate for all your—all the things that have happened in the past." Perhaps, she thought, by my using the past tense in that way I will convey to him that . . . that . . . She swallowed a sudden excruciating lump in her throat. And then her own temper stiffened and she knew that no provocation that Brandon could devise would drive her to telling him that she had said good bye to Mark Dwyer. If Brandon remained in ignorance of the fact, it would be his own stupid bullheaded ignorance; whatever he did at the behest of that ignorance would be on his own head.

He said, "There are some things no man has to sit back and take."

She raised her eyebrows. "What are you trying to do, Brandon? I am tired, you are tired, it has been the most incredibly fantastic, exhausting week. Even if there were anything to say about *anything*, this is no time to say it. I assure you," she said, with a catch in her voice which she prayed he did not hear, "it will all look quite different—later—tomorrow—any time. I am going to bed."

She rose, moving slowly and quietly. His face as she passed him on her way out of the room appeared to be less violent, but equally intense; he was staring into his glass with his strange cruel eyes in which, she remembered, she had sought vainly again and again for kindness or sympathy or tenderness. The thought of the whole burden of time to come, time in which she would labor her way under the burden of her tie to this man, was almost a paralyzing discouragement. She went slowly up the stairs, anxious to reach the refuge of her room, but heavy, too heavy to move with her accustomed fleetness. She undressed quickly; when she slid open the fastener of her dress with agility which she had for such a delicious reason concealed from Mark, she burst into one dreadful wracking sob, and then she stood, looking into a mirror as if by searching hard she could find him there, to tell her again with his dark eyes and his closed, tender mouth what he had told her before. Oh Mark, Mark, she cried in her heart, but she did not open her mouth, and she finished her preparations for bed in tight and dry-eyed silence. She got into bed in the dark, and she lay with her eyes closed, hoping to fall asleep soon and wondering with a curious sense of procrastination when she would finally decide to take one of the tablets in the gold pillbox on the night table. She could as well have taken one already, but for some reason she had not; perhaps she had hoped to fall asleep in more quiet from the memory of Mark's warm body and strong arms than any sedative could give her.

But she remained so stubbornly awake that the probings and turnings of her thoughts grew sharper; she might have expected to go off into a haze of yearning about Mark, but not at all. It was curious that once again she felt the dual balance of grief counterpoised by absolute freedom from panic. I wonder why, she thought, I wonder why? It is good, but something so good must have a strong reason. I want to know the reason.

Her eyes were closed as she lay on her back, her hands clasped beneath her head. She relaxed deliberately in mind, as if to open to her vision the gate beyond which the reason and the answer must lie. The path of these thoughts led to the future, not alone to the wide distant panorama but to tomorrow, next day, next week. Would they be as past ones had been, so many past ones all mounted up to years of futility? She weighed the question carefully, fully, wondering with another part of her brain how she could possibly be dealing with such thoughts when the most immediate fact in the world was that Mark was gone. Gone—and in what a way!

With vast surprise she found that she was not thinking now of last night, nor of any of the hours of glorious fulfillment with him, but of very different moments; of calm, brief words that he had said, of wise and subtle glances from his extraordinary eyes. What had he said, for instance, on Friday after their visit to his relatives? "The world is too old—too changed—you will go and find out for yourself." Find out, she saw, what I was so stupid as not to know, that one is only useless or helpless or lazy so long as one invites it. She thought of all that Mark had told his people, and then she thought almost with a snap of recognition, that herein, somewhere, somehow, must lie the answer for her too.

I could go, she thought, but at this fantastic pace of her thinking she did not yet know where or to what; I could go and learn and see and work; in all this ferment there must be a way for me to work again, not as I used to do, but as I could because I am older, because I have changed. She thought again with the queerest surprise that had yet struck her, of tomorrow and the next day and the next week, of notes and memos and engagements, the same old roundabout, on the pages of the blue book on the table beside her. This one, she thought, will be out, and that one I will cancel; Althea on Tuesday I must see, she will know more about all this than I know myself. George Stillman, she thought, in the process of weighing and seeking the means to her aim, I shall see at once—and not, contradicting a prior impulse, Clyde Pritchard, for that would be going backward and I want to go forward. And Mark's aunt. God knows why I think there is an answer there, but she will know ways in which I can be of use—and in the being, learn. Jessie knew sharply that here, in learning, lay the clearest answer, fundamental to all the rest.

And if it means, she thought, to be uprooted in some way, or any way: well, what have I done up to now? I love it here, I love my home, I need this city, but if I must go and be away, I must, and it will keep. And finally when she thought of Brandon she faced a leaden blank; she lay there calmly aware that if she should still find in him some element of duty, she would never again find anything else at all.

It was then that she heard the sharp click of the electric

switch on the other side of Brandon's door; and her meditative quiet vanished in cold, throbbing horror. The door opened slowly and she watched it, and Brandon's figure in pyjamas come through it, though she lay motionless in the wretched hope that he would think her asleep and go away and shut the door. But he came towards her; her heart hammered with terror as he moved to the bed and she felt his hand take hold of the covers and start to draw them aside. All at once like the total, galvanized bristling of an angered animal, she drew herself into a knot.

"What do you want?" she said, damning herself for the remark.

"Jess," he said. "Jess, I—" He touched her.

She shot out her hand and switched on the light, and sat up rigid in bed, holding the covers tight about her shoulders.

"I told you I am too tired to talk to you tonight," she said. "I want to go to sleep."

But in his face she saw that no such parry would put him off; he had come here for a reason which appeared to her to be the coldest-blooded hatefulness that he had ever conceived. Once again he made as if to get into bed with her and without thinking she sprang from the other side of the bed, seized her dressing-gown, and put it on.

"Brandon," she said, trying to control the quivering of her voice. "For the love of God, will you leave me alone. You know that I am utterly exhausted and—and—" she was uncertain what to do, whether to give in to the temptation to make one shattering hysterical explosion of nerves and tears. "I am very nervous," she muttered, and went and stood by the window.

"You brought that on yourself," he said, "like a lot of other things. I've made up my mind that you are going to——"

"Just a moment," she said. "You forget that there are two wills involved in this, and two memories. Do you know how many years it is since you have been in bed with me, by your own wish? I cannot care what you may think your reason for this now, you have done the most outrageous thing that I have ever—" she turned away, shuddering, and put her face in her hands.

"God damn it!" he shouted, "You are my wife."

"And what a moment to remind me of it," she said. "I suppose I thought your indifference had made you incapable of caring what I did, and certainly of physical jealousy. But this thing now is—" she scowled, too horrified by her own thoughts to be able to put them into words. "Like an animal," she muttered, disgusted. "Like a . . ."

"How do I know why I didn't want to sleep with you?" he said. "I do now, and you'd better know I mean to."

"Oh no," she said. She was grateful that she could hold her voice so quiet. "You've been prodded by your outrage into thinking that another man has awakened you to finding me desirable again. But that is all beside the point now. The point," she said, drawing upon a queer well of resolution which seemed suddenly to have opened somewhere within her, "is that I loathe you. I detest you in such a way that if your unbelievable ego would let you believe it, you would learn something about yourself for the first time in your life. I hate you with such a foul, bitter, physical loathing that the sound of your voice, the sight of your face, the echo of your step, the smell of your tobacco, make my stomach heave. For years I have trembled and quaked and broken into cold sweat when I was confronted with you. I have—oh, *Christ!*" she cried, covering her face with her hands and doubling over for the shame of this.

"You've gone nuts on account of that goddam man you've fallen in love with," he said.

"Even if I have," she said, looking up at him with a strange cold smile of triumph, "or more exactly, even if I hadn't!—you, being you, have seized on his identity as the reason for all this now. Why don't you admit instead that this is the only possible consequence of everything you have done to me, all of it, the whole hideous, endless, heartrending record. This is what you have asked for, these seventeen years," she said, her voice throbbing. "Now you've got it."

"What?" he asked. "You don't think I'm letting you tell me off like this, do you? Just on account of that man? Just because *you* expect to make the arrangements now, to keep things convenient for you and your lover?"

That man, she thought, dully. Your lover. Keep things . . . keep anything . . . keep? . . . oh, Mark, Mark. The tips of her fingers curled unconsciously with the fresh pain of parting, there seemed so many pains, I feel as if my heart were gashed, she thought, and what is this dragging, this pain, this pain? He is going, I tried to be brave and I tried to understand him, but he is going without even, without . . .

And suddenly she saw. Suddenly and startlingly sooner than she had ever expected, she had part of the answer for which she had known tonight that she must wait. Mark had cut her off; but had he, and why? He had cut her off, he had left her unfettered, he had made no tie, he had given no promise, he had left her free. Free—for a reason; free—in order to—she put her hand slowly to her forehead as if to shield her eyes from a fiercely blinding light, and she turned and spoke to Brandon in a voice lower, stiller, colder, than she knew hers could be.

"Get out," she said.

He stood, swaying with rage, his hands clenched before him. His eyes went to the door of his own room and then back to her.

"I mean out," she said. "Out of this house, out of my life. I warned you, and I did not know myself how much I meant my warning. I am through. One of us will leave this house now, it should be you but if you refuse, it shall be I. Get out."

His face paled as she watched it, but she could not tell whether from anger or fear. His mouth fell open, his eyes grew stony; he stood looking at her with a muddled frown, and she was amazed that he had nothing to say. But just as she thought he would not speak at all, he said, "You can't do this."

"Oh yes," she said. "I can. This looks as if it were a sudden impulse, but I give you my word, it is the longest-thought-out thing I ever decided in my life. For years," she said, "*years*, I have longed to be rid of you. I have stood in your room when you were away and dropped on my knees and prayed to God, though I don't know how to pray, that you would never come back. I have thought out every idiotic detail of what would happen and what we would do about the utmost trifles of our life—when the day came when I could be rid of you. I have looked at your clothes and your possessions and your—all sorts of things—and thought how I would use the space you keep them in—after you were gone. And do you know," she said, in a trancelike daze, "I never realized it until this minute."

"Oh," he said, breaking like a straw. "Oh, Jess."

She stood looking at him, utterly indifferent to the fact that he was suffering now.

"I wish I could feel sorry," she said. "I wish I could care. I will—later." She thought vividly of Elizabeth Betts and it seemed in an instant as if every word of that dreadful recital had reimprinted itself upon her brain. "But I don't care now," she said. "I only know that I never want to see you again. I never want to see you walk, or throw your hat on a table, or eat your dinner and leave half your food wasted on your plate. I never want to hear your voice. I never want to look at your hands. I hate your hands!" she cried, ashamed of her hysteria and helpless to control it. "They are cruel, dry and cruel, like you. I never want to hear you slam another door." Her voice sagged, and there was silence, and she heard his heavy, suffering breathing. Finally she said, "Go and get dressed and get out of here. Or shall I?"

"Oh," he said, and she could scarcely recognize his voice. "I—I will."

"Telephone to Josephine in the morning," she said, trembling with horror at her own cruelty, but unable to check it, "and tell her where you are. She will send your things. And the rest—all the rest—I will take up with Horace."

She went into the bathroom and shut and locked the door so that she would not see or hear anything. She sank down upon a stool and buried her head in her arms, all folded over on her knees, and she sat there in a state of dark, whirling wretchedness which was unlike anything that she could ever remember before. She could not think, but she could not believe that she was not thinking; she crouched there for a length of time which in all her life she would never be able to recall again. It was such a portion of time as is lifted out of one's life; and thereafter one can never again understand from where it was taken, to where it went. Finally she began slowly to lift her head and move her limbs from their cramped position, and at last she got shakingly to her feet, and groped her way to the door and opened it and went through her own room to Brandon's room, and it was empty. She went on out to the hall and down the stairs, and then without understanding what she was doing, she walked slowly and deliberately through every room in the house, sometimes groping her way in the dark, and sometimes turning on a light; and he was really gone.

She mounted the stairs again and went to her own room, and stood for a while beside her bed; and through her hands, her feet, her arms, her back, her breast, her throat, there crept the sweet heaviness of utter peace. She took off her dressing-gown, moving with the queer slowness which was part of this deep peace, and she lay down again in her bed. For a long time she lay, her eyes closed, but not in sleep, and though she would wonder tomorrow and many times again how she could not have been shaken or frightened this night at what she had done, she knew that never before had she felt so calm and so secure.

Then she thought for the first time in this hour of Mark. Tonight was heaven, she thought, and this was divine peace; but tomorrow he would be gone and sooner ,or later she would long for him and suffer. She opened her eyes and looked at the luminous face of the small clock beside her. Nearly three o'clock. Last night at three o'clock, she thought, I was asleep in his arms. His arms, his body, his size, his warmth, his voice . . . his voice. Her hand went slowly to the telephone. I can hear his voice once again, she thought. I can call him and say good night. She held the instrument at her ear, listening to the dial tone. She could call him—and if she did he would ask why, for they had said good bye, and he would not want her to repeat it; especially not in words, when the words had been eschewed before. He would ask her why. And she would tell him. The dial tone hummed on and on. She would tell him, she thought; and then, against the weird, continuing noise, she heard that strange counsel of the mind which is so often there if one will listen. If you tell him, it said, you undo what you have done. You do not use the freedom that he gave you; you invalidate his gift. Slowly, very slowly, she put the telephone down. Now there was silence. Now she felt the pain again a little; Mark. Mark. She looked once more at the clock. In four hours his plane would be gone. At the end of four hours she would no longer have a way of reaching him, she would not know where he was, she would not know when she would see him again. Four hours. Through the narrow open window she saw the clear night sky, faintly, very darkly blue before the coming of the dawn. She heard the hum of planes overhead, for all night long the planes flew back and forth to the field over there from which Mark would soon be leaving. She folded her hands upon her breast and closed her eyes and meant to sleep, but it was not easy. I am asleep, she thought, I am falling asleep, but she did not sleep. She heard the planes, she thought of the clock, she thought of the telephone. No, she told herself again; no.

But if she should really put herself to sleep, she would be sleeping long past the hour when Mark's plane took off. That was what she should do; she smiled a little in the dark, thinking that that was what he would tell her to do if he knew. She put out her hand and switched on a light. She poured a glass of water, and opened the gold box and took out a small white tablet and a yellow capsule. She put the

381

tablet and the capsule into her mouth and drank the water and put out the light and lay down again. She turned on her right side, as she had slept last night within his arms. And after a time her thoughts began to wander, as thoughts do on the verge of sleep. I feel so calm, she thought, so quiet, so calm. Fragments of memory drifted through her brain, all sweet, all faint, light, downy, feathers of memory. Falling asleep at last she heard the high shrill cry of a whistle on the river, and the scud of an automobile down the drive, noises of the river and the city which had always filled her life; and another sound, deep and warm and vibrant, like the deep voice of Mark.

MAKE YOUR LIFE
A HAPPY
ADVENTURE

Here's an amazing
opportunity to see
into your future.
Take advantage of these
forecasts to get
the most out of your life—
today, tomorrow, and
for the next five years.

HOW TO PLAN AHEAD

Arranged by Sun signs, YOUR PROPH-
ECY—FIVE YEAR FORECAST FOR ALL
THE SIGNS is a "weather report"
on the sunny days and storms ahead
—telling you what you may reasonably expect in the future so you can
plan your important moves, know
when to make major purchases and
investments, prepare for changes, be
alert for trouble. With the help of
this book, the future is no longer a
baffling mystery and your chances of
finding love, luck and happiness can
be greatly improved.

WRITTEN BY EXPERTS

This book has been produced by the
editors of EVERYWOMAN'S DAILY
HOROSCOPE and written by three
eminent writer-astrologers: Doris
Kaye, editor of the Astrologers' Guild
publication, "The Bulletin"; James
Raymond Wolfe, Jr., a serious re-
searcher in the field of astrology;
and Marya Glasser, a long-time stu-
dent of the fascinating subject of
astrology, who now writes articles
for leading astrology magazines.

A COLLECTOR'S TREASURE

This handsomely bound hard cover
book, jacketed in red, black and silver, and exquisitely illustrated, is
truly a collector's item. Only $10,
it is a book you will be proud to own.

Mail Coupon Right Away